Herbjørg Wassmo was born and bred in northern Norway, and her writing is deeply rooted in the culture and nature of this northern coastline. She became a teacher but her first book, a collection of poetry, was published in 1976, and since then she has become one of the foremost Scandinavian writers. Her previous books include the *Tora* trilogy. She received the Literary Critics' Award in 1982, the Booksellers' Award in 1984 and the Nordic Council Literature Prize – equivalent to the Pulitzer Prize – in 1987. She has also written a collection of short stories entitled *Journeys* (1995), and her latest book is a long awaited contemporary novel, *The Seventh Meeting*. Herbjørg Wassmo's novels are translated into twenty languages. *Dina's Son* is the second book in the *Dina* trilogy; the first book, *Dina's Book*, is also published by Black Swan.

DINA'S SON

Herbjørg Wassmo

Translated from the Norwegian
by Nadia Christensen

BLACK SWAN

DINA'S SON
A BLACK SWAN BOOK : 0 552 99825 7

First publication in Great Britain

Originally published in Norway under the title *Lykkens sønn*

PRINTING HISTORY
Black Swan edition published 2001

1 3 5 7 9 10 8 6 4 2

Set in 11/12pt Melior by
Kestrel Data, Exeter, Devon.

Black Swan Books are published by Transworld Publishers,
61–63 Uxbridge Road, London W5 5SA,
a division of The Random House Group Ltd,
in Australia by Random House Australia (Pty) Ltd,
20 Alfred Street, Milsons Point, Sydney, NSW 2061, Australia,
in New Zealand by Random House New Zealand Ltd,
18 Poland Road, Glenfield, Auckland 10, New Zealand
and in South Africa by Random House (Pty) Ltd,
Endulini, 5a Jubilee Road, Parktown 2193, South Africa.

Printed and bound in Great Britain by
Clays Ltd, St Ives plc.

To Ib

*If happiness were truly humanity's goal, the idiot
would best exemplify our species*

Friedrich Nietzsche

PROLOGUE

And Jesus saith unto him, The foxes have holes, and the birds of the air have nests; but the Son of man hath not where to lay his head.

St Matthew 8:20

This is me: an ant in the heather. Or a bird that has lost its way somewhere out in the universe. Far from Earth. Still, *she* is so close that I feel her breath on my forehead.

She stands with her feet firmly apart and stretches out her hands. At the same time, she drops an object. A piercing song rings out as metal meets stone. I will always carry that sound with me.

Later, when I think everything is silence, the heather moves. A dry, rustling sound. Her boots leave the hem of her skirt and slowly move backwards. Until they are outside the circle of what is.

I am inside the circle. And the man. He lies in the heather, his head covered with red foam. It spreads further and further. The red is the circle around us. Around him and me. Meanwhile, she walks backwards out of everything. We cannot reach her. She has left the hem of her skirt.

I am neither ant nor bird. I am no one. Still, I am forced to stand up. Forced to emerge from the air so she will see me.

Then I feel her hands on me. They touch head. My shoulders. My throat. My face. She digs her fingers into my eyes. Slowly. Until everything goes black. It does not hurt. But all the same it frightens me.

She takes me in her arms, as if I were something light and fragile. Holds me. Tightly.

I smell the scent of her skin. Sun-dried grass and fresh perspiration. Spiced and salty. But I cannot see her, because she has stuck her fingers into my eyes, once and for all.

Even before she pushes me away I feel her muscles tense. In her stomach. Her chest, her arms. I feel her arteries. They are a strong stream rushing beneath the ice. Threateningly close.

The cold presses against my skin. Then, alone and blind, I move out into the universe. Afraid of falling to Earth, I bend my legs. Ready for what is coming. Cover my face with my hands. Try to protect myself against the fall.

Then I realize I am floating. Hovering in the air. And her voice murmurs past my ear like a night wind through an open window:

'Bless you, Benjamin. You're the son of joy!'

It is said that a lie can also be an unspoken truth. In that case, there are more lies than we imagine.

I did not say who dropped the Lapp rifle into the heather. Perhaps I was already searching for my own truth.

Perhaps the real lies are the truths we keep silent about?

God is silent. Is God a liar because he does not speak?

It is written that we are created in God's image.

In that case: is it in the art of keeping silent we most resemble Him?

10

Only he who was in anguish finds repose, only he who descends into the underworld rescues the beloved, only he who draws the knife gets Isaac.

Fear and Trembling – Johannes de Silentio

This is also me: in a foreign city I tried to draw up the balance sheet. But nothing tallied. My life rushed past. Upside down. Backwards. The people who approached me on the streets and sidewalks wore masks. All of them. They were Dina, who used all kinds of disguises to hide from me.

The sky was a huge shiny coin at which long rows of brick chimneys spat.

Someone had written asking me to fetch Dina's cello. It was the sort of thing friends or relatives did when someone died. I did not let myself think about that because I wanted to find the living traces of her.

A woman with a large hat and swaying hips walked ahead of me for a while. It made me think about something Anders once said to me: avoid women who try to hide their heads under a hat yet look as though they are walking with naked hips. They are not as shy or as naked as you imagine.

You could think of the cello as a woman with naked hips. She was here somewhere, in a foreign city, leaning against a wall, her belly filled with weeping.

You could tell yourself that if you found the cello you would find the weeping. Or death. Or both.

You could also ask yourself whether this was a madman's doing, or a child's understandable reaction. It was equally ridiculous either way.

I did not play the cello, and had no intention of learning. The instrument was probably not so expensive that its loss would ruin me. But the decision was made. I had to find the cello and bring it to Reinsnes.

All the people hurrying past me – all the voices, the unfamiliar language, the confusion – became an inferno that opened every pore in my body. I was a little boy and Dina sat me on the horse and said she

11

would hold the bridle until we crossed the courtyard, but then I had to take the reins myself.

Already at the dirty, smoky railroad station I had the feeling I was descending into the underworld. I was Orpheus. I had to follow the traces of a woman into the realm of the dead.

During the drive from the station I checked several times to make sure the letter with the address was in my inner coat pocket. Even though I had already told the coachman the address twice and he had nodded in acknowledgement.

The house was large, and set somewhat back from the street with a high fence around it. The entrance was closed off by a wrought-iron gate with spikes both above and below. Virginia creeper and weeds appeared to have taken over the flower beds by the front steps. The house did not look particularly occupied.

I asked the coachman to wait and took the few steps to the gate, where I found a rusty doorbell. The bell growled faintly somewhere in the house. But nothing happened. I tried to open the gate. It merely gave a loud, ominous squeak, and remained locked.

I rattled the gate. Shouted. In childish rage that went on for a while. Loneliness, disappointment, weariness. It all came out in this harsh language that I did not completely master. It was Benjamin who wanted to go in to Dina. In to Mama!

I despised myself. But could not give up. Not now!

The coachman eventually seemed to find all this commotion embarrassing. He wanted to be paid and leave.

A window in the neighboring house opened and a woman leaned out and shouted something to me. I did not understand her. But the word *wahnsinning* made me realize she was scolding me. More windows along the street opened. More voices. Someone shouted the word 'police'.

Then I gave up. And, with a feeling that the house

12

did not exist except in my mind, I climbed into the carriage.

I found cheap lodgings nearby, from which I could walk to the house several times each day. The hot sun was uncomfortable. As was my dark clothing. Of course I could have bought some lighter clothes. I had enough money. But when would I use them after all this was over? Besides, my landlady said the cold weather would come any day now.

The smell of pork and sausage permeated the entire lodging house, right down to the rock-hard pillow. The bedbugs were a living, moving wallpaper pattern. So I sat outside in squares and marketplaces as leaves whirled around me. People hurried about their business without seeing me. Still, I had a nightmarish feeling of being watched.

You could imagine you did not need a heart to pump the blood through your veins. Loneliness was a force that made everything circulate. It sought out every small corner of me.

Death! it whispered.

I was Orpheus. I had undertaken to perform a fine deed. For whom?

The language exhausted me. At first everyone spoke with Mother Karen's voice. I was back in my childhood, and she read me exciting stories in German to teach me the language. I thought I had mastered it well enough to make myself understood in simple conversations. But after some hours my head was a complete jumble. I began to think people were making sounds just to mislead or deceive me.

At night, as I lay in bed under the small attic window facing a distant God, voices and words churned in my head. Had the people I tried to speak to understood what I was asking? Had I understood their replies?

I really hoped she was alive. And I was afraid lest she was.

But Orpheus needed certainty to bring home.

You could imagine she had sat on precisely that

13

bench or walked across that street. Once I thought I saw her. And followed an unknown woman for several blocks. Until she turned and hurled a furious stream of words at me.

'Don't be afraid! It's just Orpheus,' I said amiably.

Then she ran. Her handbag dangled against her thigh. It looked ridiculous. The heels on her shoes were much too high. Her steps became just tiny little clicks against the cobblestones. Scarcely moved her forward. You could easily have caught up with her again. Grasped her arm or something. It was tempting. She was almost inviting it with that idiotic running.

Three days later I was still tramping up and down the streets. Dirt and leaves piled up in front of the tips of my shoes, as if they were parts of me I wanted to get rid of.

I had risen early and decided to talk to people in the neighboring houses. I shaved carefully and put on a clean shirt.

I went from house to house ringing the doorbells. Stood listening to distant, mechanical sounds of feet. Large feet in leather-soled shoes. Smaller feet in felt soles. High heels that made a metallic, almost frightening, click. This was repeated again and again. I was part of a ritual with tiny variations. As if they were making fun of me, trying to mislead me and make me forget why I was there.

Nobody knew Dina Grønelv. Some replied politely, but distantly, as if they did not really see me. Others were irritated or nervous, as if they thought I rang the bell merely as a prelude to knocking them down. Some were cold, correct and curt. Still others looked at me as if I were crazy. A man who went from door to door asking about a woman whom he could not even describe.

By mid-afternoon I was back at the address I had been given. I rang the bell, as I had done each day.

Then the ritual was broken. Footsteps approached! Shuffling but quick steps. An old man with a long

14

silver mustache and sharp eyes appeared in the doorway. For a moment we stood scrutinizing each other. At last he said impatiently:

'Yes?'

I introduced myself and waited for some sign of recognition. But the man gave me a blank look.

'I received a letter saying I could collect Mrs Grønelv's cello here,' I explained.

At last he reacted, his face taking on a friendly expression.

'Well! So it's you? Yes, my name is Karl Meyer. You're right, I've been looking after a cello here,' said the man.

The situation was unreal. I grew frantic. All my questions spilled out at once. I stood there stammering.

The man looked at me for a while and nodded. I could not tell whether he understood what I said. Then he invited me into a large, gloomy hall. The pieces of furniture were structures that stole air and light. The man was dwarfed between a cupboard and high-backed chairs.

He proved to be the maestro. He was looking after Dina Meer's cello. The moment he said 'Dina Meer' I realized Dina used a false name.

I had to pretend to know that. At the same time, I had to get him to tell me everything I did not know.

Trembling with impatience, I shook his hand and said I was relieved to find someone home at last. We exchanged a few words as I hung my coat on a coat rack resembling a gallows. He said he was sorry that he had been away a few days. Then he led me through several overfurnished rooms. Finally we found ourselves in a large room with an enormous grand piano in the middle of a dark parquet floor. Along the walls hung a variety of instruments. Several violins, a viola, wind instruments.

I caught my breath sharply. Over in a corner I saw Dina's cello. For a moment my eyes filled with tears.

The man said he would get some refreshments. Alas,

they would have to be simple, it being the house-keeper's day off.

I went over to the instrument. Touched it. Smooth wood. Both cool and warm. A stripe on one side. I recognized it. Like a friend. A force emanated from it. I had missed it.

Sudden waves of memories. About secrets. Terror. Sorrow. And joy. I did not realize I was weeping until I heard him come back into the room.

With my back turned to him, I tried to pull myself together. Heard him put a carafe and glasses on a small table by one of the tall windows. In contrast to the other rooms we had walked through, this one had no purpose other than music. No heavy drapes. No unnecessary furniture or cupboards. No carpets.

You got the feeling you had been here before. Because *she* had been here.

'She was talented,' he said, gesturing towards the table. 'Very talented. But somewhat too old for the concert halls. Besides, she was a woman,' he added.

I noted that he said 'was'. It made me furious. Strange. Because I had been prepared for this 'was' after all, had I not?

I sat down.

'There was something she lacked. Softness of touch,' he asserted. 'She was too undisciplined. Too hard. Received expert training too late.'

He fell silent for a moment, as though thinking about her.

I asked if he knew where she was. He peered into his wine glass for a moment, then met my eyes.

'She left a while ago.'

'Where did she go?'

'That's hard to say. But there was talk of Paris.'

I tried to tell from his voice whether he knew more than he was saying. But it was impossible. I did not know him well enough to tell if he was lying.

'Difficult times,' he mumbled somewhat anxiously.

'Difficult being in Paris these days . . . I've never understood this human degradation which seems to be necessary . . .'

'What do you mean?'

'War.'

He paused. Then he said, mainly to himself:

'Charming and genteel. Attracted attention. There were certainly many who sought her company. Not all of them from the best social class.'

Why did he always speak in the past tense?

'Is she dead?' I asked.

'No. Why should she be dead?' he asked in surprise. 'These are difficult times, it's true . . . But there's no reason she shouldn't be alive. She was hale and hearty the last time I saw her, but she'd given up playing the cello.'

'Why did she give up the cello?'

'It demanded so much. She spoke of a sacrifice. Had strong views.'

I tried to explain to him that I did not believe Dina could stop playing the cello, or abandon it.

'To me, she seemed like a person who abandoned everything that couldn't be made immortal,' he said slowly.

I showed him the letter with the address and the signature I could not completely decipher.

'She was very busy, of course. Her departure . . .'

He looked at me inquisitively for a moment. Then he nodded towards the corner.

'The cello isn't particularly valuable, actually,' he mumbled. 'But it's a good instrument. Take it with you!'

'Where did she live?'

He shook his head.

'Did *you* advise her to give up playing the cello?' I asked.

'Oh no!' he said, taken aback. 'But I told her clearly that she would never be a major concert performer.'

'That was cruel!' I said shamelessly.

17

'No, it was necessary.'

'It robbed her of everything!'

'No, it gave her courage,' he said quietly.

'Courage? To do what?'

'To be herself.'

'Dina was always herself!'

We sat looking at one another. His mustache gave him the ridiculous air of a bedraggled animal.

'Tell me, did you know this woman?' he asked. 'I guess you must have, since she gave you her cello.'

I noted the fact. Without surprise. She had not talked about me. Had kept her life to herself. She used neither Anders's nor Jacob's name. She had literally hidden herself in the middle of Europe and called herself Meer.

He obviously thought I did not understand what he said, because he repeated:

'Tell me, did you know Dina Meer?'

'No, probably not,' I said brusquely.

The moment I said it, I knew it was true.

'Who are you? A relative?' he asked.

'Yes. A friend, really . . .'

'You must have been a young friend.'

I felt foolish.

There was a pause as we sipped our wine. Then he said slowly:

'I think you must decide . . . whether you're looking for the cello or the woman.'

'I'm looking for the cello,' I said with stifled anger.

'Well, you've found the cello.'

'You know more about her, don't you?'

He shook his head and grinned. Annoyingly. I had difficulty controlling myself, because I felt he was making a fool of me.

'She left you too? Didn't she?' I heard myself say.

Something about him changed. I did not know exactly what it was. A shadow in the pupils of his eyes, a movement of his hand. A tiny movement. Suddenly I knew that was what had happened. She had left him.

'What makes you think we were so close? I'm an old man,' he said with a smile.

'I don't know,' I replied.

Another slight smile, then he said:

'You mustn't draw youthful conclusions. You understand . . . I've seen them come and go. They have their dreams of fame. Just as I had. Some come early enough, but have neither the talent nor the will to self-sacrifice. Some have both the will and the talent, but they come too late. Or they're overtaken by life in some way or other.'

'Overtaken how?'

'Oh, there can be so many reasons. Family, lack of money. Love and other foolish things . . .'

'What stopped Dina?'

'First and foremost, that she came too late. A would-be virtuoso must be like wax, and at the same time possess rigid discipline. Also, one can't be overburdened with homesickness and sorrow.'

'Was she?'

He looked at me without answering.

'Why didn't she go home?' I asked slyly.

'I have no idea,' he said quickly. A little too quickly?

'Don't you know anything?' I said.

'She wasn't exactly someone who confided in just anybody,' he replied.

'But surely you're not just anybody? You're her friend and teacher, aren't you?'

'That's not the same as being her confidant in everything. What were you hoping I knew?'

'Where I could find her.'

'I'm sorry, I'm not the right person for that,' he said with a sigh.

A moment later he took out his pocket watch and said his pupil would be arriving soon. He rose and nodded again towards the cello.

As we stood in the front hall he gave me his calling card.

'Come to think of it,' he said suddenly, 'I can give

19

you the address of the theater she often went to. I think she had several acquaintances there.' He hung his cane on his arm and leaned against a solid oak table while he wrote an address on the back of his card.

I thanked him.

Then I was on the street with Dina's cello. The handle on the case was broken. So I carried it under my arm. An icy wind overtook me as I rounded a corner. Two large maple leaves fluttered towards me and clung to my overcoat.

You could dream about how everything could have been. If you had found her. But that was pointless. Orpheus was embarked on a concrete mission. You could even say the mission had been successfully accomplished. It was written that Orpheus would return from the Underworld empty-handed. Yet now he was on his way back with a cello case.

As I walked to my lodgings I recalled the students talking about their travel dreams. At the parties at Regensen or Valkendorf. Or in pubs once the beer was on the table. We dreamed of going out into the world and making medical discoveries and becoming famous.

I could allow myself the luxury of sneering inwardly. Here I was, out in the world. But what of it? Dust and dirt were the same no matter where you encountered them.

She had also had dreams of traveling. I could still see her as she boarded the *Prince Gustav*, letting the wind play havoc with the brim of her hat. To this day I hated her handkerchief that waved goodbye. I tried to imagine her features. There was a great distance between us.

What had she gained from her travel dreams? Had she found peace when she escaped from me? Escaped from the fact that I could reveal everything with a single word?

I tormented myself with thoughts about what the years had done to her. What lovers had she had? How

20

did she support herself? What did she look like? Why hadn't she gone away immediately when she realized she needed to? I tried to remember what had provoked it. What had I said or done that made her realize I would eventually betray her? Had I shown some weakness that made her doubt I would manage to keep silent?

Her cello grew heavy after a while. You could cheer yourself by seeing her in your mind as she swung herself onto a horse, or closed doors. Always going somewhere. Away from me.

This made me decide more quickly to return to Copenhagen the next day.

But I did not go to the railway station the next day. I went to look for the theater whose address the maestro had given me. Could not help myself. First I made a stammering attempt to question a man with a gray face in a small ticket window in the wall. I was looking for Dina Meer. Could he help me? He shook his head and went on eating something from a paper bag. Each time he delved into the bag his whole face disappeared, right up to his hairline. I tried to be polite, and let him understand it was important that I speak to someone who knew her.

He ignored me completely. Until it occurred to me to produce some money. Whereupon he became thoughtful, sucking air through his teeth, and suddenly snatched the note. Then he carefully folded up the paper bag, opened the door to the ticket booth, and waved at me to follow him. We walked towards a cacophony of sound that proved to be an orchestra rehearsing.

'Schröder! The first violinist!' he said pointing, and disappeared.

I waited until they took a break. Then I hurried over to the man I judged to be the first violinist. He did not seem as unfriendly as I had feared. I came right to the point. Introduced myself as one of Dina's relatives, who had come to Berlin and wanted to meet her. With no hesitation Schröder gave me the maestro's address.

'Is that where she lives?' I asked, without saying I had been there.

'Yes,' he said, and turned to the conductor, who said something I did not catch.

Judging from the worn stage curtain and soiled seat upholstery, this was a small third-class theater. No doubt with an orchestra to match.

As soon as the conductor was out of the way, I asked Schröder if he had time for a brief conversation. He hemmed and hawed, was planning to eat lunch actually. I invited him to be my guest. If there was a place in the neighborhood. But he did not have much time. He gestured impatiently towards the rows of seats and sat down.

He was of indeterminate age. A narrow face. His hair was black with a white stripe running from his right temple to a point near the top of his head. It looked strange. He knew Dina!

'She no longer lives at the address you mentioned,' I said.

'I see,' he simply said, and shrugged his shoulders.

'Did she play here?'

'No,' he said with a smile, as if the thought were ridiculous.

'How do you know her then?'

'She came with Herr Erenst.'

'Who is Erenst?'

'He owns the theater.'

'What did she do here?'

He shrugged his shoulders, and glanced towards the door.

'Attended performances. Came to the concerts . . .'

'What role did Erenst play?'

'He doesn't act, he designs and builds houses,' Schröder answered disinterestedly.

'I'd like to talk to Erenst!'

22

'He's gone away.'

'Where?'

'Paris.'

'Might Dina have gone to Paris with him?'

He shook his head rapidly. Then he turned his back to me and addressed one of the musicians who had come in. Picked up his bow and began to play. As if I were invisible.

You could of course expend a great deal of energy in thinking that the world was rude and totally lacking in understanding. I went from one musician to another, trying to get through to them with my questions about Dina's existence and the address of this Erenst fellow in Paris. I let myself be tormented by the coarse, disinterested, unfriendly, stupid people. Roughly hewn and sent into the world to crush all positive contact.

So Dina had actually spent time here! She had come here to listen to concerts. The musicians undoubtedly played as crudely as they spoke, I told myself when I got out on the street again.

The gutters stank, and the carriage wheels clattered against the paving stones. I remembered all the times in childhood when I wept in anger or fear, and wished I still could. Instead, I spread my overcoat on the jagged stone steps and sat down on it.

Later I tramped up and down the streets. But when the moon had risen and the gaslights were lit, I stood again in front of the theater. I bought a ticket without investigating what was playing.

If only I'd had a few rotten eggs.

I found my seat. When the curtain rose, I realized that no play was to be performed. The orchestra was on the stage, not in the orchestra pit. I recognized a few people from earlier that day. The conductor and the first violinist.

The theater was almost full. The cacophony of in-struments being tuned immediately got on my nerves. I had no idea why I was there. It would have been better to simply catch this Schröder outside when the performance was over.

A woman behind me talked incessantly to her companion. I gathered that she had met a man who was unbearably awkward and ill-mannered. I turned around, because she was annoying me. The woman wore a red dress decorated with lace in front. She gestured with hands covered with rings, and ignored my look.

Finally, the house lights dimmed. The woman behind me stopped talking. The violinist raised his bow along with the other string players. His shoulders were too large. Too large behind the violin, and too large for the stage. He should have been a stone cutter. It amused me that he was so ridiculously out of place.

Then the music started! And it spoke to me.

The orchestra was not third-class like the stage curtain. This was clear to me already in the first movement as I tried to determine what was being played.

I was drawn into it. Stopped linking the faces bowed over the instruments with my dismal experience earlier in the day. Stopped hating the arms that moved up and down. The necks. The fingers. The shadows on the backdrop.

Because everything was in the music. And the music was Dina.

Then I knew why she had been able to endure the people behind the instruments. Why she had come to listen to the rehearsals. The elderly cellist in his worn jacket disappeared. One by one the musicians disappeared. Only the sound remained.

Dina sat on the stage with the cello between her knees. The strings wept from her belly. Suddenly the Russian sat down in the empty seat beside me. He wore a wolf-skin cap askew over the hole in his head and leaned towards me as he nodded and smiled towards the stage. When the last movement faded away, he clapped and whistled loudly. People turned around and stared. That calmed me down. He was more shabbily dressed than I.

Were we the only ones who understood? Who knew who she was? Or was it because he understood nothing that the heather turned red that autumn?

During the intermission, I saw the woman in the red dress again. Her black hair hung down on both sides of her face. It was so heavy it looked as if it were coated with tar. She was listening to something a young man in white trousers and a dark jacket was saying. Then she shook her head, took a sip from her glass, and rolled her eyes.

You cannot always know why you do things. I walked into the circle of light around her. Between her and the man. And said in the harsh language that wearied me:

'Excuse me, do you by any chance know Mrs Dina Meer?'

At first she just stared at me. But when her admirer grimaced and tried to wedge himself between us with his shoulder, she seemed to wake up.

'No,' she said, almost friendly.

'Who are you?' the young man asked irritably.

If only he would disappear.

'Are you sure?' I asked.

'Yes,' she said. But she smiled. Her teeth were uneven and she had a rather large birthmark on her cheek. She was quite tall. Had bold eyebrows and wore far too much make-up. Still, she was beautiful.

'Was this woman supposed to be here this evening?' she asked, and held her admirer in check by laying her hand on his arm.

I felt a magnetism between us.

'Yes,' I said, looking straight at her.

'Then I wish you luck,' she said simply.

'She plays the cello,' I said in panic, seeing that she was about to leave.

'That's very interesting,' she said. 'It's hard for women to play an instrument like that.'

Then I took the two steps needed. Put my hand firmly under her elbow and led her away from her companion.

The bell rang for the end of the intermission. But we remained beside a red velvet curtain looking at each other. She was a red shadow on the curtain. It made me feel heavy. Filled up. A leather pouch filled with wine or oil.

I set my feet wide apart. That helped. I moved my fingers under her elbow. Her skin was cool and damp. It sent a thrill through me. I channeled my power through her fingers. I both saw and felt she was receptive to it.

'You're very bold, I must say, and you're not from Berlin,' she said softly.

'You're right,' I said, and added:

'I wish you knew the woman I'm looking for. She is tall and dark-haired like you. She is often in the company of actors and musicians.'

'The woman you're looking for . . . Is she your . . . lover?' she asked, saying the last word as she drew in her breath.

It was clear why she had such bold eyebrows.

'No. A friend.'

'Hadn't you agreed on a place to meet?'

'No. I lost her. A long time ago.'

'People don't lose friends,' she said.

I realized that I had awakened something in her. Not just curiosity. There was something about her breathing. I continued talking as I gazed into her eyes and took both her hands. There was a softness to them. The sort of softness you always longed for.

'Well, I do!'

'Who are you? You seem rather rude,' she whispered, without pulling back her hands.

'I'm not really sure,' I replied.

'You're a little odd. Confident, but strange . . . You remind me of somebody I . . .'

26

The bell rang again. We slowly walked in for the second half.

After we sat down, her hand brushed my neck once in the darkness. She said something to the woman next to her. It did not annoy me. I turned around slowly to catch her eye. But the darkness had extinguished the light in her eyes. My nostrils caught every small hint of her perfume. I opened my mouth to get more. Drank it. Ate it.

Then the violins began, the cellos, the wind instruments.

I did not think about the Russian. Did not notice whether he was still sitting beside me. But Dina sat on the stage in her green traveling suit with its full skirt. Her thighs wide apart and her face impassive.

While her dancing fingers forced the music into me, her garments flew off, one by one, towards the ceiling. There they were caught by the numerous arms of the crystal chandeliers. In the end, she sat in a shift, the top buttons undone.

The shadows of Dina's garments fell on people in the audience without their noticing it. Some coughed. The music rose and fell. I was not alone. The city might be dirty and unfriendly. The people might be grotesque, crude and unreliable.

But behind me sat the woman in red.

Not only did the music spring from the instruments, it played in my hips. In my skin. My groin. I smelled the garments hanging from the chandeliers. Smelled the red woman behind my neck. My nostrils flared. I leaned my head back and closed my eyes.

During the applause I felt her hand on my shoulder. As I raised my arm and took her calling card, all of Dina's clothes fell from the dark chandeliers. They were on top of me. I took the card as I squeezed the tips of her fingers for a second. Then I fought my way out of the perfumed heap of clothing and continued clapping.

'Thursday. Five o'clock,' she whispered as she stood up and joined the stream of people leaving.

I caught a glimpse of a program in someone's hand as I left. Mozart.

Dina quickly gathered her worn sheets of music, left the stage and cello, and led me out among all the people. Her shift fluttered lightly as she disappeared. Her perfume was the same as that worn by the woman in red.

The calling card said Mrs Birthe Schultz. The address meant nothing to me. I was in a foreign city.

The violinist was nowhere to be seen. I went backstage and asked for him. The others said he had already left. What did I want with him, by the way?

You could imagine you were a boat with hoisted sail in a strong cross wind. You can tack across the water and take your time, or batten down the hatches and abandon yourself to the forces of nature. The keel feels heavy enough. You can also admit you are no sailor. But bearing in mind Anders's advice, about both women and boats, you realize it is best to tack.

So I waited until Thursday, feeling a kind of triumph in my whole body.

You could have spent the time being shocked that she had broken all rules of propriety by giving her calling card to a total stranger. But you had too much raw, lonely power in your body for that. Fate had decided.

And you were accursedly doomed to go searching in this city.

I hired a carriage. Mrs Birthe Schultz lived in a mansion at the edge of town. Surrounded by large trees and thorn bushes. The entrance had spikes on top. Mrs Birthe probably had spikes of her own too.

A doorman asked whom I had come to see and whether I was expected. I nodded and showed him Birthe Schultz's calling card.

'Third floor,' he said, bowing graciously, and accompanied me up five solid steps with a brass handrail to the dark double door.

For a moment as I caught my breath, I thought about how the cotters' children must feel when they stood on the path of white sand and crushed seashells before the main entrance at Reinsnes. Before they went around the house and in through the kitchen entrance. Going up the stairs, your footsteps echoing ahead, you remembered coming up the tree-lined avenue from the boat landing and seeing the main house like a shining palace in the darkness. Before you went to the cottage to see Stine.

Surely you could indulge in such stubborn nostalgia at the main entrance of a strange woman's home, even if you also felt like a crushed child?

Dina! Your cello can rot in hell! I said to myself when Mrs Birthe opened the door. She was not red tonight. She was yellow.

What was it Anders said that time in Bergen when I wanted to go with the fellows to visit the women in the back alleys? He had not protested when I wanted to test my manhood. But he said:

'Take along a knife, and only as much money as you need!'

That time the girl was younger than I. Thin and dirty. She took me to a dark little room and set me on a ragged bedspread. Then she fumbled with me as if I were a moron. I managed to get her off me. Paid her handsomely, and left. Had I not been afraid someone might see me, I would probably have wept. Not because both the girl and the bed were filthy and repugnant. Or because all my dreams of passion did not match reality. But because I felt as if I had trampled the fingers of a young girl lying in a black pond who had seized a branch to keep herself afloat.

She had worn a blouse with no buttons in the front, and had skinny arms.

It was better to think about Aksel and the madam in Peder Madsen's Passage.

Mrs Birthe had round arms and the yellow blouse had certainly been chosen with care. It had a whole row of time-consuming buttons. Twenty-one to be exact.

She led me through a dimly lit hall and into a drawing room, and I could feel the blood pounding even in my neck. What I really wanted was to grab her and thrust myself into her with all my strength. And then: be done.

Instead, I found myself sitting on a soft sofa.

A maid brought teacups and pastries on a tray. I watched for every hint of an opportunity. For all the hints Mrs Birthe gave. It was like being involved in spiritualism and necromancy.

Meanwhile, I took medical intern Grønelv's place at the dissection table. Examined the female body with scalpel raised and ready. Dissection practice with Professor Schmidt was subject to certain rules and objectives. Membranes and muscles had to be removed from the rest of the body. The most important thing was to gather Mrs Birthe's entire bloodstream in the hollow of my hand without Professor Schmidt seeing a single spot of blood on my shirt cuff.

Mrs Birthe's body had agreed to the operation. Despite its prudish buttons.

'So you didn't find her? Your friend?' she asked.

'No, unfortunately,' I said without taking my eyes off her. I knew that the conversation was for the maid's sake. While tea was being poured, I learned she was expecting some nice friends whom she wanted me to meet. And when the maid came in after a while and asked if there was anything else to do before leaving, Mrs Birthe waved cheerfully to her and said no thank you, that was all.

The door closed, and I asked her when her friends were due. Then she climbed onto the dissection table again so I could begin work.

'My husband is away. It wouldn't look right . . . just you and I,' she said, and pushed her teacup aside. Then she offered me some sherry.

After a while I found something to say. But she did not seem to need communication. Breathing and movement took the place of everything else.

Foam. I do not know where I first saw the foam. But it came to my mind like a shifting, but eternal, image. Foam under women's hands when they are milking. Foam from huge thundering waves against rocks on the beach. Against rocks exposed at low tide beyond the large skerries. Rushing past the bow when the boat created a white plough in a show of strength. Foam. From Stine's hands when she cleaned sea mittens. Foam! When Dina washed her hair in the summer in the deep pool behind the hill. Foam from the stallion's nostrils when he prepared to mount. Mounted Mrs Birthe in Berlin. I was always in this foam. Like the movement in heavy, powerful music. I carried it with me. Was in it. Did not want to escape it. Women. The salty smell of seaweed. Lye. Hair. Rose water. Clothes from the line. Karna! The smell of Karna's body mixed with blood and pus. In the field hospital at Dybbøl.

Foam was everything: joy and fear. The ugly and the beautiful. At the same time.

Tonight there would be a secret dissection. Forbidden and intense. But, just like the breaker that draws back after the storm leaving the foam behind, I too would withdraw and could not be blamed or held accountable.

Had I not received a calling card? An invitation? Did I not get a hint at the table? Had I not undone all twenty-one buttons as I gathered Mrs Birthe's blood in the hollow of my hand?

But somewhere I had to enter the other foam. The Russian's. Red. Powerfully spurting around. Millions of tiny rosebuds that would never open into full bloom. Because the image was frozen solid.

Dina and him in the heather. First white, then red.

And then there was no longer any God. Mrs Birthe was dissected. The foam covered both her and the Russian.

Who had stood up in the heather?

From her mouth came the resounding notes of a cello. They rose and fell. As if she was trying to sing, but could not.

She had taken both the Russian's and my own ravaged head in her lap.

When I was about to leave, she asked if she would see me again.

'Perhaps.'

'My husband is away until next Thursday,' she said in a low, proper voice.

I was the wave that drew back. Far out to sea. I looked at the foam left behind. Gray light fell obliquely through a tall window. Mrs Birthe's face had become completely white. I was a stranger to myself.

It was already a new day.

BOOK ONE

CHAPTER 1

For in much wisdom is much grief: and he that increaseth knowledge increaseth sorrow.

Ecclesiastes 1:18

The boy stood in the farmyard, a wild look in his eyes. He shouted something into the air. In a kind of rage. At first they raised their heads. Astonished. In the kitchen and the barn. In the servants' quarters and out-buildings. They recognized, yet did not recognize, the voice.

Stine responded most quickly. She was the first to interpret the words. Gradually they all gathered there, down to the last person. Even Mother Karen and Jacob unwound themselves from their old shrouds and long-forgotten events and joined the others. But they said nothing, because they had not been given the right to speak.

'The Lapp rifle shot the Russian! The Russian . . . in the head! In the head!'

His words echoed from the surrounding rocks and hills. They were thrown back at him, as if to warn him, calm him down. Ask him to keep quiet. But he repeated them, growing wilder and wilder. Until Stine put her arms around him and held him close.

Then they all knew. The boy trotted ahead of the men and led them to the spot. Shouted, explained, and wept. Said they had suddenly lost sight of the Russian among the trees. He had climbed a hill to see where the Russian was hiding. Then he heard the bang. And saw the man sink into the heather. The rifle lay in the heather too. Dina had asked him to go for help. But nobody could help the Russian. He had too big a hole in his head.

Rachel in the Old Testament named the son who cost her her life Benoni, son of sorrow. But the old patriach, Jacob, changed it to Benjamin, son of joy.

No one ever discovered what Dina Grønelv meant by naming her son Benjamin. And no one ever learned what Jacob Grønelv, who was listed in the church records as the child's father, thought about the matter. But everyone could see that this sturdy, rather short boy had eyes like an old man and that his brow had enough furrows for at least two buckets of seed potatoes.

It helped that he was bright, although it almost drove one to distraction having to answer all his complicated questions about everything. Everything on earth, under water, and in the hereafter.

You could not blame the child for the fact that he had been nursed and brought up by a Lapp girl who should have been punished for fornication and sorcery that resulted in death. Nor could you blame him because his mother was more powerful and feared than loved. Powerful in amassing Mammon and making anything profitable prosper. Little loved because she made you grovel beneath her watery gaze. If the weather was fair and you found yourself out at sea, her eyes had a soft, greenish cast. But when skies were stormy, her irises were frozen solid.

It was a late autumn day in the year he turned eleven that Benjamin realized the hill folk, who lived in the netherworld, were working against him and no one who walked aboveground could be trusted either. Until that day, when human blood colored the heather at Eidet scarlet, he had believed in some sort of protection, at least for himself. Now he knew anything could happen. Anything! He also realized he was the only one who knew.

It was like looking at something under Mother Karen's magnifying glass. The letters in the Bible, or an ant that Little Hanna had pulled apart. The closeness became too much, too clear. Nothing looked the same. To see so clearly made him as restless as a snow bunting.

The heather had already been quite red. It was autumn after all. And the man lying motionless on the ground had stolen Dina from him beforehand. So he did not miss him. Up to that point, everything was just unreal. But you could bear it.

What he could not bear was that Dina was there.

To make up for it, he implied the Russian had shot himself in the head.

Dina had enough to do just watching over the body. First on the heath, where bears might catch the scent of fresh blood and rush towards it. The gentle autumn wind blowing around her face and the bright, low sun on the back of her neck were anything but warm.

Safely home at Reinsnes, she continued her watch beside open windows hung with sheets. Among flickering, dripping candles. The men had a struggle to get the Russian's large body up the stairs and into the master bedroom. That was where she wanted him to be.

Breaking all rules of modesty, she washed and prepared the body herself. As if she had already been married to it and to all its secrets. First she dismissed the servant girls who stood there trying to get a look. Then she nodded brusquely to Tomas and the servant boy to leave.

When she was finally alone, she covered the top of Leo's head with clean cloths and tied them together. Tightly. The lower part of his face had been spared. His mouth was half open with a look of surprise. As if it reflected a passing wayward thought. His Cupid's bow mouth was still and blue. It was finally at rest.

Leo Zjukovski was laid in an elegant casket and buried outside the stone church. Despite the fact that he was not a true believer, but a spy, a Catholic, a foreigner, and even worse things.

No money was spared on the funeral. People thought that Dina Grønelv could have been more frugal. And that it was not proper for the parson to bury a man who apparently had died by his own hand.

But the parson performed the funeral service. Because Dina Grønelv had her own ideas of what was proper. As well as the resources to put them into practice.

And the year's first ground frost thrust its needles through everyone.

CHAPTER 2

'She'll probably sit upstairs in her bedroom for a year now,' said Oline the day after the funeral. It was late afternoon, and Dina had not yet appeared.

Neither Stine nor either of the two indoor maids dared to respond. It could be equally dangerous whichever side you chose.

'God knows she's not much help when something is wrong. Thea! This pot is filthy around the edge. You forgot to rinse it in cold water before you washed it.'

The girl scowled, but did not complain. Just took the pot out to the water bucket in the back entry.

'She'll probably pace back and forth all night for months,' Oline continued, breathing through the corners of her clenched mouth. It sounded like a storm trying to get under the roof to tear it off.

Still no one replied. Stine was busy folding the cloths that had covered the plates of sandwiches.

She had energy from a hidden source. Not the kind often found in women condemned to doing housework for years. No, more like a wide river. Always the same, steady stream. Always coming, always gone, always present. Watching Stine work, one better understood the planets' uncontrollable orbits. Stine's work was greater than Stine herself.

'She was in the cellar last night! I heard her. And she just threw the key on the bench when she left. Anybody could have taken it! There are probably empty bottles all over upstairs. But don't let me hear a peep about this in anyone else's house! Do you understand?' Oline added threateningly.

But then the ample body doubled over. She had been a quilt cover frozen stiff on a clothes line in the wintry blast. Now suddenly a south-west breeze blew on her. The bloated cover cracked in two. She collapsed onto the peat box and covered her face with her soiled leather apron.

'The poor thing! The poor thing!' she wailed from within the apron. 'Oh, what will come of it? What will come of it?'

They were not sure whether she grieved for the Russian or for Dina. And they did not dare to ask.

Dina came downstairs that evening. Walked through the parlours a few times. Paused beside various things and touched them.

Then she came to the kitchen and fixed some food. Ate it standing at the work table. Drank water from the ladle in the bucket on the bench in the back entry. The whole time she looked as if she were trying to solve a difficult accounting problem. There were deep furrows between her eyebrows and around her mouth. But for once her hair was combed properly and knotted at the back of her neck. Her eyes looked as though someone had blown sand at them for hours. She seemed surprised and rather annoyed when she had to exchange glances with someone. As if she did not know them, or had discovered she was in the wrong place.

But everyone breathed easier because she walked through the rooms, and because she answered when they spoke to her.

Anders had been in Strandsted when 'it' happened. When he arrived home that evening, the dead man's body lay in the master bedroom.

He felt some sorrow of course. But mainly, the event seemed unbelievable. When the Russian was finally out of the house and in the cemetery, he seemed to have become a friend.

Because he was dead?

Anders always had many errands. Now he had even more. At the wharves. On the cargo boat *Mother Karen*. Away from the estate.

When he ate meals at home, he and Dina sat across from each other. He was the distant relative who politely passed the serving dishes and the salt shaker. Anders knew his place.

But he never expressed his feelings about it. Just stored it away. Like a thin layer of dust on his face. Saturday baths in the wash house could not remove it. It simply settled on layers of similar dust that had accumulated for years. To know his place!

Anders felt he was sitting at the table with ghosts. Still, he sat there. Helped himself to food. Chewed. Let others serve meals to him. Made ordinary comments. And once in a while, received amazingly ordinary replies. Sometimes he talked feverishly, if Dina and he were alone in the room waiting for the soup or dessert and had nothing to keep their hands busy. Then, for no reason, he could begin telling the latest news from the bar down at the store or from Strandsted. She usually looked at him with distant friendliness. Nonetheless, it was hammered into him every single day: she does not see you.

At first the boy sat between them like a mouse, because Dina wanted him there. But soon he found his way back to the cottage and Stine's well-scrubbed table. There they did not use tablecloths for everyday meals. But you could breathe and eat.

For a long time Benjamin had slept in the cottage where Stine and Tomas lived. The thirteenth day after the funeral, three hours after midnight, the Russian's deep commanding voice called him to the canopy bed in the main house. Wearing just his nightshirt, and armed with Mother Karen's magnifying glass on a cord around his neck, he tumbled out of his warm bed in the cottage and went outside.

Tufts of grass and ice-coated pebbles met the soles of his feet like gleaming slivers of glass. He felt burning hot, even though the night was so cold he could see his breath.

At the main house, light shone from just the two master bedroom windows. A faint golden gleam that told him Dina had lit only candles. He had stood in the farmyard looking towards Dina's windows before. He had even tried to be with her up there. But that was long ago. He was a big boy now. Big boys did not climb into their mother's bed.

It was dark. Still, he could make out the buildings. The well house in the center of the farmyard. The trees bending towards earth as the wind played with their leaves, which were heavy with frozen dew. The delicate sound remained in his head. Some trees stood half naked, like plucked scarecrows silhouetted against the sky.

He did not know where the light came from. But it shone on twisted grasses before his feet. It moved. If he walked straight ahead, it was there. If he walked to the side, it was there too. It was the hill folk trying to show him the way.

The Russian's voice was nearby and far away. It demanded something, but he wanted nothing to do with it. So he tried to think good thoughts as he walked.

The carvings above the front door now had eyes and jaws and dragon teeth. His normal thoughts turned into a stone that ground around with the Russian's voice. He opened the door. The house was a shell, and a mirage. It had been decided he should not sleep in this house. He did not want to remember how that happened.

But tonight the rule did not apply. He stood with the wrought-iron latch in his hand. The frost turned it into a scythe blade.

Then he was inside. The Russian's voice was calmer now. As if knowing it would get what it wanted. The smells were different from those in the cottage. Stine's spice smell was not so strong. Here in the main house, smells climbed on top of each other and fought for a place. Some were old forgotten thoughts. Others were recognizable. The ash bucket, cigars, books and rose water. All the smells met in the halls. Hid in the shawls and sheepskin coats hanging under the stairs. The walls smelled of the people who had lived there for a hundred years. He knew them all through the stories people told.

Everything he touched, creaked. Long sounds that fenced him in. Each black oval picture frame in the stairwell had at least two eyes staring at him. All at the same time. He no longer wanted to know who they were, even if he knew their names. The phosphorescent eyes shone maliciously in the dark. He did not dare to lower his gaze. Then they would set him on fire and turn him into a burned moth on the bottom step.

He prayed Mother Karen's prayer through tightly pressed lips and took one step down the hall.

'Our Father, who art in heaven, hallowed be Thy name, Thy kingdom come, Thy will be done . . . forgive us our trespasses, as we forgive those who trespass against us . . .'

The door to the master bedroom creaked slightly. The candles in the tall candelabra by the bed fluttered wildly in the draft. The Russian's voice came from the bed! In here, the voice was thunder and fire, as if from the beast in Revelations. He could see she heard it too. She raised her head from the pillows. A black wave against all that white.

She opened and shut her mouth several times. He went closer and put her under Mother Karen's magnifying glass. Her nostrils were bluish-white and her eyes bloodshot. She was a wax doll with terrible colors. For a moment he enjoyed that. Then he began to tremble.

43

'I came . . . because the Russian called me so much,' he whispered, fumbling unsteadily between a chair and the bed.

She looked at him with pale, wide eyes, but he saw she would not send him away.

The quilt cover crackled like a withered aspen leaf when she drew the bedclothes aside to make space for him. As soon as he felt her body's warmth, the Russian quietened down. The sheet settled gently on his skin, and everything became peaceful.

'He's not nice,' he said after a while.

'Shhh,' she murmured against his hair. 'Shhh, shhh . . .'

'Why does he call to me at night?' he asked, refusing to give in.

'I don't know.'

'But he keeps me awake and makes me afraid.'

'That's how it is.'

'Why, Dina? Why is it like that?'

'It has to be.'

'But Dina . . . why?' he wept.

'Nobody knows.'

'What are we going to do with him?'

'Nothing, Benjamin. Nothing.'

'But what if he calls to other people at night too? What if he tells everything?'

'He has nothing to tell,' she said, patting the quilt snugly around him. 'He's at peace.'

'How do you know?'

'I just know.'

He stopped resisting. Felt her warmth and fragrances enfold him. He was a baby chick under the mottled hen's wing. He was inside one of Oline's words. The word 'bliss'. He would not think about why then he did not feel very happy. Would not let it trouble him that he could not remember the last time he had been so close to Dina, or if he ever had been. Somehow there was so little to think about now.

He slept with his nose in Dina's armpit and his knees

between her thighs. He slid his hands into her shift until he found the crevice between her breasts. Her warmth was honey and caresses after frostbitten fingertips. If only the night would never end!

The night always ends. Its finger scratches towards the morning and prepares the day as if it were the final one.

Stine had searched for Benjamin inside and outside. Hanna was sent to look for him, and others on the estate finally joined the search. Nobody imagined he could be in Dina's bedroom. That was not a place one looked for lost things.

But the shouts reached the bedroom. It made waking up shameful. He tumbled out of bed and was about to run downstairs. But she reached for him and held him back.

'No, Benjamin.'

At first he glared at her defiantly. Then he lowered his eyes. Her shift was open, exposing her breasts. He had never seen her like that before. She was an unknown woman with swollen blue veins and furrows around her mouth.

He began to cry.

She nudged him back into bed. Gently. Awkwardly. Like a female animal that discovers her young one is about to fall out of the pen. Then she got up, pulled her wrap around her and went into the hall. He heard her shout to someone. Downstairs, Oline's voice was loud and worried.

'Benjamin is here with me,' Dina called down the stairs.

A warm echo rushed through his head and body: 'Benjamin is here with me . . . Benjamin is here with me . . .' Then came tears, because he did not know how to make it last. And because he was so ashamed.

She came in again and stood by the bed for a while. Then she gave him a handkerchief and rumpled his hair. He did not dare to meet her eyes. Felt her fingers clasp his hand. She squeezed. He squeezed back.

'I came because he shouted so loud,' he said in explanation.

'I know,' she replied.

'I don't run around at night because I'm afraid. But he made so much noise,' he said stubbornly.

Her eyes. Why did she look at him like that?

'I don't climb into bed with people any more!' he said desperately.

She did not answer. Just stood there.

'Talk to me, Dina!' he cried furiously, digging his nails into the palm of her hand.

'There's much noise in you, Benjamin,' she said finally.

'Not as much as in the Russian!'

'Who told you it's shameful to be frightened by your dreams, Benjamin?'

'Nobody,' he said, bewildered.

'Then why are you so angry?'

He sat there among the pillows, his head bowed.

'Only idiots don't have the sense to be afraid!' she said firmly, and withdrew her hand. Then she set the folding screen in front of the wash basin and began her morning toilette.

The smell of soap drifted into the room as he realized with a shiver that she was washing in cold water. Only his eyeballs moved as her hand picked up one garment after another that she had laid on the chair by the screen. She emerged while pinning Hjertrud's brooch on her blouse. Looking down in concentration, her fingers decisive.

You knew you would remember precisely that: Dina standing in front of the folding screen with its painting of Leda and the swan as she pinned a brooch between her breasts.

'Why do you say only idiots aren't afraid? Are you afraid?'

She turned around before the oval mirror to see if her skirt was hanging properly before she replied.

'Yes.'

'When?'

'Always.'

'Why?'

'Because of everything that isn't. And what I don't do.'

'What don't you do?'

'I need to go away somewhere . . . to a maestro who can teach me to play the cello.'

She stood in the middle of the room. As though surprised by what she had said.

He gave a start and was instantly on guard, as if she had raised her hand to hit him.

'You're just joking! You already can play the cello,' he said quickly.

'No,' she said, and went over to the bed. Shook him and commanded:

'Get up, sleepyhead!'

He felt tears trickling. It was disgraceful.

'Now, now,' said Dina lightly. 'It wouldn't hurt to have a pair of pants and a sweater, would it?'

He nodded, and thought how shameful it was not to have his pants in the house where he slept. That was why he was crying.

She left the room.

When she returned with his clothes, he had made a decision.

'Can I sleep here tonight too?' he asked, stumbling quickly over the words.

She handed him his clothes and turned her back.

'No. But you can sleep in the south bedroom.'

'I want to sleep here!'

'No. You need your own bedroom.'

'Why?'

'You're eleven years old.'

'I don't give a damn!'

'But I do.'

'I can sleep in the alcove,' he said, nodding towards the large dressing alcove where Jacob's chaise longue still stood.

'No.'

'Is it because they say Jacob had to sleep there when you were angry with him?'

'Who says that?'

He saw her eyes and thought quickly.

'I don't remember!'

'You mustn't say things when you're not sure where they came from.'

'No. But Jacob is dead. He doesn't need any space.'

It became so quiet. Why did it get so quiet?

'You once said there weren't any ghosts in the cottage. Even if Niels hanged himself there,' he said quickly and breathlessly.

'That's right.'

'Then Jacob isn't in the alcove either!'

'No. But the dead need a place too.'

'The Russian? Does he sleep here?' he asked in a whisper, swinging his bony legs out of bed.

She began straightening the sheets and quilt without answering.

'I don't take much space,' he pleaded.

She nudged his shoulder, and said:

'You take much more space than you realize. You can sleep in the south bedroom. If you have trouble sleeping, you can come and wake me and we'll play a game of chess.'

'I don't know how to play chess,' he mumbled.

'I'll teach you. You're a bright boy,' she said, so incredibly gently that he understood the conversation was over.

'Then you mustn't leave!' he said so quickly the words all ran together.

'Did I say I would?'

'You said you were afraid you'd have to.'

'I see . . .'

48

'You won't leave! You're not so afraid, Dina! Are you?'

She leaned over the bed with a pillow in her hands. Then she turned slowly.

'You mustn't think about that, Benjamin. I'll warn you if I get so afraid. I promise.'

He did not fully realize that boys do not have such conversations with their mothers. But he probably suspected it. Because he made no reference to it back under the lamplight in Stine and Tomas's cottage.

Stine did not say a word about his disappearance. But Tomas could not restrain himself.

'You ran off to your mother last night, I hear.'

The boy lowered his head and stared into his porridge bowl. Hanna looked from one to the other, sensing trouble.

'I'm moving into the main house again,' said Benjamin, putting up a bold front.

'Well, that splendor won't last long. She won't have . . .'

Tomas stopped himself. But he had already said enough.

'The hell with you, Tomas!' whispered Benjamin, and threw his spoon into his bowl, splattering the porridge. His face dissolved into tears for a moment. Then he dashed into his bedroom. They heard him knocking about wildly in there.

Tomas did not know what he should do, so he went into the bedroom and grabbed the boy by the ear in order to keep discipline in the house.

'Let me go!'

'You'd better mind your table manners,' Tomas hissed through clenched teeth as he shook the boy.

'You're the one with no table manners, Tomas! You talk about things that have nothing to do with you.'

'I've got something to do with it when you're rebellious and rude and everyone hears that. You need an upbringing like other children.'

49

'You're not my father!'

Tomas let go of the boy. His fist still hung in the air.

Benjamin stood blinking long after the door had closed and he was alone in the room. He did not understand why he could not complete a thought. The unpainted wainscoting boards had so many knots. He counted them from the corner by the headboard of his bed in the straightest possible line to the next corner. That way he had to turn his body as well. And his feet. It was important that his feet moved too.

The world was so terribly blue-black on the other side of the windowpane.

CHAPTER 3

The sheriff wanted to send word to the authorities about the Russian's tragic fate. Since Benjamin had already told everyone what happened there was no reason to trouble anyone unnecessarily. But he wanted to discuss with Dina where they should send the Russian's belongings. The sheriff was wise enough to realize there was more to the story. But he decided it would just be confusing if anyone were to hear it.

An accidental shot could be suicide. But since the Russian had no close relatives here who demanded clarification, the sheriff decided that theory would remain theory in this case. If the death had anything to do with espionage and international politics, he would just cause trouble and strife if he tried to dig into the matter. And if it had anything to do with his daughter Dina, that was nobody's business. If Mr Leo had been rejected as a suitor and it proved too much after the strain of being exposed as a criminal and imprisoned, that was bad enough without bringing the public into it.

Sheriff Holm regretted the entire affair. He had liked this man. In fact, he had harboured a vague hope that the Russian might be the man to tame Dina, even if he probably did not have much to bring to a home. The sheriff was even willing to forget the Russian had been in prison. But in any case, it was too late now.

*   *   *

The sheriff took his time and was extraordinarily calm when he knocked on the master bedroom door to talk with Dina.

She received him, not like a concerned father, but like the sheriff he was after all. The meeting was neither cordial nor ungracious on her part.

He got entangled in a long introduction that he did not know how to conclude. Finally she had to help him, so they could get it over with.

'He didn't bring much with him. Just clothes and books. Oh yes, and a silver knife. As far as I know, he has no relatives. So it's probably not worth sending his things all the way to Russia?'

'Justice is justice,' said the sheriff.

She shrugged her shoulders.

He had never felt comfortable in the master bedroom. He did not like it that she used a bedroom for conversations and business affairs, no matter how elegant the room was. It was improper to combine canopy beds and musical instruments with serious words and important matters. He had felt this way ever since the time he stood in the master bedroom and tried to force her to attend Jacob's funeral. That, in fact, was an act he regretted. He wanted to tell her so. But did not. Instead, he cleared his throat and said:

'What actually caused it? How did the shot go off?'

She raised her head slightly. As if listening to a sound outside. Somewhat surprised, she said:

'Do you want me to say I shot him?'

He shuddered.

'Don't joke about such things. I only want the document to say what happened. Do you think he did it on purpose?'

'No. He probably just didn't understand how the rifle worked . . .'

'Did you see if he carried the rifle on his shoulder? If he fell on it?'

'No.'

He nodded thoughtfully.

'And Benjamin wasn't there either?'

'Not according to what he says. But you know . . . children see what they want to see.'

'Don't you know? Haven't the two of you talked about it?'

She looked at him, but did not reply.

'Well, we'd better have a talk with the little fellow,' he said. 'Can we ask him to come in now?'

'No! It's not right to bother him with this.'

'It's necessary.'

'Do you think Benjamin fired the shot?'

'No, for heaven's sake!' the sheriff wheezed from the depth of his lungs. The silence settled around him like something unbearable he had to stop.

Benjamin Grønelv was solemnly brought to his grandfather, the sheriff, to explain how Mr Leo blew a hole in his head. Actually, the boy knew as soon as he saw the sheriff's blue outrigger gliding slowly towards the boat landing. Knew he would have to explain.

Dina asked to be excused. She refused to witness someone pestering a child to death, she snarled as Benjamin came in the door.

The situation grew so difficult that the sheriff was at his wits' end. He sent for Anders to come to the room.

After the time it takes to bridle a horse, they heard her ride across the courtyard. The sound of hoofs grew softer as soon as she started across the fields. Benjamin knew exactly where she was when he heard the sound change. It also had to do with the echo from the mountains. The mountains were calling her.

He thought about that. It was a strong thought.

Anders wanted to hold Benjamin on his lap when he saw how frightened the child was. But he decided there were enough humiliations without being set on someone's knee. So he contented himself with putting his hand on Benjamin's shoulder, and repeating loudly and clearly what the boy whispered.

'There was a terrible bang,' Benjamin began, as wetness trickled from every opening in his body. He could not wipe it away or protect himself, because his hands and feet had withered under the table.

'Yes,' said the sheriff, clearly embarrassed. 'Where were you then?'

'I don't know. I just ran ahead. And then . . .'

'And then?'

'Then . . . then he just lay there. It was red around him.'

He put his head on the table, and both hands under it. The wood smelled of wax. He thought about the wood smelling of wax. It was an ordinary thought.

'Were you and your mother together?'

'No,' came the answer from the tabletop.

'Where was she when it happened?'

'I don't know for sure . . . She was probably standing in the bushes . . .'

'And you?'

'I came running . . .'

'Why were you running?'

'The bang! Don't you understand . . .'

'Take your head off the table, so I can understand what you're saying, son! So nobody was with anyone else?'

'No . . .'

He slowly raised his head. And put his hands on the table. All the trickling stopped. He saw himself floating in the sheriff's large, serious eyes. But that did not matter. Because he had finally found an explanation for everything.

'No. Nobody was with anyone else. Everybody was alone. I was picking berries and eating them.'

He hurled the words into the room triumphantly.

When no one said anything, he thought hard about the words and repeated them. They sounded perfectly correct.

The sheriff sighed. He had done his duty. He filled out his papers with great thoroughness. They stated that Leo Zjukovski, a native of the Russian empire traveling in Nordland, ended his life by his own hand with a rifle shot in Sheriff Lars Holm's district. The man had been hunting, and there were no witnesses when the shot was fired. Dina Grønelv and her minor son, Benjamin, heard the shot and arrived immediately afterwards. But his life could not be saved.

The sheriff read the whole thing aloud. His voice grew somewhat husky when he read, '. . . his life could not be saved.'

Anders nodded imperceptibly. Then it was over.

It was then the boy first realized he had wet himself.

He went out the door last, and managed to get to his room unnoticed to find dry clothes.

That afternoon after the sheriff rowed away in his boat, Anders had the feeling he had participated in a great sin. He wondered what nice thing he could do for Benjamin. All he could think of was to take him fishing in the *spiss* boat and give him as much brown sugar and snuff as he could stand.

The boy ate sugar and chewed snuff until he vomited. And when he finished vomiting, he seemed just fine.

But Anders kept an eye on him for a few days to see what might develop. Now and then the thought struck him that she should have been with the boy when he was questioned. She was his mother. But he understood her too well. Several times he was on the point of telling her. But he did not know how to do it.

So he said nothing.

Dina's Russian was gone. And Anders felt guilty of a great sin, strange as that might be. He had certainly liked the man. Admired him. And envied him. The fellow had been so quick about everything. Had struck while the iron was hot. A fellow who did not lie around and wait for an opportunity. He went right to it. And won Dina for himself. That was the only thing Anders had against the man. Still, he had wished the man had never been born.

And now he was no more.

The first thing Benjamin did after he moved his eider-down quilt, his shells, Mother Karen's magnifying glass, and his writing materials into the main house was to go through the whole house sniffing. He had to absorb the unfamiliar smells in order to feel at home again. It took several days. He spent hours in Mother Karen's bedroom. Stared at Jacob's portrait with its cheerful mustache on the handsome face. Jacob always seemed to be hiding from the fact that he was laughing.

He looked at himself in the oval mirror above the chest of drawers to see what he had inherited from Jacob. But gave up, and decided to resume the hunt after his beard started growing.

Oline was extremely pleased.

'The boy has moved into the main house,' she announced bluntly to anyone who would listen. 'He's no cotter's boy, he's the only son at Reinsnes!'

Stine said nothing. But every day she came with little things Benjamin had forgotten, or she asked him to run errands or do small jobs for her. That annoyed Oline greatly.

'Benjamin isn't a hired hand,' she snarled one day when Stine came to ask him to help her clean the cellar.

'No,' said Stine. 'But he's strong and quick. And Hanna is so weak and careless.'

Oline took it upon herself to see to it that Benjamin's status was maintained, and exploded with a stream of harsh words. Dina walked by the half-open kitchen door just when Oline said:

'You can go home and teach that girl to do a job, without bothering Benjamin! He's been treated like a stable boy much too long!'

When Dina entered, Oline stopped her tirade and

turned to the table where she was pounding fish. The large wooden club smacked the minced fish greedily. A fire blazed in the new cast-iron stove, and test patties already sizzled in the pan. The smell of fish cakes and a hint of nutmeg wafted into every corner.

'It hasn't hurt Benjamin to do a few jobs,' said Dina.

Oline was threateninly silent.

'Benjamin doesn't sleep well at night. Has dreams. It doesn't matter if he keeps me awake, because I don't sleep well either. That's why he's moved to the south bedroom. But he can certainly do things to be useful.'

'I didn't come to make trouble,' said Stine.

'You never make trouble,' said Dina. 'And Oline has plenty to do without worrying about Benjamin too!'

'But it's not right!' said Oline. 'Not right! That a gentleman's son should grow up in a worker's cottage on his family estate and have all sorts of jobs that nobody else wants!'

She was stirred by her boldness and pursed her mouth like a postman's horn to appear even more dignified.

'There are enough masters in this world,' Dina said brusquely. 'Benjamin knows who he is. He doesn't need idle hands.'

Oline swallowed a reply, and swore never to open her mouth again.

And she kept that promise until evening.

At first he thought he could just help himself to Oline's tidbits, Stine's open hands and eyes, and Dina's un-hesitating closeness which you had to earn. But it was not that simple. Relating to the Reinsnes women proved as difficult as balancing on a hay-drying wire stretched between the barn and the bridge to the hayloft door. He often fell down, and got bruised and hurt.

Sometimes he grew weary of it. Or the Russian shouted and howled in the daytime too. Then he went to see Anders at the wharf. Anders did not ask questions or plan things for others. You could ask him about anything and get an objective answer. He was not related to anyone, married to anyone, father of anyone, or the parson's friend. He simply had a permanent place at Dina's table, and managed her cargo boats and her trade with Bergen. That was all. No one could prevent Anders from leaving when he wished, or from staying when he wished. No one tried to get Anders to clean the cellar. That was probably why he smiled so easily.

One day he asked Anders how he came to Reinsnes. And Anders answered, with his pipe between his teeth and that remarkable protruding jaw curved in a smile:

'It was because of a shipwreck, son! Shipwrecks are important for people. For life and death. You often come to new places when there's a shipwreck . . . That's certain. That's how I came to Reinsnes.'

'Was it long ago you got shipwrecked?'

'It was my poor, blessed parents who got ship-wrecked, not me. I was just a little fellow then.'

He went on to tell about Jacob's first wife, Ingeborg, who took in both his brother Niels and him. The story became so real to Benjamin that he greeted Ingeborg when he passed her portrait in the hall.

Oline had often given detailed accounts of the Reinsnes family connections. But she painted with different colors from Anders. Her innumerable stories and complicated details were exciting enough to hear. But they never ended. Anders, on the other hand, told things in a way that made you see what was big and what was small. And when Benjamin had time to compare Anders's and Oline's accounts, everything somehow fitted together.

He stopped seeing Jacob as the unhappy man who died too soon, as Oline would have it. Jacob was a lively sailor who went ashore and married one person after another. And when he got tired of that, he fell over a cliff. But Jacob always had Anders's respect and Oline's love.

That made it good to think: 'Jacob is my father.'

'If one had a father, would one maybe go along to Lofoten?' he asked one day when he and Anders sat at Andreas Wharf repairing nets in the glow of a large lantern.

'Well . . . it's not a question of . . . you can probably go to Lofoten when you're dry behind the ears. Father or no father. It depends on what sort of stuff you've got in you,' replied Anders with a sidelong glance.

'What are fathers for? I mean, what do they use them for . . . people who've got them?'

'The devil only knows. But there can be many things . . .' said Anders after careful thought.

Then he filled his pipe and started talking about his father.

'He could turn around a bowl full of hot porridge so fast that even the dab of butter in the middle didn't fall out! I can still remember that.'

'That's impossible.'

'Not for my father,' said Anders. 'He wasn't afraid of burning his hand. Ah well . . . he drowned . . .'

'And Hanna's father hanged himself?'

Anders remained calm.

'Yes,' he said.

'Why do things like that always happen?'

'They don't always happen, it only seems that way when you're from Reinsnes,' said Anders.

'Are you anybody's father, Anders?'

'Not that I know.'

'Doesn't a person know a thing like that?'

'No, it's hard for fellows to keep track of everything.'

Anders spat to control his laughter.

'Why aren't you my father?' the boy asked, looking pointedly at the man.

'That you'll have to ask Dina.'

Anders cut the thread with the small knife attached to a ring on his finger. A sharp beak that suddenly pecked.

'Do women decide who the father will be?'

'Not always, I guess. But Dina does.'

'Was Jacob such a wonderful father?'

'Hmmm . . . I don't know if she chose him because he'd be a good father. Dina was so young when she came here.'

'Why did she choose him then?'

Anders felt himself perspiring. And the mending thread had run out.

'Jacob was a dependable fellow in every way. And he owned Reinsnes. I think the sheriff wanted him for a son-in-law. But it's not my business to talk about this, Benjamin. You should ask your mother . . .'

Benjamin ignored the last words as needless talk, and asked:

'Did Dina want Jacob?'

'I think so . . .'

'Why would she want a man who only died?'

'Nobody could foresee Jacob's fate. Maybe it was mainly the sheriff who decided on Dina's husband.'

After a brief silence, the boy said firmly:

'I can't believe that!'

Anders had to laugh.

'It happened many years ago, Benjamin.'

Benjamin did not answer, just fumbled with his net without seeing the large hole he had found.

'You should have been my father,' he said.

'Why?'

'It just seems that way . . . then we could have gone to Lofoten together.'

The boy sent Anders a naked look.

The man had difficulty making his pipe draw properly.

'Do you think I'd have been different then?' asked Benjamin.

Anders took the pipe from his mouth, coughed long and thoroughly, and looked at him. Then he slowly shook his head.

'No, I think you'd have been exactly the same, no matter what.'

'So then you can be my father anyway?'

Anders hesitated slightly, then held out his hand.

'All right! If that makes you happy. But I think we'd better keep this between the two of us, because that's not what the church records say.'

They shook hands and nodded solemnly.

CHAPTER 4

Reinsnes had acquired more unseen burdens. Old log walls accepted them. Hid them in the chinks. Among dead people's eternal breathing in old buildings. Among tufts of moss and old rags already there.

Then bodies and voices filled the house to muffle the sorrow. Dina did not pace upstairs at night, nor sit in the summer house drinking wine as Oline predicted. In the morning you did not find half-extinguished cigars and empty bottles lying all over the house. Apparently everything was white and pure as fields of new-fallen snow.

At times Benjamin was awakened by the Russian's crying. Sometimes by his own. Then he went to the master bedroom to be with Dina. They played chess against fear of the dark and the thing no one could make amends for.

Since only Anders, Dina and Benjamin slept on that side of the upper floor, Anders heard every sound. He was often awakened by the boy's weeping. Then he heard padding across floorboards and creaking doors. A fire was laid in the stove in Dina's room. It made his own room feel icy cold and the bedclothes clammy. Made him long to sail away from everything. Because it reminded him of something he had never had. Anders would lie there staring wide-eyed at the black wall, knowing those two were awake right across the hall.

One morning the boy did not get up for breakfast. But Angell, who tutored Benjamin and Hanna, was at the table.

'I think that boy has turned night into day. Being awake all night surely won't increase his desire to learn?'

Dina gave the tutor a piercing look.

'Benjamin has nightmares. We chase them away by playing chess,' she said, and passed Anders the bread plate with both hands without him asking for it. One hand brushed his wrist.

Anders was not sure how to behave. He had long seen that her eyes were bloodshot and that deep furrows had appeared around her mouth. He lowered his eyes to leave her ravaged face in peace.

'Last night it was so cold the barrels under the eaves froze solid,' he said cheerfully, and passed the bread plate to the tutor.

'Winter is coming in earnest,' the tutor responded pleasantly, and was glad his slight blunder did not have worse consequences.

Sometime before Christmas, Hanna stopped being 'Little Hanna' to Benjamin. It no doubt had something to do with the Russian and Dina. He had long studied Hanna surreptitiously. That helped him think proper thoughts. For instance, how she would look if she died. Without a head, for example. He could sneak up on her with Mother Karen's magnifying glass as if she were an insect. It was impossible to imagine Hanna as a dead fly on the window sill. But he did not let himself be fooled. Because the Russian had also been like that . . . impossible to imagine dead.

Or was it just because the thought never crossed his mind? He had been a little boy then. With only ordinary thoughts.

One day they were sitting at the big dining-room table. He watched Hanna struggling to cut out a paper Christmas manger. She had light hairs on her upper lip. As if she were a cat. You could examine them under the magnifying glass and she did not mind.

Then Dina entered the room. The innermost things in Hanna's eyes closed, and her face grew sullen.

He did not like it. So he imagined she had incredibly small feet and round knock knees. That way she got punished without his having to hurt her.

The most difficult thing about Hanna was her eyes. They were brown, like coffee beans floating in a big round cup of milk. When she blinked, everything disappeared in a forest of black eyelashes. No one could blink as long and hard as Hanna.

'You don't like Dina, do you?' he said across the table after Dina left.

'Why wouldn't I like Dina?' asked Hanna, blinking long and hard.

'I can tell,' he said firmly, and put her under the magnifying glass again.

She revealed two dark brown coffee beans. They sparkled towards him. Then she blinked again.

'If you must talk about everything you see, that's fine with me,' she said while blinking.

Such answers could put him in a rage. But now he took plenty of time.

'You don't like Dina because I've moved into the south bedroom,' he asserted.

Hanna pursed her lips and cut out two angel wings before giving any sign she had heard a word. Then she sighed and said:

'You haven't really moved, because you're always at our house.'

'Am I there too much?'

'No, but what does this have to do with Dina?'

'She's my mother! Nobody has a mother who rides a horse and travels to Bergen. But I do!'

She mimicked him, tied the bib of her apron properly around her neck and went back to her task.

'Someday I'm going to leave! Just so you know!' he said.

She continued cutting out a halo for baby Jesus as she said with a sigh:

'You're really disgusting lately!'

He sat there gaping.

'What do you mean?'

'Dina this and Dina that! It's only Dina, Dina, on your mind. She's no woman! She's a . . . a devil!'

'Who says that?' he whispered.

'The men at the store.'

'You're lying!' he sobbed, as he slammed down the magnifying glass and dashed out the door.

Hanna cut out the two feet and two arms of baby Jesus while she waited for him to return. When that did not happen, she went looking for him. Without her shawl. She found him in the hay barn. He stood there tossing dry hay as if he intended to feed all the animals himself.

'Don't waste the hay,' she said in a conciliatory tone.

Then he rushed at her. Threw her down hard on the dusty floor and pulled her hair until she cried.

'That will show you, you little devil . . . you're a devil too!' he shouted, and sank to his knees beside her.

She boxed his ears weakly. He defended himself by holding her tight and putting his head against her stomach. But she had already given up. He could tell from her breathing. He wanted to roll her, knead her like dough until every sound disappeared. But he could not do that as long as she was crying.

Finally he took her and was good to her. Examined her and stroked her, smelled her, and played the secret games only they knew about. The games that were discovered long ago and were the reason they were not allowed to sleep in the same bed or in the same room.

In the midst of the game, he realized that nothing was the same as before. Because he had seen Dina and the Russian in the heather. That made the game acrid and shameful. At the same time, he wanted to do things with her that he dared not do. And if you did not dare, you were a coward.

After a while they heard Stine call across the farm-yard. Hanna straightened her clothes and ran off without saying anything. But he knew they were friends in a way. It could not be otherwise. He felt he had escaped a great danger, so he began to curry-comb the horses.

It was a day for unusual meetings. Dina came for her horse, and when Tomas entered the stable a little later he heard Benjamin's cheerful voice amidst strokes of the curry-comb and the horse's snorts.

'You don't need to bother finding a husband, Dina, even if the Russian is gone.'

Dina's voice was barely audible to Tomas. The horse stomped. The sounds came from another part of the world. He went closer and just stood. Nailed to the stable floor. His arms fell like lead weights. He did not feel them.

'We'll manage just fine,' said the boy. 'I'll be grown-up soon. At least, confirmed. And I must tell you, I asked Anders if he can be my father for now!'

'Oh?'

The hay dust made Dina cough.

'He said that was fine,' the boy added.

'And the two of you decided this all by yourselves?'

'Yes. I didn't want to bother you with it.'

'And what's he going to do when he's your father?'

'Well, I asked him about that. His father was good at turning his porridge bowl without spilling the butter in the middle. But Anders can't do that. And actually, that's nothing to teach someone. So it would have to be cargo transport and Bergen voyages and things like that. That should be fine. I can take my books along so it won't be so boring.'

'You certainly can.'

Neither said anything for a while as they saddled the horse.

'Have you often thought you should have had a father to be with?' Tomas heard her say.

'Oh no . . . no, just when it was convenient. Not so often . . .'

66

'What else did Anders say?' she asked.

'Oh, he's so much fun to talk with about a lot of things. He laughs so quietly, but there's lots of laughter in that fellow. If you'd married Anders that time you chose Jacob for my father, you'd have a husband who's alive,' he said. 'But you couldn't have known that, of course,' he added good-naturedly.

'The fact is, Benjamin, it was Jacob who wanted me, and not Anders.'

'What a lumphead that Anders is! He said it was because Jacob had Reinsnes and was such a great fellow, and that the sheriff wanted Jacob.'

'You shouldn't talk so much about that with Anders,' she said.

'But I've got to talk with him when he's going to be my father!'

Tomas suddenly came to his senses. Slipped out the door and went down to the boathouses.

CHAPTER 5

Christmas came with all its noise and commotion. Meals, party games and glasses of toddy. Some people probably remembered the Christmas when the Russian danced and sang.

The sheriff's family was there. The boys clattered up and down stairs, in and out doors. Oline shouted after them, and Thea fetched things for them and picked up after them. Benjamin's room was a rotating lair of wet woolen socks, steam-engine odors and forbidden cigar butts. Vapors from sweaty necks and sweet cocoa topped with whipped cream. The smell of Christmas holiday and boys reached way out to the hall. Coarse *lodde* oversocks lurched light-heartedly from one corner to another according to whether the blast went in or out.

Three night buckets had to be placed in the upstairs hall. And on the second day of Christmas, Thea said she could not understand how so much water could come out of people. There was more this year than last, she declared.

The boys' laughter and squabbling shifted back and forth so quickly that no one bothered to mediate. They were a year older now. And everything went on as before.

People chose not to make much of it when Benjamin quietly moved down to Mother Karen's room the first day of Christmas.

He had trouble sleeping, Dina said in passing. The sheriff's sons stared at Benjamin when she said that.

Only old people had trouble sleeping. But they did not even tease him. It was somehow a solemn thing – to have trouble sleeping. It was worse that Benjamin did not take part in the games. He sat in his room reading books of his own free will.

At the first high tide after New Year they launched *Mother Karen*. People came from far and near, and a few straggling Christmas guests also were part of the hullabaloo. The servant girls had scrubbed with green soap and joked that the lice were very stubborn in Anders's bunk. He replied flippantly that it was because the bed was always warm. Such impudence emboldened the girls, who took the opportunity to nudge and touch Anders.

Dina stood at the open window of the aft cabin. To everyone's surprise, she had come along. The day was mild, but leaden, for the sun had not yet come this far north. Still, a hint of it appeared in the south at midday and made the small islands glimmer.

The girls raised their heads when Dina called to Anders. A cheerful shout.

Benjamin lay flat in the rowboat fishing for roach among the beach rocks. He heard it too. And it seemed this would be a good day to think about.

The girls, who had finished their scrubbing and had such fun with Anders, now gathered their scouring cloths and wooden wash tubs to row back to shore. But they cast a glance or two towards the cabin as Anders went in.

'You joke with the girls,' Dina said when he entered.

'One has the fun one makes for oneself,' he chuckled.

'I brought a drop of rum to celebrate that you're ready to sail for Lofoten.'

'Oh,' he said, and sat down on a bunk. He watched as she poured the drinks.

'You don't seem much in need of a drink,' she commented.

'Well, it's just unexpected. Been a long time . . .' he added quietly.

'A lot has happened.'

'Yes, a lot has happened,' he agreed.

'But now there's daylight enough for people to live!' she said, as she handed him a glass and sat down beside him. It was the same bunk where she lay when she had forced the fetus from her body on Fold Sea.

'What do you mean?' he asked, remembering the fetus he had dropped over the railing.

'That the days are getting lighter.'

'Oh, I see,' he mumbled, and waited.

'Why are you looking at me like that?' she asked.

'Because I don't know what you want from me.'

She tossed her head. It reminded him of her horse when it whinnied while tethered out in the fields.

'It's a long time since the two of us talked . . .'

'Yes,' he agreed.

She rocked the glass between her hands.

'Sometimes you're too smart for me, Anders,' she said unexpectedly.

'What a thing to say . . . How so?'

'You don't say much about what you see,' she replied, balancing her glass between one horizontal palm and one vertical.

'What things?'

'Me, for example.'

'That's not my place,' he muttered.

He looked at her in embarrassment. The girls laughed as they rowed to shore. Ripples from the rowboat gurgled against the hull. The air was salty and pungent. They were alone. Dina and he.

An excitement rose somewhere. He lowered his gaze.

'I want you to take charge of Reinsnes for me! I'm going south. I may be gone when you get back from Lofoten,' she said.

He swallowed carefully, and calmly set the stemmed glass and its contents on the small table. It was securely bolted to the deck. He had to stretch far to do it.

70

'Where are you going?'

'To Copenhagen. Maybe even further. I'm taking the steamboat to Trondheim.'

'You're going south to Copenhagen . . . May I ask why?'

'It never hurts to ask,' she replied dryly.

The light was violet. Her fingers moved restlessly in her lap. Gleaming oval fingernails against dark woolen material.

'Is something troubling you?' he asked.

She reached for his hands and came closer. It made his skin tingle and he felt uneasy.

'It's so confining here! Do you understand?'

'Understand or understand . . . How long will you be gone?'

'I don't know.'

'What's really going on?' he asked, and began to stand up.

Then she leaned forward and gripped both his wrists. She was strong. He enjoyed it, and yet felt uneasy. When she did not answer, he said:

'It seems I must do as you say. Tell me . . . Is it because the Russian haunts Reinsnes too much?'

'What do you mean?' she whispered.

'I mean: are you grieving so over Leo Zjukovski that you have to leave the country?'

'Grieving?'

'Everyone could see he was the man you imagined as the master of Reinsnes. I saw it too.'

He wanted his voice to sound straightforward and ordinary. But did not quite know how.

'Grieving?' she repeated, staring out the cabin window at something. 'It's so confining here . . . It's all the same struggle. The seasons. The farm work. The servants. The accounts.'

'And you discovered that after Leo left?' he asked quietly.

'I suppose I knew it before . . . you'd probably think the same if you were doomed to always . . .'

'I probably would,' he agreed.

They were silent for a moment.

'But I'm not the right person to take charge of Reinsnes. I'm at home so little,' he said.

'You're the only one I can ask.'

'You're not serious about all this?'

'Yes, I am!'

'And if you got married, there would be two of you to do the work?' he said nonchalantly.

A shadow crossed them. A seagull flying past the window.

'Others have said that before,' she said.

'What did you answer?'

'It's long ago . . . I asked if they had anyone to suggest.'

'Did they?'

'Yes.'

'Who?'

'You, Anders.'

Blood rushed to his face. But he forced himself to look at her. Waited for a scornful glance. But it did not come.

'Well, people say the most incredible things. I remember they thought the same . . . when you signed the papers giving me the cargo boat.'

'Maybe they were right,' she said slowly.

'Right?'

'That it should have been you.'

'People can always think,' he said, and hastily continued:

'And now you're planning to go to Copenhagen because it's so confining here.'

'Would you have accepted? If I'd asked you?'

'If you'd asked me?'

He ran a hand through his hair helplessly.

'If I'd asked you?' she repeated.

'Yes,' he said simply.

She sighed.

'For your own sake? Or for Reinsnes?' she asked.

He gave her a long look before he answered:

'I tell you, I don't do such things for the sake of Reinsnes!'

'How do you think it would have gone?' she asked.

'Badly!'

'Why?'

'You'd have met the Russian. And I'd have escaped to Bergen,' he said honestly.

'And if I hadn't met the Russian?'

'Then it might well have . . .'

'You don't often see the Russian any more.'

'No, I don't. But I think you do,' he said.

'What makes you think that?'

'You have at least two gray hairs that I can see in this dim light. You pace your room at night, and your skin is flabby as a newly-spawned cod. There's only eyes and a tail left. And now you want to leave shore. Out into the deep.'

She had to laugh. They looked at each other with smiling seriousness.

'If I asked you now, would you have me?' she suddenly said.

There was a long pause before he answered.

'If you asked me, and then went to Copenhagen?'

'If I asked you and went to Bergen with you?'

'I'd have to say no,' he whispered.

'Why?'

'I can't live with someone who's thinking about a corpse!'

She hit him so hard they toppled onto the bunk, both of them. Then she raised both hands and hit him again. From both sides. His glass fell to the floor. Teetered there. He could tell by the sound it was still in one piece. Before he knew what he was doing, he lay full length on top of her. Broke into a sweat as he twisted her hands until he was holding her down.

'Well!' he panted.

Her body under him! He did not know which of them trembled. Both?

Then she gave up. At first he pretended not to notice. He wanted it to continue. Then he loosened his grip, let her go, and stood up. Filled with shame, he smoothed her clothes without looking at her.

'I pray for sense and reason,' he mumbled as he dragged himself out of the door.

Once outside, he began to tremble. It started in his knees and spread throughout his body. He tried to button his shirt, which had come undone in the scuffle. But he could not. Instead, he gripped the railing and held fast. It seemed like an eternity while he caught his breath. Then it happened:

'Anders!'

She called in a low voice from inside.

He put his head back and stared hard at the mountain tops. Then he heard it clearly once more.

'Anders!'

For a moment he wanted to rush back into the cabin. But something stopped him.

'All right! I'll take charge of Reinsnes for you!' he shouted hoarsely.

Then he jumped over the railing and waded ashore.

The rowboat in which Benjamin was fishing almost tipped over in the backwash. The boy shouted something to him.

He slipped on the icy stones, struggled and fought with the seaweed that tried to entangle him. He staggered up the tree-lined avenue with sea water streaming from him. Slogged across the courtyard in sight of everyone. Purposeful as a mating walrus, while he spat and panted to left and right.

No one had ever seen Anders like that. It was not just that he was wet from the waist down, with green slime and seaweed dragging from his fisherman's boots. An incredible sight. But Anders was angry! Or whatever one called it.

For the first time, Anders sailed for Lofoten without joy. Without looking forward to coming home. He cursed himself for not being different. At the same time, he realized he had harbored certain dreams all these years.

To have dreams was one thing. To carry them out was another. Dina was not for him, he had always known that. He could sail a cargo boat in storms and driving snow and still keep it afloat, but he could not knowingly start on a long voyage with a vessel that had no rudder.

That's how it was! So she would go to Copenhagen, and he to Lofoten.

CHAPTER 6

Benjamin had seen dead bodies. Dead faces. That was
not so awful in itself. Slaughtering was actually worse.
Because the animals got so badly mangled. Mother
Karen's dead face resembled the dull white vase on the
sideboard in the dining room. A clear yellowish glaze
with a pattern of criss-crossed lines. He saw her face so
clearly when necessary, it did not really matter that her
body was dead and gone.

It was different with the Russian. He shouted without a face. That was probably why it was so hard to
get rid of him. He became a slaughtered animal in a
way.

When fresh meat was served, you could imagine
Oline had secretly prepared the Russian and put him
on the platters. Benjamin did not know where such a
thought came from, and it made Oline a monster. But
sometimes it came so powerfully that everything in his
stomach turned upside down, and he had to ask to be
excused and run to the outhouse.

When Oline had used the whole man like that, and
only his ravaged head and his boots remained, you
would think that was the end of it. But the body grew
whole again in his mind. The boots creaked at night
when Benjamin turned in bed, and the shouts came
from the ghost of a headless man.

After such nights he could sit for hours in Mother
Karen's room examining his thumbnails without seeing
them. Until the tutor or someone else demanded he do
something useful. On icy mornings when no one had

laid a fire in the stove you could imagine you were a monk doing penance in a cell. Penance for the Russian.

He marked the days according to sayings on Mother Karen's calender stick. It was not actually a stick, but a framed piece of leather on which someone had painted words and useless drawings. It had always hung above her writing desk.

On New Year's Day, long before the sun returned, he had been up early to make sure the sky was not red. 'If the morning sky is red on New Year's Day, great sorrow and lamenting are in store, and the year will surely bring a great war,' the calender stick said.

He had sighed when he saw that a snowstorm raged outside and not even the icicles were thriving.

He did not really understand about these wars that people talked of. But one thing was certain: people died like flies. They did not all die from holes in their heads. Anders thought most people starved to death in the wars.

You could imagine the ragged, emaciated bodies staggering about, gnawing on anything they could find. But that did not give you the great experience of War. You needed horses and uniforms too.

Sometimes he saw them in his mind. The soldiers. They lay all over the battlefields with large red holes in their heads.

But that could not be correct, either. In a way, war stopped being dangerous this winter. Almost as peaceful as being in church. When you thought about all that could happen in real life. He lined up the tin soldiers Anders had given him. But nothing came of it. So he swept them into a corner and began reading a book of adventures from the great forests in America.

In February he began examining the light that climbed over the window sill in Mother Karen's room. Sat patiently on the floor and waited until the rays reached his bare feet. He discovered he had never really paid attention to the sunlight before.

In a way it was solemn, but at the same time so

terrible you almost had to cry. Just like when he stood looking at the rows of graves in the churchyard while people around him chattered about wind and weather. Standing there like that, he realized it was only he who knew death.

He longed to talk to someone about the sunlight, but the words lay so far back in his head. There was no use even thinking about it.

Once he had confided to Hanna that he always counted to one hundred when walking the gloomy path to the outhouse, or to one thousand when he went to the summer barn on dark autumn winter evenings. That was the law. He did not know why it was so. But he knew if he did not make sure he was at exactly one hundred when he drew the outhouse latch, all the hill folk living in the netherworld would be his enemies. What that would lead to was unclear. So he could not explain it to Hanna in a way she would understand. But she had listened anyway, blinking the whole time.

'You need to go to the outhouse. But why go to the summer barn for no reason, when it is madness?' she asked.

'You've got to visit the place you were born,' he replied, and blew rime off a blade of winter grass he held between his thumbs. It sounded like a pig was being beaten.

'You mustn't talk about being born in the summer barn. It's blasphemy! That's what Oline says.'

'I don't talk about it either. You're the one asking questions and twittering like a sparrow.'

He should have known she did not understand. She was always warning him or twisting his story. She certainly had not understood anything about the hill folk and their nature. He was sorry he had said anything, and was terrified that one day she would waylay him and prevent him from counting. Just to see what would happen when he did not get there by one hundred! That would be like her.

But she did not know that he knew the sun now, and

that he was thinking about counting the steps all the way to where the Russian's boots had lain in the heather.

On 24 February Benjamin read on the calender stick: 'Mattis breaks ice. If there is none, he makes ice.'

He had been waiting a long time for Anders to send him a letter. As all fathers did. But it did not happen. He knew it was because Anders was so angry with Dina the day they got the cargo boat ready to sail to Lofoten.

What was Anders thinking – he had shouted to Dina that he would take charge of Reinsnes for her, and then did not even send a letter!

No one had seen Anders leap into the sea before. It was awful to see that big man wade ashore with cold water up to his armpits. So completely unnecessary, because Benjamin had been lying in the rowboat waiting to bring them both to shore with dry feet.

And then Anders just went off to Lofoten. Of course, he had said goodbye and patted Benjamin's cheek, but it was unpleasant.

It had to do with the fact that wherever Dina was, things were changed and not for him. But one could still wish Anders would send a letter from Lofoten.

Nobody heard anything. He thought maybe Judgment Day had come, because Anders did not have the temperament to stay angry so long. He tried to broach the subject with Dina, but she said Anders had never been a letter-writer. The way she said it was also like Judgment Day.

'If there is no ice, he makes ice!' He interpreted the calender stick to mean that Mother Karen had intended him to do great deeds. It made him tired. Not tired so he could sleep. But tired so he could not be so afraid.

It was not just that the Russian shouted day and night. It was also that Dina rummaged in dresser drawers and dragged out her trunks. One day he heard her rummaging in her bedroom, he ran in without knocking. She was leaning over the trunk putting things into it. Then he began pounding her with his fists and said bad things which he forgot immediately. Something about her wanting him to be alone with the Russian when Judgment Day came. She did not say a word. Not that he expected her to. But it was difficult with all that ice. And he did not feel safe until he saw her drag the trunk into Jacob's alcove again.

Overcoming the fact that he and Tomas still were not friends, he asked him if there could be so much to do in Lofoten that people had no time to send a greeting. But Tomas did not seem to understand. At any rate, he replied vaguely that the Lofoten fellows often forgot to send messages home, no matter how things were.

'Not Anders!' said Benjamin.

'Anders is no better than others,' Tomas sneered.

'Maybe he's been shipwrecked?'

'Oh no, because *then* people would send a message,' Tomas said firmly.

This conversation made it absolutely impossible for Benjamin to go to the cottage when he knew Tomas was there.

The calender stick indicated George's Mass: 'Gregor's time. Day and night are equally long.' And he still had not heard from Anders.

Anders had prepared himself for how it would be at Reinsnes when she was not there. Had planned how he would get through all the days and nights. Imagined that the thought of lonely meals was not forbidding. Such thoughts had not occupied much of his time in the past. Now they were the last thing to get rid of before going to sleep, and the first thing to deal with when he awoke.

It was fine to have 'a nail in the wall to hang your jacket on', he told himself, and then added: it's not what happens to you, but how you *take* it that counts. Fortified with old adages and comforting words that barely got under his skin, he planned an early voyage to Bergen even before he left Lofoten. He conjured up

80

his longing for the hard southward journey along the shipping lane. And he reminded himself of the difference between bad luck and disaster.

Even so, he could not help feel that the land darkened towards him when they sailed into the Sound and were home. He set the wheel, took off his oilskin hat and whistled, as he normally did when he sighted Reinsnes.

At first he thought she was some sort of hallucination. But when Anton said, 'I do believe she came to the landing herself this time,' he emerged from his daze and realized it was Dina standing at the boat landing. It was a shock. He had believed Dina's word could not be changed.

He was used to looking at things in relation to the wind and seasons. That was hard enough, but allowed reasonable time for thought. So the sight of Dina at the landing was like turning winter into summer with no warning.

However, he took care to behave as he always did as long as people could see him. Shook her hand and gave her a smile. But turned as quickly as possible to Benjamin and all the boy's questions about why he had not written.

'I'm just not a letter-writer,' was his answer.

He let others take care of the crates and baggage, put his hand on the boy's head, and walked away from the landing while he told Benjamin about the package he had for him. That way he could escape.

The trees had frozen drops of water hanging from the tips of their black branches. Crows ravaged the manure in the fields. Lighter days were on the way.

The boy asked endless, eager questions. Anders replied and laughed. He could hear her right behind him. She apparently had new boots. They creaked a little with each step she took. But he did not turn around.

*   *   *

81

The crates of fresh cod were duly admired and distributed to the cotters and good customers. The fish already salted down in barrels would go into the underground cellar. But a couple of crates would also be hung to dry or be lightly salted. The men talked about all the fish that now hung on drying racks in Lofoten and slapped their pants pockets boastfully.

A whole armada of small boats gradually gathered at the landing. Everyone who had seen the cargo boat sail swiftly past the headlands found a pretext to come as soon as possible. To see if the Lofoten men had got rid of their lice or grown a beard, as they said.

Homecoming and a meal of flat bread and fat took their toll. The men disbanded early. Only Anton slept at the main house. The others went home, or slept in the servants' quarters.

The tutor had a few days off and had gone to Strandsted. The maids were still clattering in the kitchen and pantry, and Benjamin had marched upstairs wearing the helmsman's cap Anders brought him. He had worn it at the dinner table and no one had objected.

Anton had yawned three times and said goodnight. Now the upstairs hall creaked under him.

Dina sat in the chaise longue as usual, her arm stretched along its back. Her half-smoked cigar lay in the ashtray. Her eyes were half-closed. Anders cleared his throat, then calmly announced he would like that glass of rum he never got to finish before he left for Lofoten.

She looked surprised, but quickly collected herself and called to Thea in the pantry.

A tired, harried Thea put her head round the door.

'Anders wants rum tonight,' said Dina.

The maid looked in surprise at the rum bottle next to Dina, but came with a glass and filled it.

'Will there be anything else this evening?' she asked, and barely curtsied.

'You'll have to ask Oline,' said Dina.

'She's already asleep.'

'Then you're certainly free to leave. Thank you for today! There's been a lot of commotion,' said Dina cheerfully.

Thea gave her a quick glance.

'It's been fun too,' she said, and gave them a brief smile, curtsied again and left.

'It's light much later in the evening now,' Anders said awkwardly.

She did not reply immediately.

He coughed. Then he began talking about what they had earned in Lofoten. Wanted to bring numbers and accounts to her, so she could judge for herself.

'We'll look at the numbers tomorrow,' she said.

Then she rose and went to the smoking table to get a new cigar. He was about to remind her that she had one in the ashtray. But then she brushed past him and touched his shoulder. As she used to do before. Even when others saw it. Before the Russian died.

Anders had slept in cold sheepskins and endured freezing hands for a long time. When Dina carelessly sat down again without arranging her skirts, his eyes darted to her ankles. He could see them clearly through her stockings. She was wearing indoor shoes. The arch of her right instep emerged from the hem of her skirt. It had such a strange effect on him.

It took the time needed to drink a glass of rum in reasonable sips before he realized he should say something. He leaned back and looked at her.

'Have many travelers stopped at Reinsnes while I've been gone?'

'About as many as you'd expect during the winter,' she replied, returning his look.

'And otherwise? All's well?'

'About as usual.'

She took deep, pleasurable drags of the new cigar.

'You didn't leave,' he said finally.

'No.'

'Why not?'

'It occured to me that I should wait. At least until summer. And go along on your next trip to Bergen.'

The clock watched them from the wall. Its pendulum knocked the sense out of him.

'There's Benjamin, after all . . .' she said.

'I'm glad you changed your mind!'

He amazed himself. To think he said it straight out!

'I shouldn't have said what I did on the boat that time,' he mumbled.

She shrugged her shoulders and blew smoke rings, which she followed with wide eyes.

'I shouldn't have hit you!' she said without looking at him.

'It was a bit . . . sudden, that's true. You hit hard!'

He tried to laugh, but was not completely successful.

'Benjamin tells me you've promised to be his father?'

His face slowly flushed, but he nodded.

'That's what he wanted . . .' he said.

'I see.'

The pendulum nagged at him.

Anders had nerves like old tinder-dry cobbler's thread. One just had to make sure the thread did not break. He was hanging by it. He took a breath.

'You asked me about . . . about something before I went fishing. Maybe it's nothing to ponder.'

She straightened her shoulders.

'I've thought while I was away . . . I think I'll accept,' he continued.

'Anders?'

The smoking parlor was between them. The carpet Mother Karen ordered from Copenhagen. It was thick, with rows of olive green and wine-red flowers. He by the smoking table. She in the chaise longue with her back to the window. There was no moon. Just naked glass with a bluish gleam.

'Yes,' he responded.

'You know what you're saying?' she whispered after a while.

He nodded and cleared his throat. His body was immobile.

'And what you'll get?' she continued.

'No, only you can tell me that.'

'I don't know what I have to give.'

She was still whispering, as though the silk tapestry had ears.

'We'll find out,' he said, more to himself than to her.

'You don't seem especially happy.'

'I don't know what I am, Dina. I've gone for years not daring to think the thought . . .'

'Don't you think we'll manage?'

'If you really want to.'

She put down the cigar and walked across the room to him. He opened his arms, settled her head on his shoulder, and hesitantly stroked her hair.

'Do I still smell like fish, or did I manage to get clean?'

'You smell like Anders,' she said against his shoulder.

'How can you know what Anders smells like?'

'I know now.'

'It took a long time.'

'It took the time it had to take. Are you still my brother?'

'No.'

'Why?'

'Because I can't be everything.'

He sat in the smoking parlor at Reinsnes. The room in which he had dreamed of being the master, ever since childhood. The smoking table with the pipe rack and cigar boxes. The cupboard with antique goblets from Holland. And he realized they were not what mattered. Surely happiness was not found in things?

He felt her warmth. Her head against his neck and cheek. As they sat there, images came to mind. Of Dina and Jacob. Dina and the Russian. Dina when she lost herself in her music.

'There's one thing I must ask you . . .' he said.

85

'Yes?'

'Did you buy me, Dina?'

'Why do you ask that?'

'Because people will think so.'

'People?'

'Yes. The same ones who've thought for a long time that something was going on.'

'In that case, what would the price be?'

'Reinsnes.'

'And what about me? What would I get in return?' she asked, rising from his arms.

'A man to take charge of Reinsnes. Your boy.'

'Anders! Why do you say that now?'

She stood before him with clenched hands. He leaned forward, and did not look at her.

'So you will say things as they are.'

The words echoed from cellar to cellar within him.

She snorted. A sign she was very angry.

'So you think you've got me now?'

She swept over to the chaise longue.

'No,' he said. 'But I'm too old to set out to sea in the fog in an open boat without sighting land. So I need to know where I have you. Because I'm not for sale. I don't care if I own this house with all its plush and silver. I've got all I need when I can move under sail and have oars on board.'

'Good!' she replied, staring at the chandelier.

'I won't force you to say you're in love with me, Dina. I just want to know . . . This is for the rest of our lives . . . this too.'

She fumbled for her extinguished cigar and found it. Her fingers were a little unsteady and her face shone white. He got up and lit the cigar for her.

The clock's pendulum called and called.

He realized that he longed for her to say she was in love with him. To escape that thought he asked:

'What was he like? Leo. What did he promise you?'

He crossed the room hesitantly and sat down again. She still said nothing. He did not know what he expected. Rage? That she would look at him in disdain and say he was unreasonably jealous? Anything at all. Just not what happened.

She crept into the chaise longue and clasped her arms around herself. A confused ball of humanity.

He went over to her again, and rescued her hair from the glowing cigar.

'Dina,' he called in a low voice, and sank to his knees in front of her.

First he tried putting his arms onto the chaise longue. But that did not work well. So he put his arms around her instead.

'Dina, talk to me, say something . . . do you hear?'

She sounded like an old barrel organ that had stood out in the cold a long time and then been brought inside and played too hard.

'If you must cry, then do. But talk to me, please!' he begged.

'He's not here,' she said helplessly. 'He's gone! The others are here. He's the only one who's gone! Why should it be that way? Do you understand it? I thought I had him . . . But I don't.'

'Should he be here now, Dina?'

'Yes.'

'Who are the others?'

She shook her head and slowly rocked from side to side within her skirts.

'Why do you want me, Dina?'

'Because you're the one I should have had long ago.'

'How long ago?' he asked huskily.

'Benjamin is right. It should have been you, not Jacob!'

'Is your love so fleeting, Dina?'

'Love?' she said in amazement.

'Yes, or whatever you want to call it. You saw me only as a man who was in Jacob's house now and then.'

'And you? When did you show . . . love? All I can remember is that you always took care to stand where nothing was burning.'

87

'I suppose I didn't think it possible . . . When did you give me signs I didn't understand? It must have been very long ago?'

'You've always blown through the house like a wind. Before one got used to your being at the table, you were at sea, many miles away.'

'When did you see me for the first time? I mean . . .'

'When we went to Bergen. I didn't know what it would mean. Besides . . .'

'Besides, there was Leo?'

'Yes,' she said harshly.

He stood up. Tried to do it with dignity. It would not have mattered if he laughed at himself. But he did not do that.

'Who do you see now?'

'I thought you planned to propose, since you were already on your knees,' she said.

'Who do you see?' he repeated. 'The Russian, or me?'

'Can't you just let it be now? Or had you thought to make me lick clean every floorboard Leo walked on?'

'If it were only a matter of the floorboards . . .'

'If you mean me, then I think you'd better lick yourself clean,' she snarled.

With that she was gone, before he could think a single thought.

That night it seemed to Anders that the Russian tramped through the upstairs hall in sturdy boots and collected everything connected with Dina. The right corner of her mouth that curled in such an odd way when she smiled. The cowlick at her hairline. Her breasts.

The Russian put it all in his traveling bag and dragged her behind him along the hall. And deep in his sleep Anders began to wish the man were not dead, so he could have thrown him out the door with his bare hands.

He was awakened at dawn by a southwester washing the windows. He lay there for a while and could feel he was in the body of a stiff, sore Lofoten fisherman. Then he remembered the evening of his homecoming.

Despite everything, his nature was such that he saw each morning as a beginning. It had something to do with the daylight.

He rowed out to the cargo boat to get the account books and the order lists. And he was on the lookout for her when she went down to the office at the store. He carried the papers in an oilskin folder under his arm so the clerk and the handful of people sitting along the walls would know he had an errand there.

She looked up when he entered the office. Even said his name.

'Anders!' she said.

But he shut the door as a precaution. Prepared for spring tides, or even worse.

'Do you want to go through the accounts today?' she asked.

'Yes,' he said. 'I want to get it finished now, so we're not on bad terms about that too.'

'Are we on bad terms?'

'I think so.'

'About what?'

'About whether it's you or me who should clean up after Leo.'

He saw her eyes narrow and her hands grip the ledger on the desk in front of her. So he continued immediately:

'I've decided I should do it. And if you don't mind, I'd like to start right now. Will you marry me, Dina Grønelv?'

She rose from the desk instantly. Like a soldier who had just been given an order.

'Yes!' she shouted, almost angrily.

He did not quite know where his arms were. When he found them, he did something that would have been unthinkable the day before. He walked over to the cupboard where Dina kept glasses and bottles of liqueur. He handed her an empty glass.

'Here! Take it!' he said.

They both had unsteady hands. He filled the glass to the brim, until rum ran down her hand. Then he leaned over and licked it.

She did not move. Time stopped. He had never done such a thing before.

'I'm starting immediately,' he murmured over her hand. 'I'll finally have that rum you promised me before I went fishing!'

'If we drink rum this way, we'll go bankrupt,' she said.

'Then we'll go bankrupt,' he declared.

As he straightened up and floated into her eyes, he imagined he found her mouth. But he did not touch her. They gazed at each other for a long time. Then she suddenly began to laugh, tears streaming down her face.

Out in the store they could hear that the Lofoten balance sheet caused a great deal of laughter. First they heard Dina's dark laugh, then Anders joined in resoundingly. It had clearly been a good settling of accounts.

CHAPTER 7

The news of Dina and Anders's marriage was received as an affirmation, not only by Oline.

'One knows what one knows. But it's nobody's business,' she had stated. Thereby salvaging her honor. But the truth was, she had not suspected a thing. No wandering in the night, no intimate glances or caresses had revealed anything special. Oline felt betrayed. And she was not ready to forgive.

A chance to gain respect came when Thea said she had been told they should not prepare the bridal bed in the master bedroom but in the second largest room, where Johan slept when he last lived at Reinsnes.

Oline expressed copious despair that the master and mistress had such warped brains they did not realize the canopy bed would not fit in there.

Anders explained that a new bed would arrive from Trondheim with the next steamboat. And it would not be as big as the old bed. Oline opened her mouth – and shut it again. The man stood there smiling! They had ordered a new bed! Without informing *her* that new sheets and pillowcases had to be sewn. It was no way to do things!

Anders apologized, said he had not realized how serious it was. He did not understand about such things.

'But Dina should know! A man doesn't know any better. But now you know too!' Oline exclaimed.

'Don't be so angry, Oline. I'm sure we'll find a solution,' he said good-naturedly.

'I must talk to Dina about this. We'll need to have the sewing girls come out of turn.'

'But the house is full of sheets, isn't it? Can't we . . . ?'

'Oh my Lord! We're not talking about a bunk on a boat! Don't you realize we're going to prepare a bridal bed for the master and mistress? And the parson is going to bless it? Are you completely crazy?'

There were no witnesses to what caused Anders to give his first order in his own house.

Dina had invited him to the master bedroom one evening when the house was quiet and they were the only ones still up. Anders sat listening with a blank expression as music by Mendelssohn resounded from Lorch's cello.

The room listened behind heavy, drawn drapes. He sat the edge of his chair between two windows.

He watched her through thick blond eyelashes as her arms and fingers moved over the strings. Guided the bow. The fingers on her left hand were small animals that ran across the strings only to suddenly come to rest and quiver. And then take long leaps again. The look on her face moved him. The music drew him in. He could not resist, although he did not know or understand anything about music.

An old wave of longing awoke in him when she threw back her head and caught the rhythm before placing it in the instrument. Her face shone and her mouth moved as if portioning out small strangled shouts.

When the last notes disappeared into the drapes and curtains, she sat with the bow hanging down. Bent forward, as if she was waiting for something.

Then she put the instrument away without looking at him.

'It was comforting to hear . . .' he said softly.

He regretted the words before they were out of his mouth. It sounded as if he were talking to a stranger who had tried to entertain him.

'Did you know what it was?'

He shook his head and waited for her to tell him. But she did not. He grew hesitant, and the silence was uncomfortable. Because he did not know what she had played. He wondered if she thought: he doesn't even know that . . .

'Maybe it's time we gave Oline and the maid some peace so they can sleep,' he said, and got up to leave.

She turned to him with a little smile.

'Are you going to save everything until after the wedding, Anders?'

The wild spring light broke through the thick drapes, casting dark shadows on her cheek and throat.

She stood too close. He could not raise his hands to touch her. The floorboards clung to his knees, and the rows of flowers burst from the wallpaper and wound around his neck. He found no answer.

So he took her hand and led her firmly across the room. Out into the dark hall, where a gleam of light from the stairway stole across the walls.

Once in his room he released her hand and closed the drapes. He could see the pores around her nostrils when he gestured towards the edge of the bed. She sat down.

'You've got a narrow bed, Anders,' she whispered. He noticed her glance towards the wall, and remembered that Benjamin slept on the other side. But she did not mention that.

'It's not the bed, but the man, that matters,' he whispered in return, and sat down beside her.

'Where did you learn that?' she asked.

'It's nothing I've learned. It's something I must try to learn now,' he said, and gathered her hair in his hand. As if wanting to know how much it weighed.

'It's nicer in my bedroom,' she suggested.

'That niceness isn't for me.'

'What do you mean?'

He held her head gently with both hands. Began a

word. Gave up. Took another breath. Then he formed the question in an everyday tone:

'How many men have found bliss, or lain dead, on the bed in that room, Dina?'

His breathing betrayed him. But he still held her head.

'Anders! Are you starting again? You know I've been married,' she said.

'Yes, I know.'

'What is it then?'

'Your seasickness on Fold Sea . . . was that Jacob's gift, so long after he died?'

She tore herself from his hands and snorted.

'Ask everything all at once, and be done! But I want to ask you first: have *I* pressed *you* about what you did along the coast to Bergen, or in your bunk? Have I driven you into a corner because you lived a life before we two came to an understanding? Have I?'

He shook his head.

'No, you haven't. But I'm not man enough to share a *bed* with the Russian. Even if I've decided to share you with him.'

He thought she would hit him. Remembering the last time, he quickly raised his hand to shield himself. But the look she gave him was as if she were alone on a reef gazing through mist and storms.

He put his arms tightly around her.

'I don't want to quarrel about that now. But I feel . . . helpless in there.'

She did not reply. Not then. But she must have understood something, because she leaned close to him. He rocked her gently.

After a while he untied her shoes. His hands stole up her ankles, her legs, her thighs. Their heads collided.

He slowly pulled up her skirt and folded it neatly around her hips. As if performing a task in a journey-man's examination.

With a smile he examined the lace on her petticoat, and put his face in her lap. It was strange to think her odors had always been there. Now they were for him. And warm skin. Through thin material. Against his face. Her blood pulsed and pounded in his ears.

Then he felt her hands on him. She took off his shoes. As if she long had kept account of every lacing and button on his clothing. She raised him from the bed and let him step out of the last garments. Held him at arm's length for a moment and looked at him. As if looking for something particular. A birthmark or a brand. And as her fingertips glided over his organ she said in a husky voice:

'I've always seen it. You have such a beautiful body, Anders.'

He laughed silently. His skin pimpled all over. When she touched him, his whole body felt pleasure. He hid himself in her. Closed his eyes and played blind man's bluff on her skin. A crazy joy ignited deep inside him. Then a tremendous force he could not restrain overcame him. The room whirled around.

The bedclothes were smooth and cool. He drew her under the blanket with him. Wanted to warm her. Protect her. But first he wanted to have her.

The narrow bachelor's bed was a small planet sailing through the universe. She was with him! And his worry that he could not manage the flight with her vanished into thin air.

The sudden wave came. Hard. Its surges foamed until she groaned and grew heavy in his arms. He did not know it could be like that for women. He had thought it was only that way for men.

When the sea withdrew, it left only driftwood, fragrant seaweed and wet round stones at the high-tide mark. And great gusts of wind. Great gusts that gathered their fill of dew on every smooth surface.

Benjamin finally understood what fathers were for. He had heard the sounds at night from Anders's bedroom. He slept with Anders and awoke with the Russian.

Amidst these sounds he seemed to see her. On

95

eternally green fields wet with rain. Covered with motionless slimy black snails.

This was what fathers were for. That way the Russian was also a kind of father. Because, before everything ended, he and Dina had been knotted together in the heather. Was it like that with Anders and her too? The thought made him uneasy. Because you must be enemies if you acted like that?

These questions and the image of the snails made him feel guilty. Because he probably knew more than they did. Much more. And he could not warn Anders. He himself had asked Anders to be his father after all.

He had to keep an eye on Anders at all times. Because Anders was in danger. And he did not know it.

When Dina put her hand on his head and said she and Anders were going to get married, he realized that, for his sake, she had decided to spare Anders.

He swallowed and nodded. She asked if he was happy about it.

'There'll probably be dead bodies,' he replied.

'Dead bodies?'

'Yes, and he mustn't . . . die.'

She looked so strange he immediately felt sorry he had said that. But she had asked. People should not ask so many questions.

'Die . . .?' she whispered, so terribly close to his head. He swallowed and nodded.

'You mustn't think such things, Benjamin,' she said.

'I can't help thinking. You know that, Dina.'

He tried to squeeze past her.

'But aren't you glad he's going to be your father?'

'He's been my father a long time. But now he's yours too,' he mumbled, without knowing if it was wise to say that.

'Would you rather we didn't get married?'

'It's best that you do,' he said, trying to sound as grown-up as possible.

*   *   *

96

Preparations were made for a big wedding. Invitations to Grøtøy, Kjerringøy, Tjeldøy, Trandarnes, Bjarkøy and Strandsted. Johan was invited too, and he accepted.

The May days captured the smooth sloping rocks on the shore and worked a seeming miracle on the humus-rich soil. They rose to the Sound's surface and streamed down as sunshine and rain.

The bridal bed was prepared where Anders had decided. And the bride did not run through parlors wearing only pantalets and escape into a tree. No Mother Karen stood on the stairway weeping because everything was in such shameful disarray.

It was a struggle to get rid of the smell of cigars and winter men. Oline had hired five girls. But dead Jacob was inconsolable and staggered from room to room. He clung to the maids' fingers, let in smoke from the stoves, put unappetizing dead flies on the window sill. Even when it had just been scrubbed with green soap.

The wedding day arrived with snow squalls. A white wall in the Sound.

Benjamin opened his bedroom window in the morning and laughed. Captured snowflakes in his warm, open hands and watched them melt. Then he put his wet palms to his face. The Russian had forgotten him that night.

During the wedding dinner he sat between Dagny and the parson's wife. A grown-up's place. Dina and Anders sat at the head of the table. Together. He noticed she did not eat very much. But her eyes were smiling.

The past few days he had alternated between being happy about the marriage and being afraid of it.

You could be happy because she definitely would not leave when she was married. She would not shoot Anders either. Not after she had married him. But one thing clouded everything. He had to be prepared to be

97

alone with the Russian, because she would have no time for anything besides being married.

That made everything sometimes get dark because he forgot to breathe. He had collected good signs. The snow squall in the morning he took as a good sign. Snow at this time of year was unusual. And unusual things were usually a blessing. But not always.

He had been afraid up until they sat in the boat ready to go to the church. Then the Solemn Spirit came over him. When he looked at Anders he understood what Mother Karen had meant when she talked about the Solemn Spirit. It had to do with the inside of people somehow becoming visible. When Anders put one arm around Dina and the other around him as they sat in the boat among boughs of spring-green leaves, the Solemn Spirit came out of Anders. You could see it like a light across his cheeks.

He was not sure if Dina saw it.

Now they sat at the wedding table and everyone looked happy. Dina at least looked different. Good, in a way. But with her you could never be completely sure.

Johan looked stern. But it was only because he wanted to. You could easily see he liked the food.

Tomas, on the other hand, was silent and practiced the best manners he had learned. Drank moderately, and took care to use the glasses and silverware in the order Stine had told him. He had shaved so meticulously that he had several cuts on his face. His suit was a little tight across the chest. He had bought it in Tromsø after Stine had measured his whole body. A bloody high price for some miserable bits of clothing, he had said.

More than once he let one brown and one blue eye rest on Stine. When she nodded, he felt confident he had behaved as he should. He chewed slowly and thoroughly. Much more genteel than the parson's wife. In fact, it was amazing that such an aristocratic lady swallowed so fast.

CHAPTER 8

The spring weather turned cold, punishing everyone who worked outdoors. The leaves did not unfurl and the flowers wrapped themselves in their bracts.

One evening they sat in the parlour around the table with the large lamp above it. Anders, Johan, Dina, Angell the tutor, and Benjamin. The adults read newspapers and mail. Benjamin worked on some arithmetic problems that had to be finished before supper. His right hand slid over the green plush tablecloth as he guided his pencil with his left hand.

He had noticed that Angell wanted to agree with both Dina and Johan. It was odd he did not realize this was impossible. Angell admired Johan because he was a clergyman, so he agreed with him. But he liked Dina best, so he agreed with her too.

Anders began to read from *Tromsø Stiftstidende* that the Bergen prices had been set for outgoing fish. Coal fish from Nordland had risen to 96 *skilling* per *vog*. Cod roe stood at 6 *spesiedaler* 30 *skilling* per *tønne*.

Johan and the tutor started discussing an incredible thing they had read about the czar of Russia. He wanted to abolish serfdom under the motto: 'Reforms from above and down, rather than from below and upward with revolution and bloodshed!'

There was something about the word. Bloodshed. The word was unpredictable. Stuck in Benjamin's throat, making it hard to breathe. He tried to understand that the Russian czar was both good and dangerous at the same time.

Anders was clearest: he thought the czar acted wisely. But the tutor was not sure. He thought the Russian people were a wild beast that could only be tamed by force.

Johan said the Crimean War and the Paris peace agreement showed what was wrong with Russia. The Russian people were humiliated by both the war and the peace. But the empire still existed! That was why the country needed a czar who was more than an ordinary human being.

Benjamin could not do his arithmetic problems now.

'I don't see how that's possible,' Dina interjected.

'What do you mean?' asked Anders.

'To be a czar and at the same time be human!'

'They eat and drink and propagate like other creatures,' Anders said.

'Dina means humane,' Johan corrected.

Anders wrinkled his forehead a moment.

'It's good we have you to explain things, Johan,' said Dina.

'Yes, yes, that's right,' said Anders good-naturedly, and gave Dina's arm a gentle pat. 'I assume it's not possible to be human without being humane,' he added.

'Sin and cruelty aren't humane. And the history of Russian czars is based on cruelty,' declared Johan.

'Sin is widely distributed,' Anders said quietly.

'How is it among the clergy, Johan dear?' asked Dina.

Johan clearly was not enjoying himself. He fidgeted with a pipe cleaner. Squashed it quickly over his fingertips as his face turned red.

Johan wanted to be the smartest. Smarter than Anders. It was hard to tell what Anders thought about it. You could not ask of course.

Everyone around the table fell silent. It was best not to look at them. He had the arithmetic problems after all.

Then Dina began speaking, as if she had forgotten she had asked Johan a question:

100

'It would be fun to be there and see everything. It's such a big country . . . such unbelievable wealth. Not just commodities. But art treasures. Music! Here in Norway there's so little of everything, for sinners and other people. There are so few small sinners.'

She should not have said that! He began to believe she would leave Reinsnes.

Surely she wasn't thinking of going? To the Russian's country? God the Almighty. God, who had shown the Solemn Spirit could come out of Anders and rest safely on them all – He should tell her she must not leave! Otherwise there would be crop failures and poverty, and spring would never come.

Did Our Lord understand such obvious things?

He had to find something to make her forget she had thought about leaving. His eye fell on an article in the newspaper. About the English woman Florence Nightingale. He began reading aloud about how she had gone around with her lamp among the wounded soldiers in Turkey and done more than pray to God for their souls. She had dedicated her life to the field hospitals, the stench, and the blood, and had reprimanded the generals with her sharp tongue when they did not show mercy to a wounded enemy. Now the war was over, a war that no one had won and everyone had lost. The angel with the lamp had come home to England. Still alive, it was true, but ill and broken, and without faith in the goodness of people.

Everyone was quiet while he read. So he could ask:

'What kind of "goodness" doesn't she believe in?'

'She's been in the war,' said Anders. 'You don't see much of the goodness of people there.'

'Why? Do you see it better here, where there's no war?' he asked.

Anders laid the newspaper in his lap.

'At least we don't shoot people here,' said Johan.

The sounds from the kitchen and pantry became terribly important. He reached for the edge of the table with both hands. Then he closed his mouth tightly. It

101

was too hard to sit up straight. You could just lean against the table a little and it would surely go away. Nobody saw the nausea. But everything felt so wilted. His arms and his feet.

'Benjamin,' Dina called in a clear, firm voice.

She had risen from her chair.

If he just did not look at them, everything would probably be fine while he slid his feet onto the floor. Then all he had to do was stand up. He did not vomit. Far from it. He took a few faltering steps. The floor came towards him.

She was there immediately. Held him. Got him out of the room.

The men remained sitting with the czar of Russia, the fish prices, and the lady with the lamp.

The shouts came from a deep cave. Still, he knew who was calling. His eyes were caught in a fishing net. He could not free them. They were so old. And runny. Could not stand light. Could not get loose. The night spread its spores in a gleaming pattern that lived in the light. The fish net was white filigree curtains at the open window.

The Russian held him tightly. The shouts were everywhere. A stinging pressure straight through his ear canals and head. The echo reverberated way out to his lips. Time after time, the Russian shouted his question. In gibberish you could not understand. The man was sometimes so close you could feel the vapor from his mouth, and sometimes so far away you could not see him.

When he was close, you fell into a red hole that got bigger and bigger as his shouts got wilder and wilder. When he was far away, you could breathe enough to get along.

He swallowed everything that had collected in his mouth and swung himself out of bed. To bring back his eyes.

Then he realized he was standing on a slope of rocky

debris looking down at Dina and the Russian, who were humped like worms in the heather. They tugged and tore at each other's clothing and limbs. As if they could not decide whether to be distant or close, friends or enemies. Fought to get loose. Clung to each other.

Finally the Russian's head lay floating in red. He lay there motionless, his long feet sprawled to either side. As if he were a stuffed scarecrow that had toppled over in a field. The rifle lay in the heather too, and its echo wept from the mountains. All the noise was packed in wool, and the bird fluttering in the bush moved its wings so slowly that you would expect it to fall down.

He had to open his mouth to let out the unbearable silence.

Then suddenly she was there. Stood with bare feet on the rug in his room, wearing only her shift. He tried to restrain her toes so she would not come closer. Because she was still in the Russian's scream. At the same time, he wanted her to hold him. She was both dry hay and seaweed. She was a large tree with black leaves. Dangerously tall. Still, you had to climb it. Smooth branches. Deep in the trunk, something pounded. As if a bird had been locked inside. Thump, thump.

He climbed very high. Everything swayed so much up there.

Soon Anders was there too. He wore a blue dressing gown and his eyes wound themselves around you. He did not look like himself. His hands were flying crows that grasped for branches and twigs. There was creaking and crashing everywhere. Anders fell and climbed back up. Fell and climbed up again. You realized the tree was not for Anders either.

Finally you got your eyes loose from the curtain so you could cry.

'What frightened you so much?' Anders asked.

'The Russian. He's become the czar. He just lies there, and shouts, and asks questions!'

'What does he ask about?'

Things got very dangerous. Anders fell through the floor. He killed himself surely. She must realize that she had to stop him.

Anders did not know that he should not ask questions.

'Dina knows! She knows! She can speak Russian!'

Her face! It became so flat. It probably had never been there. Now she was leaving! She left. She took her hatbox and rowed out to the steamboat. So the worst had happened!

But she did not leave. And she let Anders stay too.

One day Dina waylaid Tomas in the stable and told him that rifles and gunpowder should not be left out, but be locked up. He shrugged his shoulders and promised to do as she said. But when he asked why, and heard it was because of Benjamin, he could not restrain himself.

'The boy needs to get used to growing up, even if the Russian shot himself.'

'It will be as I say,' she said.

'We can't protect him from rifles all his life. He's got the makings of a man in him.'

'I've said what I've said.'

Tomas gave her a long look. He was carrying armloads of hay to the horses, and was surrounded by a cloud of ancient dried summer.

'What does Anders say about it?' he asked.

'Anders doesn't use a rifle.'

'No, that fellow doesn't hunt,' said Tomas. The scorn was unmistakable.

'Don't bother your head about what Anders does, Tomas! This concerns Benjamin.'

'I've been concerned about Benjamin for a long time, haven't you noticed?'

'Thanks for your trouble, Tomas!'

'It's only reasonable, after all. When it comes to him, I think it's been you and me right from the beginning.'

'Tomas!'

'Are you afraid I'll tell Anders the truth?'

She had turned to leave. Now she stiffened. She raised one arm and turned towards him so forcibly he thought she was going to hit him.

'And just what would you say, Tomas?' she asked, coming so close he felt her breath on his face.

He did not answer. Just stood firmly on the stable floor.

'You're standing in the hay,' he finally commented.

'What would you say to Anders?' she repeated.

'That the boy is mine!'

She closed her eyes for a moment. When she looked at him again, she was calm.

'And do you think you'd grow old on Anders's farm if you came with such news, Tomas?'

'No,' he said curtly.

'In that case, you should think twice about your own children and about what kind of happiness they'd have with a father who went around spreading gossip. Benjamin doesn't need you.'

'He needed me before. Stine and I . . .'

'I'm grateful for that! But it's no reason for you to take revenge now. Aren't things good enough for you? Don't you live like a prince, with a tile stove and a chandelier? Don't you have food and respect? Do you need anything else? Do you?'

He lost some of his bravado during the long speech. They stared at separate walls for a while.

'If we'd been destined . . .' he began.

'We were never destined,' she interrupted.

'Couldn't you give me a word? Just one word?'

'It's dangerous to give you words. You've got a memory like a horse. And you kick backwards!'

'Have *you* forgotten?' he asked.

'I forget nothing! Nothing!'

The stable door creaked. As if by pre-arranged agreement, Dina took a quick step back from the pile of hay and Tomas bent to pick it up.

'That's what we'll do then!' she said loudly and clearly as the stable boy walked through the door.

When Tomas went to the cottage for a snack, he met a beaming Stine. Dina had been there and said she would bring her a new loom from Bergen. The warping threads in the loom Stine used now had a habit of snapping.

'It's the ten threads in the middle that always break. I've had to throw out half a warp,' she said.

Tomas nodded. Then he took off his cap and washed his hands.

CHAPTER 9

One day well into winter Anders and Benjamin had a talk while doing some work.

'How about coming along to Bergen this summer, son?'

Anders said it as if there was no question about it. That made your eyes get so very wet.

He was to work for wages and sleep with the men. But his pay would be docked for any watch when he got seasick and vomited. He and Anders shook hands on it without asking Dina.

Having this secret with Anders made him feel he had begun to grow up. One day he was sure the down on his upper lip had grown long and dark in a single night. He solemnly took Anders's straight razor and climbed on a chair to see himself better in the large mirror above the chest of drawers. But his hand was unsteady in the reflection. Things went so poorly that he cut his nose. Bleeding, he had to ask Dina for help. She did not scold, just looked at the razor and washed him until he stopped bleeding.

'It was just an idea,' he said meekly, and tried to laugh it off.

'I see. You'll probably heal this time. But next time you may have to sacrifice your whole nose.'

He nodded, then slipped past her and out of the room.

'It won't be many years before you've always got that bother!' she shouted down the stairs after him.

Then he could not restrain himself. He stopped and shouted back to her:

'You don't know what I know! What Anders and I agreed!'

She came to the head of the stairs.

'What do you mean?'

'You'll see!' he shouted, and was out the front door.

All winter and spring he asked eager questions about everything to do with Bergen. He found pictures and books from Bergen. His tutor was no longer useful for anything. Because Angell had never been further south than Trondheim.

It was hard when Anders was away, because then there was nobody on the whole estate with information. So it was a relief when Dina told him one day that she knew everything. At least she responded to his questions, even if the answers were brief.

He soon learned he should not ask about Bergen when Dina and he were awake at night because of the Russian's shouts. She got a mean look in her eyes.

When the birds began gathering materials to build their nests and the cattle were let out to graze, he told himself it was strange you could have such happiness in your body when you knew so much about everything.

When the day arrived, he understood that Hanna did not feel as happy as he about his leaving. But everything has its limits. She had no right to scold him so terribly.

'You've got to understand that I'm a man and you're a woman,' he said, and took a deep enough breath to carry a wooden box under each arm.

'I remember how you cried and carried on when your mother left without you,' she declared, wiping away her tears.

'That was long ago,' he said in an imperious tone he thought sounded manly.

'I might not be here when you come back!'

'Where are you going?'

'It's not decided.'

'Well, then I can't visit you, since I won't know where you are,' he said smiling.

'You're an idiot!'

'So are you! When I can't go anywhere without you running away.'

'There won't be anybody to be with,' she said.

He set down his load with a resigned expression.

'You can come along when I get so grown-up that I'm the one who decides.'

'It'll be forever till that happens, because you grow so slowly!'

'I can be grown-up enough to decide, even if my feet aren't very long,' he snarled, and gave her a little shove. 'I'm bigger than you, after all, you stupid girl!' he shouted, as he picked up his load and ran down the hill.

'I didn't mean it like that,' she called to him meekly.

They were friends again before he left. Neither could bear to have it otherwise. He promised to bring her a doll with a porcelain face and real hair. Just for fun, she said, because of course she was too big for dolls.

He told himself it would cost so much that, in order to earn enough, he had better not get seasick.

The morning they sailed south, the wind was made to order, but there was no sun. Anders stood at the helm and was himself. He thought much better in sea mist, he claimed.

Benjamin hung over the railing and stared at islands, beaches and coves he had never seen before. The world opened wide and became limitless as he exclaimed again and again to those around him:

'My God, how fast we're going! Hanna should see it!'

Anders glanced at the window of the cabin where Dina was. She had not said an unpleasant word about his reckless promise that the boy could go to Bergen. Had almost looked happy about it.

'It will be a bother for you, Anders, having the whole family along,' she had said. 'We don't know what kind of a sailor that young fellow is.'

'We've got plenty of time to find out,' he replied, and felt relieved that she did not mind his alliance with the boy.

The mate, Anton, showed a remarkable lack of resistance to having both a woman and a boy aboard. He seemed to enjoy all Benjamin's questions. They made him feel even more indispensable than before.

The winds were favorable for the most part. Yet not so favorable that the boy got seasick. Each time, he put a mark on a certain table by a heap of dried fish. Then he spat in his hands and went whistling to work at one of his tasks. Coiled the ropes until they lay as neatly as maggot mounds at low tide.

When not busy with the regular tasks Anders had assigned, he sat on a pile of dried fish with a spyglass and commented on things he saw. Or read a book in the cabin while the rigging creaked and seagulls shrieked. He played cards with the men. They let him barely win and had fun doing it.

'Your mother was better at card playing, when she made her first trip to Bergen,' said Anton.

'She was older, after all, and married,' Anders said with a sidelong glance at the cabin.

'Was it sixteen she was?' one man asked.

'Anyhow, I remember Jacob didn't like that she lay on deck playing cards,' Anton recalled.

'That's enough,' said Anders brusquely.

It was not what Anders said that was so strange. But the way people took it. Suddenly everyone talked about something else or began prolonged whistling at their tasks.

Once they sailed past a cluster of houses and wharves where Anders and Dina had acquaintances, and Benjamin begged to go ashore.

But before anyone could respond, he corrected himself:

'No, we have to get to Bergen before it's too late and nobody wants to buy our cargo.'

'On the trip back north we'll raid the shore and sleep in a bed and sit on chairs!' said Anders, and began telling how satisfied he was with the cargo this year. True, he had to turn away some tenant farmers who wanted to send fish that did not meet his standards.

'That might cause some hostility. It's no joke to have your fish rejected. People have no other way to earn money. But we've got to make sure that Reinsnes cargo has a good reputation in Bergen. So people have to provide top-quality goods. Isn't that right, son?'

The fish graders in Bergen were their own masters, no matter who paid their wages. Their word was law. If they sorted a consignment to be prime quality Hollender round fish, it was a law no one could change.

Anders made a long speech about these things.

'You see, Benjamin, among Bergen fish graders Hollender round fish is king. It's got to have the right blue color, be clean, and no larger than one *alen*. It can't weigh more than one and a half pounds! Preferably just one pound. Do you understand, son? Bremer round fish are the really good round fish that are too big to be a Hollender. They go to Bremen, Holland, and the Mediterranean. Wouldn't it be fun to go there, eh? Then there's cusk. It's got to have shiny white skin and flesh and be sliced to its tail. That's a prime product for Holland. It's flat as the devil in that country!'

When Anders judged dried cod he insisted it had to have been split and sprinkled with salt while still fresh and placed in wooden containers for twenty-four hours. Washed and stacked in piles no higher than one *alen*. Flesh against flesh. And then laid on clean rocks to dry. Never on grass or marshy ground. And never stacked until properly dry.

111

'I don't bring fish to Bergen that's been salted on the warehouse floor. They can depend on that!'

It was amazing how talkative Anders was at sea. About fish. Especially when you yourself thought dried fish bodies all looked the same, no matter what their names.

During the whole voyage south the Russian made no sound. He probably could not follow them. The world was very big and wide.

People on land did not know cliffs and mountains could look so pointed if they had not sailed along the coast on light nights.

And then there was the smell of the ocean. Always. Deep in your sleep. Such a powerful smell. It made people different.

The night changed too. The further south they went, the bluer it became. And people talked differently at the various places they dropped anchor and went ashore for fresh food and water.

He had read about the Tower of Babel's confusion of languages, but it was strange it could be like that all in the same country.

'Norway is as long as an intestine, that's why,' said Anton, as he cut a thin slice from the salted leg of mutton tied to the mast in a linen cloth.

'No,' said Benjamin, 'it's because things got confused at the Tower of Babel and nobody understood what their neighbours said, so they had to go out in the world and start over on their own!'

Anton forgot to chew.

'Well I'll be damned!' he said seriously, and put his knife back in its sheath. 'So that's how it happened? Just wait till you hear the women in Bergen! They must have been some of the first to leave Babel!'

When they arrived in Bergen, it was not just the language that made him listen and stare. He had to make an effort to remember to breathe. Now and then he took several noisy gulps of air, then was quiet and invisible until the next breath. Amidst everything, he suddenly noticed Dina's new hat.

'It's as fine as the garden of Eden,' he said approvingly.

But when she wanted to walk arm in arm, he leaped aside.

'No, for heaven's sake! I can't lean on a woman! You must know that, Dina?'

He walked beside Anders with one hand on his lapel and the other behind his back.

First it was everything happening in Vågen harbor. All the boats. The sails. The shouts. That was still manageable. Because everything was at a distance, so you could think whatever you wished. But when you came ashore, everything tumbled in on you and it was impossible to keep order in it. Endless rows of roofs, wharves and house gables. Carriages and two-wheeled carts, with and without horses. All kinds of people. Wearing such strange clothes you would think they were in a painting. Most women held parasols over their heads. He had thought that was just a habit the sheriff's wife, Dagny, had affected.

At the fish market everything was simpler. Even the smell seemed familiar. But there were such throngs of people coming and going that they reminded you of ants hurrying back and forth from their anthill. Without your really knowing what they were doing. In the marketplace, wooden shoes clacked against the cobblestones and people were busy constantly, just like at home. At least those on the ground. But the people sitting in carriages with hoods all looked as though they were going to a Christmas party at the parson's in the summertime.

He understood why you had to dress like a gentleman before going ashore in Bergen. Anders had taken a pocket watch and chain all that long way in order to stroll with an open jacket in the hot sun.

113

The mountains in Bergen were laughable. They looked as if they could not stand up without having people right next to them. It was a bit tiresome to have them so close. But people were probably used to them being right above their roofs. Besides, they were really just rock piles. He mentioned this to Anders as they were walking and looking around.

'I think you'd better not say that to anyone born in Bergen,' Anders said with a hearty laugh.

One day they hired a carriage and drove around as though they had errands at various places. Anders reminded Dina that they had been here before. And she smiled with shining eyes. They looked at each other, and Benjamin felt warm and happy. For absolutely no reason. They were not talking to him after all.

The larger the houses they passed, the larger were the surrounding yards and trees. Except in the city itself, where houses were pasted together so tightly you would think people in Bergen could not afford to build their own walls but had to lean against the neighbors.

As they walked to their lodgings in the city, a feeling of great amazement came over him. He had to make them understand it. So he stopped and peered towards the rooftops.

'Don't they get tired of building in a big city? Just think, that it's possible to buy and sell so terribly many things people can use!'

CHAPTER 10

On the voyage north he asked Anders where his surname, Bernhof, came from.

'The Bernhofs built up Kjerringøy island long ago,' said Anders. But he had gained little pleasure from that. His mother's relations came from Schøningene on Grøtøy. He was always welcome here at Søren and Sophie's home.

His Grøtøy relations were at Reinsnes for the wedding, and now the Reinsnes folk would return the visit.

'We've kept in touch, Søren and I. Søren was unlucky during the Crimean War. His ketch got frozen in, filled with grain, and by the time he got home with his cargo prices had fallen so much that expenses ate up his profits. Too bad. But he got through it,' said Anders looking aloft.

They sailed north across Folla Sea and in the narrow channel to Grøtøy. The evening sun had set the sea aflame with a single ray, and the Lofotoveggen mountain wall darkened behind the holms. The innumerable small islands and holms kept the breakers at a distance. But they heard the eternal song from the open sea like a warning.

'What's most frightening is when it's quiet among the holms, but the sea beyond rumbles like the deep notes of a church organ. That's a sign the wind is about to turn and strike,' explained Anton.

'You've got to watch the sails then, so you don't suddenly run aground with the wheel loose in your hand. Grøtøy channel has enough underwater reefs and treacherous shallows to turn the bows of a whole armada!' he added.

'It won't be so bad now,' Anders thought.

The trading center was located on the island farthest out to sea, but it faced the channel and the mainland. The big white main house had a row of ten windows on each floor and a high verandah along the entire facade. A solid wall kept the sea away from a large garden with trees and a summer house. Beyond lay a lively circle of wharves and smaller buildings. There was life and activity everywhere. Boats, tools and people. But not much land, and it was quite barren compared to the broad fields at home.

Benjamin wandered among the buildings and got acquainted. Forgot he was almost grown-up, asked eager questions. But he did not run, he walked. He discovered trees he had not seen before. They were brought from distant places and planted here, he learned. And before he walked over the knolls and down to the warehouses again, he was treated to cakes and cordial.

The place was so small. So close together. And still they had everything. The people were different from those at home. Or was it just now, because they had guests? It was all so orderly. He noticed it especially on the wharves. Everything lay in piles and coils, and nothing was scattered on the floor. Not like at Reinsnes. There you could drag out something to start a task, and it could lie there until the next day if it was not in anyone's way.

Only one place at Reinsnes was stricter. The kitchen. Here, there were two giggling girls in aprons. One had braids and was younger than he. But not much. The older one had already started to grow breasts and her bodice was too small. But she was the best, even if she was half a head taller than he. That was disgraceful, but could not be helped. She had short blond hair, like

116

a boy. Being near her made him sweat. So he let them continue peeling potatoes.

After investigating the place for hours, he sat down with the grown-ups in the parlor. Søren was active in the Lofoten Commission's efforts to pass a law that would establish three things: a free sea for everyone. Free fishing for everyone, no matter where you came from in the kingdom of Norway. And official supervision to ensure the law was enforced.

Søren praised Mr Ketil Motzfeldt, who was regarded as the father of this law. Anders did not say much; it was mostly Søren who talked. It was always like that with Anders.

'And the fishing-station owners? Where do they stand under this law?' Anders asked finally.

'We stand where everyone else stands,' Søren replied.

'Still, it will be those who are quickest on their feet and have the best boats who get to the fishing grounds first. And it will be like before . . . you row till you taste blood in your mouth and your sea mittens cook on your hands,' said Anders with a smile.

'Yes, but you won't be nabbed and shooed away if you enter fishing grounds where you haven't paid for a fisherman's shanty.'

'But everyone will go to the same old places anyway,' Anders maintained.

'We'll see! In any case, nobody *owns* the sea, even if they own beaches and buildings on the shore!'

'It's strange that you're so passionate about this – you, the owner of such a lot of beach and buildings,' said Dina.

'That's what I say too,' sighed Sophie. 'He sails off to meetings and argues with the important people in Lofoten to no avail.'

'The new times aren't just for important people,' said Søren thoughtfully.

Dina looked at him out of the corner of her eye. It made Benjamin uneasy.

'You're concerned about the common people, Søren,' she said. 'Where did you learn that? Here on Grøtøy?'

'Learn? You don't have to learn about justice if you're able to think! Nobody should own the air or fire or sea.'

Anders suggested it perhaps was no worse to own the sea than to own cloudberry bogs or eiderduck nesting grounds. But he was not very insistent. Just turned it into a question.

Fortunately, Dina said no more. But now and then she looked at Søren. You could wish she did not do that.

Music and laughter were heard from the courtyard, where things were set up for dancing. It was a warm evening. Doors and windows were open. Young and old mingled with each other. Servants and masters, relatives and tenant farmers. No one thought about going to bed. People's faces were like honey.

'You're probably ready for some sweet talk, Benjamin? Or haven't you noticed that we have two pretty girls working here?' Søren teased.

He could at least nod.

'Are you going to ask them to dance?' Sophie enquired pleasantly.

Fortunately, Søren started talking to Anders right then:

'As for you, old man, I guess you've stopped roaming the country looking for girls?'

Anders did not answer, but just smiled.

'I remember you said marriage wasn't for you, and you didn't believe it would ever happen. But now you're married, Anders. So let's drink a toast to love at Reinsnes!'

The grown-ups raised their glasses. But they seemed to be watching each other. He tugged at a thread in his sweater. He should not have done that. His sleeve began to unravel.

Sophie noticed it immediately and brought a needle. He had to take off his sweater so she could sew it.

That was the difference between Reinsnes and

Grøtøy. At home, no one would think of starting to sew right in the middle of a toast to love itself. Or if Dina was playing.

He glanced at Dina to see if the unraveled thread had spoiled everything. But she appeared normal. Almost. Still he regretted having worn a sweater in warm weather.

'I heard you had your eye on a girl here on Grøtøy whom they married off to Bergen right under your nose,' Sophie said pleasantly, and glanced quickly at Dina before bending over the thread again.

'That was ages ago,' laughed Søren, and seemed to want to drop the subject. Even if it did not concern him.

'When it comes to proposing, I've never been the first,' Anders said smiling, and got up to refill his glass with an air of feeling at home.

'Well, there was probably a reason. But to be as slow as you are, Anders, that takes real patience!' Søren chuckled.

Dina straightened her dress sleeve. Søren should not have said that. He absolutely should not have said that! Benjamin wanted to get up and rush out the door. But there was the matter of the sweater. Sophie had not finished sewing it. He had to thank her for her work.

'Ah yes, those days of youth,' laughed Anders.

'Actually, you weren't so young,' Sophie commented.

'I can't remember exactly . . .' mumbled Anders.

'I don't think Dina appreciates this talk,' said Søren, and raised his glass to Dina.

No, no, he should not have said that. There, the sweater was ready! Why was Sophie still fumbling with it?

'At Reinsnes we aren't so afraid of people saying things we can hear. What's worse is things said in deep darkness along the channel, when we can't defend ourselves,' said Dina.

'Oh, dear me . . .' murmured Sophie, feeling humiliated, and examined her fingertips.

The conversation stopped. The silence was dead flies on the window sill. Søren twiddled his thumbs for a moment, and then he said:

'Dina, we don't know you as well as we know Anders. You mustn't take it wrong when we joke a little in a friendly way.'

Sophie sighed and commmented that she thought it would rain tonight . . . after an evening like this. Then she held out the sweater. Her smile was completely impersonal.

He said thank you. While he was pulling the sweater over his head, Anders set down his glass and crossed to the big chair where Dina sat. Just when Benjamin's eyes reapppeared above the sweater, Anders took a cigar from the smoking table as if he were at home. Licked it carefully. Anders had such a fine mouth for licking cigars. Benjamin had seen that before. Now he almost had to nod as Anders formed his soft lips around the cigar, lit it, and took a couple of deep drags before handing it to Dina.

'Dina makes it impossible for a man to remember what foolishness he did in the past. It all becomes meaningless. And the girl married well, without any help from me,' he said.

Anders stood before Dina a moment, then squeezed himself into a chair beside her. You'd never seen such childishness. That was certain. Still, it made you happy. Because Dina smiled at him and made room for him.

A gust of wind blew through the door leading to the garden. God's finger stroked Dina's face. That's what made it happen. Made Dina turn her face towards Anders.

Later, after he had pulled the one girl's braids and talked to the other, Sophie came out and said perhaps he should go to bed since it was late. He was embarrassed because the girls heard it. Then Anders came to the door and said:

'Benjamin is almost grown-up! He did a man's job on the Bergen trip. Fellows like that don't sleep much.'

'I just thought . . .' Sophie began, but Anders took her hand and asked her to dance.

'Is that your father?' asked one of the girls admiringly.

'Yes,' he said, without thinking it was wrong.

'Yes, that's Anders, my father!' he repeated.

The girls looked at Anders.

'You don't look like him!' said the girl with the braids.

She should not have said that! Why did she say it? Was the whole world crazy? But he held his tongue and said nothing.

'You look like your mother, Dina Grønelv. She's very pretty!' said the girl with the boy's hair, cocking her head.

Then he got the idea. That he should dance with her. The other girl could stand there like a lump and watch.

He swung Bolette around and did not step on her feet very often. She was not much better at dancing than he.

'I'm not a very good dancer,' she said, out of breath.

'Me neither! But the hell with that!' he replied, and became so uncontrollably happy he felt it prickling from his throat down to wherever it was.

When they came upstairs to where they would sleep and had said goodnight, Anders closed the door between the rooms. Still, Benjamin knew about them.

He burrowed his face between Dina's breasts and floated out to sea with her. The Russian came along in a pool of thick tar that smelled disgusting. He wanted to scrape him off and let the sea take him. One should be allowed to float in peace with Dina. But the disgusting smell was always there. He shouted to Anders about the Russian. But it was too far to *Mother Karen*'s deck, where Anders was watching the channel.

A huge ugly creature that was not a snake, a raven or

121

a seagull, but a mixture of all three, flew around them constantly. Dived down, and flew into the sky again.

'She's not yours. Don't you see that?' the bird said in his ear. 'She has to leave. Because she's black!'

It was horrible. Repulsive. To float with her. He wanted to let go of her and he did not want to let go. She floated with him. Was so terribly heavy. He wanted to call to Anders again. But could not. What should he do? She floated with him. She was not his, and she wanted to leave.

The bird sloughed its outer skin and let it fall on him. He saw that it both was, and was not, the Russian.

'You must say something!' he shouted to the creature. But the bird did not answer, just waded onto the seaweed-covered beach. Into the disgusting smell!

The girl with the braids was there. She had lit a big bonfire among the stones. The heat struck his face and made it sting. He felt a burning sensation in his stomach. And in the place without a name. And all the trees along the seashore were ablaze.

'It's because you always have to get married to someone!' the girl said contemptuously. She unloosened her braids. Her hair floated through the shower of sparks. Floated towards him. Thin golden threads on a black sea.

Dina repeated his name several times. As if she had just found him and did not really know who he was.

It made him grow large and hollow inside. His eyes could see through the ocean. That seemed completely normal. All the way to the bottom. Like looking through a windowpane.

He could see upwards too. Through the sea and air. From the bottom. That did not seem strange. There was a rip in the sky. Anders fell very slowly through the hole. Like when you send a paper bird through the attic window. He landed in newly washed, sun-dried wool with sighs and groans. Because he had been in the ice slush on Lofoten Sea so long.

He felt the frostbite on Anders's fingertips. It tasted both painful and good. Just fine. The way frostbite does – inside a warm room.

CHAPTER 11

When he arrived home, it was a good autumn filled with reassuring smells. He could strut around the estate and in the store telling tales about Bergen and The World.

That was before he learned he was to go to school in Tromsø the following autumn. He heard it one day as he sat in Mother Karen's room and had not shut the door to the parlor. Sometimes doors were not shut.

Anders began reading aloud to Dina from *Bladet*. Giæver & Son advertised port wine, muscat wine, raspberry vinegar and lamp oil at low prices. There was silence for a while, then he continued reading. A notice from the General Post Office concerning an unredeemed letter to Dina Grønelv from parson Johan Grønelv. The redemption price was 12 *skilling*.

Anders's voice sounded strange somehow. As if he had tried to learn the passage by heart but could not do it.

'Why haven't you redeemed the letter, Dina?' Anders asked.

'Because I know what's in it,' she replied, as if talking about the wind's direction.

'You know what's in it?'

'Yes.'

'For God's sake . . . Are you crazy?'

'It's the same as last time.'

'I see. And what was that?'

'He wants a small sum so he can go to Copenhagen and study more theology.'

Anders almost disappeared.

'I don't know anything about this.'

'No, why should you? I didn't want to bother you.'

Then there was only the wall clock. It hacked their breathing into the walls and filled his ears with unbearable noise.

'Can't you help him, Dina?'

'No!'

'You don't mean that?'

'I certainly do!'

'But that's not true, Dina.'

'Johan has received more than enough all these years. He's never done any work other than wander around the city with books under his arm. Now it's somebody else's turn to study. It will be expensive.'

'Who?'

'Benjamin.'

The newspaper was not happy. It rustled. And large feet poked around under the table in there.

'What sort of plans do you have for Benjamin, if I may ask?'

'Tromsø Realskole! He's going to have an education in science and foreign languages that leads to an *artium* degree. The tuition alone is 36 *spesiedaler*. In addition, there's food and lodging.'

'Food and lodging! Tromsø! But Dina, he's just a boy!'

'He can't go around here and . . .'

'Does the boy know about this?'

'Not yet. But we've talked about it before.'

'He's too young,' said Anders. His voice was the same as when he gave orders to let the anchor go. Not angry. Far from it. But one could not stop an anchor.

Dina stopped the anchor:

'It's good to begin early.'

'But surely Angell is a good teacher.'

'Benjamin isn't going to stay at Reinsnes until he finally doesn't know anything else.'

Was it Anders who laughed?

Who laughed?

'But Dina, there's no hurry. He's got years ahead of him.'

'Nobody should need to sit on a reef for years!'

'Is that what it's like for you, Dina?'

Someone was walking across the floor. Where were they going? Why didn't they sit still?

'It will be hard for him, Dina.'

'Yes,' said Dina's voice.

The word shrank his head to nothing. And inside this nothing was a nut. It ached and wanted to come out. He wanted to get up and go in to the voices. But that did not happen. No, it was unthinkable.

'I presume you're the one who'll tell him he's going to leave home?'

Anders's voice was terribly near.

'Yes,' said Dina.

It was unthinkable to go anywhere.

'And I'll be informed when everything is done?' said Anders, as if speaking in a tin pail. It was not nice to hear.

'Anders, don't look at it like that.'

'How should I look at it then?'

'I just think it's best that I'm the one who takes care of Benjamin.'

'Yes, you're his mother of course!'

A smacking sound came through the crack in the doorway. Anders was probably filling his pipe. He was filling his pipe! People did the strangest things.

When the smell of pipe smoke had lasted awhile, she said:

'Why are you so angry about all this?'

'I'm not angry. I feel like a fool with nothing to say. You force us all to do things, Dina. No blessing will come of this. You'll see. I know you're used to deciding everything by yourself. But now you've arranged to have me here, so you need to accept that I want a say in things.'

'And you do have a say,' she said. Much too nicely.

'No. You've never even hinted you were going to send the boy away. And you haven't asked what my opinion would be if you were thinking about it.'

'I should have done that. I'm not used to having a husband, I suppose.'

In his mind he saw her slip in and out of Anders's thoughts. Like a weasel. She could make herself so thin that she could scurry into the tightest stone wall before you glimpsed more than her tail.

'But the nightmares, Dina!'

'He only gets sick at Reinsnes.'

She said he was sick. She knew that wasn't true! It was the Russian who was sick. So sick, so sick! Completely destroyed. Was she lying to save herself? Did Dina lie like everyone else?

He stood in Mother Karen's room and reached out his hand. Wanted to console himself by stroking the lamp with the green glass shade above Our Lord's cherub. One needed something. He spread his fingers. All at once. Then it happened. Mother Karen's lamp did not want him either. It took revenge! Slivers of green glass stuck in his leg. The room smelled of oil as the Russian trickled out of him in tiny red blisters.

He stood like that long after they came from everywhere and began talking.

CHAPTER 12

Oline should not shout like that, he thought. He and Oline were the only ones who shouted at Reinsnes. But it was so much worse when she did. Dreadful. Because somehow she had a right to do it. She was Oline.

'God the Almighty punishes those who misuse His gifts!' she shouted, looking quite red.

Open doors were unsafe. Now it happened again. Maybe he should move back to the cottage. But that was not safe either. Tomas was there.

'The mistress can't treat cornmeal the way she does!'

Shrill, dreadful words streamed from her mouth and her tears splattered. She probably intended that only Thea be a witness. But you could not help hearing when you had ears. Dina had long since gone to the stable with the round wooden meal container.

'She didn't take very much. There was hardly enough to cover the bottom of the container . . .' murmured Thea in there.

'I'll cover *your* bottom!' Oline shrieked.

A moment later, a loud slap was heard. As though a wet dishcloth had been thrown onto the table. He could of course act like a man and stand there smiling and regard it merely as women's foolishness. But that was not so easy.

'I saw what she took. It's blasphemous! And a terrible sin! One doesn't give horses God's gifts of food – but the custom isn't followed here at Reinsnes. This will be punished! We've seen it already. The punishment that comes when Dina takes grain and cornmeal to the horses.'

He decided to be a grown-up and go into the kitchen. Then she would surely keep quiet. But Oline paid no attention to him. She stood very close to cowering Thea and began to whisper. Loud and threatening, as if she were practicing witchcraft and Lapp magic.

'Why does such bad luck befall people and horses at Reinsnes? Why? I'm just asking in all innocence. First, the horse bolted and snapped the carriage shaft, and Jacob perished in the canyon. Then, Dina had to kill her riding horse herself. In the past few years our work horses have become sick or died. That's the truth, girl! I'd repeat it to the parson. And it's all punishment for Dina's misuse of God's gift!'

He asked if there was some pitch-stained cord in the drawer. He needed a small piece to wrap around a knife handle that was so slippery to hold.

But she did not see him. He was in the midst of the storm.

'Dina knows about horses!' he roared, and realized he was trembling.

'Knows about!' snarled Oline, as if she were talking to Thea. 'And why do we have such bad luck buying horses here at Reinsnes? The last work horse has such bad shanks it's a disgrace. That's what Tomas says! And what do you think caused it? The stallion has sort of sunk together and his legs get more and more crooked every season. And he's had both spavin and colic.'

'But that happens other places too, doesn't it?' said Thea, looking pale.

'You mustn't talk like that!' he said threateningly, and marched over to Oline. 'Nobody cures colic better than Dina. She gives the horse a big spoonful of lactic acid mixed in a half-liter of water, or a half-liter of diluted vinegar, which she tastes herself!'

But Oline was crazy today. Could not be stopped.

'She stops giving the horse fodder, and rubs its belly with warm cloths herself,' said Thea to help him.

Oline looked as if she wanted to spit at them. But instead she narrowed her eyes to thin slits from which she spewed fire and brimstone.

'She violates God's gifts! That brings punishment. I tried to move the meal sack way under the supplies table, behind a crate, so she wouldn't find it. I couldn't believe she'd ask for it. And she didn't. But fresh traces of meal clearly showed she found the hiding place and robbed it! What can you do? When a housewife sinks so low that she steals God's gifts from her own pantry. To give to a stupid horse.'

When she sighed it reminded you of someone plopping huge halibut heads into a salt bin.

'What's so special about horses anyway? Can any living soul tell me what's so special about horses? Compared to cows, which give milk and butter and calves? Riding horses are no good for anything. The last foal became knock-kneed, and has hindquarters like a brooding hen. That's a punishment. For misusing God's gifts! How can Anders dare to sail the wild sea, when his wife breaks the simplest of all rules!'

'You mustn't talk like that about Dina! Or . . . or I'll shoot you!' he shouted.

Then she finally became more like herself. She shut her mouth so her cheeks quivered, and looked at him.

'God protect us all! Poor, poor boy! And now she's going to send you away!' she sobbed, and threw her arms around him.

He was inside a world of sweet and sour and white flour.

You could begin to think again. It was over.

He went to warn Anders about Oline's punishment. That way you did something, even if it did not help very much.

Anders was walking along the wharves checking provisions for the Lofoten trip.

He wrinkled his forehead and said:

'Did Dina hear that?'

'No, she was in the stable.'

'It's nothing to bother her with. Oline is so full of superstitions.'

'It was awful to hear,' he said.

'Just forget it! Oline needs to scold once in a while. She's like a steam engine! She works best when she can let out steam. Stay here instead and help me count and stack things.'

Anders smiled slightly, but you could see he was a little frightened.

'A Lofoten sailor has, in contrast to the horse, a 200-year-old right to a three-month food supply,' he said. He smoothed out an old list and read aloud:

' "One steelyard pound of butter, ditto sour milk cheese, and two milk cheeses. Two *vog* of flat bread. Also, two steelyard pounds of barley meal for herring soup, one smoked mutton soup bone and some salted meat. Twenty *lefse*, a half-firkin of herring. One cask of vinegar, a two-liter tankard of brandy and some *marks* of tobacco. Each man shall also have free grain for cooking communal porridge, and syrup for simple needs." All for the price of ten *spesiedaler*.'

'Will they eat all that?'

'That, and more. If you want the best crew, you must figure too much rather than too little. The crew I can manage myself, regardless of what Oline says, but Our Lord controls the fish. Still, if the fish come in huge numbers, it does little good unless you have a willing crew.'

'It would be fun to see what it's like . . .'

'So many crews! I've heard there are 20,000 men fishing in Lofoten. Each man has his outfitting and provisions. That's many boxes of flat bread and many chests. And a whole lot of oilskins and leggings. The sea mittens are tied behind the boat to keep them clean and free of ice.'

In your mind you could see a band of 40,000

gray-and-white cod fishermen's mittens in the Vestfjord waters. It was a serious thought. Why hadn't anyone told him about that before?

'If Oline complains about Dina giving meal to the horses, you should know that many years ago your mother set up complicated accounting methods for how much cheese and butter and snuff are needed in Lofoten each year. That's how I started chartering to other markets. Oline thinks about everything from the kitchen at Reinsnes, poor woman . . . Dina and I look at it a bit differently.'

'Dina and I,' he said. That made everything all right. Anders was part of it. Then it must be Oline who was mistaken.

'Let me tell you, son . . . even though you're going to Tromsø to read books . . . Fishing, that's freedom and adventure! It makes you sleep well. It gives you swollen fingers and a cheerful spirit. If fishing is bad, it's still a blessing to get away from home. Everything else, everything you can't atone for, must wait until after fishing.'

'Can I go along to Lofoten?'

He saw that Anders was at a loss. Still, he repeated the question.

'I'll talk with Dina,' Anders promised vaguely.

But they both knew. There was no use thinking about it.

Anders cleared his throat and said:

'You've got a good head, son. You'd better use it before you get old and foolish.'

'But you've got a good head too, haven't you, Anders? You're not sent to strange buildings in Tromsø because of that!'

'No, things were different when I was young. You had to be glad somebody was willing to take you in and feed you. Besides, in my business I don't need to read books.'

'I want to be a cargo-boat skipper, Anders. Tell Dina we decided that!'

'Dina doesn't think you'd be a good skipper.'

'Why? I'll show her!'

'I don't think you'd be a good skipper either.'

'Will I be a total failure in Tromsø, if I'm not good enough to be a skipper?'

'No. You're the luckiest boy I know. We think you're going to be something great. So you need to go to school.'

'What will I be?'

'You'll discover that eventually. It will be something great!'

'I thought you were going to be my father and help to decide. And now she's the one who decides after all!'

You could not help getting angry. And now it was said, and could not be taken back. Anders stared at the floor.

'Your mother probably sees things better.'

'Look how things went with Johan. He just lies on the chaise longue in his clerical gown and begs for money!'

Anders had to laugh.

'He's made differently. He's not Dina's son,' he said pleasantly.

'What do you mean?'

'There's different stuff in you, Benjamin.'

'How do you know?'

'I see it when you get furious. And when you're good-natured too.'

'But we're both Jacob's sons, Johan and I, and you know what happened to Jacob. Now he just hangs as a decoration on the wall and haunts the alcove in the master bedroom.'

'Who says he haunts the alcove?'

'Dina says he's there.'

'I see,' said Anders thoughtfully.

'He's not dangerous.'

'That's good.'

Anders finished filling his pipe and lit it.

'Do you believe in phantoms and ghosts, Anders?'

133

'Those creatures haven't bothered me much.'

'They bother me.'

'What kind of ghosts?'

'The Russian. He's going to move to Tromsø with me. And in Tromsø I won't have anyone to play chess with at night.'

'Do you still dream about the Russian?'

'Yes.'

'What does he do?'

'Shouts and asks questions.'

'What does he ask?'

'If I'll be his witness.'

He should never have said that! Knew it the moment the words were out. They should be unsaid!

'Does it still bother you that the sheriff asked so many questions that time?'

'I don't know . . .'

'You can't forget he shot himself?'

'It was the rifle!'

He repeated it several times so there would be no doubt.

'Yes, it was the rifle!' Anders agreed.

'Do you think it's all right for people to shoot each other?' he asked, even though he knew he should not ask.

'It's not all right here.'

'Why not?'

'You'll go to prison for the rest of your life. It's only all right to shoot people in a war.'

'Do you know anybody who shot somebody?'

'No! Thank God!'

'Think about it! Think very, very carefully!'

It was like having an operation. You could not escape it. He had said the words.

'Stop it now, son! I don't have to think about that.'

You could stare in an ordinary way at a small creature with a black back – a beetle apparently – moving slowly across a board. Black, shiny shell. Suddenly he had to do something. Everything became so empty. Unbearable. He got up and squashed the beetle under his heel.

'That wasn't very nice. The beetle hadn't done anything to you, had it?' said Anders quietly.

'Dead Russians aren't so nice that it matters, but they haven't done anything either,' he said, and realized he had plopped down on a barrel. It teetered back and forth. The floor was so very uneven.

'You're probably right,' said Anders.

'How can she . . . go around as if everything is all right?' he heard himself ask.

'She's not going around as if everything is all right. She just doesn't give in to it,' said Anders. He had such a large face. You would think it was Anders who knew everything.

But Anders did not know anything.

'She has you!'

It was so remarkably easy to say that: 'She has you.'

'You also have me, Benjamin.'

'Anyone Dina has, nobody else has!'

'Maybe that's why she wants you to get out in the world and learn about something besides being Dina's son.'

'Do you think so?'

'Something like that,' said Anders, looking a little odd.

'And the Russian?'

'He can stay here. If he doesn't, let me know and I'll come and talk to him.'

'And if you're in Lofoten?'

'One can sail from Lofoten too.'

'That takes so long.'

'But it can be done. In the meantime, you must manage as best you can. That's what a man has to do.'

'Do you think I'm an old lady who's scared of a dead Russian?'

'I've seen bigger men than you frightened by miserable bad luck,' said Anders seriously.

'Are you sometimes afraid, Anders?'

'It happens.'

'Dina says everybody is afraid.'

Anders looked surprised. He did not know much. Anders believed the best about everything.

'Oh, she says that?'

'She says she's afraid herself.'

'What's she afraid of?'

He had said too much. You could not simply talk to people. In order to get along, you must not talk to people. You could not give in. You just had to talk about something else. So he said:

'Probably ordinary things that aren't very dangerous.'

Anders nodded and asked no more questions. He was a wonderful father in many ways. Knew that everything had to end. Instead, he told a story about one of his voyages. He had been so afraid that he had vomited without being seasick.

'It's all forgotten when you get safely ashore,' he added with a smile.

The next day Anders told Benjamin that, unfortunately, he had to be kneaded in grammar and baked in numbers until he went to Latin school in Tromsø. There was no time to lose, so the Lofoten trip would have to wait for another year.

'She's not very nice!'

Surely he could dare to say that much to someone who was supposed to be a father.

'There may be good reasons,' said Anders, and turned away.

He often sat in Mother Karen's room thinking a person should not remember everything. There was no blessing in that. The more he thought about it, the more he remembered.

Sometimes the thoughts came into the books he read and spoiled everything. The thoughts spoke to him in a frightened voice that was his own. Right through the

fairy tales and novels he heard himself tell everything
he should not remember.

It was almost worse than the Russian's howling.

Now and then he saw himself from the outside. Like
a speck of dust someone had put under Mother Karen's
magnifying glass. Sometimes he thought he had put
himself there. And that the part of him that did it was
an unconquerable giant who tramped through outer
space with the starry heavens over his shoulders like a
cape. But mainly he felt as though he was under the
magnifying glass. Sometimes he was a moth that flew
through the room without anyone bothering to notice.

He often wondered why he did what she decided.
Was it really she who decided? Or did he try to guess
what she wanted for him?

Sometimes he clearly saw it was not her fault. Or
anybody's fault. But he did not dare to keep that view,
for then everything became his own fault. Because he
was a coward. Because he was not as good as he should
be. Because he shouted and cried worse than Oline,
with no right to do so.

On really bad days he thought Johan was Jacob's
favourite son. And the one Mother Karen was most
proud of. Johan was a good person certainly. If he hit
someone, he had a reason. A good reason.

One day after Anders and Dina's wedding, he had
tried to talk with Johan. After all, you only had this one
brother. And Johan seemed so happy that day. So he
went along uninvited when Johan took a walk on the
beach. But it became obvious that you were a bother.
Of course, you could pretend not to understand, and
just endure it. But that was not the same. It was then
you showed what a bad person you could be in com-
parison to your brother.

Suddenly he said it. He was grown-up enough to
know you could not say such things to people.

'You have to sleep by yourself at Reinsnes this time,
now that Dina is married to Anders.'

Johan stopped short and stood motionless among the

137

stones as waves lapped against the rocks. The sun turned the sea green in the shallows and everything was calm. Just a gentle wind blowing. But inside yourself, it was cold. Johan was as pale as the sand and crushed shells on which he stood. A distress signal. A white brother fluttering in the wind.

'What do you mean?' said this brother, scarcely moving his lips.

He knew Johan could not stand the answer. So he replied:

'You used to sleep with Dina before, when she lived in the cottage. Didn't you?'

'Where did you get that idea, Benjamin?'

Johan took two threatening steps forward. You had to move aside and feel your heart pounding even in your fingertips.

'I saw it!'

He felt Johan grip his shoulder. Johan's nails dug into his skin. It almost felt good. They shared something in a way.

'Hush! You've never seen anything like that!' shouted Johan, and squeezed even harder.

He had to scream. But that did not matter. You could certainly scream when you were being squeezed. Then you knew why you were screaming.

'Is that so bad?' he howled, as he tore himself loose and ran ahead.

But all of a sudden he could turn around and say new words that made Johan chase after him and never doubt that he had seen.

'You will not tell this terrible lie to a single person!' panted Johan.

'It's not a lie! But if you're so afraid of it, I don't have to talk about it!' you could shout to your brother. It made things so easy. This way you could share something with Johan.

Johan could not get away without thinking about him. Thinking about what they both knew.

CHAPTER 13

The sheriff's family had come for a pre-Christmas visit. At the table, the atmosphere was strained. The boys had gone on the sleigh with Tomas to distribute Christmas gifts to the tenant farmers.

Things did not improve when the sheriff commented over the halibut that he heard a lot of commotion at night. People going in and out of bedroom doors. It wasn't proper.

'Benjamin still has trouble sleeping,' said Anders brusquely.

Dina sat stiffly aloof and picked at her food.

'Every night?' asked Dagny.

'Yes, lately,' Anders admitted.

'That's amazing! Isn't he . . . being raised a bit delicately?' asked the sheriff as he devoured the rest of his second helping.

'It's because of what happened to the Russian,' said Anders quietly, and passed him the fish platter.

It smelled of vinegar and bay leaves. The fish meat was white and firm, with a surface like uneven mother-of-pearl and strips of fatty skin at the edges.

'But that was long ago,' the sheriff said, and took another helping.

'He was there. That could affect a grown man too,' Anders replied.

'But he was so strong right afterwards,' said Dagny. She wanted peace at the table.

The sheriff regarded her a moment as he chewed. Then he nodded and said emphatically:

'One can't coddle them too much, or they become a bit odd.'

'Like me?' asked Dina.

'Now, now,' said the sheriff.

Anders and Dagny each began sentences, which collided in the air.

'Were you there when he fell?' Dina continued.

Her words had an unpleasant effect on the sheriff, but he held himself in check.

'Now, now . . .' he repeated kindly.

'Were you there when Hjertrud fell?' whispered Dina.

Sheriff Holm grew pale and suddenly clutched at his heart.

'Dina, Dina, let's have some peace,' Dagny pleaded, half rising from her chair. Her knife fell to the floor. The silver handle was coated in sand. It sang a long time under the table after settling there.

'Were you there when Jacob plunged over the cliff?' Dina continued coldly. She clasped both hands in front of her plate and stared stiffly at the sheriff's closed eyes.

'Dina . . .' Anders begged.

'Were you there when Niels hanged himself from the ceiling?'

The air around her grew frosty.

'If you'd been there, you might have had to spend a wakeful night over it. So don't be so appalled!' she said.

She calmly pushed back her chair, folded her napkin and laid it beside her full plate. Then she nodded to each person in turn, and left the room.

Anders managed to stay through the meal. But then, saying he was tired, he bid everyone goodnight. Upstairs in the hall, he had to stop outside the door and pull himself together before he entered.

She was undressing behind the folding screen. He went over and stood staring at the top of her head until she stopped and looked at him.

'I can't stand the friction between you and your father!' he said without preliminaries.

'And what do you want to do about it?'

'I want to be away when they come if you make things intolerable for a man at the dinner table,' he said, taking off his jacket and shirt at the same time.

She hung her blouse over the screen without answering. He saw just her hands and her hair in the dim light. Outside, it was snowing. He closed the drapes and finished undressing.

Once he had spoken his mind, he softened. But she continued what she was doing. It became unbearable after a while.

'Something else, Dina . . . and this is more important. We can't send the boy to Tromsø in his present state. He never sleeps!' he said.

'It's better for him to have other things to think about than to stay here,' she replied.

Anders realized he was angry.

'You're hard on the boy.'

'What do you think I should do?'

'Let him stay home until he's over this.'

'And if he doesn't get over it?'

Anders looked at her back while she brushed her hair. As so often when he watched her without her knowing, he had a helpless expression.

'What if it continues? Forever? Should he go around with his nightmares here at Reinsnes?' Dina added.

'Have you tried to talk with him? About what's wrong?'

'I know what's wrong,' she said wearily as she came from behind the screen.

'Yes, the Russian. But have you told him it's not his fault?'

She turned quickly and fixed her eyes on him.

'It's not a question of guilt!'

'No! But does he understand that? We must be able to help . . .'

He was silent for a moment. Then he said slowly:

'Maybe you're not the best person for this task, Dina?'

'What do you mean?'

'You were there and found the Russian too. It might be better if someone else talked to the boy about these things.'

'And who should that be? The parson?' she said contemptuously.

'No! Me!'

She eyed him carefully as she put down the brush without seeing where she placed it.

'You've got a high opinion of yourself, haven't you Anders?'

He felt the cutting sarcasm.

'Yes, and haven't you? Got a high opinion of me?'

His face broke into a sort of smile.

'Of course. And it's nice of you to offer, Anders,' she said absent-mindedly.

After they were in bed, she said into the air:

'It's not you who shouldn't be here. It's me.'

'And how would that be? Would your family visit me when you were away?'

'They may have to do that.'

'What do you mean?'

'I think I need to leave.'

The room held only silence.

'Now again, Dina? Why?' he finally whispered.

'Someplace where a maestro could teach me the cello.'

'The cello! Good God!'

He heard only her breathing. The room was very cold.

'You've threatened this before,' he said, and took such a deep breath that it helped. Then he continued:

'So it lasted no longer than this? You're sorry already? About getting married?'

She shook her head and hid her face against his chest.

'What's troubling you, Dina? Is the Russian still affecting the whole household?'

'It's so confining here.'

'That's what you said that time on the boat, isn't it? Then you wanted me to make up for it. But now that's no longer good enough!'

'I can't help it.'

'Who can help it then?'

She did not answer. Lay quietly, as if she wanted him to think she was asleep. It made him furious. But Anders did not like to show his rage.

'Are you still grieving?' he finally asked.

'Grieving . . . what's that?' she asked in return.

'I know what it is. For me . . . But I don't know anything about your grief, Dina.'

'Neither do I,' she said barely audibly.

He felt dead tired. Still he persisted. Had to make her say something.

'Maybe you should find out? You must have grieved your whole life. First your mother, then Jacob. Then Leo . . . Maybe you should have found out *before* you asked me about marriage, Dina?'

Footsteps sounded on the stairs. Dagny and the sheriff spoke softly and carefully closed the master bedroom door behind them. When everything was quiet, Dina took a few deep breaths.

'Getting married has nothing to do with my grief,' she said.

'Oh? Would you have asked me if Leo was still a guest at Reinsnes?'

'Oh Anders, are you starting that again?'

'No!' he said.

They lay close together under the big eiderdown. Motionless. So long that he had to shift his position.

'A herring net for your thoughts?' he said, and hugged her.

She did not reply. But she put her arms around him. That was something at least.

'Dina?'

'Yes?'

143

'Do you think . . . we'll ever manage to have . . . a little love, or whatever you . . .'

He was at a loss for words.

'Love . . .' she began.

'Yes, it's easy for me to say it,' he murmured.

'Why?'

'Because I feel it.'

She stroked his hair and the back of his neck. It only made him feel pitiful.

'That surely can't be wrong?' he asked against her hand.

'No Anders. No, no, it's not wrong!'

He had asked her something. Didn't she understand that?

Finally he sighed and said:

'Maybe you should talk about him? About Leo?'

She made no reply. But he felt the words moiling inside her. She held her breath. He drew from the eiderdown to look straight into her eyes. But it was dark. For a moment he glimpsed them, like two distant stars. Then she disappeared.

'No. Can we go to sleep now, Anders? It's been a long day,' she said, wanting to slip under the eiderdown again.

'You think you're to blame? Because he shot himself? And because Benjamin saw it?'

'Can we go to sleep now, Anders?' she repeated.

He forced her face up to his.

'No! Why do you want to leave?'

He was angry. He heard it himself. Angry because he was afraid.

She sat up with her knees under her chin and arms clasped around her legs. Rocked slowly from side to side. He tried to put his arms around her. But she twisted free. She held her hands in front of her as if expecting a blow, while words came spasmodically:

'If I told you . . . he didn't . . . do it himself . . . what would you do then, Anders?'

'What do you mean?'

144

'What I said . . .'

'That it was an accident?'

'No.'

Something was wrong with the shadows by the door. He did not know what caused them.

'Dina . . . ?'

'Yes.'

'You don't mean . . . ?'

'Yes!'

When only their breathing existed in the room, she repeated loudly:

'Yes!'

It was dark. Anders was a little boy. He sat on Mama's lap. But Mama had drowned years ago. Nobody knows anything about time.

He found Dina's hand. Laced his fingers with hers. Loosened them and intertwined them again.

'Did the boy see it?' he heard himself ask. From far away.

'I don't know,' she replied, so softly he had to listen into the darkness awhile before he understood.

Then he laced his other hand in hers. Gripped so hard the bones cracked. But she did not feel it.

'What will you do now?' she asked.

He cleared his throat several times. Then he realized they sat there shivering, and tucked the eiderdown around them.

'Damned if I know!' he finally burst out, and held her very close. As if it were the only thing he knew to do.

Time flowed back to them, like sand that a wave leaves behind when the tide goes out.

'What had he done to you?' he asked.

She shook her head. The shaking spread into trembling throughout her body. He could not tell if she wept. But her face was dry against his chest.

'Dina?'

'I couldn't let him just leave. Snakes and fire came . . .'

'And you say that! You, who threaten to leave me! Are you saying I should load a rifle . . . ?'

She looked at him. Her eyes gleamed in the dark.

'Yes!' she said firmly. 'If you love me enough to do that. Then do it! Until somebody finally dares, we'll keep doing the same things we've always done. For ever and ever. Somebody has to dare!'

He stared at her.

'You don't mean what you're saying!'

'Do it, Anders! Take it away from me! Like that! It's written that love is never in vain! That it survives everything. But it's not that way for me. He doesn't come any more . . .'

Anders felt his heart chopping his body to pieces. Its powerful blows cut up bones, cartilage and flesh, until his head lay alone and rolled into Dina's lap.

'Dear God, protect us both!' he gasped, embracing her with wilted arms.

He had stood at the helm in storms with waves as high as church spires. He had separated men attacking each other with knives. Had called upon devils and divine powers when the blows got too heavy. But he had never put his arms around someone who had . . .

But if that was his life, then he accepted it.

'What will you do now?' her voice broke in. Distant and hard.

He took a breath. A deep breath.

'I'll hold my arms around you until you tell me everything I should know. And then I'll keep holding you! But don't run away from me! Do you hear! Don't leave me!'

'Can you bear everything?'

He did not answer immediately, but then he said firmly:

'I can bear everything you're willing to bear with me! Everything I know something about!'

'Now you know!'

She laughed in hoarse shudders, and pulled herself free from his arms. Before he could stop her, she was out of bed. Shuffling about like someone looking for something when only half awake. She leaned under the bed for the chamber pot and squatted over it. He heard the trickling. Moments later the sound was mixed with weeping.

He got out of bed and hunched beside her in the raw odors of urine and sweat. All he could think to do was to untangle her hair with his fingers. When she was finished, he helped her back into bed.

He lighted a candle with trembling hands. Set it on a chair over by the door so it would not bother her. Went to the washstand. Poured water from the pitcher onto a towel and clumsily wrung it into the porcelain basin.

When he came back to the bed and wiped her face and throat, she murmured something he could not understand at first.

'I've met them all. The patriarchs. The disciples. John. Judas. Simon Peter. They're still here. Lie, deny and betray. I don't think they even know it themselves. And Christ is only a baby, even though so many whores lie at his feet.'

She paused, as if not knowing how to say the rest.

'But you . . . Anders! You've got too heavy a burden. You won't be able to carry it!'

'I can do what you can do.'

She shook her head and handed him the towel.

'Everything repeats itself. We've always done the same deeds. Always. And you haven't realized it before tonight. But now – now you've seen! Anders!'

He put the towel on the floor.

'I remember thinking Leo wasn't the sort of man to stay with anybody . . . But I thought that was what you wanted. Oh dear God! Could I have done anything, Dina . . . before it was too late?'

She shook her head.

He gripped her shoulders tightly, and said:

'Then we must simply decide it isn't too late, Dina!'

Somewhere outside himself he heard a horse and sleigh come into the courtyard. Torchlight spattered blood on the drapes. Soon afterwards the front door closed respectably and three pairs of noisy feet tried to find their way to bed.

Snowflake after snowflake clung to the windowpane outside. Combined into one huge flake. Became too heavy and fell down. Without a sound. Then you could see out into the night for a while. Until new specks created new flakes. The process repeated itself continually.

The next morning they met each other's watchful gaze. As if neither could believe the other was there. Although they had lain entwined all night. If, the day before, someone had told Anders you could go on living with such knowledge, he would have denied it.

Just the same, they got up. First she. Then he. He walked behind the folding screen and put his arms around her. Nothing was said.

At breakfast he happened to look at her hands as they spread butter on a piece of bread. Long fingers that clenched the knife and held the rye bread in place on her plate. And suddenly he saw the hand lift the Lapp rifle to her cheek. Heard the shot. It reverberated through the whole house without anyone noticing.

The nausea. One just had to admit it. Accept it and hide it.

CHAPTER 14

Benjamin had heard old people say that time passes much too quickly. That was already true for him. Ever since he learned he was being sent to Tromsø. His life only consisted of studying and Angell the tutor. It was as if he no longer belonged among the living.

Anders sailed to Lofoten and made an early voyage to Bergen alone. He was never at Reinsnes any more. And Dina's eyes were fixed on something no one else saw. Hanna had so many duties you would think she was ready to get married.

He began to regret that he had avoided Tomas so long. Even if all that fellow did was to dig ditches from the day the ice in the soil began to melt. Tomas had forced his ideas through, and had taken the Agriculture Association's advice about draining the land to yield better crops.

Now Tomas had convinced Dina to buy an Ayrshire bull-calf from Trøndelag. They talked about that calf as if it were the only calf on earth. Anders would get it on his way north from Bergen.

Many interesting things happened as a result of Stine's new loom.

'Bless this loom! Such a strong beam and good handle. Wide, but easy to pull. It's like a miracle,' Stine sometimes said.

To leave no doubt as to who owned the loom, Dina had Stine's initials carved into the beam. She could move it to America if she wished.

Neighboring wives came to Reinsnes to use the loom. With yarn, rags and daughters. Because the loom was not to be moved! They settled into the largest room in the servants' quarters, which was actually the farmhands' common room. But the men thought it was more fun to have a weaving room with women in it, even if they had to go out to the back steps with their smelly pipes in the evening.

The women exchanged rags and helped each other with warping and cutting. They laughed, gossiped, and sang. They made Benjamin think of freshly churned butter or babbling mountain brooks.

The weaving girls did not all arrive at once. No, they came like small ripples against the pier. One and two at a time. It began with a rustling of skirts up the tree-lined avenue. Then: joyous shouts and low laughter behind the outhouse and in the servants' quarters. Whispered conversations through open windows at night. And high-pitched, sparkling voices during the day. He was not the only one who paid attention to what the visiting creatures did. All the men on the estate noticed. He heard them ask if they should fetch someone in the *spiss* boat. Or chop extra wood? Or hang more lamp hooks? The youngest farmhand was eager to build shelves for their rag baskets to get rid of the clutter around their feet. It was easy to hire men to work at Reinsnes when Stine's loom was set up for the weaving girls.

He too found errands in order to see them. One had such a tiny waist you would think she could not hold together. They all leaned over the loom's beam and pulled until the fronts of their blouses quivered.

More people than usual streamed into the general store. It began in February. They came in small and large boats to see their wives, sisters and sweethearts. Or someone they hoped to meet. And they all bought syrup and snuff and other things once their boats were pulled ashore.

Even Angell the tutor forgot himself now and then.

Leaned from the open window and stopped in the midst of dictation. That was always when one of the visitors walked past.

It was one of the last days in May. He stood on a sturdy stool and got turned around slowly with his arms straight out. If he made movements he should not, he received nasty pricks from several dozen common pins.

'Stop fidgeting, and this will go faster!' said the seamstress.

He supposed it was the only way to escape the enemy more quickly.

'You haven't grown much this past year, Benjamin,' she said with her mouth full of those hateful pins.

She wore a blue cotton apron and her hair was pulled into a tight bun at the back of her neck. He wished she would swallow the pins. All at once. That was a shameful thought of course. Yet quite natural, the more he thought about it. But he stood extra still a long time so God would forgive him.

'He sleeps so badly at night, and eats so little, he can't grow!' said Thea, looking at him as if he were already shriveled up and dead.

'What's bothering you, young man?' the fiend asked ingratiatingly, and pricked his arm a little.

He did not reply. Found something better to do. He blew his nose on the sleeve, leaving a white stripe. Of course he had to sneeze afterwards. That was unplanned. He immediately regretted it, because everything came undone and the pins all had to be put in again.

Stine scolded him quietly about the snot, and went to the kitchen to find a cloth to wipe the sleeve.

He said nothing. Let them fool around at their tasks and talk nonsense about his not growing. He would not hinder them.

Dina came in, cocked her head and looked at him.

'Shouldn't he have clothes that fit him right now?' she asked.

'Clothes must be sewn to grow into! Otherwise he might walk around Tromsø half naked before Christmas comes,' said the seamstress, and showed how she allowed extra material in the pants cuffs and shirtsleeves.

Stine and Thea agreed with the seamstress. They had taken the large mirror down from the wall, and held it up for him. Both he and the clothes looked as if they had been borrowed.

Dina nodded, but it was clear she had not seen him. She did not care if he looked like a scarecrow. But that did not matter to him.

He let the seamstress turn him around under Stine's gently appraising eyes. He was a wooden figure that had to be dressed and sent to Tromsø. Before that, he also had to stand in front of the congregation at church and defend the articles of faith and their explanations. But that would be all right, as long as Anders returned from Bergen in time for Confirmation Sunday.

Hanna did not understand about anything except finishing her tasks. Sometimes she sat with him quietly. And listened while he read aloud. But it was only because she did not like to be alone. A few times she had even fallen asleep while he was reading.

He never got to examine her any more. She insisted they were too big for such things. He had no reply. There was nothing to do about it. But sometimes he was allowed to smell her hair. At the back of her neck. It made him feel strangely warm. But she would not sit still very long. That did not matter. He was going to leave anyway.

He preferred to be alone. Because there was so much you had to think about. Otherwise things just floated past and you could no longer take hold of them. Probably for the same reason that his body did not grow any more, he thought. Even the downy straws he once saw on his upper lip had stopped growing.

As long as he just sat in Mother Karen's room and

caused no disturbance, nobody paid any attention. If he just sat there a little longer each day, maybe they would not notice that he suddenly was gone entirely.

He often sat in the summer barn. The light coming through the small window always had a bluish tinge. The air smelled of cows, manure and clover. He could sit in the open doorway and think complicated thoughts about who he was, who others thought he was, and who he had to be so they would not discover anything.

You could be tempted to ask: who are you living for? Do you live for yourself? Or because you must be a witness who reveals nothing?

He never found any answers. Just got used to the uneasiness. His head had become much too big for his body. Straightening his neck, as Stine told him to, did not help.

He did not know when he first had the thought. That no one could ever save him from anything. He had to save himself. The thought became white maggots that crept into his spine. They swarmed and crawled and kept giving birth to more maggots. In the end, he could scarcely hold himself erect. Had he even dared to be properly afraid? But he could not be afraid. Because then he would die. So instead he had to live with uneasiness and maggots. Since the maggots devoured everything, it stood to reason that everything was empty. You could not think about it all the time, but you knew it anyway. That everything was empty.

He saw that Dina was waiting for Anders too. She went to the flag mound day after day. She was so thin she could have been a flagpole herself. She did not care how he looked or what he wore. Why should she? She had her hands full with her own concerns.

He tried to be at the flag mound with her. Watched for her. As if it were a meeting place. Just for them. But actually, he knew she was not waiting for Anders. She just went there for the Russian's sake.

She never got angry when he followed her, but she did not say much. Just stood there with her hair flying in the wind like a dark mainsail. If the sun was shining, they both shaded their eyes with one hand. As though it were a pre-arranged meeting.

They stood like that in the wind when *Mother Karen* glided into the Sound under full sail. He shouted, and ran to the house to change into the long trousers and big jacket and white shirtfront. He felt like a late migratory bird. Had shifted to protective colors, as it were. Soon he would be out at sea himself.

His boots were so big he had to adjust his stride to keep from stumbling on rocks and stones. He had been waiting for Anders to return. Yet he did not feel happy. So he laughed loudly several times and gave a shout. After that, he just stood on the ebb-tide beach with all the others and waited.

They launched the small boats into the water. One after another. Their voices floated on the wind over the small waves and whitecaps long after the words were spoken.

Then came the moment Tomas had been looking forward to for months: the young bull was taken ashore at Reinsnes with as much excitement as if it had been a negro from Africa. The animal had an upset stomach, because they had met stormy weather on the trip home. The crate the calf stood in, and the boy who had to hold the animal, were soiled higher than the tops of the boy's boots.

Anders looked relieved when they got the royal bull muzzled and had it on solid ground again. Then he ordered the boat to be properly cleaned.

'A bull is a person too. But it doesn't belong in a boat,' Anders said with a smile as the boat scraped the rocky shore.

'He's named Tore Hund and cost 30 *spesiedaler*,' said Tomas to anyone who would listen.

'A greedy price for an animal,' commented one of the cotters as he leaned under the bull and fiddled with it.

The other men watched with interest, but the women looked everywhere else while this was happening. The bull bellowed loudly and leaped against the side of the handcart.

'We'll earn that back,' Tomas said proudly.

'What's the price for a mount?' someone else asked.

'Six *spesiedaler*,' replied Tomas, and clapped the angry bull.

'You'll be passed over for cheaper bulls,' the man remarked.

'I give cotters a discount,' Tomas said quietly.

No one had seen a more powerful young bull, everyone said.

Then Dina came to the beach. She shook Anders's hand and bid him welcome. It grew quiet around the bull and Tomas. Now it was just Dina and Anders.

The weather had long been misty and raw. But it was as though Anders was a woolen blanket brought ashore. Benjamin noticed the effect on Dina too as they walked from the boat landing. It was as if Anders strode up the path with the Russian on his back, light as a feather. And later, when Anders put his elbows on the table and began telling about all he had seen, it was easier to breathe than before.

You could not complain, even though you were packed into trunks and chests to be sent away. It could have been worse. It could have been she who was leaving.

One afternoon Anders and Benjamin stood by the dovecote watching the doves flying to and fro. Suddenly Anders said:

'I'll come and get you at Christmas. It will be Christmas before you know it! I'll come and get you, even if the most terrible weather breaks loose!'

He had to nod. The words were kindly meant.

*　　　*　　　*

155

The sheriff's family came to the Confirmation dinner. Dagny praised Benjamin for doing so well at church in reciting the holy faith and the catechism's detailed explanations.

The sheriff said such a bright boy ought to make something of himself. He had already given Benjamin gold cuff links the night before.

Oscar and Egil did not fight with him any longer. All the fun was over. Oline did not shout through the house: 'The sheriff's boys are killing Benjamin!' Oscar and Egil followed Dina around. They talked with her, and about her, as if they owned her. He never got used to her being a sort of sister to the boys. And his being the youngest did not make things better.

He got even by getting acquainted with Dagny. This summer she had changed in his eyes. From being someone who always comforted and covered up, she now became a marvel. Dangerous. Someone he had to be near. Her hair. The weight of her when she leaned over his bed to say goodnight. Because she continued that custom, even if they were much too big for it, as she said.

She was a distant cloud. It felt unbearably delightful. He used every trick, both those he had learned and those he had not learned, to get Dagny to see that he existed.

When they returned from church, the women gathered in and outside the summer house before dinner. He walked past the open door. Shadows of leaves danced on faces and fronts of dresses. He floated into the fragrances. Among the skirts and the bodices. It was not especially manly. But surely you could have it for a little while?

Dagny leaned towards him to look at the cuff links he had received. Brushed against his hand. That was a bit strange. She said something about his having grown handsome.

His head became a soft clump. His hand raised itself.

It could not help brushing against her breast. She did not move. Just stood there while she hid his hand against herself. As if taking part in it. Making sure nobody would see. Then he became a puppy that stuck its nose into her low-cut neckline. Just for a second. Then it was over.

But the fragrance remained for days.

CHAPTER 15

Tomas said it looked as though 1859 would be a good year for the crops. Especially for potatoes and root crops. Rain at night and good weather during the day made the grass tall and green. Benjamin helped with the mowing and haying. Books were simply books right then. All the grown-ups agreed about that. They generally agreed when it concerned him.

One day after haying season a woman from Bjarkøy came to use Stine's loom. She brought along a girl with pale skin and braids that reached to her hips. He had never seen such a girl before. Completely unlike Hanna.

Nonetheless, Hanna took her as her own. In their work. In giggling over something nobody else knew about as they cut up rags for weaving. They went to the outhouse together. And their laughter floated across the courtyard like the wild shrieks of kittiwakes.

Now that Hanna had found a girlfriend in Else Marie, she had a good opportunity to punish him for going to Tromsø. And he could not retaliate.

He tried to approach them a few times to talk with the new girl, but Hanna whispered something that made her friend giggle with her hand in front of her face.

Early one morning as he crossed the courtyard he saw her. Else Marie. She stood by the well drawing up the water bucket. Her unbraided hair blended with the low sun. Her feet were bare. Light streamed over her and clearly outlined her body through the thin linen material. After a quick glance around, he was at her side in an instant.

She did not hear him because of squeaking from both the crank and bucket handle. When he came from behind and tried to take the crank to help her, she got startled and let everything go. He felt the iron crank scrape his hand. And the bucket landed in the well with a hollow splash.

He stood holding his hand as they looked at each other.

'I wanted to help,' he said.

'Oh.'

'Else Marie? Is that your name?' he asked, and grasped the crank. Blood dripped on it.

'Yes,' she said shyly. And the next moment:

'Good heavens! You're bleeding!'

He began turning the crank.

'You're bleeding,' she repeated.

'No, I'm not.'

'I see the blood. Should I bandage it?'

'Don't be silly.'

He cranked like a madman, and she said no more.

'Do you like cutting rags all the time?'

'No.'

Then she apparently thought of something terribly funny. She doubled over and started to giggle, glancing at him out of lascivious blue eyes. Totally unlike Hanna's brown eyes. He was so close to her he could see small light freckles on her arms and across her nose. And even down to her neckband, which was not closed properly.

He shifted his gaze and diligently continued cranking. The bucket came over the edge with a thud, splashing water on them both. A dark spot made her dress cling to her body. Right at her lap. He could not take his eyes from it. There were such strange curves on her. She was so round.

'Do you know who I am?' he asked, as he lifted the bucket from the hook.

'Yes.'

'Who am I?'

'You're Benjamin Grønelv of Reinsnes,' she said.

'How do you know that?'

'Everybody knows that.'

'Do you think it matters?'

She put both hands over her wet lap and looked at him through half-closed eyes.

'No,' she said.

'Why won't you talk to me then?'

'I didn't say that . . .'

'I'll show you something. By the summer barn. After supper. After they've milked the cows and everything is quiet. But you have to be there before the sun goes behind Kobbholm, or you won't be able to see it.'

'What time is that?'

'You have to figure that out yourself.'

'Where's Kobbholm?'

He turned and pointed.

'What are you going to show me?'

'I can't tell you.'

She giggled and bent over her wet skirt. Lifted it and let it fall again. You could see how it got sucked in. That did something to you. He could not breathe.

He put the wooden yoke on his shoulders and hung both buckets on it. Holding the bucket handles in each hand, he said:

'It has to do with the hill folk.'

The moment he said it, he realized how stupid it sounded. But it was too late to take back the words. He swallowed and felt his face flush. Then he turned as fast as he could with the full buckets and carried them to the doorstep of the servants' quarters.

Later that day he helped Tomas bring hay-drying poles from the fields in a handcart. You had to carry them

160

even if you had a large wound on your hand. Tomas had little sympathy for such things.

The change from studying and Confirmation celebration to farm work with Tomas was miserable. He did not say that. It would have done no good anyway.

How could he be so stupid as to brag about the hill folk to Else Marie? He had nothing to show her!

Moreover, he did not like being with Tomas. Felt Tomas was watching him, as if trying to prove he was only half a man. Something about Tomas made him take roundabout routes. But he could not say what it was.

The farm work began the day he passed the open stable door and heard Tomas's voice inside:

'The boy is pale and sickly, and just sits and reads. It's going to make him ill.'

Dina's voice said something he could not catch.

A moment later he heard one of them come out. He ran off with a feeling of intense dislike. Why did she talk about him to Tomas? Why did she do that?

Today his job was to haul poles.

He itched all over his body and felt Tomas's eyes on him. But he had to put up with the man's attempts at conversation.

'It's warm today,' said Tomas.

'Yes.'

They each carried some poles and put them in the handcart.

'Soon you're going to Tromsø to study?'

'Yes.'

'Won't that be fun?'

'I don't know.'

'It's easy to carry learning . . . Easier than carrying poles.'

'Mmm.'

'You'll probably like it.'

'Yes.'

'It's going to be lonesome for Hanna.'

'Mmm.'

'Are you coming home for Christmas?'

He let the poles fall into the handcart like a land-slide. Then he stood erect. His face felt like a dark red knot.

'Why do you ask?' he demanded.

It was not right. Still, he had said it. Tomas's gaze wavered, and you could see he did not know what to say. You could feel sorry for him. But you would not!

The man calmly set down his load, stared at the ground, and said:

'Because I want the best for you.'

You could laugh at such behavior from a grown man.

'I heard you tell Dina I wasn't much of a working man!'

'When?'

'A while ago . . . in the stable.'

'I said you should be outdoors more, not just bent over your books.'

'What's it got to do with you?'

Tomas wet his lips with the tip of his tongue.

'You are probably right . . .'

This time he whispered. It was eerie. As if Tomas knew that one of them would soon die. That it was important he say precisely those words: 'I want the best for you . . .'

He swallowed. His anger disappeared. Something was definitely wrong. Nobody should have to hear such things while hauling poles. Things you could not defend yourself against and did not understand.

Suddenly he grabbed the shafts of the cart, though it was only half full, and pulled it wildly towards the barn. The poles danced and the sun stung. You had to save yourself.

As he stormed past the garden fence with the cart, he saw Else Marie and Hanna. They were sitting on a bench in the garden cutting up their everlasting rags. He whistled, despite being so out of breath. Hanna did not look at him. Else Marie raised her hand. Just barely. But it was enough.

He dashed to the barn with the poles. Shoved them under the floor. The wound on his hand opened up. Everything got very red. Suddenly he felt nauseated. The blood flowed out. Red. He had not noticed earlier today that his blood was beautiful. He felt sweaty. His face was dripping.

Else Marie! Else Marie! Else Marie! he shouted to himself. But he was careful not to let a sound come out. Instead, he sat down for a while. Blew snot into the hand that was not bleeding. That helped a little.

When he went back to get more poles, the girls were by the garden fence staring at him. Hanna gave him a haughty look. Then she leaned close to Else Marie and whispered something. They snickered behind their hands.

You could not help that something tore loose. Inside yourself. He did not know what it was. Suddenly. A nasty little troll? Who made his eyes dry as tinder. Who turned his head into a viper's nest. Who gathered the rage into a terrible force. He brought the cart right next to the fence. It was just high enough so the sheep could not jump over it. Painted white. With a point at the tip of each board.

Before he knew what he was doing, he had leaned over and grabbed Else Marie's waist and lifted her over the fence. He met Hanna's dark look as he set Else Marie down. It took his breath away.

He forced himself to do it. Breathed in so hard the sound roared in his ears. Then he lifted the new girl again. In outstretched arms, high above his head. Her shoes barely scraped against the fence. Her breath was a long sigh as he set her in the cart. He turned his face towards Hanna again and tried to smile. But he did not know if he succeeded.

Else Marie sat there with a stripe of blood from his wounded hand. Red all around her waist. Now she was his!

He gripped the shafts and stormed down to the fields with the girl in the cart.

*   *   *

She actually came to the summer barn that evening. He had hidden behind some bushes and saw her walking up the path. She had such terribly light hair and skin. He did not know people could be like that. When she passed the wild raspberry bushes she reached out and picked several berries, which she threaded on a straw. That was not nice. To take Hanna's raspberries. But it was not his fault.

Suddenly she seemed to sense she was being watched. She stopped short and drew herself erect. Looked right at him without seeing him. He felt a pleasant tickle. A small thrust far down in his belly. Out towards each thigh. Then he realized he had no hill folk to show her.

It was best to get it over with. He came out from the bushes and raised his hand. She slowly walked towards him, carrying the red berries on the straw. When she got quite close he saw that her face was perspiring. Small beads of sweat shone on the skin above her upper lip and on her forehead. Underneath, the skin was completely white with those wonderful small flecks.

He could stretch out his hand and touch her face with his fingertips. Now. Like this.

She stood absolutely still and peered at his fingers. That looked odd. He had to laugh a little, even though they had not said anything. She laughed too. She was as small as Hanna, although she was fifteen years old. They stood like that as he ran his index finger across her cheek, nose and forehead, while he began telling about the blue-clad hill lady who came from the netherworld to bathe in a human stream.

He had never heard the story, but that did not matter. Because it was there. Waiting to be told. After a while he noticed she had stopped breathing.

'The hill lady stood under a huge waterfall and the water poured over her,' he continued.

She still did not breathe. Just gazed at him wide-eyed. She'll choke to death, he thought. And it was his fault. But he could not help that he enjoyed having her just stand there and choke while he told the story.

Just when you might have thought it was over, because she began to sway, she breathed again. The final sway brought her closer. So close she had to put out her hands to keep from falling on him.

The warmth of her hands! He had never felt anything so strange before. They were alive. Terribly alive.

He put his fingertips on her face again. Such a light face! So much brightness! Maybe the light lived in her and made her sway? Maybe he was the only one who knew?

'When the hill lady returned to dry land she took off her blue skirt. It had become so wet. She laid it to dry on some underbrush. Just like this underbrush here,' he said, and pointed. Pointed very quickly. Because he could not bear to leave her face very long.

'Then the hill lady lay down to sleep in the grass. But she shouldn't have done that! A dark boy saw her and thought she was pretty because the sunlight lived in her. He wanted to have her, but didn't know she was a hill lady, not a human being. And the moment he touched her cheek, like this . . . she woke up, and realized she was naked. She felt so ashamed that her shame was felt all the way into the mountain where the other hill folk lived. And they rushed out and cast a spell on the boy, so he was never himself again. As for the hill lady, she couldn't go home to the mountain again. So she always sits, naked and shivering, under the waterfall, or wanders in the underbrush . . . Shhh! Can you hear her, Else Marie? How she still wanders around here? Shhh!'

She listened, and looked a little anxious. So he took her hand. She did not laugh even once. And dusk fell thickly around them. The air smelled of cows and unused summer. And she still had not said a word.

He got her to sit down in the thick underbrush. Hesitantly, he reached towards the straw she held.

Then she came to herself and handed him a berry. He shook his head and placed the berry against her lips. She opened her mouth and put the fruit inside. One of the tiny bubbles had broken. The red juice painted a dot on her chin. He had to remove it. The juice stuck to his finger, and since he did not know what to do with it, he had to lick it off.

The whole time she kept looking at him. Just at him. It made him tremble. To sit and be looked at while you ate raspberries without saying anything about anything.

When the berries were gone, she still did not mention what he had promised to show her. But you could not be sure she had completely forgotten. So he put both hands on her waist. Very lightly. In a trustworthy way. So she would not feel threatened. Then something happened. She closed her eyes. Did not press them tightly together as if not wanting to see. No, they just glided shut. Lightly, lightly. Like tiny wings, her eyelashes spread onto her cheek. They were so blond you could hardly tell they were real. And her eyelids were very white with blue veins. As if someone had used a tiny brush and painted them on. The whole time they quivered and tried to hide how frightened they were.

He swallowed and touched her. In front where her breasts were. Not right on them. A little to the side, so it could just as well be something he had not meant to do. It was almost unbearable that she just sat there for an eternity with quivering eyelashes, not saying a word.

He swallowed again, and let his hand glide down to her neckband. Her skin was damp and soft. It was amazing she sat completely still.

He was about to undo the top button of her bodice when they heard crackling in the bushes down the hill, and Hanna's voice called:

'I know you're here! I know you're here!'

Else Marie instantly leaped to her feet and ran down

the path. He felt something like a cramp. In both his belly and his face. As if he were about to cry for no reason. The world was completely blue. He heard twigs crackling from her long after she was gone.

It did not matter. A little later, he heard them laughing down there.

He went to the cows in the summer barn. They breathed on him and chewed the tufts of grass he brought. He touched their warm bodies one after another.

'I'm Benjamin Grønelv of Reinsnes. Do you know me?' he whispered to each creature. They chewed, standing or lying down as the case might be. One or two looked at him with big eyes and nodded.

'But now I have to leave.'

The last cow breathed damply on his face.

'I'm no good at hauling poles.'

The cow turned resolutely away.

Without knowing why, he kicked its rump with all his might and shouted:

'I'll show all of you! I'll show you! Do you hear!'

Then it happened.

All the cows stretched their necks and opened their jaws wide towards the ceiling. The shadows of those big heads were frightening. Mooing surged out of them with terrible force and knocked him into the manure trough. He lay there, trembling and terrified, as cow shit oozed between his fingers. Soaked into his clothes. The cattle bellowed. Stamped. Breathed in more air and bellowed again.

He got to his feet and walked backwards to the door.

The eyes! They followed him. Shone towards him blankly. There were more and more with each step he took. Finally they were one huge cow eye.

Then he felt the door behind him. Staggered out, and fastened the latch.

The trees outside were like ghosts. They both saw and heard. They tried to grab him, scratched and whispered. Still, you had to run through them. Towards the stream. For a moment he stood looking at the deep bubbling pool that had an underground spring in the middle. Then he threw himself into it. He had to wash his shadow. It smelled of manure.

His body floated in the cold water. He found the deepest spot and sank in up to his chin. Let the water flow. Past him, past him. Clear and icy cold. The bubbling and rushing made him dizzy. Everything was so crazy. Everything was going to pieces. You had to hold out. It never lasted long. Something whispered to him. At first he thought it was the water. Or the hill folk. Then he understood. It was the Russian.

He did not know how long he sat there. His body was washed away. He did not feel the cold. His arms and legs were gone. He was a head that lay in a stream thinking ice-clear thoughts that floated away. Bright cow eyes stared at him from an immensely purple sky.

BOOK TWO

CHAPTER 1

When the child must be weaned, the mother has stronger food in readiness, lest the child should perish. Happy the person who has stronger food in readiness!

Fear and Trembling – Johannes de Silentio

One dark blue autumn day *Mother Karen* slipped into Tromsø Sound. Benjamin was to become a proper fellow, and perhaps a learned man.

Anders did not much like that anyone had to learn something he had not asked to learn. But he took off his oilskin hat and sighted the channel. As they glided towards the harbor looking for a suitable spot to anchor, Anders suddenly heard Benjamin say something behind him. It sounded more like a plea than a reprimand:

'The men of Bjarmeland came here in 1250 because the Tartars had taken their land in Russia. Håken Håkonsen said they could stay if they became Christians. So they built churches in Ofoten and in Tromsø. Then people came to buy and sell. And now Dina sits at Reinsnes and sends me here! Without even a piece of trash to sell!'

Anders kept watch, but was a little distracted.

'Where the devil did you get that from?' he finally asked, after shouting a brisk order to the men preparing to anchor.

'Some is my own thoughts, and some of it I've read . . . like everything else,' said the boy with a mature air, and took off his cap too.

The helmsman steered clear of a large English brig and a Russian *lodje*, and Anders shouted:

'Let go the anchor!'

As so often when Benjamin said things Anders had never heard before, it was like receiving a gift of wisdom. It made Anders remember Mother Karen. But she had been old and well-traveled. This fellow was just a boy.

As they rowed to shore, Anders pointed to buildings and wharves and mentioned them by name. Over there, apart from all the others, lay His Majesty's Royal Ammunition Depot and pier. There, were Merchant Giaever's impressive dock works and Figenschau and Steenson's piers and warehouses. And rising proudly beyond the city, Ebeltoft's wharves and the rectory.

The buildings leaned towards each other in the blue light. In between were yellow-green vacant lots and clumps of trees. Some of the large white wooden houses had picket fences and full-grown rowan trees. Roads and paths wound up the gentle slope of the mountainside like threads in a spider web that disappeared into the blue and white afternoon sky.

Along the beach stood small unpainted or weather-beaten huts with sad thin curls of smoke rising from wretched chimneys. On the other side of the Sound everything was terribly green.

The houses were lined up in rows with a wide street between them. Fewer and smaller than in Bergen, but connected the same way with gates and sheds. Some were built wall-to-wall, as if terrified of being alone in the world.

As they walked behind the wagon carrying his trunk and parcels for an entire winter, Anders pointed and gave names to buildings, signs and roads.

'Just wait till it gets dark and they light the lamps! That's a grand sight!'

*   *   *

But first he had to walk up the hills and into the tanner's house. A two-storey yellow ochre building with brown window frames. Had it not been that he went there with his trunk and parcels, he would have thought it an elegant house. Nothing rattled or came loose in the wind. It had geraniums in the windows and a gate with silent hinges.

You did not have to worry that roof tiles might fall on your head if you walked by. They were firmly fastened. The front door did not squeak either.

Still, something began to vibrate somewhere the moment he entered the house. As if it had been determined long ago. That he was here.

There was something about the smell. He had never known one like it before. Not a stable smell. Not a spice smell. Not the smell of lye or chamber pots. Not sour wool or rotten meat. But perhaps a bit of them all. When the tanner came home, the smell got so strong Benjamin thought Anders would comment on it. But Anders did not say anything.

Mrs Andrea had received them when they arrived with the luggage. She was tall and dark-haired, and you could not look at her hips very long without having to swallow. It was too much. If he set the small water pitcher from his night table at home on her hip, the pitcher would probably stand.

She had a lot in front too. Somehow he could never fully measure that with his eyes, because it made him blush. Her dress was severe and buttoned to the neck. Brown, with a silver brooch at her throat. You could look at the brooch if you wanted to look at her from the front.

Even so, he could not help turning red. Her hair was combed back from her face. So tightly that the skin at her temples was pulled up and her eyes slanted like a cat's.

Dina's hair was never pulled back tightly. But you did not see much of her face, unless she wanted you to. Andrea's face was terribly visible,

173

but still you could not look into her eyes.

You could not avoid Dina's eyes. That was the worst, and the best, thing about being in a room with her.

His first evening in the ochre house Andrea grew larger every minute. She undulated among them. It was probably the way she walked. Like a wave cresting over the reefs when the wind was from the west. Sudden and slow at the same time. With vibrations you merely suspected. Or perhaps it was her slanted eyes? You might think she was a witch or something. No, not that actually. He was not afraid of her. It was completely different. He did not really know. He sort of wanted to be the oatmeal biscuit she held in her hand a while before closing her lips around it.

At first he wondered if Anders had thoughts like that too. But he acted quite normally.

When they arrived, a shriveled figure was standing behind Andrea wearing a blue cotton dress and a white kerchief down to her eyes. She nodded silently several times. Then she shook hands with Anders and him in turn, and disappeared into the house.

Anders was right. The street lamps by the market square and outside Røst's bakery were a sight to behold. He had seen large wharves in Bergen, so Holst Wharf and Wadel Wharf did not impress him even during the day. But the oil lamps were a marvel.

Already the first week he learned that under the lamps was where you gathered to smoke rolled tobacco on the sly and see what made the girls giggle.

Never in all his born days had he seen so many girls at once! They stood in small groups hiding their hands in muffs and their noses in fur collars and scarves. More and more layers as the cold weather set in. The girls under the oil lamps in Tromsø were beyond comprehension!

The clock in the town hall was lighted too. As if in

this city it was absolutely necessary that people always knew the time.

They came from a certain street. The girls. Early in the afternoon little girls from Søndre school created restless shadows under the lamps. They fretted and complained about the nasty boys from Nordre school who swore, spat and cast sarcastic remarks and, later in the year, snowballs.

Sometimes an untidy figure walked by. With a gait like a worker coming from the pubs. But he was sober enough. It was the headmaster, Hans Baade Theting. He staggered along waving his arms and mumbling to himself as if he had just escaped from the insane asylum. Nobody was afraid of him. They made way for him just to avoid unpleasantness. Once in a while some tough fellow confronted him and began to tease. But the man flailed his arms and warned that the 'rascal' would suffer for his pranks. After thumping his cane on the ground a few times, the headmaster raised his hat absent-mindedly and walked on as if he had forgotten his anger.

Some teachers were despised, and some were admired. And some were the object of envy. The latter applied to those who taught the girls at Søndre school or worked with Miss Thesen and Miss Braeck.

Rector Blom was a newspaperman and did not count. He sat with his articles while the students did German translations. He was inside his head in a way. But his body and eyes were present. So you could not be sure he did not see. He was not someone to joke about. He commanded a kind of respect, which you could not really explain. Probably because he wrote in *Tromsø Stiftstidende*. Somehow you could not overlook that.

From the first time he walked along the sidewalks on Fredrick Lange's street to Skipper With's house at the shore, he reluctantly had to admit he enjoyed this place of banishment. He forgot everything he had imagined would be frightening and strange.

175

The smells. The people moving about. Sounds from the craftsmen's huts by the sea, the boats flying foreign flags, and men who rowed ashore in unusual clothes. He even liked the steep mountains on the other side of the Sound which prevented him from seeing the open sea. They became a kind of protection. If he had to be sent into the world, it was good nothing reminded him of Reinsnes.

At first it felt as if someone had put him into a fairy tale. You could not really know how to react to such a thing. When he realized nobody was going to take him out of the fairy tale, he decided the city was created then and there for his sake. Sometimes it was a chapter in a book he was reading.

But as soon as Anders left for home he understood you could not shut the book and walk out of it. He had to live and breathe here for years. He had to submit.

Every evening when the tanner came home and they sat down at the table to eat, the house seemed to fall under a spell. He was locked up with a dragon and a bewitched woman with an inscrutable expression. The house had many rooms he must not enter. Because if he did, the terrible thing would happen.

They had given him the best room, they told Anders. It had two tall windows that stared blankly at a shed and a wooden fence. And a black stove that always smelled of stove polish because it needed to be so shiny.

He had to sit at the table with this large dark-haired woman who must never show her husband her true nature. The tanner cleared his throat and his eyes always had a hunted expression. As if he mistrusted everything and everybody. Or feared they suddenly would say something unbearable. Something dreadful that broke the magic spell.

You could not tell if the tanner liked or disliked having him in the house. Neither of them said anything that would lead him to believe one way or the other.

The words were locked up somewhere. It had been decided ages ago which words could be said.

As long as Anders was there, they behaved more or less normally. But when he left, they changed a little each day. They became less and less real. There were many signs of this. For example, Andrea could see through a hidden eye at the back of her neck. She always turned around quickly if Benjamin tried to imagine setting the small water carafe on her hip as she stood with her back towards him.

He had to get used to more than just the house's smell. The man had unpleasant hands. The first week they were almost ordinary. But they slowly turned copper as the days passed. And regardless of the color, the backs of his hands were covered with black hair. All the way to the joints.

He tried not to stare at the tanner's hands. But it was not easy.

The food was unreal too. Or bewitched. It all tasted the same, no matter what it looked like. That was not so strange. Because the atmosphere at the table was like being in the ocean's depths. Dark swaying forests of kelp and slippery rocks, chasms and crevices. Creatures swimming about with open jaws and sharp fins. The rows of snuff-brown flowers climbing the dark dining-room walls were actually billowing seaweed and slimy bodies. The room was filled to the ceiling with words that would never be spoken. No words could survive here. Not even with gills.

Secrets floated around and made it impossible to see properly. Something about it reminded him of Lofoten fishermen's sheepskin blankets after two months' use. The smell too. The way it probably smells when you never undress before going to bed.

But it was strange how quickly you got accustomed to it. He became so used to no conversations at the table that he would give a start, as if caught cheating, when they suddenly said something about the weather. There was nothing dangerous about it. The weather

177

was either good or bad. The wind was either from the north or sadly from the west. Or both.

The awful thing was that the words probably concerned something else. Something horrible! Even though it sounded as if they concerned the weather.

He sometimes saw a smile. It was she who did it. And always at him. Never at her husband. The first time it happened he felt a tightening far down in his belly. Because her eyes rested on him. Because her mouth spread out so he could see inside it. She became a large animal that was ready to take him. Not swallow him. But lap him up.

That was how she first came to him in his dreams too. She fell over him somehow, with the rippling corners of her mouth ready for action. Everything grew heavy with forbidden, unmentionable images. They came closer and closer. Until he disappeared in them. Deep inside the large, fleshy lips.

But that was at night. At the table she always kept her lips tight together. As if she had a toothache. Except when she smiled. He could not recall she smiled at anything that was said, or because she wanted to be friendly. It was nearly always when she turned around quickly and saw him watching her from behind.

She could stand at the sideboard arranging dishes and silverware. Suddenly her movements froze, she turned, and her lips spread to each side. Then it appeared. Her smile. And drew him in helplessly.

From the moment he entered the house he knew you did not touch one another. So it became a sentence passed on him: to dare to touch her somtime. When she stood like that with her back half-turned to him.

He heard about witches and werewolves, beings who lived double lives. As ordinary people by day, and as wolves at night. That was it! The thought made him grow heavy and big.

He knew if he touched her when she stood like that and thought no one was looking at her, he could reveal her true nature. And then the most terrible thing would happen.

The city of Tromsø was more than Mrs Andrea. There were duties and constant seeking for affirmation by others besides Benjamin Grønelv from Reinsnes.

In 1858 Rector Blom had received permission to establish a so-called extension school. Dina's son was one of nineteen students from outside the city who lived in strangers' homes or with distant relatives. He would be equipped with learning and discipline. Before he finished his third year he would read Book 9 of Herodotus, works by Plato, the Olympic speeches of Demosthenes, the Books 5–7 of Homer's *Iliad*. He would also study morphology, syntax and grammar, as well as a comprehensive Latin curriculum: Livius, Book 1 beginning at Chapter 44, and Phaedrus, Books 2, 4 and 5. Virgil's *Aeneid* and Horace were required reading too.

Every two weeks they had to write themes in German, English and French. They had to learn geography by rote, and drill in arithmetic and geometry. Everything was oriented towards the final examination. They needed to show competency in Latin composition, translation and speaking, as well as in history, religion, Greek, geography, arithmetic, geometry and Norwegian composition. They also had to pass tests in singing and declamation. The latter was something he really enjoyed.

Each month the teachers' council gave demerits, in addition to the daily register of sins in the grade book. For all this punishment and learning Dina paid 36 *spesiedaler*. Almost every day he heard comments from the teacher's desk about what a grand sacrifice the 'dear guardians' had made.

You constantly learned new tricks to escape all the punishment deemed 'appropriate' if you did not submit.

The first commandment was to be absolutely silent when a teacher was present and had not asked you anything. The second commandment was to be polite without groveling. He quickly learned that every student who groveled met his nemesis sooner or later. Either through the teacher or through his fellow students.

But things went fine when you had no talent for groveling.

On the other hand, he had much to learn about keeping his mouth shut. At Reinsnes, only Dina and Stine repressed their words. And they did that of their own free will. He had learned, without anyone directly saying it, that at Reinsnes each person had the right to voice an opinion without reprisal, as long as you did not curse or swear around Oline.

Perhaps the Latin teacher was correct in saying he was as stubborn and verbose as an untamed oracle. But it was not a mortal sin, as long as you showed you were willing to improve.

This was a school for the sons of merchants and government officials. But a few students' fathers were craftsmen or sailors. In Tromsø it was no shame to work with your hands. Nonetheless, the difference was there.

You could always tell who came from the uncultured homes. Even if they tried to modify their language. Especially those from homes that permitted slovenly talk at the dinner table. Meals at school were a bewildering hodgepodge of so-called cultured and un-cultured speech.

He gradually understood what the sheriff meant the few times he had roared that Dina allowed her son to talk like a stable boy. But that only helped him to control his love of talking.

Some things were refined and some were vulgar. He felt more comfortable with carpenter Beck's son Sofus than with anyone else. Sofus swore softly, and kept quiet in situations demanding cultured speech. He was silently absorbed by the girls under the street lamps. You could even like his smell. The fellow was resin and newly chopped wood.

Sofus, with his broad nose, beanstalk figure and sullen expression, became a person you could count on. But they did not talk about that.

CHAPTER 2

Mrs Andrea was much younger than her husband. The thought gave him a somewhat triumphant feeling. He could not know what she did during the day, because he was at school then. He thought about asking her. But that would not do. Somehow he would have to find out. That was certain.

The husband was in his tannery down by the sea. But that did not make him less dangerous. Quite the contrary. You could imagine him standing over a steaming vat, stirring a seething mass of blood and bones with a huge wooden ladle. You knew that one tanned the skin. But all the rest? What happened to it? One had to get rid of it, no matter how horrible that thought was. And the tanner got rid of it surely. That was why his hands were so unreal.

He had never seen such hands. The tanner's hands seemed to grow a little every day. Sometimes he thought he could see them right through the bedroom wall. They were huge sores that placed themselves on her body under a big blanket he had not seen. Sometimes the sight also came when the tanner folded his hands on the white tablecloth and said the table prayer. The nail on one index finger was filthy as a sewer. That was the secret! That was where she put her poison and held them all prisoner.

At first he thought she did not see him. Not properly. Whereas at home, even if Dina and the others did not always appear to see him, they did. He had always understood that. He had his secret hiding places at Reinsnes, but somehow people always sent for him.

Here, nobody asked. They did not look at him when they talked to him. They were not real.

No outsiders came or went in this house. Only the old woman, who was both cook and housemaid. She lived next door in a little annex which apparently was once a stable or a shed. She could have lived in the house, because it had at least five bedrooms. In any case, there were five doors in the upstairs hall. But the old lady undoubtedly knew what she was doing when she left the house each evening.

At Reinsnes, many people came and went. Many of them he had never seen before they suddenly were there. Everyone, even the parson, stopped in at the kitchen and the store. It did not matter whether you had an errand there, even if you often acted as though you did.

It was different here. After a month in the tanner's house he still had not been anywhere but in the dining room, the stairway, and his room.

At Reinsnes the doors and cupboards had bolts and hooks. But that was so you had something to grasp when you opened them. Even when the office at the store was locked, the key stayed in the door. Oh yes, the wine cellar was locked. But the key hung on a key hook in Oline's room, or lay upstairs in Dina's room because she had not put it back in its place.

In the tanner's house you locked all the doors before you went to bed. Each room had its own key. Which was used. Every evening he lay quietly and heard keys turning. Then came footsteps on the stairs, the creaking of the landlord's bedroom door, the tanner's hawking, and finally the sound of a key being turned from the inside.

Already during the first weeks he realized that the day when, for some reason, this ritual stopped or did not occur as in previous evenings, the terrible thing would happen.

He lay under his blanket and held his breath until everything was quiet. He counted footsteps on the stairs and keys turning.

Still, he was unprepared when it actually happened. One evening in the early winter before Christmas. The final locking sound did not come!

The night was as threatening as the coffin hanging in the hay barn at home without anyone knowing who would lie in it. Of course, you could get up and light the lamp to save yourself. But that meant actually doing it. And he could not.

You could tell yourself to simply go to sleep and get away from everything. It was not certain the curse applied to him. It could be a trap the tanner had laid for her. Not locking the door. But deep inside he knew the curse applied specifically to him.

He did not know if he had heard the sounds from the landlord's bedroom before and just become used to them like everything else. But after a while they were unmistakable. They entered his ears and created an excitement it was useless to avoid.

Someone moaned. Someone groaned!

You had to pull yourself together and save yourself somehow. He got up in the cold, dark room. Threw on some clothes. Felt an empty warmth when he stuck his feet into the coarse socks. His groin and hands were completely stiff. The stiffness became all-important. He both wanted it and did not want it.

He fumbled his way to the windows and pulled back the curtains. Moonlight streamed in and transformed everything. It was a clear sign. Also the sounds! They forced him out.

He walked without touching the floor. Opened his door without anyone seeing or hearing. He did not exist. It was a floating, but stiff, feeling . . . to not exist.

In the hall, the sounds were clear. Half-choked whimpers and rough groans. Surely he had known it the whole time! That the tanner would expose her secret, would realize she put poison in his index finger.

Now the time had come. The tanner needed a witness! He was going to shoot her!

He had known this the whole time. This was how it had to be.

He did not think about whether he dared. So he did it! Opened the door to their bedroom. It silently swung open. It was part of the judgment! Took part in it! He had to endure it. He was here because he had to endure it.

At first everything was just darkness and chaos. But moonlight broke in through the curtains. The tanner's large back was outlined in a white nightshirt. Beneath the shirt, his legs were twiggy pine trunks. His body operated with power from a large invisible bellows. You could hear them. It was unreal. Suddenly, the tanner straightened up and swung to the side a little.

He held something in his hand. A tool of some sort. A Lapp rifle! A knife? He had laid a trap for her. She had shown him she was a werewolf. So he had to kill her.

Her thighs! The moon shone on them with a white glow. Terribly white.

The moon shone on what the tanner held in his hand.

Nobody could have such a thing loose in his hand. It was supposed to be attached to the body. So probably she had doomed him to that. To have it in his hand. Completely unattached. That was his judgment!

Now the tanner would take revenge. He held the revenge in his hand!

She realized everything was over. She groaned as the man leaned over her and sank the tool in her. Held her down with one arm and worked with the other.

The room was thick with all the words that would never be said. Thick with the tanner's revenge and her groans.

185

It was impossible to escape. You just had to get it over with. Not scream. Just be absolutely quiet. He saw her convulsed in a spasm. Thighs and legs on either side of the tanner's broad back. The moon bathed it completely white.

Suddenly the tanner stiffened with the tool raised. Did he notice someone standing there? But no. He leaned down and thrust it between her thighs again. The movements! The moans! She was still alive!

You just had to stand motionless and be a witness. They performed a kind of dance. They were enemies. And they were doomed to each other. It was the end. Soon the bang would come. And the blood.

She suddenly gave a choked gasp and her feet dropped and lay quite limp beyond the edge of the bed.

You were already in a grave. In silence unlike anything else. You just had to wait for clumps of earth to tumble down and bury you.

The tanner had tricked him into being a witness. Now he was like them. Unreal.

He did not shut the door again. Just got himself across the hall and into his room. With their odor clinging to his hair and skin. The tanner's breath was his breath. The smell of their bed became his smell. He could not escape. Was inside it now. With them in their bed.

The next morning, everything had happened. Still, everything was as before. Because she was not dead yet. He heard her through the wall. She talked to the tanner. Quite normally. That proved nothing was real.

You had to do what you usually did. Go down to breakfast. Eat. Go to school. Only by doing absolutely ordinary things could you save yourself. He set one foot on the steps. Then the next. Held the railing.

He stood at the edge, ready to leap into the haystack. He was dizzyingly high up. He could not see if there was hay down there. Now he jumped. Aaaah!

The dining-room door needed to be opened. That

was a job. He must open it quickly so they would not see he had become like them.

When he entered the room, they sat there already. He had not considered that possibility. That they already sat there. Because then they could watch as he went to the table, pulled out his chair with a scraping sound, and sat down.

Once you were seated without having tipped over anything, you could not get up. You had to sit.

The tanner cleared his throat and mumbled:

'Good morning.'

She moved her mouth without looking at him.

She knew! She had seen him in the doorway!

She passed him the bread plate. The bread was surely poisoned. Nevertheless, he had to take a piece. He helped himself to butter from the square dish with a gold border and 'butter' written in ornate letters. The butter was hard as rock. It made a hollow in the bread and would not spread.

He reached for the jam. Currant. Terribly red. It seemed to flow across the whole room. He felt nauseated and reached for the cheese. That lay in another square dish that said 'cheese' in ornate letters.

It was written what he had to do.

Probably it was written that he had to stand in the doorway each night to make sure the tanner did not use a knife or a Lapp rifle.

This was why they took him into the house.

Or: was it just she? She who saw what he could be used for.

He chewed as he looked at the two square dishes in turn. You got accustomed to it.

But he could not raise his glass of milk. The same color as the moon and her thighs. You could not drink it just like that.

He had chewed safely through the piece of bread and over to the door, when he saw it: her smile. It spread across her face. Across the entire room. Her lips undulated towards him without showing her teeth. Her eyes! Sleepy, but terribly watchful. Like a cat's.

The tanner cleared his throat and said:

'Not too bad – the weather today!'

He rushed from the dining room, fumbled into his overcoat, and left the house. The key burned in his pocket. He had not locked the front door as they had told him to do.

He began sleeping with his pillow over his head. Still, the sounds were there. In his sleep too. He knew how they carried on. Eventually he, not the tanner, took the big tool in his hand and performed the motions. Thrust into her. Some nights they functioned together. The tanner and he. Other nights he was alone with her. She was large and soft. The corners of her lips dissolved. Her mouth became a huge chasm into which he could drive the tool. She whimpered and sighed, revealing her large fleshy lips the whole time.

During the day you could not live with the knowledge of the night. He scarcely dared to look at her during meals. The thought of touching her was the first thing in his mind when he awoke and the last thing before he fell asleep. If you touched her, you would die.

Still: he knew he had to!

When in the house, he constantly needed to think about a chance to touch her, and at the same time avoid all the traps she set for him to do precisely that. He began to see her body as a sign under the severe dress. It was important always to see the signs.

He was safe as long as they did not notice he had a face.

CHAPTER 3

One of the tanner's relatives died. The sign could not be clearer. He knew it was his fault. He had long wished something would happen to give him an opportunity.

It must be somewhere in the bedroom. The tanner's tool.

He could not feel regret for the death being his fault when Andrea said with a blank expression that they had to leave town for the funeral. They would be gone four days. But he would get his meals and care as usual. The cook would be there.

That afternoon he sat doing his Latin conjugations and waiting for evening to come. The cook shuffled into his room in her coarse gray oversocks and said she was going to a Free Church meeting. She had prepared some sandwiches for his supper. They were in the dining room under a napkin.

He could not help it, he smiled at her. But he should not have done that. She looked at him suspiciously and said:

'Be sure to lock your door!'

He hastened to look serious again.

The moment he heard the front door lock behind her, the Latin verbs and conjugations no longer existed. He rushed to the hall window to make sure she indeed waddled down the street clutching her worn handbag.

Then he was standing in the hay barn again. The haystack lay below. It was just a matter of jumping.

You knew the feeling. The pull. The excitement. The tension. Did he dare? Could he do it?

Maybe the door was locked? Maybe they stuck pieces of paper between the dresser drawers to betray him? Or even worse: maybe she had not gone? Maybe she lay in bed waiting? He had not actually seen her leave the house. Maybe they wanted to trick him into coming into the bedroom. So they could catch him?

He paced around his room a few times. But sooner or later you had to make a decision. So he decided. Stole into the hall and over to the door. It felt as if his blood rushed through his ear canals and onto the floor.

He put his hand carefully on the brass door handle and pressed down. It lowered silently. The door swung into the room, still without making a sound. Was it a trap? That the door was unlocked? They always locked it after all.

Then he was inside. The room expanded. Ice-blue light streamed through the windows and lay on the bedspread.

She was not in the bed!

He shut the door and stole into the room. The house watched every step. This bedroom smell was totally different from that at home. Summer and haying season never reached here.

The bed was a ghostly cargo boat. Dark and high. Above the chest of drawers a large mirror angled out from the wall. He gave a start at his reflection. A blurred figure with overly long shirtsleeves and a chalk-white face. His eyes were wide and dark. He wanted to rush from the room. But some unknown thing was stronger. He stayed.

His head thundered like a rockslide. He realized he had forgotten to listen for whether the cook had returned. Could she have forgotten something?

He hurried into the hall again and listened down the stairway. But no. There were no sounds. No noise from the parlors or the kitchen. Not a single click of a door. He stole back into the bedroom and took a deep breath before opening the door of the nearest nightstand. It contained a covered chamber pot. An unmistakable odor struck his nostrils, although the pot was certainly empty.

He opened the small upper drawer and found a box covered with yellow silk. Inside it were orderly piles of embroidered handkerchiefs. There was also a small box containing rings and pins. So it was her nightstand! In a long flat cardboard box lay a tiny half-completed cross-stitching of a girl holding a lamb. The lamb had many needles stuck into it. Neatly beside it lay small skeins of embroidery thread. Red, yellow, blue, orange and black. Beneath were some letters tied with a silk ribbon. He did not touch them.

The husband's nightstand was locked! He knew it would be. Still, it drove him wild. He shook and tugged the handle. But the door would not open. He had to sit down. But did not dare sit on the bed. At the foot of the bed was a stool. He sank down on it. His throat was full of sand and plaster. He stared straight ahead and saw himself in the mirror above the chest of drawers. His hair was standing on end. The look of a madman. He had gone into it willingly!

His desire came in waves. Powerful. You had to help it. You had to loosen your clothes and handle yourself. While you stared at everything. The organ that grew large in your hand.

He had fallen into her trap. Could not do otherwise. He collapsed over his lap when the spurt came.

Did the front door click?

Could you be choked by your own heartbeat? You had to get up. Make your pants hang right. Like that! It still burned down there. Wet and sticky. He got back to his own room. But she had him all the same.

Utterly exhausted, he sank onto his bed and slept.

At school the next day he thought about only one thing: how to open the locked nightstand. That afternoon as he sat alone eating smoked herring and potatoes, he felt brave.

He got through his school work after a fashion. But the words would not stay in his head. Then it was evening.

First, he made sure he was really alone in the house. Went to the cellar and found a file, an awl and a hammer. No matter where he was, he sensed the smells of their bedroom.

It was even more frightening than the day before. He laid the file, awl and hammer on the chest of drawers and patted the bed gingerly. Was it warm? No. Then he lifted the bedspread and looked under it. Dark!

He brought the lamp from his room and set it on the chest of drawers. The light went in and out of the mirror.

Positioned by the nightstand's brass fittings, his courage failed him for a moment. He took a deep breath and tried the awl first. To no avail. The lock was more complicated than he could master. The file was too large and the hammer was unthinkable.

Then suddenly he had it! He rose quickly and pulled the nightstand slightly out from the wall. He was right. The back was a wooden board attached with nails. He turned the nightstand completely around to reach the back more easily.

But he found he could not manage without pliers. The nails were in too securely. He got them out far enough so the heads were free, but then everything stayed absolutely firm.

Had he seen pliers in the cellar? He put down the file and took the lamp with him down all the stairs. It smoked terribly because he could not hold it straight. The whole house was dark creaking corners.

What was that? Was it somebody walking? Utterly beside himself, he stumbled up the narrow cellar steps to listen. But no. All was quiet.

He did not find any pliers, but he remembered seeing

sugar shears hanging on the kitchen wall. That might be useful. He got the shears.

He had become like them, like the tanner and Andrea, he told himself. Then, with his head in a red fog, he launched his attack. The fog spread to his lower belly. It was a tremendous force that squeezed his breath out of him and filled him with exciting expectation.

The board slid away and he could put his hand into the nightstand. It had two shelves. On the lower one, papers and books that looked like ledgers. On the upper one, a piece of checkered material rolled into a small bundle. He took it out and felt something inside it.

The material opened like a sling.

The tanner's tool fell to the floor.

At first he stared at it, unable to move. Then he picked it up carefully. The tanner had gone to the funeral without his tool!

It was made of soft, smooth, light-colored leather. So long it stretched the length of his open hand. It had a finely formed head and two large pouches at the end.

He knelt holding it in his hand. It was made of six leather strips. Painstakingly cut into its remarkable form and sewn together with small stitches in brown silk thread.

His fingertips glided over the seam. You could hardly feel it. Probably stuffed with sawdust. Firm, but flexible.

Herds of stallions emerged from the mirror. Galloped with the tanner's tool under their bellies. They had a goal. Hooves and fluttering manes. Muscles straining under their hides. Loud whinnies. They thundered towards their goal. It was she. In the bed. The place for the tanner's tool. Lips.

Images flew round his head like cuffs on the ear. Then he joined the herd of horses. The tanner's thing was warm in his hand. He stared at it. Smelled it.

Followed it into her. Grew so strong from it. Inside her, with all the whinnying horses waiting their turn.

It was a necessity! To get there. All the way there! That was what she wanted.

He coaxed the tool and the board into place, turned the nightstand around and went downstairs with the sugar shears. It was like descending a steep rocky slope in pitch darkness, even though he carried the lamp. The glass was completely blackened with soot.

Taking a chance that nobody needed the file, awl and hammer, he put them in the drawer of his own night-stand.

The fire in the stove had gone out and a cold moon looked in his bedroom window. His head filled with red folds of skin, he returned to the tanner's room.

He had to lie in her bed. How he would do that without anyone discovering he had been there, he did not know. But he had to do it.

Tremendous forces exploded and made him hiccup. He slipped under the bedspread on the side by her nightstand. Buried his face in her pillow and took deep breaths of her scent. Frightening. Close. Delightful. So unmistakable.

He had smelled it when she entered the dining room. Sometimes an inkling remained in the halls. But all of it was here. Heavy. Body, breath and night.

He blew out the lamp and threw his arms around her pillow and eiderdown. It was she! She was warm. She touched him and caressed him and turned him into a huge leather thing with silk seams.

It was painful. Nonetheless, she dragged it out. Held him there. And he enjoyed it, until he could take no more and gave in.

For the first time it was not just a game that made him ashamed. It was very serious. He had forced himself into her bed!

The tanner might find out and hang him from the chandelier. Or beat him black and blue. Or report him

194

to the rector. Or write a letter to Dina and Anders. But none of that mattered. He was invincible. A grown man who spurted into both her and the sheet.

He awoke when he heard footsteps on the stairs. The cook. Coming to wake him! He did not dare to breathe. His eyes stared at the door handle even before he was awake. He had slept in the landlord's bed! He would be discovered!

The cook knocked on the door to his room. The sound shattered the world. He barely could keep from replying, just to get it over with.

She took a couple of steps out there. Or shifted her weight to the other foot while waiting for his reply. Then she called him again:

'It's seven o'clock! Time to get up!'

He held his breath. They both waited. Now she would open the door! And see the empty bed! He began to pray. That she would go away. Forgot that his situation was so shameful it was hardly wise to draw Our Lord's attention.

He heard her call a third time. Sharply. Everything was silent for a moment. Then his prayer was answered and the stairway creaked.

He was on his feet at once. Tried to get an overall idea of the bed. But it was too dark. He pushed his heart far down in his stomach because it was hammering crazily. Meanwhile he smoothed the bedspread like a blind man trying to erase his tracks. He remembered to take the lamp with him into his room.

It was not a moment too soon. The cook came upstairs again. He coughed loudly so she would hear he was up, and hoped she would not ask questions. But it only resulted in her calling:

'Are you sick with a cough today?'

'No,' he shouted in a voice nobody had heard before. 'I'm coming! I'm coming!'

She mumbled something and the stairs creaked again.

*   *   *

195

As he tried to make the best of sitting at a hard wooden desk with a fellow student, the uneasiness began. What if the cook went to the tanner's room and found the nightstand ruined and the bed slept in!

When the teacher asked if he was ill, since he was so pale, he willingly admitted he felt terrible and got permission to go home. Now he could inspect the bedroom and remove all traces. While it was light.

The cook's shoes and coat were gone. Relieved, he entered the forbidden room. As he had feared, it was quite evident someone had lain in the bed. The hollow made by his head was clearly outlined, even though he had pulled the bedspread over it. He fixed it as well as he could. But making beds had not been among his duties at Reinsnes.

He waited until evening and the cook had gone home before he put the tanner's leather thing properly back in its place and hammered in the nails. It felt as if he had hidden a fellow conspirator. Someone who knew everything.

He thought about her coming home and lying in the bed where he had lain. As he sat doing his school work he thought about that.

The evening they returned from the funeral he was in one of showman Pettersen's public halls putting on an act, as people said.

The Norwegian literature teacher had asked him to read a poem by Henrik Wergeland.

'Benjamin Grønelv has a good voice and a talent for declamation,' the teacher had said.

So he stood at a podium and put his secret into every word. The poem was to Stella, the 'heavenly bride'. The words formed themselves in his mouth. It was just a matter of letting them out.

'Feeling – oh like the slow
          and gentle blow
That set worlds in motion, that let

Suns burn hot and waves grow
With Promethean fire that must glow
In the pale blood of plants yet!'

It did not matter that his jacket sleeves were too long and his trousers rubbed his shoes. The applause was loud and long.

You had to try not to fall as you left the podium. You had to walk confidently.

In the front row sat a whole line of girls. He glanced at them as he went to the foyer to get a cup of hot chocolate during the intermission.

They stared at him! All of them! At him? He forced himself to pass them when he returned with his full cup of cocoa. In the middle of the row sat a red-haired girl with fur cuffs on her jacket.

Then he saw it! She held the tanner's leather thing in her hand. You could not help giving a start and spilling the hot cocoa.

The red-haired girl rose quickly, hid the tool in the folds of her skirt and took the cup from him. She was still staring at him. It had happened so fast. He bowed in confusion and said:

'Thank you!'

Then he began to feel his hand burning. It made him grimace. Holding his cup in one hand, she took out her handkerchief. Her breasts rose and fell. Like two animals. Her plump white fingers wiped the back of his hand carefully.

'You read so well!' she said. Her eyes were terribly blue. But you did not forget she had hidden the tanner's tool in her skirt.

'Thank you! Do you want my cocoa?' he said breathlessly.

She curtsied and took a sip immediately. She too burned herself. He saw that. She tried to hide it. But she did not stop looking at him.

When she looked up from the cup there was a light brown stripe between her mouth and her nostrils. He wanted to lick it off. But instead he smiled as best he could.

'I'm Charlotte Wickstrøm,' she said a little shyly. But just the way she said her name showed he ought to know who she was.

She stole a sidelong glance at her girlfriends, as if she had started the whole thing on a wager. So he bowed in his best manner and told her his name.

'People know that,' she said acting grown-up, and fondled the tanner's tool in the folds of her skirt.

'People know the Grønelv family from Reinsnes,' she added.

'I see,' he said faintly.

'People know Dina Grønelv.'

He was about to ask her who 'people' were, but that did not happen. Because now she stuck out the tip of her tongue and licked off the chocolate stripe. It made him dizzy. His hand burned. But he did not look at it. Her tongue was pink. He tried to adjust to his painful hand and stood very straight.

Then she blushed and lowered her eyes. And when she gave him a brief nod and went back to her girlfriends he realized she thought he had mimicked her. He had evidently done like her, stuck out his tongue and let it deliciously travel around his mouth. You could not make up for such a thing. What could you say?

He wanted to run after her, but she had already disappeared in the crowd. He should find her. Explain to her. That he had not mimicked her but merely licked his mouth. He had to explain. Because she was a sign. She hurried away with the tanner's precious tool in her skirt.

As he walked home from Hegelundssal at Skippergata 12, he thought about two things: that they had returned from the funeral now. And that Charlotte Wickstrøm had fled with the tanner's tool. The tanner probably knew everything. Had seen how he broke into the nightstand and lay in the bed with her.

The seriousness of death creaked in the snow and wept under the soles of his shoes.

His mouth was dry and his glance unsteady as he let himself into the ochre house and tried to steal upstairs. Halfway up it happened. She came into the hall and talked to him. She talked to him!

'Was everything all right while we were gone? You got your meals?'

He mumbled something and nodded several times.

'My husband went to check on things at his workshop,' she said soft as a cat, and looked up at him. Right at him.

The sweat! He was a fool desperately trying to stop a spring flood. His face. The upper lip he had shaved for more than six months. Dripped. And his nose. It was a bonfire.

Did she have to hold the lamp so high?

'I hope you don't mind that supper is delayed? That we wait for him?'

'No, no, no!' The words tumbled out.

He rushed up the stairs.

When she called him to come down for supper the tanner still had not arrived.

'He's so behind in his work, he won't come until later,' she said, pouring milk into his glass.

A sweet darkness shadowed everything for a moment. He put down his sandwich on his plate, just to be safe. Could not say anything either. Something was wrong with his tongue.

On the sideboard was a brass samovar. It glittered coldly towards him when his eyes tried to escape in that direction. The lamp above the table was lit. It swayed a little. Why did it sway? And throw fire in his face.

He leaned back in his chair and stared at the samovar. Then he swallowed a bite of bread without having chewed it.

He had been discovered! He saw it on her. All he

could do was give up. He sighed loudly. Drank his milk in a great hurry and thought about her thighs in the moonlight.

She passed him the milk pitcher. His whole body caught fire as he grasped the handle and two of his fingers touched hers. He held the pitcher across the table in his outstretched arm until she withdrew her hand. The movement made the brooch between her breasts glisten faintly.

Suddenly the tanner's tool lay on the table between them. You could be grateful to the red-haired girl. Then it began to dance! Powerful, satiated plops on the white tablecloth.

Her eyes! You had to avoid them. Hidden there behind heavy eyelids. Her lips expanded from her face. They moved. Wanted to have him. They sucked him in. And the tanner's tool danced.

He knew it. He was discovered!

You could not know whether it was death or desire. But in any case it was quite useless to escape. Her lips spread wide. Her front teeth showed slightly. The corners of her mouth trembled.

The tanner's tool thundered. Until the glass of milk spilled.

She rose and came around the table. Leaned her body over him with a napkin in her hand.

Now was the time! He remembered at the last second. That he had to touch her first. He raised his hand. Did it! Put his hand on her bare throat. She was utterly soft. And warm.

She paused for a moment. Then she put the napkin between him and his plate and began to wipe up. He sat completely still. Kept his hand on her throat. His hand moved with her as she wiped. Like a part of her. Strange.

When she finished, she put the napkin on her plate. Then she picked up the pitcher and filled his glass again.

Then he did it! Tipped the glass!

200

'Uff da!' he heard her say. She bent over him with a cloth napkin, heavy with skin. Whiteness flowed over his hand and dripped into his lap. All that whiteness seeped through his pants and stuck to his thighs.

She wiped carefully, without showing her eyes. Said something about changing his pants. Touched his clothing. Her fingers were hungry. They were on him. Pressed. Touched him. He leaned his head back. His arms fell to the sides of the chair. Behind closed eyelids he sensed her shadow. A sultry shadow. It was dangerous surely? But could not be avoided. It breathed heavily.

He felt something that could have been pain. But it was not.

The stove had been cold for several hours. The locking and the rituals with doors and footsteps on the stairs were over. Sleep was part of the house. Part of the vague wind roses on the windowpanes.

She entered the room without him hearing the door open. But he heard she locked it from the inside. The night was pitch dark. Still, light fluttered over her. First over the folds in her robe, then over her body wrapped in thin white material. Her skin spilled out. Great waves he could not escape. Masses of heavy velvet fell from the ceiling and buried him. Buried him in her scent. He recognized it. And knew he must have it.

At first she was one with the darkness and glorious damnation. Death and terror. You let yourself be led through it. Without resisting. Surrendered yourself in her moist warmth. Hid yourself. Crept into her. Whimpered. Made movements like a fish that did not know it could swim. Until it swam. He was hers now.

And she let him spill milk over all her white table-cloths.

CHAPTER 4

He was up early the next morning. Like someone
uneasy to the point of sleeplessness about a task. His
task was to leave the house before anyone else
awoke.

He wandered through empty streets and watched
the city come to life. All the way to the church. Up and
down Strandgata. Past the midwife's house and Sheriff
Irgen's place, past merchant Giaever's home. You could
count and categorize the houses according to size and
color. You could try to remember the names of people
and buildings.

Finally he found himself at the shore among the old
shelters for people who came to church by boat. He had
never been here before. A fellow who clearly had not
been to bed gave him a furtive look as he staggered
towards home. The rank odor of urine and old garbage
was everywhere. A scraggly cat of indeterminate color
leaped from a wooden fence and hissed when he
almost stumbled into it.

He was at the bottom of a well. Doomed. And he
owned the whole wide world! He could not go back to
the ochre house again. Never! The tanner would slit
him open. Pull out his intestines. Toss the blood under
the stairs. He would strip off his skin and make it into
a silky soft tool stuffed with sawdust. One consolation
was that you knew who it was intended for.

The tanner would probably cut off his head and
organ and hide them in a closet. Perhaps salt them in a
firkin like pickled herring. Later he would take them

out to devour in great secrecy when the cook was at her prayer meeting.

Nobody would miss him. Aside from little Charlotte Wickstrøm. She would ask about him a few times. Then she would forget him for something else.

As he thought about Charlotte, he tried to remember if anyone had told him where she lived. Perhaps he could get her to plead his case with the tanner. But he rejected the idea. Because he would first have to tell her the whole story. And it was not like Wergeland's poetry. Absolutely not for Charlotte Wickstrøm. She understood nothing about the tanner's tool.

He trudged through town towards the school. Realized slush and mud had soaked through his shoes. That was somehow cleansing, even if it felt miserable.

What was it Oline always said? The Son of God's suffering purifies humanity. You could feel in your icy feet how much Christ had suffered.

He would just keep walking here. Then perhaps he would be purified. But his thoughts were as lewd as before. All he could think of was the leather tool and her skin. And a tremendous pressure. Down there.

You wondered if you would ever get used to it.

He would deny everything. No matter what the tanner could prove, he would deny everything. It was the only way out. Or should he use the tanner's own tactic? Silence. Not a word. Eat in silence and leave. And if the tanner beat him? Beat him senseless? It would not matter. The tanner would kill one of them anyway. Perhaps both of them. In the end.

No, no! She would not let it happen. She would save him.

He gathered some courage. Decided to go to school. He would see what happened afterwards. In the midst of this thought he plowed into a rock-solid body rounding the corner. They both fell to the ground and lost their book bags.

He heard an oath and saw a bloody nose. It was

Sofus Beck. After finding all their scattered things, they stood up and brushed off the snow.

'You could have looked where you were going!' snarled Sofus, as he looked for something to wipe his bloody nose.

'The same goes for you!'

After a few silent moments, they both realized things were bad enough already. He handed his handkerchief to Sofus. Who took it without saying thank you, and put it over his nose. But the bleeding would not stop.

'Put a clump of snow in your nose. That helps,' he said, patting a handful of snow on Sofus's face. With no fuss. The bleeding stopped.

'My father knows a man who can stop bleeding,' said Sofus.

'Now you do too,' Benjamin said with a smile.

They talked like men about everything imaginable as they walked. Their teachers and their studies. You could allow yourself that. The day already had enough problems.

Whether because of Sofus or something else, he returned to the ochre house after school. No matter what happened, it was better to get it over with than to wander around in the cold.

You could get used to being a squashed snail in a wheel rut. If you were so loathsome nobody would touch you, then you would probably be left in peace.

She had touched him! That could not be changed.

During dinner, the unpleasantness began. The tanner spoke! Asked if he was now so disciplined that he left the house before others got up. If this was to continue, they must set out sandwiches for him so he did not go hungry.

The tanner had not said so many words in a row since Benjamin arrived.

'It was something I promised to do for someone. Work . . .'

The tanner grunted and folded a pair of yellow hands while he said the table prayer.

She ate the meat soup without looking up. Tiny, well-mannered spoonfuls. Without showing her teeth. She merely spread her lips over the spoon.

He could not breathe. But he had to do something. He gripped his spoon.

Perhaps the tanner had a weapon hidden under the table? Was he just waiting for the right moment? When you least expected it? Was she waiting for that too?

She spilled a little soup from her spoon into her soup dish. Small drops. Sat as if it was important to listen to the drops. She did not look at him. Was she on the tanner's side? Had they agreed about everything? No, she protected him. That's how things were.

The meat was cut into very small pieces. Still, some were large enough to be red with beads of fat on them. You could not look at them. The sight settled far down in your belly.

She had thick eyelashes. Dark, like old barbed wire. They lay on her cheek now. She was pale. You could imagine Christ's crown of thorns. She had a crown of thorns on her cheek. Because of her sin?

Her breast raised and lowered the silver brooch. Raised and lowered it until he began to tremble. Then it happened: she raised the two small crowns of thorns and looked at him. Straight at him.

He fell. Fell further and further, as he pressed his thighs together and stopped breathing.

But more days and nights followed. He went to school and worked hard at his studies. He went with Sofus to look at the girls under the lamps. But that was just to conceal himself.

Sometimes he promised to better his ways. That lasted until the evening ritual approached. Then came the restlessness. The desire. The longing.

Most dangerous of all were the evenings the tanner

returned to his shop after supper and the cook was at a prayer meeting.

He took off all his clothes, blew out the lamp and went to bed. The desire to grow was so strong. He was the beam supporting the ochre house.

CHAPTER 5

She once said she would send him word before she left. She probably sent it with the wind.

He heard it little by little after he came home for the summer. Oline was an old freight barge who was not quite sure what she would transport to him. But eventually she stacked everything in place so he understood.

Dina had left. In May, after Anders sailed to Bergen. First she paced back and forth in her bedroom every night for a whole week. Then suddenly she was at work before anyone else opened their eyes. Within a few days she settled her estate. Placed accounts and papers in the old safe. Took the store clerk into her confidence and gave him complete authority until Anders returned.

Then she packed her hat box, travel chest and Lorch's cello in the time the sun took to cross its path on the horizon.

'The oystercatcher had come north long before and was sitting on its nest at the edge of the field. But Dina left everything and traveled south with the steamboat,' said Oline.

He had always known she would leave. Now she had done it.

Oline told him the sheriff had received a letter authorizing him to turn over to Anders all rights and duties for Reinsnes and 'the boy' for an indefinite period. It sounded as if you were part of the estate. A copy of the letter lay in a large sealed envelope with Anders's name on it. In the office safe.

He could go and look at the letter of course. At the envelope, that is. The key was there. It was not like the ochre house.

He also learned that at first the sheriff wanted to telegraph along the whole channel to find her and bring her home. But Dagny dissuaded him. Instead he telegraphed to Bergen to contact Anders. He received a surprisingly calm telegram in reply:

'My wife decided to travel abroad to learn to play the cello. I am coming home soon God willing. Respect-fully your son-in-law Anders.'

God willed that Anders came home. But was stern in other respects. He took *Mother Karen* on her voyage north from Bergen. With her crew and cargo.

Benjamin was standing on the beach when Anders arrived with the steamboat. Felt ashamed that people saw him crying. But was not really sure why he cried. Dina was gone, but not dead. Anders was empty-handed and had lost his ship, but he was not dead either. Many stood there weeping for those who were dead.

Anders walked among the people gathered on the beach. Embraced those who had lost a family member. He had once said a shipwreck changed everything. So he knew this from before.

'You're waiting, Benjamin. This time I don't even have a present from the city for you,' he said. But it was hard to know what he was thinking.

Not much was said about his not having insured the boat and its cargo as the sheriff explicitly advised. There was little reason to insure the men. They were, now and for ever, gone.

Anders invited the remaining family members to a memorial gathering at Reinsnes. There would be sleep-ing space for everyone. In beds and on the floor. So they could all be together for a day and a night. No effort or cost would be spared. The parson came too, and spoke kindly to people.

Things were especially difficult for Peder Olai's widow on one of the tenant farms. She had six small children and was in debt for a barn and a *spiss* boat. Anders saw to it that collection boxes were set up in the store and other places people frequented. There were no voyage profits to divide, because the small money chest lay at the bottom of Fold Sea.

'Bad weather and storms. A lot of snow. The mast cracked like a twig. We couldn't maintain our course. The rudder struck a reef. Then we were in the stormy sea!'

That was what one said when Our Lord demanded His own.

Anders and the rudder had been saved on the same reef. A fisherman found him there a few days later. They found the cook's helper too. He got a grave on land. Nothing was known about the others.

After the memorial gathering a deathly silence fell over the estate. And Anders went inshore fishing. Two days with no food or drink in the boat. He had gone in a *treroing* meant for three rowers. Alone. That in itself was the act of a madman.

When he did not return to shore the first night, Oline wept and prayed to Our Lord. People had a saying: 'God is strong, yet three men in a *treroing* is also something.'

But Oline created her own variation:

'Dear God, when there's just one man in a *treroing*, we must put our trust in You! And let the good weather last!'

They could see the boat from shore. A floating shadow. Sometimes just beyond the jetty, sometimes out in the Sound. You could wonder what was wise to do when your mother left home and your father fled

209

to go inshore fishing. You could laugh about it. But that did not make things better.

Finally he told himself that if he were in Anders's shoes he would wish someone would row out and talk some sense to him. So he rowed out to hear how Anders was. It took three hours. Back and forth. With rowing and everything.

One could not really say the conversation between Anders and him was profound.

'Are you going to stay out here the rest of your life, Anders?' he shouted through the evening mist when he got close enough.

'It looks that way, son!'

'What are you doing?'

'There's lots of small coal fish!'

'Have you cooked some on board?'

'No, but the gulls around me live well.'

'Can you save some fish for people ashore too?'

'I haven't decided yet, for God's sake!'

'How long does it take to decide?'

'Are you waiting? For me?'

'Yes, but it's not much work. Because right now I haven't got many people to wait for.'

'That's true.'

The boats bumped into each other.

Anders had a steel-gray beard and his nose was one raw wound. The sun had been strong.

'You look like a ghost,' Benjamin ventured to say, holding the boat rails tightly together.

'Yes, I'm a ghost!' said Anders. 'On my very tiptoes in hottest hell, cellar to attic and every other place in this damn green, glowing hot, devilishly burnt hell. I'm a ghost! And Satan and Our Lord can just scratch their gnat bites over not destroying a ghost! They can see forwards and backwards and everywhere, but they'll learn that Anders didn't live like a long-suffering idiot all these years just to go to the dogs! So! Lash the boats, you little devil! And hop aboard with me!'

*   *   *

With no fuss, Benjamin did what his ghost of a father ordered. Then he sat down and gripped a pair of oars. And Anders continued:

'Just think, she took that damned cello and left! Eh, son? What do you think? Can you figure it out? How in inner Bals Fjord can a damned woman be so dumb? Whether she's your mother or not. God forgive me, she'll never set the world on fire this way! Now let's get moving! We'll row right through glaciers and flaming hell!'

Anders stopped being Anders that summer. His hair turned white. But his rage gradually diminished. Later he seldom mentioned them: the *Mother Karen* and Dina. When he did, it was because they belonged to the story he needed to tell.

In daily life Anders acted as if no one had done anything to him. But he stopped going to church. You could understand that if you knew him well: he had become a ghost.

In a way it was a relief to go to Tromsø in the autumn. He stopped thinking about Dina being gone and Anders becoming a ghost.

If you told yourself those things were in one room and Tromsø was in another, you believed it in the end.

Autumn was not too bad, even though it was frightening.

He had his hands full with each day's demands, and Reinsnes was far away.

And then there was Andrea. Perhaps he had known it had to happen. In fact, things really should have been much worse.

Andrea never specifically promised after all. But he thought she would protect him. Not that she should shoot the tanner. She should not do that! She should just ask him to take the big leather mountain in his colored hands and leave the city. Then his smell would disappear too.

Afterwards they could paint the ochre house. White. He could study and she could do the things you needed her to do. And nobody had to know how things stood. Because there was no law against having lodgers.

But that day just before Christmas when the tanner came home earlier than expected and held his short talk, she walked out of his room without a word.

He knew the two things had no connection. That Dina left and that Andrea simply walked out of the room. He was grown-up enough to realize that. You could have become used to people disappearing. Were it not for the emptiness.

The tanner did not kill him.

Did not chop anything off him.

Did not threaten to have him expelled from school or anything.

The tanner gave some sort of speech and cried at the same time. There beside Benjamin's bed. He had known it the whole time: the tanner was not real.

It was the cook who saved him. She made a bed for him in her annex for the next few days until he went home for Christmas. But he could not recall her saying one word. Her place smelled of camphor and iodine. It made him feel sick. But that was nothing to worry about. He had stopped fearing something would happen. It had happened.

When he came home to Reinsnes he discovered it had been decided that Hanna should go to Anders's relatives at Grøtøy. To learn a little more about etiquette and refinement.

He could do nothing about it.

Hanna had become a bit strange after the summer with Else Marie, so she was no longer for him. Now she felt triumphant about going away. That was like her.

As if Grøtøy was anywhere to go!

You could have become used to it, were it not for the emptiness.

CHAPTER 6

'It's amazing how you've grown, son! I think you'd better come along to Lofoten this year,' said Anders.

So he did not have to go to Tromsø right after Christmas.

Anders did not say everything he knew or saw. He simply decided.

'We need to get rid of your moodiness,' said Anders. 'Besides, we have to contact people we know about finding you a new place to live. But that's a simple matter,' he added.

He was not sure what he had imagined about Lofoten fishing. He had heard Anders talk about the freedom, about the waves, the camaraderie and the fish. Fantastic quantities of silver straight from the black sea. But Anders forgot to mention the infernal amount of frostbitten fingertips, snot and wet leggings. And sore hands! His hands went to pieces and reminded him of Mother Karen's descriptions of lepers in the Bible. He could not even feel his hands for hours out in the salty mist. Which was just as well. When they got inside the cabin and should have had peace, then suddenly the devil struck. Then all he did was feel.

It was soon evident he was not a good fisherman's apprentice. He rushed around energetically, trying to satisfy everyone, no question about that. But if something could be tipped over, he tipped it. If something could be broken, he broke it. He lost his hammer and gaff hook in the ocean. Intoxicated with sorrow and blind energy, he could not learn anything.

At first they cast furtive looks at the books he brought along and suggested he hoist them up the mast so the gulls could learn something too. When they saw how clumsy he was in all practical work, he first had to endure silent sidelong glances. Then it fermented into small stinging words.

It got so frightening that he repeated the words aloud for everyone to hear in order to make them harmless.

For a long time they left him somewhat in peace. He had the unpleasant feeling they felt sorry for him. It was also that they respected Anders.

But one Saturday night, everything broke loose. Anders was away on an errand, and the men had set a kettle of cooked fish on a metal slab by the stove.

He came in to hang up his wet clothes to dry. Was probably thinking he must not drop his mittens in the kettle. But as he took a step to hang them up, it happened. He stepped on the kettle handle. The cod stew spilled all over the floor.

The men had downed a few drams while waiting for the food. Some had downed quite a few. Rage and disappointment over the spoiled food was a spark in dry hay.

It began when two men grabbed him, one from each side, and swore he had to lick up the pieces of fish and all the livers from the floor. A third man suddenly shouted a better punishment:

'We'll baptize the witch's boy in the liver barrel. We'll baptize him in the liver barrel!'

They dragged him into the bait room. The next moment he closed his eyes and tried to hold his breath as long as it lasted. At suitable intervals they let him up for air so he would not choke.

Their job well done, they paused to evaluate the situation. He stood there trembling and squinting at them, his head covered with icy livers. Did not dare to move for fear of what punishment that might bring.

When they saw how awful he looked, Satan seemed to possess them. One man shouted they should wash the little devil as clean as a mountain of dried cod at sunrise. That started a whole revival-meeting chorus of: 'Yes, yes, yes!' from the others.

They tied a thick hemp rope around his waist, pulled him to the edge of the pier and threw him in. Quite a good punishment in February.

He was already prepared to die when in the barrel. Now he was dead. The icy water knocked his breath away and closed over his head. The shock made him briefly lose consciousness. Then he opened his eyes and ears in the Beyond, and from the depths he heard the slow clanging of a bell. He not only heard it. He also saw the clanging move. It was lovely.

You might well die. But you would never forget the sound.

That must have been about when Anders came rowing across the harbour. Benjamin saw him for a moment as they pulled his body to the surface again. They must have pulled in panic. It happened so fast his eardrums were going into his head. Nonetheless, he sensed Anders in the boat. Standing between the thwarts. Still gripping the oars. They hung straight up and down in the sea. Like plucked wings.

Anders's voice was an enormous landslide that came simultaneously from all corners of the world. Bringing with it a huge storm that ripped the air and shattered the last daylight to pieces.

The men realized this was serious. They probably did not intend to dunk him into the sea again. But nobody wanted to admit holding the rope. This time he dropped all the way to the bottom. But soon he felt a powerful tug under his arms and was pulled upward.

He was drawn onto the pier in an uneasy silence. At first he lay stiff and calm. Then he vomited, no matter how dead he was. All the men were upside down

215

and the sky lay in the sea. Everything swung round and round very fast.

So he would not only die, he would be turned upside down too.

They carried him into the cabin and took off his clothes. Anders gave brusque orders about hot water, woolen underclothes and sheepskin blankets.

The cook's boy shrilly shouted he was not to blame for anything. He drew away and was about to leave. But Anders's voice slashed the air:

'There will be no shore leave tonight! Everyone is to remain in his quarters. I plan to have something to warm my knuckles on!'

Angry muttering broke out. But everyone stayed.

He was wrapped up and laid in his bunk. Anders identified the four men who had participated in the fun. He was calm now. Called them by name, like a parson about to give the holy sacrament.

He heard it all as he lay with his eyes closed and his shame like a sack over his head. Exhausted as he was, he did not understand the first sounds. Everything tumbled around in his brain like straight pins in a tin box. Then it was as if Oline were pounding ground meat in a wooden trough. The first sounds must have been when Anders cleared a space among the benches, tools and barrels. The following sounds were probably when his fists struck the men.

You forgot how worn out you were and opened your eyes.

The first man took the blows with a dreamy expression. But gradually the others began to get between them. Then Anders turned into a powerful windmill. Waved his arms and legs in a systematic hunt for flesh. Benjamin would never have thought Anders could do such a thing.

'He's gone crazy,' someone managed to say before he was silenced with a blow to his face and sank behind a stack of crates without a sound.

Anders rushed at the next man. The others could

216

have overpowered him. If they had really had a reason. But they seemed to have lost all strength in the face of this holy wrath. To tell the truth, they let themselves be totally beaten.

Finally one of the most avid watchers of the liver-barrel baptism gasped from a stack of crates:

'Stop it, Anders! Stop it for God's sake!'

Anders leaped on him with a wild howl. The other was not a big man. But stocky and strong. Moreover, he was somewhat sober. You could fear the worst. But when Anders finally got up and gathered what clothes and limbs belonged to him, the man lay with a bloody face against the rough planks. He slowly wiped his face so he could see, forced a smile to maintain some dignity, and sniffled:

'All right, Anders. We know you can keep discipline. We know! The boy is no fisherman, but he sure as hell was lucky with the stepfather he got! I'll help you take care of the boy. Now stop!'

They had to come to his bunk and shake his hand, one by one. It was no fun. He could not say a word. And he never told Anders they had called him a witch's boy. He was sure that would be the end of the poor fellow who said it.

From then on he was treated like a gem that might prick you. Anders had shown the men a side of himself they had never seen before. True, he went around with rags on both hands for days. He tried to hide them under his sea mittens. Being a giant had been hard on his knuckles.

What you learned from the whole thing, besides that Anders had turned into a windmill for his sake, was that grown men could be ashamed of themselves. They were like a flock of cormorants on the mountain. All turn at the same time when the wind shifts.

He felt responsible for their being so ashamed. And forgave them all. What else would he do? Everything was hard enough as it was.

The uncomfortable atmosphere. The silence that clung to him. And the nauseating odor that rose when they cooked a new kettle of cod and crumbled flat bread. It would prevent him from ever again enjoying freshly cooked cod.

When they returned from Lofoten, heavy with fish waste and homesickness, Oline had hired Else Marie from Bjarkøy. She was to take Hanna's place and learn housekeeping in a large house.

Coming home after the hard, crowded life with only men was like getting out of bed after being sick with a high fever. He almost forgot Dina was not there.

First was the Lofoten bath in the wash house with the crew. The sun thrust flaming swords through the steam each time someone came in the door. The women fetched water and carried firewood. For brief moments they saw a man as he was. Naked.

You could easily be deathly afraid. Being naked and one of the men was entirely different from being a boy wearing clothes who wandered in and out among the bathtubs. His body was developed, but still it did not look really finished. It was shameful. Nobody must see it. One consolation was that he had grown taller. Some people said that already on the beach:

'I think that Benjamin fellow has stretched out, both in his feet and his mustache!'

'We fed him codliver oil and stretched him between the drying racks,' Anders replied good-naturedly.

That ended that. But the disgraceful thing was that they talked about him as if he were a calf.

He had realized long ago there was something special about all the men bathing at the same time. While the women ran back and forth serving them.

One by one the men left the wash house with dripping hair and shaved beards. Some had not yet fastened their suspenders or buttoned their shirts. It was a matter of displaying their hairiness. In a respectable way of course. Hair oozed out everywhere on them. He had seen them reach for the girls hurrying past. Something they would never dare to do if it were just an ordinary day in the year. On bath day the girls stood still and smiled. Maybe that was how girls were: touchable on just one or two days? Then came the emptiness.

Girls were forbidden. Yet they were not forbidden. If you understood how everything was arranged. Or had enough hair and beard for it.

Now at least he had bathed with the men in the wash house. As well as he could. Naked!

The air was heavy. Steam and soap smell. Thea dumped more hot water in the wooden tub while he got dressed behind a sail hung on a line. Anders waited his turn to have his back scrubbed and chatted good-naturedly with the others. You could hear his splashes as he teased Thea about being too rough.

'You're rubbing so hard, you must have quarreled with your sweetheart?'

'Puh! I don't have a sweetheart, but you can certainly try if you wish!' she retorted.

She would never have talked that way to Anders if it had not been bath day. That much was certain.

The laughter showed the others enjoyed her pert reply. Anders laughed too. You could see his back as he sat in the tub with his hairy legs and arms hanging outside. You could wish to be like that. Had he been Anders's son, he would at least have known what to expect in the years to come. Jacob hung on the wall and was just a handsome face. It was impossible to say what the future would bring as far as his body was concerned. But he must see to it that he grew up.

He was putting on his shirt when a pink face crowned with tousled blond hair appeared in the opening between the wall and the hanging sail. Two wide blue eyes fluttered like a leaping trout. He stared back. It lasted only a moment. The face turned deep red and disappeared. It was Else Marie from Bjarkøy.

'You mustn't disturb the young fisherman behind the sail, girl!' shouted a fellow named Trond.

'I didn't know . . . I was just getting the green soap on the shelf,' she defended herself.

The men laughed. He felt as if someone were tickling him with a straw over his whole body. His skin became nubbly against the clean shirt. He slid his bare feet into his wooden shoes and trudged from his hiding place to show she had not seen him naked.

The girl was gone. But her face lay like a veil over everything he looked at. He stood in the doorway and wanted to conjure her to him. Wanted her to come very close. Like a piece of clothing. Like a wind. Even if it lasted only a moment.

But nobody must see it!

He went into the kitchen and made a fuss of Oline with the present he brought her from Lofoten. But it was for Else Marie's sake.

She was chopping onions for the liver casserole. He wore wooden shoes but no socks. Came in out of the cold. She looked up with tears in her eyes. That was nice. But it was the onions no doubt.

You could think about how Anders would behave. So he straightened his shoulders and gave Oline a hug and the package containing material for a dress. As he leaned towards Oline, he could leisurely look at the girl by the onion board. Good curves. Better than he remembered. Had he thought about Else Marie? It was hard to recall. He had been so far away. In both Tromsø and Lofoten. But now he certainly did. Think about her.

He talked with Oline without blushing.

'You amaze me,' she said, stroking the material with both hands.

'Thank you, thank you,' she added, and he had to let himself be hugged and listen to her say he was a generous and very thoughtful person.

It did not matter that Else Marie heard that.

'I see you've got new help?' he said.

'That's Else Marie. She'll be here until the autumn,' said Oline with a kindly nod towards the girl.

He strode across the room as well as he could in wooden shoes. Shook her hand as he had learned you should do when new servants arrive. Her hand felt cold and damp. The onion was a smelly chaperone.

Her blond hair was unruly at the temples. But otherwise tamed into two long braids. Just like when he ran across the fields pulling her in the wagon. She had fewer freckles than in the summer. But there was even more light in her than he remembered. You could imagine it came from the hill folk.

He created errands in the kitchen so often that Oline commented on it. Not in a teasing tone. Quite the contrary! It was a clear warning.

'I know you're a man and not a kitchen maid, Benjamin!' she said after several days of his kitchen visits. She narrowed her eyes to two slits and scowled through them.

He tried to be enough of a gentleman in that he winked at Else Marie when Oline did not see it. But the girl did not dare to look at him.

He stayed away from the kitchen, but was on the lookout for Else Marie when she had errands in the barn or elsewhere. The mere thought of her made the day wild and good.

He also stuck his head over the stairway from the second floor and called for hot water, for towels, for anything whatsoever. When he guessed the others were busy and only she could bring it. The first few times she brought things she was like an ermine in the narrow door opening. Out again before he could say thank you. But the third time he reached her fast enough and grasped her arm.

'Wait, Else Marie,' he said breathlessly, and closed the door to the hall.

'I've got a lot to do,' she said, trying to catch her breath too.

'What do you have to do?'

'Dust the south bedroom, because someone is arriving with the steamboat,' she said.

There was so much sea and sun in her. He pressed her against the door and put his arms around her. Tightly, in case she should decide to run away.

She tried to escape – at first. Then she became quite still. So still you could wonder: what should you do now?

They were breathing unevenly. He lifted his hand and touched her cheek. Then she sighed and moved one foot. The whole time she kept looking at something on the other wall.

'Will you meet me at the summer barn after supper?' he finally whispered.

'I don't think I can.'

'Why not? You did it before.'

'Because of Oline.'

'Oline doesn't own your evenings.'

'No, but . . .'

He did not know where it came from, because it was a ridiculous thought, but still he said in a manly way:

'But I own Oline, and everything else.'

She opened her eyes wide. Looked straight at him and asked:

'Do the masters at Reinsnes own the cook and everything?'

'Yes,' he said, laughing it away as a joke.

'Then I don't dare come to the summer barn,' she said, and tore herself loose and slipped out of the door.

He hunted for her. Waylaid her. Made no secret of helping her with the water buckets and wood basket.

He remembered she was a servant on the estate, of course, but that meant nothing. He had to have her.

One day Oline called him into the service area between the kitchen and dining room. She was sitting on one of the brocaded armchairs that stood there because they were not for everyday use.

222

'I see and hear, Benjamin,' she said.

He stood by the door and knew what was coming.

'You keep trying to be alone with Else Marie.'

It was best not to grumble.

'I'll tell you one thing, Benjamin! And that is: I'm responsible for this girl.'

He just had to stand there until she finished.

'You're grown-up, Benjamin! Do you know why people have to walk above my head to get to the maids' room? Why do you think none of the girls – except poor Stine many God-given years ago, and that was in the office . . . Why do you think, God help me, none of the girls ended up in trouble at Reinsnes? Well, I'll tell you why. It's because Oline watches out for them, and sleeps as lightly as a butterfly.'

'I won't do anything to Else Marie.'

The blush covered not only his face but his whole body.

'Show me that!' she said sternly.

Then she seemed lost in thought, and you could think she was about to cry.

'Oh dear Lord, you look so much like that blessed Jacob . . .'

Then she struck without warning:

'But the devil take you if you run after Else Marie and get her into trouble.'

'But Oline . . .'

'Hasn't anybody told you it's not proper to run after a maid when you're the master of Reinsnes?'

'Noooo . . .'

'Well now I've told you,' she said, and slapped her thigh so hard that everything quivered. Then she stood up.

He did not know what on earth he should do to get back in her good graces.

'I like Else Marie so very much,' he whispered.

It was as if the sun came out in Oline's face. She went towards him with outstretched hands.

'Oh Benjamin, Benjamin, you're the spitting image of

Jacob,' she said, wiping her eyes quickly with her hand. 'But you see, at your age love is so fleeting. And you don't want to ruin things for the girl, do you? Give her a bad reputation? Spread gossip and nasty talk about her?'

'No,' he said.

There was something stuck in his throat.

'Leave her in peace then. She's engaged to Evert Steinbakken from Hasseløya and has to learn to take care of a house. Besides, she's at least two years older than you. You're still just a shrimp. But good as gold . . .'

She almost broke into tears again. That alone could make you feel ashamed.

Apparently you were not to have anything. In any case, he went to Tromsø without having met Else Marie at the summer barn. Of course, you could laugh and tell yourself it was not the season for it either.

CHAPTER 7

Anders had not asked why he had a falling-out with the tanner before Christmas.

Sometimes it seemed as if Anders knew everything. Other times you were sure he knew nothing. There was so much people should not know. Your head got all filled up with it, and you had no room for other things.

But Anders had not said anything. Just arranged for someone to get the trunk and parcels in the ochre house and move them to the home of merchant Sørensen, who lived near the market square. Everything was there when he arrived.

His room was in the garret. All by itself, with a pitch-dark drying loft between him and the steep stairway. At Sørensen's they were a family of seven at the table each day. Eight with him. The mother talked most. She knew everything about everyone, and wanted everybody else to know it too. He wondered if she knew why he moved from the tanner's. Did he know that himself?

He contented himself with the thought that if she had known she could never have kept it to herself.

One must work to atone for one's sin, the Scriptures said.

It was March and the rector said he regretted the illness that had kept Benjamin away so long. But if the young man wanted to do extra reading and take his examination, he would be permitted to do that.

Illness? He was about to ask. But fortunately you did

not ask the rector questions at the wrong time. It was Anders, no doubt. He knew from before that Anders had a gift for good explanations.

Now he just had to start studying.

It was much too light to walk up to the ochre house to see if anyone still lived there.

He knew which streets the tanner took to and from work. So he did not walk there. Sometimes he had to turn around because he thought he smelled her scent. But it was always someone else.

About the time he returned from Lofoten and did not get to meet Else Marie because she was Oline's, he developed some sort of sickness. Or maybe it was just the emptiness after Andrea walked out of the room without defending him?

In any case, whenever he smelled the scent of women he had to discover the source. Like a fat man who simply eats and eats. Even if he is so full he is about to vomit, he still has to eat. As if the food protects and saves him from all that is painful.

No matter what they said or did, if they turned away or smiled encouragingly these creatures existed, and he had to find out about them before they disappeared.

Andrea had already disappeared, even though she was still up there in the ochre house.

Merchant Sørensen's house was painted white and was full of life. Children's shouts, laughter and good times. The first thing he noticed was the unlocked doors.

'Even if it's bad, there's some good in it,' said Madam Sørensen when something came up that could be regarded as a little unpleasant.

The husband traded with the Russians. And now there was to be a royal decree allowing lumber to be brought from the Arkangel region to northern Norway. This meant the business he had long carried on would become much simpler.

Sørensen put his thumbs in his vest as if he had

written the decree himself. And they celebrated with meat dishes until the gravy splattered on the table-cloth. Even so, you could sit there wondering what Andrea was eating.

The Sørensen family was too numerous and too noisy for him to really enjoy them. There were many people at Reinsnes too. But moderation in everything. You could shut doors at home, even if you did not lock them.

So he often studied at Sofus's home. The Sørensen children were much too eager for his company.

He had grown taller. That was what he had always wanted. But even so, he was unhappy with his shape. It was something about his wrists and shoulders. When he came home for the summer he had to get new clothes. He refused to climb on a stool to try things on for the seamstress. Just smiled a little and pinched her cheek lightly.

He thought about Hanna now and then. And about Else Marie. But they were gone.

When he came home for Christmas he learned Else Marie was married. And Hanna had become indis-pensable at Grøtøy. He thought about the strange life girls lived. So quick, even if it appeared slow.

He smelled and touched the new girls at Reinsnes a little. But in moderation, because Oline had an eye on each finger. And next time he came home they were gone.

In Tromsø he had Charlotte Wickstrøm. But she was only someone to sniff under the street lamps. She would never take a walk on the island. Or sit in front of him sleighing down hills.

'Mama doesn't like it. The police might take the sleigh when we go so fast,' she said, and put her hands in her muff.

Still, he hung around her just for her smell.

He had to study too. And smoke sliced tobacco plug with Sofus. It was no life really. But time passed, as old

227

people said. Soon you would be old without having met anyone you could touch.

The last two times he had been home at Reinsnes he had not asked Anders if he had heard from Dina. Nobody talked about her any more. Not even in corners. That was for Anders's sake.

Anders became more and more ghostly. He did not say much, but worked all the harder. Yet one day as they sat alone in the smoking room he said:

'You've started your third year in Tromsø. This summer it will be two years since she left.'

He wanted to ask what Anders thought. But he could not. And when he went back to Tromsø in darkest January, he still did not know what Anders thought. He felt it was his own fault. Before, when he was young, he had asked about everything. And Anders had always answered.

One night he dreamed he was walking down to the shore. He followed the smell. To the tannery. The tanner stood on a board over a large tanning vat. In the vat floated hides of all shapes and sizes. They looked slimy. He shouted a greeting to the tanner. But he should not have done that, because the tanner fell into the vat and disappeared for a long time. People came from everywhere and pulled him up. The tanner was completely ochre. You watched for a moment. Then somehow all you had to do was sit down at the table with the Sørensen family and act as if you had not been there.

'Is Magnus the tanner dead?' asked the oldest boy. He was fourteen years old that day, and had received the tanner's tool as a gift. It lay on some gray paper on the table.

You could laugh afterwards to think that in the dream this was not the least bit odd. Nor was it strange when Madam Sørensen sighed and said:

'Yes, the poor thing . . . his color was completely ruined . . .'

'Eat nicely, dear! Don't spill your milk!' she said to the youngest child.

People said the queerest things in dreams. The odd thing was that what they said was so similar to what they said otherwise. Still, it was something to laugh about.

He had never known the tanner's name was Magnus.

In the dream he thought: sometimes you have to move, or people have to die, before you know their names.

He still had not walked by the house to see if Andrea was there.

That night Sørensen's son became ill. Maybe that was why Benjamin began thinking about whether he should become a doctor. He certainly thought about it long before he went home for Christmas. The day the rector came into the classroom and told them a disease, an epidemic, had broken out in the city. People said it came from Trondheim. So they called it Trondheim sickness. It began as a sore throat and killed people.

It was springtime now. Sørensen had taken his son aboard a boat that arrived from Trondheim. At first there was a great uproar in the house. Then it got terribly quiet. You could hear them saying they did not have a chance to swab the boy with silver nitrate before it was too late.

He had known the whole time. That his name was Søren. But had he not known, there would be no question about it now. For Madam Sørensen began shouting it at her husband. The night the boy died.

'You shouldn't have taken Søren with you! It's your fault! Your fault! You always dragged that little boy with you everywhere. Now Søren is dead, he'll lie in the cold churchyard! And it's your fault!'

His garret was right above their bedroom. The name Søren was all that existed in the world. You could not sleep, so the only thing to do was to get up for a while and think about perhaps becoming a doctor.

When the night sun reached his room, he sat down to study Latin. There was such good light that night up there in the garret. Exceptionally good light. But much noise from the seagull. It had a nest on the roof. He put a couple of cotton wads in his ears. Poor Madam Sørensen screamed so loudly. Everyone woke up. At any rate, several were crying.

After a while he saw Sørensen walk down the road, his pea coat fluttering, wearing no hat. Seen from the garret window he was just a black dot. He looked as if someone had simply left him. And in a way, that was what had happened. But when worst came to worst, it was not Madam Sørensen who just walked out of the room. The trouble was, she did not defend her husband either. So Sørensen had to leave the house.

He was at school when they went to the cemetery with Søren. That did not matter to them. He could do nothing after all.

But he thought he should have said a friendly word to the boy. Before he died. The boy had come up to his room many times. Wanted to talk and look at his books.

That was probably the reason. Why you would get the idea you should become a doctor.

As early as February the Health Commission set up specific rules: remember cleanliness and fresh air! Wakes or funeral processions are forbidden for people who die from the throat disease. Burials must take place as soon as possible. Bedding and clothing must be disinfected, and rooms must be thoroughly scrubbed and aired.

Nevertheless, many would die from the disease. Far too many for him to learn their names. Still his head was full of them.

And the weeping. They wept so much in Tromsø. Søren was only fourteen. The oldest person who died was twenty-three.

*　　*　　*

On graduation day the rector was to give a speech because they were finished and had passed their exams, but nearly all he talked about was those who had passed away in the springtime of life. And Sofus Beck was not in his place that day. The rector understood the message. You knew immediately. It was Sofus's turn.

Sofus was somehow a fellow you could be with. They laughed a lot when not studying or looking at girls strolling arm in arm. Sometimes they walked all the way to the island and around the lake, and he told Sofus he had not been sick, but in Lofoten, that time. And Sofus swore never to mention it to anyone. Of course, there were certain things you did not tell Sofus either.

You had to go through it again. The disinfecting. The Sørensen family were pink and shiny all over from washing. When you were one of them, and had often visited Sofus Beck, you had to scrub yourself. They did not want to lose anybody else.

But even if he had disinfected himself, he went to see Sofus before he died. He planned to say there was something to what Dina said: the dead are always with us, no matter what. He was old enough to realize it was mostly to comfort himself. Sofus had enough to deal with. But Sofus's mother would not let him in. She put her arms around his neck and wept.

'It's the Health Commission,' she sobbed. 'They say nobody can go in to see Sofus, poor boy.'

He said it did not matter, because they had been together so much, and everybody had to die sometime anyway. But he should not have said that. It was strange how you said the wrong words when you thought you ought to say something. She started weeping so terribly.

He did not dare to touch her.

*   *   *

It was not a proper funeral. That was against the Health Commission rules. He was grown-up, and understood it had to be this way to protect other lives.

But he went to the cemetery and stood outside the picket fence. Sofus's mother cried, but she nodded to him from a distance. To think that she saw him on such a day!

Now you just had to wait and see. But if you escaped, you could take it as a sign you should be a doctor.

Each day that passed and he did not get sick he thought he should go to see her in the ochre house. But that did not happen.

The tanner did not get sick and die either. All who died were young. Sofus was number sixteen.

It was enough now.

Anders came to get him in the new cargo boat named *The Swan*.

'What the devil have they done to you anyway?' he said the moment he walked into the garret.

That made him realize Madam Sørensen had stopped saying, '. . . there's some good in it.'

After a while he handed Anders his diploma to make up for not looking so good. They looked at it together while Anders rubbed his forehead and said:

'Well done! Well done! Come on! This is no place to be!'

He might be right about that.

BOOK THREE

CHAPTER 1

Every movement of infinity comes about by passion, and no reflection can bring about a movement. This is the continual leap in existence which explains the movement.

Fear and Trembling – Johannes de Silentio

You can ask yourself what determines the choices. Or if there are choices. After sailing with Anders for months, I realized I was neither a sailor nor a merchant. I do not know if Anders was disappointed or relieved the day I said I wanted to study in Copenhagen. But at least he did not try to dissuade me. And he did not warn me it would be expensive.

On Johan's recommendation, I installed myself at the home of the widow on Bredgade, as everyone called it. The street was actually named Norgesgade, Norway street, so that alone should have been good enough. Johan had lived there some years ago. Madame Frederiksen was not particularly wealthy, but evidently high-born. She immediately concluded I did not resemble my brother. It was several months before I realized she meant that in my favor.

The city terrified me at first. But I could not live in constant terror, so the only alternative was to give in to curiosity and the senses. Only someone who has been in the same situation knows how I felt when I entered the university foyer the first time.

I got initiated into student life and learned the student songs. I also looked into Møller's book of contemplations about women, although I would admit to no one that I learned anything new from it. A student should not admit, he should study and discuss endless approaches to problems. He should go to pubs and be invited to dances.

I regarded the tall trees with thick trunks and massive crowns as new acquaintances. They became my direct contact with the sky, as the mountains at home had been. Ever since childhood, the trees at home had given me a metallic taste in my mouth when autumn turned them into bristling branches. The trees in Copenhagen kept their foliage until far into the winter. The leaves became glazed and transformed by the frost, but held fast.

I could not share these thoughts with any students I met of course. It made me realize that ever since Mother Karen died I thought like an old man.

I got used to the tall buildings, the crowds of people and the language, and settled down. But just beneath the surface lay a feverish desire for The Great Experience. What it would be, I did not know.

> What power o'er student atmospheres
> Doth heaven hold?
>
> A student counts the mountain's years
> Day or night, he has no fears.
> Though the world may stand or fall, he hears
> The songs of old.
>
> While men enslaved all fight for land,
> Clear thoughts are his sole treasure and
> His gold.

That was Møller's message in the student songbook. I went to Regensen collegium and sang along while beer bottles were passed around like peace pipes. Later I gained entry into Valkendorf collegium. There each student usually had his own bottle. And the parties bore the mark of generous pocket money.

At Valkendorf I met Aksel. A clergyman's son from Limfjord whose father knew N.S.F. Grundtvig. Aksel enjoyed being the worst of all Danish parson's sons. Blond, tall and sardonic. With a voice like a judge and stories like a ditch digger.

We eventually understood each other. Read *Philosophicum* together, and attended lectures by Sibern or Rasmus Nielsen. We also made serious plans to do the required reading in zoology, physics, botany and chemistry. Because we needed that to take the preliminary examination for medical study, which everybody just called 'Kantussen'.

The professors said the reading initiated you into 'a view of nature and its wonders'. But the wonders were rather dry, and we soon discovered Copenhagen had other wonders worth studying.

Aksel had contacts. We went to dances. But I quickly learned that girls at dances cannot be touched. They are someone's daughters. You could not even dance with them without signing up on their dance cards. A person from the North Pole could find that a bit frightening. But you got used to it. And they often served good food and drinks.

I learned to dance again. Aksel said the dancing I learned in Norway would scare even elephants. The two of us practiced in the Valkendorf corridors amidst swearing and hubbub. Aksel had more to learn than I. He claimed one did not dance in Danish parsonages.

Few students studied for their own satisfaction. Most of our classmates were content just to feel ecstatic about getting away from home, to escape secondary-school discipline, or to poke around the royal city. Novels and stories were something reserved for women. They were not for men.

Men studied, listened to lectures and discussed politics. That shocked and disappointed me. But I was careful not to show it.

*   *   *

Yet literature made Aksel and me blood brothers. One evening well into the new year I tried to tell Aksel about my dreary Christmas at the widow's on Bredgade. I had, with great difficulty, read right through Gustave Flaubert's *Madame Bovary* in the original French.

We sat in the Apothek pub and I tried to make him understand that Flaubert merely confirmed what I already knew. Aksel probably saw through my attempt to seem wiser than I was, but he was nice about it.

'Intelligent human beings are placed on this earth to accept – yes, even bless – the fact that everything repeats itself,' I said tragically.

'That's fine with me,' he smiled.

I ignored the disrespectful reply and continued my lecture. He tolerated it with a hint of boredom.

'Not only the trivial things of life, like eating food, expelling it from your body, putting one foot in front of another, falling in love, pursuing intrigues, etc. But also generational patterns. Everything repeats itself in an eternal circle dance. Everything has but one outcome. Namely, a meaningless death!' I said in two breaths.

Aksel took care to sigh when I breathed. He also corrected my Danish a few times.

'I know Flaubert wants to show us a great tragedy too. But I see through the form. It's dull, vulgar.'

'Stop trying to act so grown-up! So bourgeois! I read that the bourgeoisie wanted to imprison Flaubert,' Aksel chuckled.

'Bourgeois? Me?' I said indignantly.

'Then why are you so angry? It's just a story, isn't it? What's so special about that book?'

'It tries to be shocking,' I said sullenly.

'How?'

'Oh, it's this Emma,' I said impatiently, wanting to be philosophical again.

But Aksel did not want that.

'Tell me what's shocking about her,' he asked eagerly.

'Well, you see . . .' I said slowly, 'it's not easy to explain.'

'You mean one shouldn't write about people like Emma?' Aksel asked with a smile.

'She tricked her doctor husband into performing an operation according to modern principles. The operation was unsuccessful. There's a lesson there for you and me, since we're going to be doctors. But on the whole, I think I could have done it better myself. The book, that is,' I bragged.

'Well, first you'd better lose your virginity,' he said good-naturedly.

I was taken aback for a moment, and blushed. You never could tell what this parson's son might blurt out.

'You haven't read the book,' I said, annoyed.

'No, I haven't read it. And your babbling bores me. Let's talk about Baudelaire instead,' said Aksel.

'That will be hard,' I admitted.

'Why? You recite his poems the moment you've had three beers!'

'That's different,' I said.

I could not talk to anyone about Baudelaire's poetry. I was ashamed it made such an impression on me. True, I had recited his poems a few times. I regretted that. To me, Baudelaire's poems were pure magic. I lost myself in descriptions of long funeral processions. And of his hope, which planted its black flag on his bowed skull.

'The best thing about Baudelaire's poetry is the women,' I said, trying to find a common interest. But it was true.

'Really?' said Aksel.

'Bestial. Reckless and inhuman, violent and dangerous.'

'You mean one can take them to bed and not miss living women?' he asked.

'I don't know,' I said uncertainly.

Aksel shrugged.

'I don't think you care about poetry, man! You just

brag about everything you think and know, exactly like a Norwegian,' he chuckled.

I protested, feeling insulted. And admitted how the poems affected me.

'They make you feel sexual?' he asked, livening up.

'Well . . .'

'Sexual from Baudelaire's poetry! It's only worms and death. Isn't it? Sexual, how?'

'I want to do things . . .'

'With women? Or . . .'

'Everything! Do everything!' I said.

'My God!' he exclaimed, very impressed.

That was how he slyly got me out of my head.

'I once knew a woman . . .' I began.

'Yes?' Aksel said breathlessly, licking beer foam from his lips.

'Andrea . . . She was . . . She came to my room at night.'

'Really? When?'

'Long ago . . .' I said wavering.

He stared at me until I blushed again.

'The hell with that! What did she do?' he asked eagerly.

'Touched me and . . .'

'And?'

'Well, you know . . . Everything!'

Watching his face as I told about the tanner's leather dildo, I began to doubt the story was true. Maybe I had just made it up? Dreamed it?

'She must have been perverse,' Aksel said with shining eyes.

'Do you think so?'

'Could she . . .? No! Hold your tongue, man! You made up that story to shock me!' he said firmly.

I did not answer. Just shook my head.

'How was she?' he asked after a while.

'Wonderful,' I said.

'Yes, yes. But how?'

'I don't remember too well.'

240

'That's a lie! You remember! You're just embarrassed.'

He tried to laugh.

'It was awful,' I said suddenly. That was not what I intended to say.

'Why?'

'Her husband threw me out of the house.'

'That's what I'd have done too!' said Aksel.

'He was crying.'

'Crying? Ugh!'

'I wished he was dead,' I said.

'One doesn't wish people dead,' said Aksel.

'I did.'

'You only think so. Don't tell me you were that brave! I bet you were scared to death. It's a hell of a thing . . . that you did it anyway!'

'This is just between us,' I said threateningly.

'Damn right, man!'

Aksel held out his big hand to me.

At that moment, some sort of huge wave enveloped me. We owned something together. Aksel and I. Perhaps that great word which came and went. Happiness? Or whatever you call it?

When we left the pub, Aksel began to joke about taking time to visit the 'side streets'.

'I think I know a clean place,' he said vaguely.

I just have gaped at him. Because, he added, he had only heard about them. But he knew which streets . . . they were easy to see. The women. They sat in the windows.

'I've seen them, of course!' I said boldly.

Two were twice as courageous as one. We counted our money. It seemed to be enough.

'What does it cost?' I asked.

'Hard to say. We won't take the most expensive.'

We walked decisively to Holmensgade. Both of us had seen that women there even showed themselves on the street. We knocked on the two doors Aksel knew

241

about. But tonight they were all busy, because nobody opened. And no one was to be seen in the windows.

'The high and mighty renamed this street,' Aksel said with a smirk.

'What was it called before?'

'Ulkegade, the street of old tars. Every sailor in the world knew about it. It became too much for people living at the proper end of the street. But changing the name didn't help much.'

We laughed and trudged through the slush.

'No matter what its name, we can't walk around here all night,' I said.

Aksel looked a bit chagrined, since he was supposed to know the area.

'And you claim to be so persistent,' he teased.

'That was my youth,' I laughed.

'You want me to believe that,' he chuckled excitedly.

'Magstraede! We can go there!' I exclaimed, pulling his arm.

'No, you know what – in Magstraede they receive you in rooms with plush furniture, and have strict madams who wear men's hats. It's sure to be expensive!' said Aksel.

'What vast worldly knowledge the boy has in his head . . .' I murmured.

We ended up in Peder Madsen's Passage. A narrow passageway leading from Svane pharmacy towards Grønnegade.

A cramped, dirty ditch of a place that shouted warnings to people from good society. At least those of the female sex. Three-and-four-story houses clung to each other on either side of a pigsty whose gutters were brimming with garbage and dung.

I suddenly recalled a professor mentioning in a lecture that records over a five-year period showed that of 80 children born in this street only 19 lived to the age of five.

I did not remind Aksel of this. What good would that do? Confound it, why did I have to be so concerned with numbers! Still, I shuddered so violently he thought I regretted everything.

'Cold feet?' he taunted.

'Not at all!'

Two or three women sat in the open windows and had already seen us. It was too late to turn around. I looked at Aksel and was about to ask if we should split up. But was afraid he would say yes. Now you could be sorry you had boasted about your experience. I cleared my throat and smiled at the nearest window decoration. She had a large bloated face and hair elaborately piled on top of her head. She wore her working clothes. A loose-fitting white dress decorated with a lace collar and a brooch. She was not fat, but close to it. Still, I thought she looked nice. To talk with. To sleep with? No!

Aksel had a different opinion. Or he wanted to show off. He shook off the slush, stuck his head in the window, and said to her:

'Nice weather!'

She smiled and stood up. The woman in the window on the other side of the passage waved to me. She was smoking a pipe and was not particularly young. But none of them were . . .

'Come in! Come into my office!' she shouted.

The two women started bickering about us. For them, it was perfectly normal. I tried to make Aksel keep walking. But he just stood there with a stupid smile.

Then the door opened and the madam came out. The women in the windows instantly fell silent.

'Please come in! Don't pay attention to Jenny. She's just a fishwife!' the madam said with an ill-tempered nod towards the woman who did not belong to her 'office'.

The next minute we stood in a little hall so dark you could not see your hand. But at least we were together. My heart was leaping out of my vest. My Adam's apple felt like an abnormal growth, and I did not know what to say.

The madam opened a door and yellow light from a tiny parlor filled with fringes, tassels and curtains fell on us threateningly. As if that were not enough, a pygmy version of a dog leaped towards us and bared a set of pointed teeth. Drooling and loose-bellied.

'He's so happy when strangers come,' the madam said.

The room was crowded with furniture. A chest of drawers on which were three flower vases, a pipe rack and a half-empty liquor bottle. A round table with a rainbow-hued tablecloth and four glasses on it. Behind the table: a sofa where a buxom woman sat with another dog in her lap. This one was mangy, but friendly. On two of the three chairs at the table sat women in loose yellowish-white smocks with heavily made-up faces. They nodded and smiled invitingly, as though sitting on stage at the Kongelige Theater.

The yellow light came from a paraffin lamp above the table. The only beautiful thing in the room. It looked like the lamp in the dining room at Reinsnes. The arms holding the flask and lamp globe were shaped like twining roses and it had a yellow shade. Three dusty pink wool pompoms dangled from the handle beneath. On the smoke-stained wall hung a portrait of the King. I could see no windows. The room smelled like a combination of old rose water and sweat, with a fresh sprinkling of raw onion. The two women at the table had a bottle of lager beer each and a plate of green biscuits.

Dazed, we let them offer us each a chair. The women and dogs crowded onto the sofa. Aksel had great diffi-culty maneuvering his legs under the table. The table was too low, or the chair too high. And the only place he could put his legs was under the table. He sat at the edge of the chair, leaned backward and carefully slid his legs underneath.

Who could have imagined there would be so many of them? I looked at Aksel. But he just sat there.

'This is Tilda, this is Olga, and this is Birthe. Who can I offer?'

The madam gestured impressively with her hand. She wore a loose-fitting dress, but it was not typical working attire. Mottled brown, with gold cords spiraling down the yoke. The spirals trembled on her breast when she moved. You could not take your eyes from them. Her face was stern. Almost attractive. Her age was indeterminate. A tarred pirate ship adrift.

The youngest woman was maybe twenty-five, maybe younger. She seemed normal. Aksel looked at her, even if she was not pretty.

Birthe, the woman with the dog, was a proper full-rigger. Her stomach quivered if she even moved her plump little hands from the table into her lap.

'Surely you couldn't do it here? In sight of everyone,' I thought, aware of my organ. Like an earthworm in a dry desert.

I could tell Aksel was getting sober, and it made me feel even more lonesome.

The women looked at us questioningly. I shrewdly avoided their glances. Finally the madam asked:

'Would you gentlemen like a beer before going to the office?'

'What does it cost?' I asked, and cleared my throat.

She stated the price and noted the beer was free.

'For each one?' I said, taking the lead.

'For each one,' said the madam, rolling her eyes towards the ceiling.

'We don't have that much,' I said dully.

'That's right, we don't have that much,' Aksel said with relief, and nodded several times.

The madam looked us over. Up and down.

'We only accept cash, and we don't give discounts,' she said firmly. Clearly, she did not believe us.

'We've got only half that much between the two of us,' I said, and stood up. Aksel jumped up too.

But he did not reckon with his legs. The women reached quickly for the beer bottles and the stemmed plate of green biscuits. We stood like tin soldiers just escaped from the war.

The women looked at each other. They had obviously communicated with their eyes before.

'You're young?' the madam said, silky as a cat.

'Well,' said Aksel, drawing out the word.

'They're pretty, especially the dark-haired one with the beautiful eyes,' the madam said, as if talking about the dogs.

The fat woman in the sofa laughed, making everything jiggle. The madam gave her a look that could have killed an ox. Everyone immediately fell silent. They all took a swallow from their beer bottles, one after another. As if it were a ritual. The madam lit a pipe. Very slowly, then regarded us through the smoke.

'The big one isn't so pretty, but she has good shoulders,' said the madam, nodding towards the women on the sofa.

'I agree!' the fat woman said amiably.

'That doesn't help!' said the youngest, giggling wildly behind one hand.

She has pimples and bad front teeth, I thought vindictively, and turned to leave.

'Wait, gentlemen!' said the madam.

Chills ran down my spine.

She went to the sofa and whispered something to the fat woman, then she turned to us and said gently:

'How much do you have?'

Aksel and I looked at each other. Our faces flamed. Then we stuck our hands into our pockets and fished out what money we had. The moment we put it on the table, four heads rushed over simultaneously and began counting.

Finally they looked up. The madam said dryly:

'For that amount, one can't go to the office, my young friends. One only gets women along Volden, or in the cemeteries, for such a small sum.'

She nodded graciously to us. Then she smoothed her hair with one finger.

'I'll take them to the office,' she told the others, as if we were deaf.

The fat woman was about to protest, but restrained herself. The other two looked thunderstruck.

'But Mother, that makes no sense!' said the fat woman.

The madam sighed and said:

'It's Sunday. I guess one can do good deeds on a Sunday.'

Then it was too late. Everything was too late. Sweat poured off Aksel too. We were led into a dark little room which had no windows either. The thought struck me that if there were a fire we would burn straight into hell, because we could not escape from here.

I had heard so much about palpitations of the heart. Had experienced them too. Of course. But right then my heart stood still. I did not dare to breathe either. Clinically dead.

In the middle of the floor was a bed whose contents you could not see because the room was too dark. You could dimly make out a washstand behind a pitch-black folding screen.

The madam had brought a small lantern with a candle, which she set on a stool behind the screen.

'Please make yourselves comfortable!' she said, nodding towards the bed.

When I did not move, Aksel poked me in the ribs. I just barely could see he tried to smile.

I sat on the edge of the bed and stared towards the screen at the madam. She poured water into the wash-basin. Then she stripped off the tarred old hull with its spirals. For a moment I saw her contours, and an infinity of skin and creases, through the cracks in the screen. Then, very slowly, she slipped a white smock over her head. Aksel swallowed next to my ear.

Then things got going. She came from behind the screen with the dim light behind her. It made her hips

247

and thighs show through the thin smock. Everything swayed. Not only her. The whole room.

She slowly began taking off Aksel's clothes, while she talked to him as though he were one of her dogs.

'There, there, you'll see how good it will be!' she said, and patted my arm with each button she undid.

'You'll see how good it will be. Now you just have to wash yourself. That's important. Everyone knows that. See, like this! You'll see now.'

She undressed us from the waist down. We even helped her. I could not look at Aksel. Stared at the wall during the washing ceremony. If Aksel had protested, I would have too. But he pretended not to notice. He almost seemed to be asleep.

The bed was too small for three. We were about to be shipwrecked. Then the madam spread the blanket on the floor with a sheet on top.

She lay between us, touching us as if we were one body. Her hands were as skillful as Oline's when she made wheat bread.

I think I was the first to give in. But Aksel was the first to come to the mill.

Suddenly she turned her rear end to Aksel and pulled up the smock. A white mountain emerged. It moved in coquettish circles above gasping Aksel.

She knelt with one knee on each side of me and pumped my organ while she offered him her rear end! Then she spilled her breasts from her smock.

'Come here!' she commanded, leaning over me with two full skin sacks. In a measured rhythm.

I do not think I prayed. But I should have. Look in mercy on us poor sinners!

Aksel! Slowly, he moved behind her on his knees. Slowly, a rhythm was established. His groans were alternately pitiful and terrible. She spoke reassuringly to him. Turned half around and helped him.

And then there was hell to pay. He threw himself on

her like a wild animal. Pressed her over me and went at it like a madman. I died for a while, squeezed between her enormous breasts.

You can keep from thinking about it every day. But you never forget it!

Finally Aksel lay there. His breathing was a locomotive trying to reduce its speed.

I do not think I ever got the courage to tell him how amazing they were. His thrusts. How the devil can you say something like that? You should not even have noticed them.

As for me, she could not get me going. I almost cried with shame. Aksel went behind the screen when he realized how things were. But that did not help. Her hand could have worked on me the whole night. I was in the ochre house again. Was a wild, pleasure-filled force in Andrea's skillful hand. But the moment she tried to help me in, I shriveled up. Again and again.

Finally she gave up. Patted my thigh and said comfortingly:

'That's all right, you're so handsome and young. Your time will come. You'll see, it will come!'

Never in my life had I felt such shame.

Out in the street, as I stood shivering in the cold wind, Aksel said:

'We need a schnapps!'

'No, I'm going home,' I mumbled.

'You damn well better not desert me now! I've never done anything like that before!'

We found a pub that was still open and stole into the darkest corner. So we did not have to see each other too clearly. We let ourselves be scarecrows for a while. At least I did. Aksel had passed the test after all.

'I'll give you back the money you paid,' he said suddenly, staring into his schnapps glass.

249

'Why?' I mumbled, staring into mine.

'Damn it, I couldn't have stuck it into a hole full of someone else's stuff either . . .'

He never mentioned the humiliation again. Not even when I tried to take Anna away from him.

CHAPTER 2

Oh yes, I heard about it! How just a short time ago Sweden and Norway's king, Carl XV, had met Denmark's Frederik VII in Copenhagen and in holy brotherhood promised to sweep Germany and Austria off the playing field.

But that was with fanfares and fine-sounding words. When things got serious, the Norwegians and Swedes never appeared.

I was so new in the world. By my second semester I felt the shame of being a Norwegian in Copenhagen. Despite the university, the beer and Aksel. The country stood alone against two huge bloodthirsty armies.

I preferred not to speak my own language. Practiced short Danish sentences and a pleasant expression, and otherwise kept silent. If I revealed my native tongue, I heard about Carl XV's compliance when the Swedo-Norwegian government realized things were serious and would not risk blood to defend a brother.

In the pubs and at student gatherings people told coarse stories and sang broadside ballads about Queen Victoria's love for Bismarck. About the Queen's many pregnancies, and which ones the English could thank Bismarck for. And about that dastardly Napoleon III, who was such a coward he did not dare shoot off a fart, let alone fire a cannonball at the German and Prussian lines.

Shopkeepers and small grocers still bought *Adresseavisen* with its abundant advertisements. But otherwise people began to read about the war wherever they found it. On small pieces of paper that floated everywhere. Or they heard the latest news in the pubs.

On 13 November the state council approved a new joint constitution for Denmark and Slesvig. The Germans got what they were waiting for. And winter set in.

People said:

'Bismarck came with iron and blood!'

'Karna!' I exclaimed, when she told me her name. 'Nobody is named Karna!'

'I am,' she replied sullenly.

She sat in a cattle cart holding a wounded lieutenant's hand. The stench of blood and excrement reached to the edge of the road where I walked holding the reins.

I have many people to thank for my meeting Karna. For example, the Prussian and Austrian troops? The night of 1 February 1864 they crossed the Eider. Or perhaps I should thank Bismarck. The cynical brain behind the Slesvig occupation.

Already in December, students knew the situation was critical. But we could not imagine the outcome. Everyone in Copenhagen believed the Dannevirke rampart would stop every German.

We discussed the possibility of war over a drink in the pubs. I, an innocent from north Norway, was not the only one unable to imagine war. That most loathsome kind of heroism.

Throughout my childhood I had wondered what happened in war, but no one gave me an answer. In the Copenhagen pubs you heard stories about old General C. J. de Meza, who played the clavichord and went around in his dressing gown worrying abut his bad stomach. While all the other brave men went to be slaughtered.

Few people knew Bismarck. I always wondered if that man played chess. Did he believe life was a chess game?

Meanwhile, the Danish army withdrew from the Dannevirke and fortified its position at Dybbøl. It slunk back like a pack of convicted thieves, without hope and in sorry condition. Those who came to Copenhagen and could speak told about standing on their feet day and night, without proper food and clothing, while snow, slush and cold gnawed at their bodies and death watched from the Austrians' campfires.

One despised government official had come to inspect them – wearing galoshes, and under an umbrella! The King had fled, and the rest of Norden sat around its well-decked tables with its eyes closed and exchanged remarks. Such as:

'It's terrible! It's a shame! So tragic!'

Despite what I heard, I did not understand. They were just exciting stories. And in the streets you saw many highly polished boots, weapons and blue uniforms. Some students talked about enlisting. The university had a long tradition for that in troubled times.

After a student gathering in the Regensen courtyard, when songs and beer turned us all into heroes in knitted wrist warmers and student caps, I signed up for military service. Aksel was going to enlist too. But his mother came and botched that plan. I did not have such a mother.

Since I was Norwegian and also a medical student, I found myself on the battlefield picking up bodies for the field hospital.

At first I regarded this as a degrading insult. But I had not hurried across blood-spattered fields many times before I realized I was fortunate to get this assignment. If one could use such positive words in ice-cold hell.

Had they known what good cannon fodder my young body was, they would have given me a weapon and put me in the line of fire.

But the generals probably did not believe in the war either.

*   *   *

We were billeted in a stable. The animals provided
some warmth. As did the old hay. We washed as best
we could in the water trough in the courtyard after
poking holes in the brittle layer of ice formed during
the night.

A fellow named Paul collected bodies with me. We
roamed far and wide. First to the straw-roofed snow
huts of the advanced positions and to the hated earth-
work. Actually, there were ten earthworks. All equally
hated. We were so frightened we hardly spoke. The
cold pounded our ears and froze us into our clothes.
Even so, our sweat ran like rivers, then hardened into
lumps of ice.

We were not sent out while the cannons thundered
their worst. But when the shooting had lasted for a
while and the Prussian shells had hit their targets, we
came and saw it all.

The military surgeon and us. Sometimes he was so
tattered and dirty you could think him a vagrant tramp.
He plodded along with his medical bag, or sat on the
cart and dozed a few minutes. Once he fell off and cut
his forehead. I bandaged him as best I could while he
called me an idiot and a cripple.

I offered to tie him to the cart so he could sleep in
peace. But the cannon roar was so loud my words
disappeared.

They marched to the earthworks. Staggered, and
crept back. Our boys. In and beside the carts. They
were already dead. Those who were walking too.

One day I heard a voice say:
'The German positions are 450 meters from our
earthworks.'
He got no reply.
That's how it happened. That's how I met Karna.

The first time the Prussians crossed to Als with 15,000
men Our Lord muddled the whole thing with drifting

snow and blessed bad weather. But they bombarded us and dug in closer. Prussian shells were an endless, cursed sunny day that spewed death on us. On 9 April, the Danish artillery fell silent.

When the military hospital was full, we got orders to bring the wounded to farms and provisional field hospitals in the area. One was a small farm near the church. We were many insignificant, deathly frightened heroes who drove and carried hundreds of wounded soldiers.

Old nightmares about the Russian were banished to a corner. You simply did what was necessary with mechanical self-control.

Afterwards you could think. About justice, for example. Did it occur to me to study law instead of medicine? Nonsense! The time at Dybbøl taught me that justice is ridiculous and useless. True, medicine is merely first aid, but it's still a better thing to devote your life to.

Death was all that lasted. But I was much too afraid to admit that. Fear was a black horse. It trampled me time after time. Yet I got up again. Did not dare to do otherwise.

My restless sleep in the stable made me see Dina in an entirely different light.

If men loyal to Prussia and Austria could allow hundreds of Danes to be maimed and slaughtered because they were sent to defend land, why couldn't *she* fire a shot into just one Russian's forehead because he had crossed her?

It was comforting somehow. To see Dina from this perspective. The Russian had been badly shattered, because the shot was fired at close range. But he had a humane death. Quick and effective!

One night the nightmare was not about the Russian's cry, but about Dina riding forth in a military uniform. She was an army general who, swiftly and humanely, shot every single Prussian and Austrian soldier. Using a Lapp rifle! With perfect marksmanship and great

255

effectiveness, she freely hunted generals behind the enemy's lines. Hunted for epaulettes and golden tassels the way she collected hats. A herald accompanied her to gather the masculine decorations from vanity's battlefield.

I awoke in my temporary bed and realized it was not Dina the sharpshooter that made the dream a nightmare. Nor the nameless horde of soldiers behind her. No, it was my own role. For I was the deathly frightened herald scurrying between the corpses and horses' hooves. It was I who carried all the medals and uniform decorations in a sack on my back.

I had become old as the hills inside my head.

The field hospital seethed with blood, pus and bitterness. Deep into stumps of legs, gangrene and disfigured faces. Yes, even into death. If you could do nothing on the battlefield, and had lost faith that this war could be won, at least you could pour out hate and despair through your mouth.

I had never tolerated humiliation. But at Dybbøl you learned to tolerate. I felt humiliated three times over. My cowardly countrymen stayed away while the Danes fought an impossible battle. Dina was hiding somewhere behind the enemy's borders and I did not know where. Those to whom I gave all my time and effort disdained me the moment I opened my mouth. Unless they were so wounded they could not. As long as they were too injured to notice, they tolerated me. But as soon as they regained a little health and hate, they let me know who I was.

Why did I stay? I had enlisted, by God! Put my name on some piece of paper! I did not know the difference between fear and rage. Perhaps they had become the same thing. One woman who worked on the farm we used as a field hospital called me 'the Good Norwegian'.

I did not bother to ask what she meant by that.

*   *   *

256

The women on the farm worked day and night to feed and care for the wounded soldiers and us.

I needed something besides blood and fear. So I looked at them. Smelled their scent. Got as close to them as possible. Turned them into a campfire to yearn for as I ran across the frost-covered fields. That way I could keep the other things at bay. The cannon. The fires. The men's ruined bodies.

Those who returned from the field each evening sufficiently intact surely had thoughts like mine. They smoked and pinched girls, drank and slept. Once in a while they sang. One had an old photograph with him.

Women were like music. Fearfully present. Under your skin. And yet inaccessible. Something that provoked or moved you. An object. Never permanent. Sooner or later they left the room.

Books and dreams, on the other hand, you could take with you. Even to this place. To hell.

I do not know if I have had any dreams since I killed Karna.

He cried out for Mama. The first man I saw die at the field hospital. Later I realized men usually do this when they die.

His right arm and shoulder were shot to pieces. His face was gray beneath blond wisps of hair on his forehead. His bloodshot eyes were the only desperate living thing about him. He had lost so much blood and was in such terrible pain, it was amazing he uttered a sound.

'Mama! Mama!' he groaned, fumbling weakly for Karna with the hand he still had.

A pitiful little boy's voice:

'Don't go! Don't go! Mama, don't blow out the candle! Don't go!'

Karna Dons rocked him and whispered to him.

She was a servant girl on the farm. Before we came. Before Bismarck. About my age. Well-built. Her hair was a large dun horse. Her face pale and serious. When

257

she helped me get the poor fellow up the stairs and onto the hospital bed, I realized how strong she was.

There was something about her embrace as she drew the brave fellow close. Her hands. Hard work had made them red and swollen. Her eyes always focused on a point above my head when they turned towards me.

Suddenly, I was overwhelmed with a desire to lie with Karna. It knocked all common sense out of me. When I saw her with death in her arms, I was captured.

The crumpled blue laundry apron that told of strenuous night duty. The rolled-up sleeves that revealed winter-white skin and dimpled elbows. The strong, plump fingers that spread around the male bundle in the bed. The stench of death that blended with body odors. It all kindled my desire.

I realized I was waiting for the man in the bed to die, so it would be my turn. I wanted to have her.

From that moment, Karna's body was all that mattered. A few hours later, after we had carried out the corpse, I waylaid her. She was fetching bandages and sheets in the shed we used as a storehouse.

I slipped in and closed the door. Then I pressed her against the shelves and let my hands move freely. I do not know why I did such a stupid thing. I could have used cunning and charm, and possibly received what I wanted.

She did not even scream. Just set her knee in my groin until I let her go.

Later that evening I noticed her looking at me as we sat across from each other eating our meal in the cramped kitchen. Suddenly everything began whirling around, and I rushed out to vomit. It was total disintegration. And obsession.

When I came back, trembling and miserable, she nodded amiably. She seemed to have accepted that all men, both the dying and we others, would force their attentions on her.

Karna became an acrid lead taste in my mouth, and a murmuring desire. She did not start rumors about me among the other girls. I would have noticed that. So the scene in the storehouse was not my shame alone. As long as she did not betray me, it was her shame as well. She probably knew that.

Then I was out with Paul and the terrified horse that pulled the cart. Everything rose and fell in the raw fumes and stench of suffering. And she was part of it! I drove the open cart with bodies for her. Carried them in to her. And she let them die in her arms while they cried out for Mama.

Already the next day she met my gaze over a whimpering, shattered body. I did nothing about it. I waited.

We were the most desired death helpers at the field hospital. Somehow dependent on each other. We searched for each other's hands around a wounded soldier. Brushed each other's skin when we could. But I stayed far away from the storehouse when she was there.

I waited.

We heard the students had held demonstrations. They had spat at the royal family. But I did not need to participate. My days and nights belonged to Dybbøl. I waited for Karna while the Danish army dug in and prayed for the embankments to hold. As they had held during the Three Year War.

But the army's prayer was not heard. The blood ran thick. So thick that mutiny and desertions became common. They came to us as hunted youths, crazed with shock and the fear of death. Some had wounded themselves to escape the fighting.

I was off duty when the Prussians stormed Dybbøl on 18 April. Then, while the cannons thundered and blaze after blaze scorched the earth and sky, she waylaid me at the door. Led me behind the buildings and into her small room. Karna Dons.

There was a hook on the door and a narrow bed in the corner. Above the bed hung a colored picture of the angel Gabriel with a wreath on his head and a torch in his hand.

She was not as well-built as I had imagined. Her breasts were smaller than expected. But they were warm mounds in a cold world. She had pale skin and her veins ran like signals under my hands wherever they roamed.

Juices flowed from her like water. As though she had been saving them since the day I tried to take her in the storehouse.

We did not say a word. Now and then we lifted our heads and waited until the cannons paused. Then we tried to find each other again. The whole time, I floated in a leather sack with Andrea and the tanner's dildo.

But still I was with Karna. I do not know if she got much from it. But she took it calmly. Just as she took death calmly.

Afterwards we ate potatoes and herring and drank cheap schnapps. I was shy and tried to find out how she felt. But I did not dare to ask.

The bottle was almost empty when I suddenly started crying like a coward. Wept and stammered something about death and war. She nodded. With dry, friendly eyes. I could have loved her for the way she responded. But I did not. She was a weight in my body. I did not know if that was good or bad. She was already part of me. My conscience and sorrow. And I did not know anything yet.

I do not know what I expected when I saw madness at close range and hurried across the battlefield until I tasted lead in my mouth. I only know I became thoroughly cured of the Russian.

The same day Karna became part of me, Paul and I ran through the graveyard at Dybbøl church carrying a man wounded by cannon fire. He had no nose and his teeth lay like poorly strung pearls outside his mouth. In all that red. He did not even cry out for his mother.

But I cried out, and literally frightened water out of Paul. Or maybe it was that the cannons were so close. In any case, I shouted to the man without a face:

'Everything will be fine. Just lie still. Your mother is coming! She's coming soon!'

The iron gate squealed across the barren churchyard. The row of snow-covered graves seemed the only orderly thing in the world. A peaceful blanket of snow covered the stone fence, and icicles glistened along the roof of the small building by the pump. The bare trees around the church bristled towards a red sky that devoured the shouts and thundering bombardments out there.

Inside my empty head, I drifted without direction. Like an old piece of flotsam. Amidst everything, a thought rushed through me:

'Dina, help me not to faint. Shoot this man! Help him die! Quickly!'

Then we ran across the coarse gravel and stiffly frozen grass with the man. His blood ran a race with my prayers. And the earth drank it beneath our feet.

Afterwards, whenever the scene came to mind I saw the winter landscape more than the people. I did not see the results of six hours of constant shell fire that the Danes did not return. Did not see the wild terror in all the eyes I met. Nor the gunsmoke above the Prussians' overpowering army, which was closer to the embankments than our army. I did not hear the commanders' furious shouts and the screams of pain. My common sense knew it was there.

But what I saw was an utterly silent winter landscape in which men tumbled over each other in slow, macabre movements. And the red snow. Diluting black craters of upturned earth.

On 18 April, Denmark lost 5,000 men. Of all those I carried on the stretcher, the man without a face showed himself to me most clearly. Along with the poor fellow who died in Karna's arms, he chased the Russian away.

Instead, there was Karna.

One day we patched together a poor little girl whom the war had trampled. She had Hanna's eyes. That made me feel weak. But just for a moment. Then I went on. To the next bed.

The following day both she and her gypsy family were gone. They were called 'night man' people, like the men who help executioners.

I thought about saving myself and going home to Reinsnes. Doctors were of little help as long as Bismarck existed.

But I did not leave.

When I returned to Copenhagen, a letter from Anders awaited me. He explained why he sent less money for my living expenses. He had been forced to take out a loan. Fishing was poor, and the new cargo boat was so expensive. At the end he mentioned Hanna had married and moved to Lofoten.

When summer came, I thought: it's summer at Reinsnes now! In my mind I saw the sun turn above the holms without disappearing into the ocean. And I could suddenly be struck by a painfully intense smell of sun-scorched, seaweed-covered beach, no matter where I was.

Actually, it was just a vague sorrow that time had gone on without me. I could not even remember Hanna's features properly.

Reinsnes was a place I had read about in a book.

When the London conference broke down at the end of June, and the ceasefire with it, I had a childish hope that wherever Dina was, she would telegraph or write: Come! We're going home to Reinsnes!

But she did not do that.

Then the Prussians crossed to Als and the humiliating peace was a fact. On 30 October, with the stroke of a pen, Holstein and Slesvig were ceded to the Austrian kaiser and the King of Prussia.

I decided I would never say another word in Norwegian. And I would never set foot on Swedish soil.

Copenhagen was paralyzed. Some people thought about their bank savings, others filled chests with food and fled out of town. Late that autumn Aksel said my Danish was improving. I should hope so! After all, I lived in a betrayed country and was studying medicine.

To my surprise, I returned to Copenhagen as a hero. Because I had picked up bodies at Dybbøl. Such were, and are, the myths of manhood.

Another surprise was that Karna came to Copenhagen too. Her body was not the same in Copenhagen as at Dybbøl. I understood that, and I did not understand that.

Perhaps the intoxication of being a hero among the students went to my head. Once I got drunk and shouted to Aksel and other boon companions:

'Do you know a murderer?'

But they did not know any murderers. They just stared at me as if I had gone mad. I got so furious I yelled and pounded the table:

'Where the hell are all the world's murderers? Can you tell me?'

They did not even bother to shake their heads.

'He got that way after he met the Prussians,' mumbled Aksel, and told me to keep quiet.

Two fellows marched me out between them and got me home to the widow on Bredgade.

Of course I knew where they were. The murderers. In jails and prisons. I worked at a jail for a while. And met a few of them there. Without becoming much wiser.

Just confused. About how innocent they were. Meek. Groveling. Miserable. Broken. Or raw and repulsive with the language of a neglected, hated child. They did not resemble Dina. She had eyes and thoughts like glass.

CHAPTER 3

One night Aksel and I were out drinking with a fellow student. Claus. We were celebrating that we had passed a test of manhood by dissecting cadavers for hours. Pulled out their intestines and organs, stuffed in newspaper and straw, and sewed them up again. We were thirsty and enthusiastic, and arrogant with knowledge about mankind.

Claus started talking about the well-known person we had opened up, who bore all the signs of advanced syphilis.

'Shhh!' said Aksel, when Claus began giving details.

'I didn't say his name,' he said defensively.

'If we report your blabbing to the medical director, you'll be in trouble,' said Aksel.

'I didn't know such men visited the side streets,' said Claus.

'Now you know,' I said, trying to hide that I felt nauseated. To tell the truth, I had felt nauseated all day.

'Poor devil! He was a clergyman, you know,' said Claus.

'Hush! Don't let anyone hear you. Or you'll be an equally poor devil,' said Aksel, looking around.

Claus began talking about the general lack of morality and intelligence among dead scholars.

'But a cleric in the side streets!' he exclaimed at the end, refusing to give in.

Aksel and I exchanged looks.

'Haven't you been there?' I suddenly asked.

'What?'

'To visit ladies of the night?'

'I beg your pardon?'

'I'm just asking,' I said.

'One doesn't go to such places,' he said in confusion.

'You've got to lose your virginity somewhere,' I said provocatively.

'Aww!' he said, and looked at Aksel for help.

'That's right!' said Aksel, refusing to help him.

It could have become unpleasant, because we realized he was not one of us, and I wanted to needle him a bit.

But Aksel took positive action, and began entertaining us with stories about his childhood town, the bourgeoisie's double morality, and his father who forgave their sins at church each Sunday. It was the same general topic, but more harmless. Aksel should have been a diplomat.

Instead he consumed sandwiches and raw eggs in one gulp, like a trained wolf or large dog. That is: he opened his mouth very wide and somehow managed to put everything into it without spilling on his beard. Then he closed his mouth and began chewing like mad.

His strict upbringing had made a deep impression, because he did not talk while doing this. And he chewed with his mouth closed. But the rest of his body was in a trance. Trembled, as if very cold or in convulsions. His head and throat created deliberate spasms which spread throughout the upper part of his big body. When the huge mouthful was down safely, he took a large gulp of beer. Half a tankard, to be exact.

Then he continued his wild stories about the judge's wife and her lover, ignoring the fact that while he was chewing Claus and I had become friends. And that we were discussing prospects for getting a hospital internship when we finished our coursework.

*   *   *

Then I saw Cecilie. She had just come through the door to serve beer. She leaned towards us across the bar, revealing the cleavage of her breasts at her neckline. Utterly paralyzed by Aksel's eating technique, she let beer spill over the glass's rim while she stared at him.

Finally, feeling sorry about the beer, I put my hand on hers. It was cold from the dark beer. She looked at me. At that moment I decided something wonderful had touched my life.

She became a fever in me. For a long time. I stopped going to see Karna on Store Strandstraede. And the war grew very distant.

After our first time in her bed while her girlfriend was at work, Cecilie decided to become the doctor's wife at Reinsnes.

I felt skeptical, but Cecilie was practical and useful. She poured beer for me, washed my clothes, took me to her bed when her girlfriend was away, and scolded me when she thought I acted improperly.

When we quarreled, which happened quite often, she made fun of me with her girlfriend. She liked to play to an audience. So everyone knew when we quarreled. It provoked a rage in me that was somehow ennobling. More than once I grabbed her when we were alone. Hard. But she simply looked at me with defiant flashing eyes and endured it. Just before she spat at me I let go of course.

There were no sensible reasons for the quarrels. Like a volcano, they arose in an interior we could not control. They spewed out with tremendous force and died away.

I do not know if she also felt the lava hardening around her. Thicker and thicker at each eruption.

We had some good fights. Even Aksel had not heard their like. I had learned little tricks in my encounters with Hanna. And I took advantage of Cecilie's long hair. Held her fast until she was checkmated. But always, when I thought I had her, she managed to thrust a knee or an elbow into some tender spot. She obviously had learned dirty little tricks too. Once she stuck her thumb in my eye and I could not see out of it for several days. And as if that were not enough, I had to comfort her when she realized she had nearly blinded me.

I gradually realized the outer aspects of my relationship with Cecilie took so much energy I could never finish a single thought.

Aksel kept urging me to find a sweetheart from a better social class.

'One doesn't fight with women!' he said in a fatherly way one day when we had to leave the pub because Cecilie and her girlfriend made us feel as if they had put arsenic in our beer.

'Find a sweetheart like Anna!' he added.

I could not bear to discuss it with him. It was early evening. It was raining. And life was bitter. Of course I could have asked what he got from Anna. What I knew about her was not exactly exciting. A much too respectable professor's daughter, whom you could only be with at a dance, or in Tivoli, or at the Alhambra. Or even worse, at the Kongelig Theater.

Since Anders had begun saving *skillings*, I had no budget for such things. Nor the patience either.

So I simply said:

'Shut up, you middle-class social climber!'

'I don't feel like fighting with you. You haven't got the brains for a decent attack!' he spat at me.

What saved Cecilie and me was a sergeant in the royal army with a new scar on his forehead. Women are attracted by scars. Or wounded men. Strange as that seems.

It was not the sergeant's fault that my relationship with Cecilie ended. It began several weeks earlier. The day a letter from Anders fell out of my pocket when I was with her.

For the first time, Anders's letter contained a request. Not specifically stated. And in the stilted, old-fashioned language of someone who does not usually express himself in writing. He wanted me to come home when I finished my classes. Or to take a break in my studies. Between the lines lay his concerns about Reinsnes. They could really use me at home.

There was nothing in the letter I could report to Cecilie. I think I was ashamed. Realized it was thanks to Anders's hard work I had lived in Copenhagen for almost four years. He was probably worried I would be no use for anything when I came home. Just like Johan.

While Cecilie chattered about how wonderful it would be when we went to Norway, I tried to put away Anders's letter.

I could not imagine treating infected fingers and writing prescriptions for pills and powders in northern Norway for the rest of my life. But I could not explain all this to Cecilie. She tried to snatch the letter from me. Annoyed, I pushed her away.

At first she was hurt and angry, and claimed I was keeping secrets from her.

'It's just a letter from my stepfather,' I said.

'Why can't I read it then?'

'Because it's mine!' I said coldly, and realized I was on the verge of moving Cecilie out of my life.

I do not know if she realized it. In any case, she shifted her strategy. Began asking questions about Reinsnes, the people there, the places, the boats, the sea.

At first I felt flattered that she sat quietly at my feet while I responded to her questions. I exaggerated. Selected the best stories, the best places, the most legendary people. I grew flushed and eager as a school-boy who is finally tested in a subject he knows.

Then she began asking about Dina. Carefully at first. Because she had asked before and received scant reply. But now, since I was talking about Reinsnes, she became bolder. Pressed me for answers.

'What's she like? Your mother?' she asked.

'She's living abroad. I said that before . . . I haven't seen her for years.'

'Why? Are you enemies?'

'Not at all. I'm not at home either.'

'Why don't you want to talk about your mother?' she asked. 'Aren't we sweethearts? Am I not the person closest to you in this terrible world?'

Talk like that always annoyed me. People should be no closer than you can bear. And I could never stand being asked several questions at once. It reminded me of a graduate student who lectured to us in Tromsø. He always fired off all the questions at once. And that way prevented any answers or conversation.

At that moment, as I struggled to reply in a way that would avoid a quarrel, I realized how intensely weary I was of Cecilie.

'Why won't you talk about your mother?' she persisted.

Instead of answering, I attacked her. Lying between her thighs while sucking her breast, other images burned in my mind. Of Dina washing herself behind the folding screen. I saw her shadow and sensed her scent. Like snips of horror, I saw the Russian's head with a huge hole in it. And the soldier's head in Karna's lap. Everything moved with the same rhythm as the body beneath me in the bed. It floated in Cecilie's hair. Finally, the Russian and the soldier emptied their blood spasmodically between us. Until we lay there motionless, glued fast in it.

But I said nothing. Cecilie was already rejected. She was not a person you could send your soul through without its being crushed.

We still quarreled a while longer. Until the sergeant arrived. I do not recall that I felt sorry. Just that I disliked the sergeant.

The discussions, the quarrels, the laughter, the pipe-smoking. It gave me a feeling of belonging. And kept at a distance the smoldering longing I did not understand.

But when I was free of Cecilie, Reinsnes suddenly came clearly to mind. A bird soaring above the islands. A cutting in the herb garden. Leaves turned wrong side out in the wind. Rain! The smell of dust, books and lavender.

Students still had lively disputes about Kierkegaard's stinging scorn for official Christianity and his idea that individual martyrdom was the only thing of value. He affirmed this personally by wearing himself out completely. He collapsed in the street and died. Although he had been dead since November 1855, the students were not finished with him.

Some never forgave him for the contemptuous scorn he showed towards Grundtvig.

These students rallied around Grundtvig's thesis: be human first and then Christian, this is life's only law.

I was bewildered by people's unwavering enthusiasm about taking a stand for or against another person's thoughts and writing. Where the great thinkers were concerned, I always discovered something I did not understand. And thought it more productive to discuss things until I understood than to be unilaterally enthusiastic or negative. I could not choose Grundtvig or Kierkegaard.

At first I naively believed those who spoke as experts had met or known Kierkegaard and Grundtvig. But often it became evident they had never met the great men. Just heard about them. Some made it seem they had studied the men's writings better than they actually had. And people constantly exposed one another.

I think the debate initially attracted me. As an example of Mother Karen's theory that words are false, or at best distorted. And it is dangerous to love books without being clear about this. So there is no reason one wise saying need shut out another. As if life could be divided into forest plots and chopped down according to precise markers? As if someone could decide how many fish he would draw up from the sea?

Or decide his own beliefs and doubts before they were tested? As if love for your neighbor and personal opinions had anything to do with each other?

A few times I went to Borch collegium to hear a man who attracted much public attention. His name was Georg Brandes. I think I was a better listener than debater. When someone made good arguments for Grundtvig, I told myself Kierkegaard was the more serious thinker. Had the best brain. But, medical student that I was, I always stopped myself with the fact I had not seen these brains from the inside. And if I had, I did not have enough knowledge to interpret what I saw.

I evaluated the pros and cons the way you would if you had a choice between a juicy piece of meat with dessert afterwards, or a plain onion soup and a good wine. What you choose depends on the time and your state of mind.

When someone presented good arguments for Kierkegaard's excellence and effective satire, I always defended Grundtvig as the better human being and the one who lived most genuinely.

I read books, speeches and articles by and about the two men, but came no closer to clarification. I was, and remained, neutral. I thought I could use them both, without really knowing for what.

But there were other topics I was eager to discuss. One was guilt, which I provocatively brought up whenever possible. It always ended in a dogfight about religious philosophy.

The other was women. That was a difficult topic because the students always distorted things by boasting, to hide the truth about themselves.

Aksel and I knew about each other. But Aksel did not discuss such things. He acted. Or left things alone.

I could scarcely see anyone of the female sex without regarding it as a tangible gift from heaven for use in my fantasy. I did not always fantasize about concrete actions. Far from it! I understood my limits. But I put the women into my dreams. I stored the best examples and took them out on appropriate occasions. There were many examples. I filed them according to color, size and age. And could summon their images whenever I wished. Sometimes so clearly that if they had suddenly walked through the door I would have seen no difference. But most often they were half hidden and embellished with crêpe and drapery. Or set in a vulgar context, position or situation. Or made innocently pure and passive. All according to what I could use.

Now and then I tried to talk to Aksel about the collection, but he wanted to laugh it away.

'They think differently, Aksel. They are different! They stick in your thoughts even if you don't want them to.'

'You explain so much about girls. One would think you knew them from the inside!' he said.

That made me feel like a hermaphrodite.

'Maybe you should visit the side streets again, and run out of the door when you've finished,' he chuckled.

'That's not what I'm talking about,' I said crossly. 'In fact, why don't you go there yourself? Anna isn't exactly available, is she?'

I almost wished he would hit me. But he did not. Just gave me a contemptuous look.

'I'm sorry!' I said after a while.

We sauntered along the lakes in the wind. A few people were skating on the ice. Circling here and there like dolled-up ducks.

'You can't go there after what you see when you dissect a cleric,' Aksel said dryly.

'But if you weren't so afraid of syphilis?' I asked.

'Well, yes . . .' he said, squirming a bit.

'Did you like it?' I asked.

'Benjamin! Hold your tongue, man!'

'What did you like? Was it the smells? The fear? The big hams?' I persisted.

'The smells? No! The other? The light was out, after all.'

I was careful not to laugh.

'Do you mean it makes no difference whom you go to bed with? Because the light is out?'

'Of course not!'

'What do you mean then? What do you want to experience?'

He just shrugged his shoulders.

'I've had enough of your philosophical nonsense,' he said firmly.

'But you must have some ideas and dreams about what a bordello can give you, when you say the only reason you don't go there is your fear of diseases? At the same time as you tell me to find a sweetheart who doesn't do such things!' I shouted.

'Hush! I didn't say that! . . . But you're right. It's . . . I don't know . . . easy.'

'Not exciting?'

'Be quiet!' he said, and walked away.

I ran after him on the icy road. Slid long distances. The whole time I had the feeling I had torn off his clothes. Publicly.

The next day I handed him a note as I walked past him in the lecture hall. On it I had scribbled: 'The reason I don't go there is that I'm afraid I'll be unsuccessful. But if there are two of us, and one is successful, it's not so bad. Doctors can examine whether or not the merchandise is tainted.'

I saw him put the note in his pocket with a smile. Then he raised his hand as a sign he had forgiven me.

CHAPTER 4

We postponed our visit to the side streets. But Aksel got me invited to dinner at Anna's parents' home.

The professor was a lively fellow with large sideburns. During his lectures he would often rise on his toes and then fall back on his heels with a loud creak. This ritual ruined for me most of what he said.

Aksel's father and the professor had been students together. Which may have been the reason behind Aksel's pure and innocent love for Anna. But I did not say that. In any case, he got the dinner invitation to include 'the student from the most barren and distant Norwegian mountains'.

When I asked Aksel how he managed it, he said sardonically:

'I have to save you from women like Cecilie and Karna, or whatever their names are. You need to get into respectable society. And there's another reason,' he declared.

'What's that?' I asked, filled with misgivings.

'You have such a powerful ability to *will* things, people around you feel guilty and think it's their fault if things don't go the way you want. You've been cross several times when I went to Anna's without you. That's why you're invited!'

The professor lived in an elegant apartment on Store Kongensgade. A black-and-white-clad parlor maid opened the door and took our coats and hats. I wore gloves for the occasion. But only the black-and-white-clad girl saw that.

In my excitement I attempted a smile at her. Which made Aksel hiss through clenched lips:

'That's the maid . . .'

She took the chocolate Aksel and I had bought together, curtsied, and showed us into the parlor.

The apartment was a blend of impressive good taste and threadbare humanity. Some furniture bore the venerable stamp of C. B. Hansen's establishment at Kongens Nytorv. In one of her subordinate clauses the hostess revealed that the furniture maker was appointed royal 'Court Chairmaker'.

Already in the front hall I noted a heavy cigar smell. That helped to make you feel at home. I began thinking about Reinsnes. The rooms. The sounds. The smells. The photographs. Especially the photograph of Jacob. The brass candlesticks and the lamps. The hum of lighted stoves. Everything I remembered showed that the things and the people belonged together.

I had met Anna and Sophie before. But just in passing. A handshake on the street. They never came to student parties. It was as if Aksel had Anna somewhere else. As if she were not truly alive.

Sophie and her mother did most of the talking. That was already true by the main course. But before the dessert arrived I had decided to make contact with Anna.

She did not say much, but I was well aware that she looked at me from beneath lowered eyelids. She was quite slender, but Our Lord had still given her all the feminine forms. The beautiful long fingers on her narrow hands had a good grip on her knife and fork. Her face was golden, even though it was midwinter. I have seen the same skin color on newborn babies with jaundice. She seemed foreign, like the rest of her family. There was probably something to what people said about the professor being Jewish.

Her hair was dark brown and smooth. Except for curls around her face. Thanks to a curling iron or God. You never knew in the case of women. In all this golden and brown, her eyes were a shock.

I could not understand how I had missed them the first time I saw her. Intense blue eyes that went right through whatever they focused on. But there was much I had not noticed before. Her nose, for example. It was curved and stern, with large nervous nostrils. Her shoulders looked like a wall against everything and everyone.

Aksel looked at me and smiled. For some reason that irritated me immensely.

Sophie was absorbed in Grundtvig's teachings, and talked about the importance of making education available to ordinary people. She wanted to work as a teacher in the Grundtvigian spirit. When she had gained more knowledge herself.

The professor nodded with pride.

'My Norwegian friend prefers Kierkegaard,' said Aksel with a teasing look at me.

'I don't see why one can't admire them both,' I said, feeling my face flush.

'*Fear and Trembling* is so terrible,' whispered Anna entranced.

'That's why it's not something for young ladies,' laughed the professor.

'What do you think is so terrible?' I asked. I had the feeling that Anna's family and Aksel disappeared into the large front cupboard and closed the doors behind them.

'It's this terrible thing . . . about the sacrifice. Abraham, who's willing to sacrifice his own son, Isaac,' she said, staring right through me.

'But God commanded it! I explained that to you, my dear,' the professor began.

She ignored her father and looked directly at me as she said:

'A God who gives such commands can't expect

277

human beings to ever improve, even if thousands of years go by.'

'Anna dear!' her mother exclaimed in alarm. Then she turned to her husband and said regretfully:

'I've told you Anna doesn't have the nerves for reading such things. She takes everything seriously. That's not good. Writing like that shouldn't . . .'

'Shouldn't I take God seriously, Mother?' Anna interrupted.

She should not have said that, I thought. She should not have let her mother out of the cupboard.

'Why do you think Kierkegaard wrote about this?' I said, turning to Anna.

'Because the Holy Scriptures disturbed him. The story is in the Bible, you know.'

'He should leave the Scriptures in peace, and instead write so people can understand what he wants to say,' said Aksel.

'I'd like to solve the Bible's enigmas too,' I said. 'So it's not strange that someone like Kierkegaard tried.'

'What interests you most?' asked Anna, as if we were the only ones present.

'Sin and guilt!'

'Not angst, like Kierkegaard?'

'No . . . but that's probably the same thing.'

I paused, because the thought suddenly surprised me.

'You young people certainly have gloomy table conversations,' sighed Anna's mother. 'But I must say, Grundtvig is more human. He's a marvel of enlightenment. He believes in a better world, if we just want it ourselves!'

'If only people in power were like Grundtvig!' she went on, and launched into a long speech about that disgraceful Bismarck.

He had demanded that all clerics, teachers and government officials in Slesvig and Holstein swear an oath of allegiance after the territories were annexed to

Prussia. And those who refused were discharged for no reason.

'For the good of humanity, someone should put a bullet through Mr Bismarck,' Aksel said darkly.

I suddenly felt very uncomfortable. My whole body broke into a sweat. For a long time I did not know what was being said. Finally, in the middle of something the professor was saying, I leaned over the table towards Anna and asked:

'What do you think about Grundtvig?'

The room grew silent. I had obviously been impertinent.

'I don't know him,' she said indifferently.

'Anna is only interested in music and poetry,' said Sophie with a sigh.

'What kind of music do you like, Miss Anna?' I asked, looking straight at her, but at the same time protecting myself from her gaze.

'Actually, I don't like music. The others think I do, because I play the piano a little.'

'Anna dear, how can you say such a thing!' exclaimed her mother.

I had to cough into my napkin a few times. Flushed and perspiring, I raised my head again and tried to keep my dignity. But I had to find my handkerchief and blow my nose. Meanwhile, everyone at the table maintained a sympathetic silence. Not even Aksel came to my aid. When my pulse calmed down, I said stupidly:

'I've always wanted to play an instrument.'

'It's only a matter of doing it,' said Anna.

'Surely it can't be that simple?'

'It just takes a lot of time. In principle, it's like crocheting tablecloths or antimacassars for the chairs.'

'But Anna! Making music is an art!' exclaimed the professor.

'Art has little to do with moving your fingers across the keys,' she said, looking as if she were about to yawn.

'Then what is art?' I asked curiously.

For a moment she looked bewildered, but then she replied:

'Art expresses what humanity, not nature, has created by drawing on all its sensitivity.'

'Do you think experience gives form to art?' I asked.

'No, but without experience, that of both the one who creates and the one who receives, art is invisible and has no value.'

'So do you think art hidden in burial chambers has no value, because nobody sees it?'

'No. Because people dream about seeing it.'

I held my breath. What a revelation she was!

I almost shouted across the table to Aksel:

'Damn! Now I understand why you don't visit the side streets.'

But I did not say that. Besides, it would have been a very poor reply.

CHAPTER 5

I truly planned to go home that summer. With the thought somehow of doing both Anders and Reinsnes a favor. Maybe I was influenced by Grundtvig's ideas about educating the masses. His follower Schrøder and others founded folk high schools and got farmers to join them.

In Copenhagen, many so-called intellectuals tried to trivialize and ridicule it all. But after a while, most people were stirred by the idea of educating the masses. Everyone wanted to go out and free the common people to be educated. Possibly I blended homesickness and missionary zeal.

But the whole time my brain reeled with Kierkegaard's words: 'The true Knights of Faith are witnesses, never teachers . . .' It seemed to be a judgment I could not avoid. Moreover, I had had no chance to talk with Anna alone. One slight comfort was that Axel did not get a chance either.

The sisters always did things together. I had the distinct feeling Sophie was told to keep an eye out because my reputation was not the best. Still, we four became well enough acquainted to allow me to call the women by their first names and walk arm in arm with them.

One day when Aksel and I had been in Tivoli with Anna and Sophie, Anna asked if I knew a Norwegian writer named Henrik Ibsen.

'I've read about him in the newspapers,' I replied.

'I read his last book. We have it at home. *Peer Gynt*. You can borrow it.'

'Thank you,' I said.

'Ibsen is living in exile. Like you. But he probably has different reasons?'

I shrugged, feeling skeptical about reading a Norwegian author. It must be impossible for a writer to be Norwegian. Everything I appreciated about literature bore no resemblance to anything Norwegian. At least not after picking up bodies at Dybbøl.

I do not know if I would have said that. But I forgot it, because suddenly Karna stood on the sidewalk in front of us on Ny Vestergade. She carried a large basket. It looked heavy. What was she doing here?

Behind her came a funeral cortège with mourners on foot. It blocked the sidewalk, so we had to stop. Our eyes met. I do not know what she saw, but when I greeted her, she just walked right past.

'Wasn't that Karna?' asked Aksel.

'Yes,' I replied.

After a pause I said:

'Anna, do you know where Ibsen is living in exile?'

'Do you know her?' asked Anna.

'Who?' I said.

'The servant girl with the basket.'

'Oh yes, her. I think she worked at the field hospital at Dybbøl,' I answered.

Anna said no more. Neither did Aksel. He could have said many things if he had wished.

When we went home with the women, I got the book. *Peer Gynt*.

I do not know whether it was because I saw with Anna's eyes, but I did not put the book down until I had read the last page. I despised and admired this fellow Peer. And I liked the dancing rhythm. But at the same time, the book irritated me. The self-deception. The cowardice. The lies. Even the humor irritated me. It made me uncomfortable.

That night I dreamed about Karna. But I could not fully recognize her. Something was wrong. I awoke and lay thinking. Then I realized that in the dream Karna had Cecilie's face. Or was it Hanna's?

It was because she was on a chain around my neck. Like the silver cross Mother Karen left to Johan at her death. I dreamed I stood on the Nyhavn quay in the rain playing with Karna as if she were an amulet. Letting her glide between my fingers. Suddenly I made an abrupt, involuntary movement. The chain broke. Karna glided into the water. The chain stung my palm and glided after her.

When I awoke, I remembered something I had heard or read. Or maybe the dream made me form the thought myself: you must forgive yourself much, before you can forgive others.

I did not know if Karna still lived at grandmother Dons on Store Strandstraede. But I went there the next evening.

'She cares for patients at night at Frederiks Hospital,' said her brother, staring curiously at me.

'When will she get home?'

'Tomorrow morning.'

We stood looking at each other.

'It's a long time since you were here,' he said finally.

'Yes. Please say hello from me.'

'I will. Are you coming again?'

I thought for a moment.

'Maybe,' I said.

The next day I wandered through the streets after the lectures. I had avoided Aksel, and left the university without talking to him. I realized he must think that strange. I also avoided our usual meeting places. Made sure the Round Tower, that emblem of student hunting grounds, was always out of my sight.

Then I gathered my courage, sat myself down on

Gammel Strand, and scribbled a letter to Anna. The problem was to get it delivered.

First I walked to Kongens Have park and imagined I was strolling in the sunshine. Then I went to Anna's door.

The maid who opened the door was the same one I met when I came to dinner. She recognized me and curtsied as she stared in surprise. I wore neither a proper coat nor hat, and undoubtedly looked like the student I was.

'Does the gentleman wish to wait?' she asked.

I nodded. She left the front door open and went into the house. I sat down on the stone steps to wait, my ears cocked. So I could leap up quickly and stand at attention if anyone came. Who this 'anyone' might be, the maid or Anna, was unclear to me.

When Anna stood in the doorway, I knew I had not expected her. Blushing, I met her gaze.

'Hello!' she said, her voice slightly questioning.

I haltingly started to repeat what was in the letter.

'I was just ready to go to my piano lesson. Perhaps we can walk those few blocks . . . together?'

She looked over her shoulder watchfully, as if expecting someone to call her inside. Then she added quickly:

'You can walk ahead, as far as Kongens Have!'

She told me a meeting place, which I did not understand because my pulse was pounding so in my ears. Then she was gone.

I walked unsteadily down the steps and along the street. Now I knew she dared to do forbidden things. Dared to meet me alone without anyone knowing!

I did not go into Kongens Have. Stood right at the entrance so I could see her coming. Withdrew a little and waited among the large trees. Something was wrong with both my breathing and my heartbeat. I hated myself for it, but that did not help.

Not long afterwards, I saw her. A dark shadow in a fluttering short cape. Her skirt billowed towards the cobblestones. Her clicking heels were a fanfare. It said: here comes Anna to you!

As she came nearer, the light transformed her. She sloughed off her dark outer casing and became a vision in thin yellow material. The sun grew powerless under the trees.

I wanted to pull her close. My arms seemed about to free themselves and follow their own will. But I knew she was no Karna. No Cecilie. No Hanna. She was the professor's daughter, even if she had agreed to meet me alone. If I thought about her being Aksel's Anna, I was unaware of it.

She smiled briefly when she entered the shadows.

'I don't have much time, a half-hour. I really do have a piano lesson,' she said quickly.

As if it had occurred to me to doubt that.

'We can walk along the path between the trees here. There's a bench . . .' she continued.

I still had not said a word. Simply nodded and followed her.

'So! You've read *Peer Gynt*? And you think Ibsen was writing about you?' she said over her shoulder.

It took me a few seconds to remember I had written something like that in my letter to her. Was she making fun of me? Or was she serious?

'It's probably got to do with living in exile,' I stammered, but could go no further.

'I knew it!' she exclaimed. 'I knew you'd like the book! All the people he betrayed! All the tests he failed!'

Still, I was unprepared when she went straight to the point:

'Have you betrayed anyone?'

'Well . . .' I said evasively.

'I understood the thought of Peer Gynt's betrayals was what made you send me a letter.'

I could not interpret her voice. It was as neutral as a sound in nature. Still, it contained *all the questions*.

'That's true,' I admitted.

'It's true? And yet you don't want to talk about it?'

'I wanted to meet you, Anna,' I heard myself say.

We had come to the bench. I brushed it off and gestured gallantly with my hand. She sat down without a word. I seated myself at the edge. Turned my whole body towards her.

'You've met me several times . . .' she began.

'Not alone!'

We sat for a while without saying anything. The words I had planned were gone. Then she looked at me and said:

'No. That's true. Not alone.'

I felt as if she had touched my skin.

'Aren't you alone with Aksel either?' I began.

She gave me a sidelong glance and smiled. I did not know how to interpret it.

'That's different.'

'Oh?'

'We know Aksel.'

'Do you?' I asked, thinking about Aksel behind the madam in Peder Madsen's Passage.

'You don't have a particularly good reputation, do you?' she asked. As if she knew what I was thinking, but forgave Aksel.

'What do you mean?'

'Sophie's friends are allowed to go to student parties at Regensen,' she said. As if that explained everything.

'It's the same at Valkendorf,' I said. That way I dragged Aksel with me.

'I know.'

'Oh?'

'That he lives there doesn't mean everything, does it?'

I could say no more.

'What do Sophie's friends say about me?'

'That you have many sweethearts,' she said honestly.

'What else?'

'That you're smart and good in every way, but don't frequent the most proper student places.'

I was about to say I usually went with Aksel. But restrained myself.

'Anything else?' I asked instead.

'That you want to go back where you came from when you finish your studies.'

'Did you ask about all this?'

'Yes.'

'Why?'

'Because it interests me.'

'Why?' I whispered.

I did not dare to look at her. Just at her hands. They had large, strong thumbs. Her wrists were as bold as a boy's. Her fingernails curved and were clipped short. Had I not known better, I could believe she worked with her hands.

'Why, Anna?' I begged.

'Because you're different. I think it was because you asked me about art . . . Or that . . .'

She interrupted herself and kicked something on the ground.

'May I hold your hand? I want to hold your hand. I've been looking at it so much, you see. It's awfully important for me to hold your hand.'

She smiled then, and hid her eyes.

'All right, one hand. I still have the other for myself.'

Of course I was not satisfied with one. I edged my way close and grasped both her hands. Feeling quite dizzy, but very happy. The fragrance of the woods. Raw and fresh after the rain. And of her. Lavender? Rose water? I did not know. It needed no name. Her hair? Strange and exciting. And yet as if I had slept with its fragrance on my pillow every night.

'You're different . . .' she said, almost as if to herself.

'How?'

'You seem to talk . . . to me . . . about what's alive in me.'

I wanted to carry her through space.

'I really want to . . . you see . . . I really want to discuss . . .' I began clumsily.

'Yes? About Peer Gynt?'

'No.'

'What then?'

'I really want to discuss the nature of love with you!'

She blinked unevenly a few times with both eyes. Then a look of some secret understanding glided across her face. She nodded and gently moved one finger in my hand. I felt a jolt far down in my belly.

'So what do you think . . . is the nature . . . of love?' she asked seriously.

'I think it isn't specifically connected with physical love.'

'Oh? Then what is it connected with?'

'I think it's a power.'

'Oh? What kind of power?'

'I don't know,' I said, leaning closer.

I was captured. Shackled. So close to her I felt her breath. But shackled. Until her fingers again began to move in mine.

'I think I have to go now,' she said breathlessly.

'No, don't go,' I begged.

'I thought you wanted to talk about Peer Gynt's betrayals.'

'Yes, I do. I'll talk about anything!'

'Sophie says she's heard you have affairs with barmaids. Several at a time!'

'Where did she hear that?'

'Where she goes to study Grundtvig.'

'I see,' I said dully, beginning to hate Grundtvig.

'Is it true?'

'Don't you like barmaids?'

'That's not the point . . .' she said.

Was she hurt? Was she *really* hurt? Dear God, if only she had shown me she took it to heart!

'Yes, for a while I had a sweetheart who worked in a pub.'

'What happened with her?'

'She went off with somebody else,' I said.

'Hmmm.'

We were silent.

'Why did she go off with somebody else?' she whispered.

'Because we didn't love each other.'

'What did the two of you do?'

She was bold now. As if she were a fellow classmate. I sensed her curiosity was greater than her modesty. Still I lied, because I didn't want to risk her running away. Peer Gynt and the Bøyg lay in my hands and pretended they were Anna's fingers.

'We met now and then. She was cheerful . . . and . . .'

I met her gaze. I saw it on her. She knew I was lying.

'Why did you want to meet me?' she whispered.

'I think you're one of the people I absolutely must meet. Alone.'

'Tell me why!'

She was still whispering.

I tried several times to find something to say. It was nothing but babbling. Finally I just sat shaking my head. If only I could have thrown my arms around her! One should not have to talk about everything.

'You came to me because you'd read about Peer Gynt. You wrote that this book was about you,' she said, pulling out my letter.

She was no longer holding my hands. I was completely alone!

I snatched the letter from her, crumpled it up, and stamped on it.

'That wasn't nice! There's no reason to be so angry. You say the barmaid left you for somebody else because you didn't love each other. Why do you want to talk with *me* about these things?'

'I already told you.'

'Oh?'

'I needed to have you to myself. I don't believe all that stuff in the books . . . I know you and Aksel . . . But I think I'll come to . . . to love you . . .'

I said it. I heard that I said it.

'I really must go,' she whispered close to me.

Then she rose and took a few steps. I sprang after her like a foolish dog without a leash.

'Don't go,' I whimpered, taking her hand.

'I must.'

'Can I meet you again? Here? Tomorrow?'

'That's impossible.'

'You're going to be late for your piano lesson anyway,' I shouted triumphantly, and tried to hold her back. She shook herself loose and kept walking.

'You're going to be late! That's just nonsense about your lesson! You only said it so I wouldn't know you wanted to meet me!'

She stopped walking then. Turned and looked at me. As if looking at something in a glass showcase.

'I'm going to keep the book! You won't get it back!' I shouted desperately.

'You're a madman,' she said quietly.

Then she turned her back on me and walked away. With short, firm steps. Right through the birds' twittering. Right through the tree trunks. Through the sun. Right through. Everything.

CHAPTER 6

I do not know when I first realized I did not accept death as a final separation. It must have been in Mother Karen's bedroom. After her death.

For years Mother Karen's voice seemed to lie behind the words when I read books. Stories I would not have understood if she had not read them. Explained them. Looked up words and said:

'Benjamin, here is the origin of the word. This is how they diverted it, so it became different from what it was in the beginning. And this is how they use it today. Words twist our reality, Benjamin. Can you see that? A word is never what it appears to be. In other realities, in other times, people gave the words other meanings, other inflections. Expressed different things. God, for example. God has changed much in the last hundred years. Before, God was easier to understand. Now we've used the word so much for everything we try to avoid with lies that we don't understand who God is.'

'Who is God?' I asked breathlessly, and believed the great mystery that darkened the world would be solved.

'God is the love in you, Benjamin. Without the love in you, there's no God!'

Sitting alone on her bedroom floor with her big book in my lap, it was a paltry answer. But she was right. Words were false. You had to live your words, and yet understand that without love there is no God. Mother Karen made that clear to me long after her death. Her body was unnecessary.

I could have wished she stroked my cheek of course. As a boy I pretended she put me in her lap and strands of her white hair tickled my cheek. But that took all my concentration, so I did not hear what she said. Besides, I always started crying with self-pity because I knew she was not there. So I chose her voice. That was independent of her body. I carried it in my head. Into my bed. To the summer barn. Out into the world.

Eventually, every book I opened was a voice from Mother Karen. Even the dull descriptions of the body's accursed anatomy became Mother Karen's.

Of course, the old woman and I had tough battles when I would not accept her words. At Dybbøl I had no love and no God. I had only the stench, the nausea, the blind angst my body let out in sweat, piss, tears. I remember I tried to make her a connecting link between me and my absent God. But she gave me a clear answer. She would not bother God with me as long as I had no love.

'Mother Karen, you must understand I don't have time!' I shouted into the gunpowder smoke and the groans of the wounded.

'Look at people,' she said. 'Don't run around crying like a coward, son! See people! Experience their suffering, and you have God.'

'But I can't pray, Mother Karen! I don't believe in it.'

'Haven't you understood anything yet? You don't have to believe. Only fools spend their lives on prayers and rules of faith created by people. It's love that counts. If you have love, all the world's prayers are answered. If you don't have love, there's no God! It does no good to die for an absent God! Then you're doomed to toss about in the skeleton of your dreams for ever.'

That was how she talked to me. That was how she taught me what was in the books that would have been written had the words not been twisted and destroyed on the way.

*   *   *

It was June 1868. Soon I no longer would need to report at precisely eight o'clock at With's clinic. There would be no more lectures and examinations. No more nerve-wracking tension to see if your marks hung in the balance between the two top grades.

Aksel hung in the balance. I shared his agony. It helped me a bit too. Because at times I had to think about Anna without saying anything to him. How the devil could you say such a thing to your best friend? Especially when you were not really sure what you thought.

One comfort was that Aksel had little time to attend balls with dancing and smorgasbords or to stroll with the women. He was smitten by pale, hysterical study sickness.

My first oral examinations went so well I could saunter through the last one, with O. Bang.

The topic I got was spinal cord diseases.

'The spinal cord is the brain's tail . . .' I began.

O. Bang was smiling already. Later we got into a battle. At the end he said:

'Much learning hath made the young man mad with desire for examinations, I believe!'

Then it was over. We wandered out with stiff knees and solemnity like a cowl over our heads.

'It was a damn easy exam,' I exclaimed. That was unnecessary.

'I sure as hell didn't know the spinal cord has diseases!' Aksel burst out, his face pale.

'Remember the master's words: if in doubt about the diagnosis, it's wisest to remember the natural thing is always the most natural!' I said arrogantly.

I immediately regretted my words. But it was too late. Aksel left without saying anything. I was a damned poor friend. But I could not bring myself to run after him. He had Anna after all. He was probably going to her home for a celebration dinner.

*   *   *

When I came outside, suddenly Anna stood before me on the sidewalk. Just then a carriage rumbled past, sending a shower of gutter water onto my trouser leg.

The rumbling carriage, the dirty water and the sight of Anna confused me. They did not fit together. I think I even tried to walk by without acknowledging her presence.

She grasped my arm and exclaimed:

'So! Aksel was right. You look like the living dead!'

I stood there like a bumpkin. Without saying hello.

'Aksel said he thought you were studying yourself crazy,' she continued, drawing me back as another carriage rumbled past.

'Oh,' I finally said – and let myself be drawn.

She wore light colors, like the last time I saw her. Her hair was gathered under her hat. Her face lay in shadow. In profile, her nose had an independent curve. A mountain slope covered with warm skin. I was so close I saw the small pink crevices of her nostrils. The light caught her mouth and chin more clearly. On my rapid exploratory expedition I observed a small pimple by her eyebrow. It awakened something in me.

'It's been a long time . . .' I mumbled.

Then she took my hand. I saw she said something. But I could not understand what. She was too close.

She began walking me along the sidewalk in the opposite direction from what I had intended. I felt I was disintegrating. Her elbow poked me in the ribs.

Woman came from man's accursed rib, I thought, and tried to find something I could say aloud.

If only it had not been so warm! I wanted to un-button my jacket, but could not do that with just one hand. The other was hers. She held it.

'Aksel said you were working so hard. You didn't see people any more.'

'Well . . .' I said. Pulled myself together and continued:

'Can we sit down somewhere?'

She looked around, as if suddenly afraid someone was watching us. Then she squeezed my arm.

'Of course!' she said cheerfully, and strode off as fast as her skirt allowed. It was tight across her hips.

I swallowed.

When we were seated at a table on Brolaeggerstraede, each with a glass of sherry wine, she leaned over to me and said:

'I've got permission to invite you to dinner. Sunday.'

I nodded speechlessly.

'You aren't at all pleased?'

'Yes, of course.'

'You don't have to come.'

'I know.'

'Are you going to come?'

'Yes! Thank you.'

I could see the blush spreading above the neckline of her blouse. As if her blood felt imprisoned and unhappy.

'Your blood wants to come out to me,' I whispered.

She turned bright red and drew her shawl around her.

'Don't be angry,' I begged.

'You're so . . . so tactless!'

'I'm much better than you think. Even if I've stolen *Peer Gynt* from you . . .'

She fiddled with the tablecloth and stared at me. As if wondering whether I was making fun of her.

'Nobody heard anything from you,' she said.

'Should they have?'

'You make fools of people.'

'How?'

'You just talk nonsense . . . What you say to people . . . It's not true.'

'What do you mean?'

'The last time we met . . .'

A sweet sense of having the upper hand spread throughout my body.

'Yes?' I asked blankly.

She looked at me defiantly. Blushed even more and did not budge an inch.

'You said that you . . .'

Dina would have liked Anna!

'Yes,' I agreed.

'And now?'

'It was true,' I whispered.

We were silent.

'And now?' she said, after arranging something in her lap which I could not see. Then she laid her hands on the table. She expected me to say something.

'Come with me to my lodgings,' I whispered, grasping her naked hand.

Her breath came in a long gasp.

'You purposely want to ruin my reputation.'

'No. I mean it.'

'I'm no loose woman.'

'I want you anyway!'

She tried to get up. I tried to stop her. Our heads collided over the table. She was hard-headed. But her glass tipped.

'Don't go, Anna!' I said, looking her hatpin in the eye.

The waiter came by and stared with interest.

There was nothing she could do but sit down again. I did the same.

'I meant what I said to you. Both in Kongens Have and now!' I whispered when the waiter disappeared.

'What are you going to do about it?' she said seriously.

'Do you have a suggestion?'

'Yes. I'll tell you after the dinner party,' she said in a businesslike way.

I do not know where the intense happiness came from. Maybe it was chemistry. Or sound waves? Or smell? Between us. In any case, we gave up, leaned our heads together and snickered. Then I stood up as gallantly as I could with a soiled trouser leg and a lap full of sherry.

We hired a carriage and had the coachman put up the top. Hid ourselves as best we could as we drove out of town.

'Do you know what Father says?' she asked after a while.

'No.'

'That I have an unrealistic relationship to the opposite sex.'

'Why does he say that?'

'Because I don't want to get married.'

I was suddenly on guard.

'One doesn't discuss such things with a professor,' I said laughing.

'I have to, when he tries to make me get married.'

'To whom? Aksel?'

'Who else?'

The coachman turned around. The carriage bumped along awkwardly. Hooves against cobblestones. Klakk, klakk, klakk.

'You can't marry Aksel,' I said calmly and decisively.

'Of course not! I'm not going to get married. I'm going to London . . . I have an aunt there.'

She sat smiling. Inhaled with closed lips and flaring nostrils.

'Did you come looking for me to tell me this?'

'Ugh! That was nasty!' she said offended.

'Where do I come in?' I asked as sarcastically as possible.

'I need you. A scandal will make me completely impossible for Aksel's clerical family. So I'll have to be sent away for a while . . . And I'll ask to be sent to London.'

'What scandal?'

'Having an affair with his friend!'

The humiliation was absolute. I kept my eyes fastened on the horse's rump, and wondered what would happen if I jumped out quickly and landed between its hooves. But I sat there. When I glanced sideways I saw she was no longer smiling.

'Do you have enough money to drive further?' she asked in an everyday tone.

'N . . . no,' I stammered.

'Then we need to turn around.'

'What will you do in London?'

'See the world. Play the piano. Be free. Be a woman . . .'

I told the driver to turn around. Loudly and angrily, as if he were a thief far off in a field.

For a long time we just sat there listening to the uneven rhythm of horses' hooves. I was desperate. This day was pure madness.

She wanted to get out at a safe distance from the windows of her home.

I hopped out to help her. Paid the coachman, and trudged alongside her. The happiness had vanished. The tableau was ended.

'We'll separate here,' she said with assumed cheerfulness.

'What do you want me to do?' I asked.

'Show everyone you love me! We'll see you Sunday at six then? On the dot? Aksel is coming too,' she said, and waved goodbye. Then she was gone.

Had I known before that women were devils?

I went from pub to pub looking for Aksel. When I found him at Cafe Sorgenfri on Brolaeggerstraede we were both too drunk to fight. He sat with a group of students from Valkendorf collegium, and did not exactly brighten when he saw me. Still, he shouted cheerfully:

'Well, if it isn't young Grønelv, out on the town for a change! Where have you been all my life?'

'Congratulations on passing the exam!' I said matter-of-factly.

'Thanks. Same to you! You disappeared like a hunted dog afterwards. Was it your delicate Norwegian nerves?'

'Damn it! You're the one who got mad and disappeared!' I said curtly, and squeezed onto the bench beside him.

I was not sure whether he understood anything, or if he was just bubbling over with relief at getting through the exam.

'We got ready for a party at Valkendorf. And bought champagne! We looked for you at the widow's on Bredgade. But no luck! And now suddenly you're here! Alive!' he snuffled.

'I know where he was!' a fellow named Otto suddenly shouted, slapping his thigh.

'Well, spit it out!' Aksel demanded.

'He was taking a pleasure drive with the professor's virtuous little Anna!' Otto said triumphantly.

I heard Aksel's silence. His large head shrank to a small lump before my eyes.

'What the devil?' breathed one after another, not just Aksel.

'I didn't know you fished there,' said one.

'I thought you stuck to hospital workers and barmaids!' shouted another.

Sometimes you want to hit somebody. But here it would be suicide.

'She invited me to dinner,' I said feebly, looking at Aksel.

He nodded.

'Have you got money, man? It's your round!' he said firmly, looking me straight in the eye.

I paid for the next round and the others stopped thinking about Anna. But Aksel did not.

When we had sung and toasted student life and women awhile, and stood out on the street ready to march in procession to Regensen to continue the party in the courtyard, Aksel was beside me.

'Let's go!' he said.

'Why?' I asked guardedly.

'This is too worldly for a parson's son! I need spiritual nourishment.'

'I'll take a few turns around Holy Ghost church with Aksel, so he can get a little spirit and fresh air!' I shouted to the others.

After they disappeared, Aksel said:

'You went for a drive with Anna?'

'I met her on the street, we took a drive, and she invited me to dinner with her parents' blessing,' I said lightly.

'Why?'

'Why? Why do you ask? Must I ask your advice before taking a drive with a woman?'

'You know,' he said more gently.

'Know what?'

'Anna and I are going to get married.'

'Yes, she mentioned that.'

'So?'

'So what?'

'You're hanging onto her.'

'She wanted to take a drive!'

'That's a lie,' he panted. 'It's you who pours on that damned ingratiating charm and thinks you'll get an internship at Frederiks Hospital just because you're courting the professor's daughter.'

'That's enough, damn it! Is that how *you* think? You . . .'

'I can tell you're in love with her,' he interrupted darkly.

'All right, all right! Can I help that?'

He sort of collapsed. We sat down on the church steps and swore in turn.

'Is it serious?' he asked after a while.

'I don't know,' I said.

'This is supposed to be a happy day,' he wailed.

'Pull yourself together!' I commanded.

'You've got to stay away from her,' he said savagely.

'You don't own her!'

'Aren't we brothers? Didn't we visit the madam in Peder Madsen's Passage together . . . you and I?'

'Did you tell her about that?' I asked.

300

'You really don't understand,' he exclaimed in disgust.

I don't know what it is about Aksel, I thought. Damn it, I think I'm fond of him.

'Damn it, I think I'm fond of you, Aksel!' I said with my head in my hands. 'But sometimes you demand too much.'

Then he started to cry. He was infinitely far from my image of a crying man. So I turned my eyes away the moment I saw him begin. He was probably more drunk than I.

'There, there,' I said, rocking him back and forth. He towered over me like a huge tree.

'Maybe we're doomed to each other?' I said into the air.

He blew his nose into his hand and did not answer.

'Maybe Anna is for both of us?' I wondered.

'What the devil! What are you thinking, man?'

'All right, all right! Don't be so moral! Weren't we together with the madam?'

He reached out his hand and nailed me to the church door.

'Don't talk like that about Anna!' he shouted. 'Anna is an angel! A flower, a . . . a . . .'

He could not find words and began crying again.

I lit a cigar for us to share and said no more. He calmed down after making a long speech about Anna's beauty and excellence. Some things I doubted, but I agreed with most of it. However I was careful not to show him whether I felt one way or another.

Late that evening we came to Holmensgade. Aksel knew a clean place there. Filled with brotherly camaraderie, we pulled ourselves together and knocked on the door. The madam came out in her white working smock and made a quick overview. Then she shook her head and yawned.

Filled with shame, we tramped around awhile. Quivering like moths blinded by light. Our arms clumsily around each other for comfort, we sang one raucous drinking song after another. Whole and partial verses. Life was worthless. Exams were over. The war and emptiness and women. Were they anything to live or die for?

We slept foot-to-foot on a park bench. And were awakened at sunrise by a policeman.

Back on our feet, Aksel laughed:

'You sure as hell livened up again, my good Norwegian!'

As we passed Regensen on our way back to Valkendorf, she was standing there near the old brick wall. Right on the corner of Store Kannikestraede. The night light made her transparent. Her head was covered with a white shawl. She held something in her hands. A bundle of clothes?

'Isn't that Karna?' said Aksel.

I stopped, but was too exhausted to cross the street to her at once. By the time I collected myself, she was gone.

'Wasn't that Karna?' Aksel asked with a loud hiccup.

'No,' I mumbled.

CHAPTER 7

Having slept off my drinking bout and dressed in my
good clothes, I went with Aksel to Anna's home for
dinner. Four other people were there besides Aksel and
me and the family. Afterwards I did not know what
they looked like or what they had said. But there were
two of each sex.

Sophie bemoaned that they had spent the whole day
polishing the furniture and dusting the parlor because
of the celebration for Aksel that evening. It sounded as
if he were the only person in Denmark who took exams
that year.

'And all the food we prepared! Dear me!' said Sophie.

'Sophie!' her mother warned.

But Aksel was full of praise for the efforts, and
complimented the food, the mother's dress and the
platters of sliced beef tongue. The latter was for
the men. The women ate raspberry compote.

Aksel, who detested parlor games, suggested
they play 'Boston' or 'Halvtolv' with the ladies before
dinner.

'Did you know we're going to have *kransekake* for
dessert? But first you should peek at the smorgasbord
table,' Sophie cooed.

'Really, Sophie!' her mother said sternly.

Roast goose lying on its back with paper fringes
around its carved thighs made me feel bold. I tried to
find Anna's eyes. They played hide-and-seek with me
under the chandelier's glow.

Desperate with desire, I tore off her dress without

anyone noticing, and placed her among the smoked salmon and beef cold cuts, the anchovies and salty red meat.

Then we did it. On the table. Her thighs curved willingly around my hips. I saw them through two carafes of wine and Danish brandy in the center of the table. Dear God, how golden they were!

Her breasts lay in the bread basket. I put my fingers around them. Held them in my hand. Opened my mouth around them. And later I took her lips out of a dish! They tasted of currant jelly and *kransekake*. A long time.

We did not take part in the table conversation. I was in Anna's movements. Saw only her.

Once I noticed Aksel. He sat stiffly on his chair talking with the professor and Anna's mother. I could have stroked his cheek. But one did not do such things.

After dinner the double doors to the library were opened for us men. That was where you could smoke.

However, I was not finished with Anna. She was not finished with me. But she had put on her dress again.

'She's going to disappear now. And then I'll have to sit with Aksel, the professor and the two faceless men drinking cognac and smoking cigars,' I said to myself.

I do not know where I got the courage, but suddenly I said:

'Please join us in the library, Miss Anna!'

First she stared at me, then she sent her father a questioning look. He pretended not to see it. But she came with us.

She broke completely with custom. Perhaps she would be reprimanded. Later. But it was unthinkable to reprove her in the guests' hearing. The professor wanted a reputation for being liberal and modern. He believed women should be admitted to the university.

Anna sat on a hassock at the professor's feet. Her back straight and her face serious.

To think I had not seen it before! Anna was a figure

from one of Mother Karen's books. I did not know exactly which figure. Simply that I had met her there.

The library was filled with expensive books. Suddenly I remembered the atmosphere when Mother Karen received a crate containing many books. The expectation. Sometimes they came from far away. The last year of her life a crate came from this very city. Copenhagen. There were German books too. Mother Karen read German, but translated in her own words for me. That was how I got my first German lessons. She read Heine aloud, constantly taking off her lorgnette to dry the eye that always got irritated, as she put it.

I did not get much out of the poems. Yet I listened without moving. Her voice uplifted me. Though I did not know it then.

Today I could sit looking at Anna and realize I was the only one Mother Karen could share poetry with. Even as a boy I understood the poems were full of moonlight and pain.

If it was daytime, shafts of light came through the tall window and did a slow dance with the furniture and rows of flowers in the wallpaper. If it was dark, she lit the tall lamp with a green porcelain shade. A cherub wrapped in black iron held the green lamp globe high above its head. The light spread moss on the book's pages and on Mother Karen's hands.

The lamp no longer existed. It got knocked down when I heard I was going to Tromsø.

The crate stood in the middle of the floor with its many smells. Dust, paper and old newspapers stuffed between the books to protect them during transport. A faint odor of moisture or mildew.

Once I recognized that smell in a second-hand bookstore in Copenhagen. You would think it gave me a warm, nostalgic feeling. But I stood among the bookshelves feeling intense physical pain throughout my body. I had to rush into the street in order to breathe.

305

In the professor's lavish, leather-decorated library I realized Mother Karen's bedroom was clearer in my mind than much of what I experienced daily. She was mine. I carried her with me.

The shaft of light in her room. *Uncle Tom's Cabin*, Hans Christian Andersen's fairy tales. Henrik Wergeland's *The Jew* and *The Jewess* and *The English Sea Pilot*. Everything lay there in the pillows and wallpaper at home. No one could ever light a lamp in that room without all the figures coming to life.

Now I sat here among strange bookcases and looked at Anna.

In the professor's library everything was larger, colder, more suitably masculine. The last time I was here it did not make as great an impression on me as now. Probably because then I was so curious about Anna I saw nothing else. Now I noticed the room because she intensified the difference between here and at home.

'Do you still read Kierkegaard, young man? Or have work and medical books taken all your time?' the professor asked.

'Since you ask, I must admit I've thought of reading again about Abraham's sacrifice of Isaac,' I said, taking the cognac glass he handed me.

'Well, the old patriarch couldn't escape God's judgment. Or what do you say, Aksel, as a theologian's son?'

'Theology isn't my strong point,' said Aksel.

'Yes, that's exactly what I didn't understand in *Fear and Trembling*,' Anna interjected.

The professor graciously poured sherry for her.

His talk about Kierkegaard was a warning sign to me. It made me reckless. I gave myself away.

'It's strange. Kierkegaard's words came out of the book in my grandmother's voice. She was a believer, and she read to me . . . It must somehow be a key to my search for a father figure,' I said, and sat down on an empty chair directly across from Anna.

'How . . . ?' began Anna, but the professor interrupted:

'A father isn't something you search for, he's there.'

'Possibly. My father died before I was born.'

The room grew silent. Everyone stared into his glass.

One of the men said something I did not hear. I waited until he finished, and then continued:

'Maybe that's why I react so strongly.'

'What do you react to, young man?' asked the professor.

'The righteous, god-fearing father figure. Abraham the believer, who would sacrifice his son to God without bothering to explain anything to Isaac, the person concerned. Or to his wife Sara.'

'So you take a single episode from the religious myth and look at it in an ordinary, human way?' smiled the professor.

The smile, more than what he said, annoyed me. But I restrained myself.

'If the father myth is a single episode founded on concealment and fanatic sacrifice to the deity, perhaps I can be glad my father died,' I said dryly.

Painful silence. Which was intensified by the professor's creaking shoes.

'Abraham could not say anything. That would have been a crime. Against God,' said Aksel indifferently.

I suddenly realized the worst thing about Jacob was not that he was dead, but that he concealed so much. That he just hung in a black oval frame with a stiff, handsome smile and was no more to me than to others who entered the room.

In that smile lay no warning. That I would be sacrificed.

'Just as a slaughterer purifies himself by looking into the eyes of the sacrificial animal . . . you should be honest with a son you're going to sacrifice for some reason. Abraham has always been dishonest and cowardly in my eyes, even if both my grandmother and Kierkegaard admired him. It's one thing to obey

307

God's commandments, but how you do it is something else.'

I took a deep breath after this long speech. The professor sat smoking his cigar with a wrinkled brow. Aksel looked worried.

Then Anna said:

'I agree with Mr Grønelv. I've never understood how Kiekegaard could ignore something so important as that concealment is a sin too. One who's to be sacrificed should know why.'

The other man without a face said something I did not feel like listening to. When he finished, the professor said:

'You young people are so absolute. You have no sense of dimension, of the myth's true message.'

'What do you mean?' I asked politely.

'Well, yes, what do I mean . . . ? Abraham was chosen by God to make a sacrifice. He also had to bear the burden of concealing what it involved from those he loved most. His relationship to people was subjugated to his relationship to God.'

'I don't see why he couldn't have done both. Told Isaac and his mother that Isaac had to die,' said Anna.

'And what do you think Sara would have done?' Aksel interjected with a sigh. The conversation clearly bored him.

'She'd sacrifice her son to remain friends with her husband, who in turn had to remain in his God's good graces,' said Anna boldly.

'And Isaac?' asked the professor, sounding as if he was enjoying himself.

'He'd have to let himself be sacrificed because he had nowhere to hide,' I replied.

'Interesting,' he said.

His glance went from Anna to me. And back to Anna.

The black-and-white-clad maid entered and said coffee was being served in the drawing room. I gave in again. When everyone turned their backs to leave, I boldly let my hand touch Anna's wrist. She did not withdraw it. Just looked attentively at her father, who was already expounding on modern medical training.

And Aksel? Did he see us? Strangely enough, that did not worry me.

'It's very important to have close connections among hospitals. And head doctors must fulfill their duty to hold clinical lectures for students. Also, we need a better system to ensure that medical students volunteer in a hospital as early in their training as possible.'

'Yes, it's a shame that for so long doctors have been able to practice medicine without any internship experience,' Aksel observed, with a watchful eye on Anna and me.

We seated ourselves around a low coffee table. The women too. I shamelessly wedged myself between Aksel and Anna.

Aksel gave me a disdainful look.

'Benjamin has certainly been a good example. You've had experience in both war and childbirth, haven't you?' he said with a sarcastic smile. As sarcastic as only a good friend can permit himself to be.

He was referring to a time I helped deliver a breech baby.

'Experience in delivering babies isn't a matter of course,' said Anna's mother. 'One can surely demand a certain modesty, a certain respect for privacy, even if doctors need training.'

'The fact is, we've come no further than to give clinical training in childbirth only to doctors who've finished medical school,' the professor said mildly, and patted his wife's hand. Then he continued:

'I think students need at least two semesters before they are mature enough to perform such services. But we need a better internship system for practical clinical training.'

'Yes, but you must remember that female illnesses should not be made public for just anyone,' said the hostess firmly.

'I'm sorry, but I must disagree. You can't take modesty into consideration where complicated births are concerned. It's important for doctors to know more than midwives about such things. It can save lives,' I said.

I should not have said that. I saw on Anna's face I should not have said that.

'Of course. But you mustn't insult women by using them as objects of investigation. That's tasteless, young man,' said Anna's mother.

I had obviously offended her.

'A doctor can't be compared with other men,' said the professor in a conciliatory tone.

'He's still a man,' Anna's mother said sharply.

'I still think we should be glad this young man doesn't avoid painful practical tasks, my dear,' said the professor.

'Uff! All this medical talk is boring! Can't we talk about summer? About our trips to the country?' said Sophie.

'Are you going home to Hålogaland now?' the professor asked me.

'That's not decided yet. It's not easy to get an internship in the city hospitals here. At least not right away.'

'I'm trying to convince him to come home with me,' said Aksel.

I guess I looked at him open-mouthed.

'I'd like an invitation in return,' he added teasingly.

'How nice, then maybe you can attend the engagement party,' Sophie burst out.

There was a painful silence, until Aksel said:

'Exactly!'

'Oh dear! I hope I didn't say anything that was supposed to be a secret? Benjamin Grønelv is Aksel's good friend, isn't he?' Sophie said flushing.

'Of course!' Aksel said with satisfaction.

I do not think I said another word in the conversation. Just sat and stared at Anna.

After a while the hosts let us understand the dinner party had lasted more than long enough. Aksel got up to go, and we left. Together.

As we stood in the hall saying goodbye, I clung to her hands. Sucked myself into her eyes. Tried to touch her brain, so she would understand.

I was unable to ask her. If she understood.

I tramped with stifled anger down the tree-lined avenue, my hands behind my back. He followed, whistling nonchalantly with both hands in his pockets.

'You can't marry her!' I said furiously.

'You're going to be my best man.'

'Go to hell . . .'

'Now, now! Don't get excited. Let's have a schnapps before going to bed.'

'I don't enjoy drinking with you any more.'

'For heaven's sake, let's not quarrel.'

'Why not?'

'There, you said it! Finally! Are we rivals?'

'No!' I said.

'Well then, say you'll come! At least to the engagement party.'

'No! She doesn't want you!'

'Of course she wants me,' he laughed good-naturedly.

He trotted up to me. Then began shouting and singing at the top of his lungs.

'I'll tell her you go to whores,' I said maliciously.

He stopped and turned towards me.

'You wouldn't be such a damn coward!' he said.

His eyes and mouth were narrow lines in a moon landscape.

'But you don't love her!' I said as calmly as possible.

He stopped short. Carefully took hold of my jacket lapels and forced my face up to his.

'You're the one who doesn't love her!' he snarled.

'Do you know more about love than I do?' I said, tearing myself loose.

'This isn't some damn relay race in love,' he said furiously.

'What is it then?'

'We're talking about finding a wife one can endure things with. Anna has class. And she's not . . .'

He got no further. I do not know where the hell it came from! But suddenly I started crying. Did not know myself how it happened. I tearfully excused it by saying that I had been studying so hard and staying up so late. That I could not tolerate the cognac and wine.

We stood in the middle of Kongens Nytorv. People stopped and stared. Some laughed, shrugged their shoulders and walked past slowly while turning their heads. Two young louts confronted us. One laughed, and the other mimicked me impressively.

I heard a sound like crushed cartilage. A moment later the fellow who mimicked me was lying on his back. Aksel had thrown him to the cobblestones. Two women screamed. A crowd of theater-goers stopped.

'What's wrong here?' asked a man in a top hat and cutaway.

'The fellow on the street spat on my friend, who's crying because he's unhappy!' said Aksel furiously.

The group glanced at the young man on the street. The women wrinkled their noses. Then they left.

A police constable was already hurrying towards us. Speaking with authority, he too wanted to know what happened. Aksel repeated what he had said before. But now the fellow had revived enough to begin scolding us loudly. He should not have done that. The world is not fair to people like him. The constable accepted Aksel's explanation, took the young man by the collar, and off they went.

We were impeccably dressed. And I had not said a word.

When once again we were as alone as it is possible to be at Kongens Nytorv, Aksel snarled:

'Now I want that schnapps even if it costs me my life of freedom!'

I trudged alongside him.

After three schnapps in eloquent silence at the Apothek, Aksel said carefully:

'You do understand you can't have her?'

I stared at him furiously without replying.

'Do you want to marry her? Bring her to that god-forsaken place you come from?'

I still did not say a word.

'She'd come running back to me within two months,' he said dejectedly.

'Go to hell!' I replied bitterly.

'You're welcome to follow!'

We sat for a while.

Two students at the neighboring table had trouble staying on their chairs and were advised by the bar-tender to head home to Regensen before they had to be taken in a wheelbarrow.

'You're a hypocrite,' Aksel suddenly said in the same tone as the bartender.

The word 'hypocrite' brought me to life.

'What right do you have to say that?'

'You tease girls like a cat with a mouse. But when it's somebody else's girl, you do everything possible to get her.'

'I don't tease girls.'

'Yes, you do!'

'When? What girls?'

He rattled them off. Had an incredible ability to remember names. It must have been due to memorizing all those hymns in his childhood.

'Whew!' I said without defending myself.

'We wondered if you'd got syphilis, since you stopped so suddenly, and finally passed your exams instead.'

'Who wondered?'

'Oh . . . several people. Including Anna.'

'Did you discuss this with Anna? You filthy bastard!'

'No, she discussed it with me.'

I slumped despondently in my chair.

313

'And what did you say about me when she asked?'

He shrugged, and downed the rest of his schnapps. Wiped his mouth.

'That I didn't know what to believe. You just lived in your room with your books. You'd got as skinny as a scarecrow, and hardly washed yourself . . .'

'What did she say?'

'That you ought to be rescued.'

Suddenly I realized it was not by accident she met me on the street. I needed to be rescued! But why? Because she cared about me?

'She doesn't want you!' I threatened.

'She'll come to want me.'

I spat on the floor to demonstrate my disgust and protest.

'She's going to run off to London!' I burst out.

Now I had betrayed her, I told myself.

But Aksel looked at me calmly.

'Women of good families don't run off, even if they talk about it,' he said.

We were on the verge of real drunkenness. It was not a happy intoxication. We sat without speaking for a while. Finally he gave me a friendly clap on the shoulder and said:

'Let's stop this now, Benjamin. I'll have one more. We don't have much time left. Together. Student life is over soon . . . It's been good. I'm going to . . . Yes, damn it, I'm going to miss you! But we'll get internships at Frederiks. We'll see each other there!'

He clapped my shoulder again.

'Did she think I had syphilis?'

'That doesn't matter. You're certainly more interesting *with* syphilis than without it,' he said laconically. 'Women like Anna love to save people.'

CHAPTER 8

In the days that followed, Reinsnes seemed like a place beyond the rainbow. I did not know how I would get there alive. And certainly not how I would get back. For several years I had imagined I no longer thought about Reinsnes as 'home'. But now it surged into my brain and took form. It was like finding a childhood photograph album and sitting down with it, but not daring to open it.

I told myself I should go home for Anders's sake. And because it was uncertain whether I would get a hospital internship in Copenhagen.

On the wharves in Bergen I learned powerful forces were moving to establish an annual congress in Norway to keep the Swedo-Norwegian king in line. I did not get involved. I had been away a long time. Even felt a certain malicious pleasure that Norway needed to represent itself. I had not forgiven it for leaving Denmark to stand alone when Bismarck attacked. The thought still made me feel ashamed.

The further along the coast I traveled on the smoke-spitting steamboat, the more I regretted being on my way home.

A fellow passenger kept me awake at night with his snoring. And started the day about six o'clock by coughing and hacking. That he spoke my language in an unending stream made things no better.

I replied in single-syllable words. At the same time, I remembered disdaining Johan because he spoke like a

Dane when he came from Copenhagen. I decided to keep silent as much as possible.

My fellow passenger watched for chances to get closer to the table where I usually ate. Like someone making a great show of circling his victim. When a place became vacant because someone got off in Brønnøysund, he sat at the same table as me.

I knew I had seen him before. After a few minutes he began to plague me with questions. It was hard to avoid them. He had already let me know several times that he knew who I was. Without introducing himself. I did not ask. Instead, I tried to remember where I had met or seen him.

Now he sat down at the table with a self-satisfied smile. For no reason, I began to perspire. As if I were afraid he would reveal something terrible about me.

At first he was silent. We passed the platters and chewed. Then he began to talk about Reinsnes. In a high, sniveling voice. I was perspiring and felt increasingly anxious. It was not what he said that was threatening, but his expression. I alternated between ignoring him, giving short neutral replies, and being overly polite and obliging. But he did not understand the warnings. The situation became quite painful, because everyone else at the table understood I did not want to talk with this man.

The man was stocky and well-dressed. His large, elaborate sideburns made his face look much broader. It was as though you saw him through a cracked mirror. He had a high, thin voice. And spoke with exaggerated slowness. As if expressing eternal truths. He seemed to be constantly calling attention to vital messages. His words churned in me, without him having said a disparaging thing.

I became a little boy who imagined this passenger was The Catastrophe. From the moment he mentioned Dina as if he were a member of her family, I could not eat in his presence.

He said he had been in Trondheim on business and

let me know he was a thoroughly respected person. The underlying assumption of his own excellence was clear to everyone. In a roundabout way he told me he sold herring nets and that he gladly assisted with capital. The captain, who sat at the table too, mentioned the name of an acquaintance and asked if the passenger had sold him herring nets.

'No, Lord preserve me from that fellow! He's quite insolvent now!'

The captain said no more. No one said anything. So the man continued:

'I don't fish myself. I'm only concerned with refining "silver of the sea". Poor people get work. The wheels turn. Everything improves. As long as someone knows how to make it happen! But at Reinsnes, things have gone up and down. Isn't that so?'

I gave up and put down my knife and fork. Why had he focused on me, I wondered. Why hadn't he seen benefit in one of the other passengers? Was he provoked because I did not ask to hear more about his excellent qualities? Or was it something I did not know about?

'Yes, I heard from a reliable source that Reinsnes has had certain liquidity problems. But you know that, don't you? It's not new. Ever since the cargo boat sank. Of course the shipwreck was an accident . . . Anders is a capable man. But everyone has his limits. He probably doesn't understand about running a store and such things. It was Dina Grønelv who . . . Everyone knew that. Why things went as they did. People talk, you know . . . Yes, Anders also tried his hand with herring nets. But was unlucky, or whatever you call it . . . It seems Strandsted is taking all the business. He couldn't get rid of his herring.'

I had an uncontrollable urge to hit the man. Or to clamp shut the wide, pink opening in his face. Instead, I looked at the man's mouth with intense disgust, and decided it looked like a pig's hind end.

'I know your mother from the old days,' he continued.

317

I wanted to leave. The sun baked through the windows of the dining room. To leave the table, I had to pass much too near his body. My dinner was in my throat. He regarded me through two greedy slits of eyes, and would not give in.

'She was truly masterful, your mother was.'

The man leaned over the table and blocked my exit.

'It was strange she left, wasn't it? She had just married?' he continued with a contented sigh.

'Excuse me,' I managed to say as I pressed past him and floundered out to the deck.

In the smokestack's shelter, unseen from the dining room, I let go. Vomited, while sweat and shame trickled from my body. Finally I sank onto a crate in third class.

Third-class passengers stayed on deck day and night. Slept, and ate at their own expense. They stared at me in surprise, but left me in peace. I sat without an overcoat for hours.

As the paddles drew us forward, my energy returned. I began to lay a battle plan for how to survive the days and nights on the steamboat.

Point 1: I must prepare intricate questions for the man. About personal things. Family. Finances. I must act as if I knew he bluffed about various things.

Point 2: I must ward off all comments about Anders and Dina and anything concerning the Reinsnes family.

Point 3: From beginning to end, I must make him aware that his hawking and snoring are unappetizing and deprive others of sleep.

I grew calmer. In the end, I even managed to see the ridiculousness of the situation. I was on my way home.

It occurred to me that all societies have their own laws. Those which applied to the pubs or the medical faculty in Copenhagen were useless on this foul-smelling steamboat winding along the rocky Norwegian coast. Here, envy and malicious pleasure had other voices and other forms. I must relearn the

318

patterns well if I was to manage. I probably never learned them properly as a boy. Because I had lived a protected life at Reinsnes.

By supper time my plan was ready. I felt like an inexperienced theater director when, sure enough, the man hurried over and asked if my nausea was gone now that the sea was calmer.

'I'm very sensitive when it comes to being at a table with others. Sometimes stupid talk makes me sick,' I said.

The man halted his thickset body on its way into the chair, and his face grew red. But of course he did not dare to ask if I was referring to him. I had won the first round! But it did not last long. He asked in a seemingly polite way what I did in Copenhagen.

'Study.'

'Oh, yes, I heard that years ago. And what will you become?'

The waitress came with a coffee pot and I used the opportunity to change the subject without answering him.

'You don't have sons studying in Copenhagen, since you ask so many questions?'

'No, not exactly, but . . .'

'No, not every man can afford that. It's so terribly expensive. Was the coffee good?'

'Yes,' he said in confusion.

'Do you have coffee and tea and brandy in the evening at home?'

'No,' he admitted in bewilderment, and tried to laugh.

The other passengers at the table had noticed the strange conversation, and listened with interest.

'Perhaps you aren't married? For that matter, I can't say I've heard of you. Your family name isn't so well known perhaps?'

The man chewed hectically, but fell into the trap and answered between mouthfuls that it was true, he was not married.

'That's what I guessed. Please don't take it amiss,' I said. I enjoyed being a theater director.

The man lowered his eyes, then glanced quickly at the other passengers before beginning to heave in food again. As if he were stoking a steam boiler.

The couple at the table with us had been involuntary witnesses during both meals. I saw I had them on my side. They were going to Tromsø to visit a daughter. But beyond this I knew little about them, for they had said nothing because of the inquisitor.

'You mentioned Anders. When did you meet him?' I asked, and grimaced when the man slurped his cofeee.

'It was . . . Yes, was it in Lofoten in '61?'

'Oh? You did business with him?'

'Not exactly . . .'

'Visited him on the cargo boat?'

'No,' he replied evasively, and pushed aside his plate.

'But you knew him well? Had been at Reinsnes to visit Dina Grønelv?'

'No, not exactly . . .'

'But you knew about the business and the store?'

'Well, one hears things . . .'

'Yes, perhaps that's the best way to keep informed where you come from? One hears things? And then tells others? That's a kind of business of course. Is that how you got rich?'

He could take the impudence no longer. He rose heavily. Braced himself with his palms on his knees for a moment and looked down at the deck. Then he walked from the dining room with a face like a sunrise and a forehead like sea-washed dried cod.

No one spoke at the table after he left. And I did not try to make excuses or carry on further conversation. Somewhere deep in my brain I knew I had gone too far. You could not take such thorough revenge on a person like that. Simply because his maliciousness was so much greater than his intelligence. He did not realize how deeply he could hurt people. Nor did he know the

320

mere mention of Dina's name started an avalanche of forces and feelings I could not control.

I alternated between regret and triumph. But it helped that the gray-haired woman nodded when I met her glance as I passed her the herring platter.

'It's so nice that daylight lasts longer and longer the farther north we go,' she said mildly.

'Yes,' I replied gratefully. 'I'd almost forgotten that.'

'This is our first trip up here. We're so enthusiastic we scarcely can sleep. It must be hard to leave here to study in Copenhagen?'

'Oh, it's probably good to learn, and to see things one doesn't see at home,' said her husband.

'That's true,' I replied.

'It can even be hard to come home again. Especially when you're the object of that kind of attention,' the husband said pleasantly, nodding towards the door.

'But you managed well this time!' whispered the wife, cocking her head.

That night I slept well, despite the snoring. Or maybe he did not dare to snore. I never got any proof. But the next morning he had moved to another table. And soon his inquisitor's voice could be heard across the dining room as he exposed a bankruptcy and two family scandals with slow marksmanship and a satisfied expression. His table companions silently bowed their heads lower and lower. Meanwhile, the huge paddles propelled us across Vest Fjord.

The man went ashore and no one seemed to miss him. The air improved, both in the men's cabin and in the dining room.

That night I awoke from a dream. Felt a dull pity spread through my body. I knew I had dreamed about the disagreeable passenger, but could not remember what.

The pity had something to do with seeing how malicious he was. Many people had witnessed that. But beyond the unpleasant feeling, I did not remember the dream.

*　　　*　　　*

I do not know what I expected when I saw the buildings at Reinsnes emerge from the green fields. It was hard to stand there with all the strangers. I busied myself seeing to the luggage, and rummaged in my travel bag a few times to check on some papers and two letters I wanted the postal clerk to mail. I took out eight skillings for the letters and saw them disappear in the clerk's mail pouch as the rowboat drew alongside.

I had an overwhelming feeling of being a total stranger. But I pulled myself together when I recognized Anders in the small boat. He was rowing himself. For a moment I thought I was going to cry. But I did not. I waved and shouted 'Halloo!' because I thought that was what one should do.

I had not expected Anders to have grown so old and gray during these years. Had not expected a new boat and an unknown young boy in the bulkhead. Did not remember the sea stretched so far beyond the holms. Or that they looked so small and abject in the sunshine. Or that Anders had such toil-worn hands.

I did not recognize the wharves either. Wasn't the paint peeling badly on Andreas Wharf? Hadn't the buildings shrunk? How could such thin curls of smoke rise from the cookhouse? And the people on the beach? Why did they look at me as if I were a ghost? Was I a ghost? Had I returned home, or was I the guest of strangers who had only read my name in the newspaper's passenger list? What in the world would I do here?

Was this how it should feel to come home after being away so long?

Suddenly I felt the way I had heard people say they felt when drowning. My life passed before me. Terribly fast. Dizzy and tenderized, I gripped the railing tightly and let it happen. And Peer Gynt's idiotic life got mixed up in everything. A coward, a cad and an adventurer. Like me. A whitecap utterly lost in the ocean. And when it finally came to shore, it was on a strange beach.

Tomas and Stine's daughter, Sara, had the regular task of reading the mail and the newspaper to Anders in the office at the store. Now she read that the herring were swarming into all the fjords and Strandsted was already overflowing with barrels and people wanting to salt fish for payment or a share of the catch.

'We'll take our chances salting here at Reinsnes,' said Anders, gazing at Sara as though she were his partner.

'Here's wishing us luck! We'll buy more herring nets!'

Anders pounded his fist on the desk resoundingly. His chin thrust forward and his eyes twinkled. He was like the willow trees on the flag mound. In storms they bent to the ground. But they did not break. When the wind died, they rose and shook their crowns as if nothing had passed over them.

Anders had noticed on the last Lofoten fishing trip that his night vision was worse. At first he blamed the Lord's bad weather which had raged all late winter, forcing fishermen to stay ashore and causing much damage to boats and gear. But it was not just snow showers and strong south-west winds. It was something about his eyesight itself, he complained.

Tomas gave me a friendly look with his one brown and one blue eye. I could not understand why we had any misunderstandings before I left. But we did not talk to each other much.

Hanna was a witness to everything I did. But she was not there.

'She's fine. She doesn't come here often,' said Stine in her terse way.

Sara had grown up. A rare wild flower with a great thirst to arrange letters of the alphabet so they had meaning. Anders had hired her to read the newspaper to him this winter. They had a firm agreement about a large paper cone of brown-sugar candy each Saturday and dress material when he returned from Bergen next summer.

The child was born ancient. One foot dragged a little. I saw she had a hint of a club foot. Took her in my lap and massaged her foot.

She sat quiet as a mouse.

'You look like Hanna, do you know that?' I asked.

She nodded and settled herself more comfortably.

'You don't look like anybody here!' she said, gazing at me with solemn eyes.

CHAPTER 9

While looking for traces of Dina in closets and drawers,
I realized I was breaking the promise I made to myself
as a seventeen-year-old: never to make connection with
her unless she reached out first!

One evening when Anders was working in the office,
I went down to see him.

A timid wind stirred the treetops along the avenue.
The bitter smell of frost was in the air. I missed the
pubs and student life. All this nature gave me pangs of
conscience and made me restless and lonesome. I was
not a fisherman, nor farmer, nor hunter. Nor was I a
storekeeper. She had seen that too. I had done little
more for Reinsnes than Johan. But this evening at least
I would break the pattern.

With the last Havana cigars from Copenhagen in my
vest pocket, I went to see Anders, not quite sure how to
approach him.

He was clearly happy for the interruption. Closed
the ledgers and pushed them aside. Then he poured
us each a glass of rum and invited me to sit in the
chaise longue that had been there since Niels's days. It
was very worn, with streaming feathers and pitiful
tufts on the arms. Covered with stains from untidy
fishermen and drams that had sealed business
deals.

I asked what he was working on. And Anders
talked about the prospects for buying herring nets. I
let him go on for a while, as I nodded and asked questions.

When he got up to refill our glasses, I said without warning:

'I'm thinking of writing to Dina.'

He stood with his back to me, but I saw a small movement of his arm and at the back of his neck. Then he stiffened, and seemed silhouetted in the air for ever. Finally he turned and looked at me.

'Nobody can tell you not to.'

He handed me the glass.

'Do you have her address?'

He raised his glass to mine and drank slowly. Then he said:

'I sent letter after letter . . . To an address in Berlin. But never got any answer. I gave up long ago. I'm no letter-writer. Now I've stopped all that. I just hope she's got a good life.'

I swallowed, and felt rage rising in me. Had to stare at the floor awhile.

'Your letters weren't returned?'

'No.'

'Then she must have received them!'

'Hmmm . . .'

'But she didn't answer,' I said grimly, and took a large swallow of rum.

He said nothing.

'You have the address?'

'Yes, but she's probably not there. Berlin is a big city.'

'Yes, and the world is even bigger,' I said dryly.

He looked at me and said:

'Why do you want to write now, when you didn't write before?'

'There's a time for everything,' I said evasively.

He nodded.

'These have been hard times . . . But now I'm going to buy nets. I believe in the herring . . . What are you going to write? Don't say that things aren't going well. That's no news to get.'

'No, it's not.'

We were silent awhile, then I continued:

'I'm finally going to write about my hate.'

His eyes looked like those I saw when I picked up bodies at Dybbøl. There was life in them yet.

'Do you hate your mother?'

'Yes. I can't help it.'

'You're clever but harsh,' he said slowly.

'And you? You're clever too. Have you had the sense to hate?'

'No,' he said, straightening up and looking at me. 'I'm not made for gambling on such a high card. Hate? No.'

'How did you manage then?'

'Work!' He tried to laugh. Slapped his thigh and ran his other hand through his white hair.

I did not help him laugh. Acted as if I had forgotten how men avoided difficult subjects.

'Haven't you ever blamed her for being gone when you came home from Bergen and had lost everything?'

'She didn't send the boat to the bottom,' he said firmly.

'But she was gone when you came home!'

He leaned forward, his elbows resting on his knees and his hands dangling. Like a tired fisherman who comes safely to shore and sends his weariness up in smoke with his first pipe.

'She had her reasons,' he said finally.

'What sort of reasons?'

He looked straight at me. His look was so stern I was taken aback. They were not Anders's eyes. They were a ghost's.

'You should know that better than anyone, Benjamin.'

'What do you mean?' I whispered.

Had I longed for this for years? That someone would say: I know everything! Now maybe it would happen. Then it would be Truth. Could I take that?

'What do you mean, Anders?' I repeated.

'She told me why she left. Asked me to take care of everything here.'

I could not see his face. It was turned to the floor's darkness.

'She blessed me and everything I did,' he said quietly.

'Blessed you?'

'Yes, like the old patriarchs you read about in the Bible . . . she gave me her blessing.'

'Before you left and *Mother Karen* went down with its crew and cargo?' I said. Could not help asking.

'She left her blessing behind. In a letter. But before then, she told me why she had to leave.'

The oil lamp was empty and sending smoke into the room. I got up and extinguished it. The darkness brought us closer together. Threateningly close. I walked over to the window.

'May I see that blessing?' I asked.

'I burned it right away.'

'Why?'

'Someone might see it who shouldn't.'

He knew! My head was on the executioner's block and I waited for the ax. My mouth was dry and my brain would no longer function. It had quit. Anders had known everything, without saying a word to me!

'It was such a strong blessing you had to burn it?'

I tried to make my voice sound normal. Even tried to add some childish jealousy.

'Yes, that's right. She put a lot in that blessing,' he said.

'And you didn't want to share it with anyone?'

'No!'

'Not with me either?'

'Especially not you, Benjamin.'

I stared out at the black seaweed along the shore. Remembered being afraid of it on dark evenings as a boy. Afraid of its smell too. I stared at the moon. A solitary yellow comma on an endless, empty violet page.

This is what I wrote:

Reinsnes, 15 January, 1869

Dina,

I, your son Benjamin, am writing to you about Anders and Reinsnes.

It is a long time since you left. And Anders has heard nothing from you. He has had difficult years. *Mother Karen* was shipwrecked, as you know. All the others drowned. Including Anton. Nothing was insured. Fishing was bad two years in a row, and the store clerk had to be replaced several times.

Anders probably told you this. And it is not the reason I am writing. I beg you to let Anders know if you are alive, because he needs to get married again. He is what you would call lonely. You can release him from the marriage, or send a different message. If you do not give some sign of life, I do not know how things will go.

All is well with Tomas and Stine and their child. Oline is beginning to get old. The sheriff and his family are all fine as far as I know. Hanna is married and lives in Lofoten.

Your son,
Benjamin Grønelv

PS. If someone other than Dina should receive this letter, I ask that you reply in her stead.

B.G.

I rowed out to bring the letter to the steamboat myself. As if I were afraid the store clerk would see it and get his own ideas.

I could have told her how long I would be at Reinsnes, or that I had finished my exams and hoped to get an internship somewhere. But I did not write for my own sake. I wanted her to see that.

What was she living on? Anders had not sent her anything, according to what he said. Now and then I saw her sitting under the bridges in some city. With a grimy face and dirty, unkempt hair. Her body hidden in tattered clothing that had not been washed for months. Now and then I saw her on a concert stage in a black silk dress, her smooth shining hair flowing onto her shoulders and the cello between her knees as people solemnly listened.

Anything in between did not exist.

I tried to question Anders further about what he thought. But quickly realized this only caused him pain. She had taken an important part of Anders with her when she left. Perhaps he did not even dare to look at the damage.

Sometimes one does foolish things that prove to be a penitential journey. I went to Lofoten with Anders. More because I thought I would be a comfort than a help.

My job was to keep order in the records and the cargo hold. And to help anywhere else one could use me.

We sailed with the new cargo vessel and both *fembøring* boats. So there was more space for us and for the gear. Transporting cargo was a good business. Especially towards the end of fishing season when those with small boats quit. Then we stopped fishing to earn money transporting salt and other cargo.

I stayed in the cargo boat to keep the accounts. Anders probably put me there to spare me from frost-bite and rusty fish hooks.

He himself preferred fishing. It was freedom and adventure. It gave you infected fingers and a bold spirit.

'Even if fishing is poor, it's still fun. Everything else, everything you can't atone for, has to wait till after Lofoten,' said Anders.

It was a philosophy he shared with his men. They regarded him as a good captain. But something about him kept them at a distance. Something in the air around him separated him. He could be dressed in fish-gutting clothes and oilskin hat and blow his nose in his hand like the others. Still, you could see from afar that this was someone with authority. You could joke with Anders from Reinsnes to be sure. But you did not do it behind his back. He never used curses and devilish rules to earn respect. It was his look. His whole aspect.

I was glad to see that.

I tried to hide that I did not enjoy being in the cabins with all the monotonous talk about weather and wind direction. And the smell of fish entrails and sour wet clothes. I tried to make amends. For what?

I never saw Anders check my work. Yet I knew he did. I told good stories about my own stupidities. Then we all had a hearty laugh. But I found no chance to tell about my life or stupidities in Copenhagen.

I received status as a doctor not only from the Reinsnes crew. Sometimes men came from other fishing boats too. Sought advice about infected fingers and hangovers, hernias and fevers.

One did not bother about trifles on the Lofoten sea. That you had not had an internship made no difference. If someone needed a doctor, and people said you had studied in Copenhagen to become a doctor, you were good enough to use. One looked at the big picture. Calculated victory or loss. Life or death.

You got respect from being a doctor, even if you were terribly incompetent otherwise. Sometimes I thought a dunking in the liver barrel would have been better than the condescending esteem and oblique glances.

But when I said I did not want a full share of the catch, I offended them. The moment I said it, I knew it was a mistake. But then it was too late. They saw I did not take their hard life seriously. I did not have the necessary respect. Nor the will they needed to endure.

The witch's child could give away his share of the catch because he was a doctor. The witch's child had no need to be an adult fisherman, because he joked around in a coat and vest. But they did not grumble.

Had fishing been poor, as on my first trip to Lofoten, they might have done something to me. But this year fishing was good. That made them as slow to anger as the cod they pulled into the boat.

When Anders stood on deck in the rolling sea, his face reflecting the same calm as the mountains, I was envious. Anders was the sea. At such times, he seemed to need nothing else.

I did not dislike the men nor the work they gave me. But it was not my life. They understood that.

She had probably seen it, she who banished me to books?

I was careful about liquor, and about teaching the men that the world was a little bigger than back and forth to Lofoten. That would have been stupid too. Like under-evaluating an opponent just because he had different weapons from mine.

You only had to be brought to your knees once in a south-west gale on the open Vest Fjord. Or to lift onto a bunk someone you had treated for bragging when he was drunk. Then you understood.

We were quartered in a reasonably large cabin. But it was crowded nonetheless. Anders and I shared a bunk. I had a rack overhead for my books and writing materials. Nobody touched them or joked about them. But they cast glances.

On my first Lofoten fishery we had a fellow on the crew named Tore. He read aloud from the Bible every single day. Until people fell asleep. Everyone thought he was very religious, so they left him alone. But the first Saturday he tumbled into the cabin drunk, they realized their presumption was wrong. And when they reminded him about his everlasting Bible-reading, they discovered he had just learned to read. It was an obsession with him. He was almost fifty and had just learned to read! The only book he owned was the Bible. His only listeners were the other crew members.

In my mind I could see the man solemnly spelling out the gospel for a crew that fell asleep from weariness and boredom. While he went on reading and reading.

Now suddenly I thought about Dina and the cello. I remembered waking up at night because she forced the music into all of us through the walls. All night long the cello rumbled, wept and laughed from the master bedroom. I understood a little better what it was like to give something nobody wanted to receive.

Maybe you can make only one choice. Either you go into something and give in, as I did in the tanner's house.

Or: find the strength to break out.

In either case, you pay the price.

Of course, you can escape if you are a clown. Who causes laughter, but also fear. Fear, because everyone is a potential target of the clown's humor.

A clown can laugh at himself, but nobody knows what he thinks or the real object of the laughter.

But you cannot choose to be a clown. That's something you either are or you are not.

I do not think I am.

I was glad the man with the Bible was not along this year. I read silently and with as little light as possible. For me, it was a waste of time to share words I read with the men in the room. I felt no pride in being able to read. I had not struggled to learn how. It was something I took for granted.

My achievements were in flux. As if my life were more a passive exploring expedition than a battle. I do not think I can fight. I do not understand the rules. Once I had a talent for conquest. But I go too far, and get thrown out completely.

Is it because I am an unsuccessful clown?

*   *   *

We arrived home from Lofoten on 17 March.

Mother Karen's calendar stick said on this date you could go to bed without having to light a candle. But no letter from Dina had come.

On the other hand, I got an internship at Frederiks Hospital.

In May when I left with Anders on an early trip to Bergen in order to travel on to Copenhagen, there was still no letter from her.

Now I was leaving, and I had not given her a Copenhagen address. If she wanted to be a mystery to me, then I would indeed be a mystery to her. She would have to go through Anders.

Anders sat on the aft cabin roof, waving, when the schooner I had special passage on glided past *The Swan* and out of the Bergen harbor. It was summer, but Anders had winter in his hair as he waved the handkerchief he did not use for blowing his nose.

'I never liked blowing my nose in the tablecloth . . .' was a confession I remembered from boyhood.

Then Anders's face was slowly erased. His figure shrank. The slightly stooped neck. His shoulders. His arm. He wore his new pea coat in honor of my departure. It turned his whole figure into a dark spot among the masts.

Then the handkerchief blended into the sky.

I felt I was the grown-up abandoning Anders and he was the boy who had to stay at home. Maybe that was not important. Who was the father and who was the son.

The most important thing was to not be abandoned.

You could wonder why Anders had not asked if Dina had replied to the letter. Or tried to convince me not to return to Copenhagen.

Now Anders was going home. The evenings would get darker. The main house at Reinsnes would be large and desolate. With the hollow echo of solitary steps in drafty halls. And empty parlors with muffled sounds from the pantry and kitchen. Then the homeless wind would come and play havoc with everything. Large and small. Biting frost on the windowpanes. Worst in the rooms where there were no people. He would walk among the dead and the living. Yet he had no one to make the fireplace's warmth come alive.

I had carried her hatboxes down to the shore, and had seen her disappear out to sea. It had been summer. Even so, I had frozen to death a little each time.

How had Anders managed to survive?

CHAPTER 10

Copenhagen was hot in July.

For a few days I sat on Bredgade with the curtains drawn and refreshed my medical knowledge in preparation for what I would face as an intern at Frederiks Hospital.

Occasionally I had to go outside. I would end up in one of the pubs near Regensen. I met few people I knew. The students were either working or in the country. Aksel was home with his family.

I could regret coming to Copenhagen in midsummer. But I made the best of it. Read, slept and drank beer.

One morning I did the impossible.

Changed my shirt, made myself elegant in a top hat, and went to the professor's home for a visit. It was not entirely proper since Aksel was not along. But I thought an intern at Frederiks Hospital could allow himself to do such things. Perhaps the visit would result in an invitation to a summer ball somewhere. Or I could suggest that Sophie and Anna go to Tivoli with me.

A maid, who was probably new, stared at me with curiosity when she opened the door. No, the professor was at the hospital and his wife and daughters were in the country.

I did not ask where 'the country' was. It did not matter. I could not visit them there in any case.

*   *   *

After indulging in sufficient self-pity and loneliness, I went to Store Strandstraede one evening and asked about Karna.

Grandmother Dons came to the door. She was of indeterminate age, with a worn-out voice and face. But her movements were quick and her eyes alert. She must be much too old to work so hard. She sold newspapers. Swept streets. Did laundry for people. And comforted herself with an old clay pipe while she sold newspapers or had five minutes on the steps in the hot sunshine.

She told me Karna had the good fortune to work as a night nurse's aide at Frederiks Hospital this summer too. If things went as usual, she would come home and sleep a few hours the next day.

Her words held a vague friendliness. I had been away a long time.

Karna? Had I thought about her while I was at home?

Now she became a necessity. I had to see her. I mustered courage and walked to the hospital that evening. Went through Grønnegården to see if the oldest nurses, the ward nurses, were sitting outside with their cocoa enjoying their evening break. If so, Karna might be working alone or sitting in the small enclosure in the corner of the ward.

They sat on benches and chairs around small tables rotating their feet. Cups of tea and hot chocolate set nicely beside embroidery and knitting. Had you not known this was outside a hospital, you might think it an institution for women in blue cotton uniforms. Their buns and braids were fastened neatly on their heads, but their aprons were not always completely clean.

When you heard their voices or laughter, you realized the nurses were camouflaged women.

I assumed a natural expression, as if I had an obvious errand. But I chose to go through the back courtyard. Only once did I see an old nurse cross the corridor. I

337

paused then, as if waiting for someone. It was unwise to let such women question you. They were worse than Oline. Because even if they did not know how to keep up with 'antiseptic development', as the professors called it, they were veritable dragons where discipline was concerned.

Grandmother had said Karna worked in 'XY' on the top floor, known as The Attic. I knew that part of the hospital. You got there by a steep, narrow staircase. The story was told about a newly operated-on patient who fell out of the basket and down three flights because nobody took time to put a lid on the basket. Fortunately, the patient was already at the hospital.

The Attic consisted of two wards. One for women and one for men. As far as I recalled, there were just three beds in each. This was where they put patients who had contagious diseases or were delirious.

I also remembered that the head nurse in The Attic was kindness personified and that she used to make *epleskiver* for supper if she had time. She made the small apple-filled pastries on a stove in the dark hall up there.

Sure enough, you could smell baked apples far down the stairs.

She stood by the stove. Karna! Half hidden behind a cabinet and a chest of drawers which there was surely no space for in the 'room'. That's what they called the small enclosure for the nurses' use in the corner of the ward.

When I got upstairs I smelled more than apples. The odor from the toilet was unmistakable. The buckets were not emptied until midnight, so this was the end of a long day.

It was not so bad you could not stand it. And you could determine that none of the patients had diarrhea.

I looked at her back and her waist. She had not heard me come. A voracious cough from one ward drowned

338

out everything. Her uniform was too big, and her apron straps and waistband too wide. Still, her curves sprang towards me willingly. She had tucked her hair inside her kerchief the way I remembered from the field hospital.

I grew sentimental and excited at the same time. Strange as that may seem. I had a raw desire to force myself into her from behind, and at the same time almost wept.

The door to one ward was ajar. The light from the green lampshades by the beds cast its glow into the hall. You could imagine that Karna stood by a stove in a wild green forest waiting for me to take her from behind.

A gray cat stole from beneath her skirts and came towards me mewing. She turned then, and saw me. I do not know if she looked happy, but she smiled.

Someone cleared his throat and spat heartily in there under the green forest light.

'You?' she said.

'Yes,' I said.

It was always like that with Karna. The moment I was alone with her, she became a state of being. A force in my body. I could not separate her from myself. I could not separate her from my body until I had her.

'How did you get in?'

'The back courtyard. Past the piles of bedpans and bloody sheets,' I whispered lustfully.

'She might come!' she said when I pressed myself to her and held her hips.

'She' was the ward nurse.

'She's sitting in Grønnegården embroidering and drinking cocoa,' I said.

'You're lying! She's got a headache and went home to sleep. I have to serve the apples,' she said calmly, and put her arms around my neck.

'I'll wait,' I said, my mouth on hers.

'No, you can't stay here. The girl before me was fired because a man visited her behind the stove while the

339

nurse took a nap in the "room",' she whispered, her arms tighter around my neck.

'So no one will think you'd dare to do the same,' I said.

It immediately became an obsession. To take her behind the cabinet there in The Attic.

New rounds of coughing and hawking began in the ward. Someone came up the stairs, but the footsteps stopped at the floor below. She quickly pulled herself free and left with the apples. But first she put a glowing hot *epleskive* against my lips to make me back away.

The toilet barrels were emptied and the noise from the heavy barrel wagons had died away long ago. For a while I sat quiet as a mouse on a chair behind the cabinet while Karna went back and forth with bedpans, spittoons, urine bottles and cloths covered with blood, slime and snot.

With excited pleasure I watched her body walk through the doorways. The green lamplight met the blue light of the night sky coming through the small attic windows. When the light struck the wall it disturbed the cockroaches' enjoyment of life and they fled into the corners in great hordes. I was as excited as the cockroaches. The cat, however, lay calmly in my lap. Once it rose and, with silky soft tread, turned clockwise in my lap. On balls and a swollen organ.

Also, the ward nurse returned unexpectedly. But the hall was dark enough for me to disappear among some bedding hanging behind the cabinet. The cat almost gave me away. But a friendly kick made it understand I needed to be alone.

The old woman sighed and complained about her headache, and asked if everything was all right. Karna chirped a long 'yes', and said she could certainly manage alone for the rest of the night.

'The rules . . .' sighed the old woman, and went her rounds in the wards.

I realized if I did not leave now I risked her seeing

me when she came into the hall again. So I scurried down and hid under the stairway.

Despite the rules, the old lady was on our side and went back to a bed somewhere.

After a while I heard snoring from two rooms behind the wall. The patients were asleep. Soon I would be a released prisoner! Life was full of immediate meaning.

Karna came to the door. She held one hand over her mouth and with the other beckoned to me. I pointed behind the cabinet. I had thought about what to do. To move the bedpans a little and put her on the table with her opening towards me. A suitably low table. In fact, it would look quite decent with her skirts around me.

But she did not want to go there. She drew me into the ward, past a screen she had already placed in front of the only bed occupied by a patient. He was sleeping noisily under the green oil lamp.

Then we were in the 'room'. A dark corner with Karna.

It had been so long! She smelled of oatmeal compresses and arnica liniment, baked apples and fresh perspiration. With a dangerous underlying scent of pus and sweet blood. Secret and internal. Fresh and damp.

I gasped for breath.

We had exactly what we needed for the occasion. A sofa by a wall. The table and chair were not used that night. She did not want to be taken on the table. Besides, its legs were probably not strong enough.

We floated in secretions and heavy breathing in the 'room' in The Attic. Two *alen* wide and five *alen* long surrounded by thin walls. We did not dare to do much about taking off and putting on clothes. Precise resourcefulness and trembling impatience can take you far.

Karna! Bless your absolute concentration, even when the coughing patient turned and groaned his pain over us! Bless your ability to look beyond scabs and pus, hemorrhages, and unwashed flasks and containers.

Bedpans! Those droll earthenware dishes with leather rings stuffed with horsehair. They never got completely clean, you know! Karna!

You initiated me into internship at Frederiks Hospital. You did that! Even after I had insisted to Bang that 'the spinal cord is the brain's tail'.

Karna!

Later I got self-confidence and 300 *riksdaler* in internship pay. But this night we did not say much. It was not a place for talking. It was a time for action.

I whispered her name once. That was too much. She closed my mouth and rode away with me.

Afterwards I stole down the stairs, light as a night moth. Here and there I stumbled in the darkness between the rays of green light coming through cracks in the doors. Between the odors and possible disclosure. And was happy to be in Copenhagen!

Karna! This was before I began to think like an old man. It was before I killed you.

It was while I still dreamed about letters from Dina.

Sometimes I awoke in the morning and could recite them by heart. But nothing came in the mail.

Autumn, on the other hand, did come. I was not to be just a night moth in The Attic at Frederiks Hospital. I was among the fortunate ones chosen to report for work as an intern.

The same porter I remembered from when I worked as a volunteer at the hospital sat in his little wooden house keeping an eye on things. He looked as if his life had stopped when I last saw him and began to function again the moment I appeared. Everything was exactly the same. Even the stain on his jacket. The questions and the tone of his voice were precisely as before:

'What do you have in your satchel? Where are you going? Are you expected?'

You could smile, if you could bring yourself to do it. He was clearly not as frightening as the first time I went through the iron gate. Before I took preliminary exams. Then I had greeted the porter as if he were the king's closest guard. Now I simply said:

'I'm going up to the resident surgeon's!'

He nodded distrustfully, acted as if he did not recognize me, and began to explain where I should go.

'I know the way,' I said curtly.

The resident surgeon recognized me. That gave me courage.

I asked about Aksel. Learned he was en route, as they say.

And where was I born? The surgeon wanted me listed in his papers.

When I replied, he said as his pen scratched:

'Yes, yes, that's right. You're the Danish-speaking Norwegian.'

I was not sure if he was making fun of me, so I did not answer.

'Then you're one of the ten who'll meet tomorrow. At 7:30 precisely, in P Ward where we begin rounds. We'd appreciate if you enter through the front courtyard, go down the classroom corridor to the narrow hall next to the 'church', and hang your wraps there. Too often the volunteers and interns arrive at the last minute and come straight in from Amaliegade with their wraps and everything. That's not proper!'

'I know the rules,' I said with a bow.

'Everyone knows the rules. But Dr Saxtorph intends that they should be obeyed.'

I said no more, simply bowed and walked towards the door.

So I had entered a new life. Reinsnes was infinitely far away. Anna was a severed arm.

When Karna was working, I slept, and vice versa. But occasionally I went to The Attic. Sometimes she accepted my need. But now and then she wiped off perspiration and waved me away. The Attic at Frederiks Hospital was no place for loud arguments.

But she accepted small presents. Especially on

343

Sundays when I went to her house with them. Grandmother still looked at me with polite skepticism.

One day when Aksel and I were drinking coffee in
Grønnegården I said, as if into the air:
  'Anna! How's Anna?'
  He looked at me quickly before he replied.
  'Anna is in London!'
  I nodded and asked no more.
  I got a letter from Anders. He was counting heavily
on net fishing and on salting herring.
  This is how our lives were.

CHAPTER 11

'War is a natural condition for human beings,'
Bismarck declared. He had made his best move: getting
all of Europe to remain neutral. No one helped France
when Bismarck came with his 535,000 men and turned
France's 'triumphal march from Strasbourg to Berlin'
into a bloody defeat.

People told malicious stories about how Empress
Eugenie sat in Paris and refused to let her husband
return from the battlefield with his tail between his
legs. In my mind I could see the sick emperor being
carried around like a troublesome object among the
baggage and war materiel. His royal cape was shabby
and bloodstained, and the last champagne cork had
been popped long ago.

When Bismarck overpowered the emperor, the
empress fled to London. Like so many others, I identified with the emperor and despised the empress who
fled.

Meanwhile things fermented in Paris. People
claimed Bismarck laughed and said: 'I'll give one good
day to the revolution in Paris. I'm on my way!'

And he was too. Suddenly Paris was frighteningly
near Copenhagen. The siege was a fact. An iron belt.
Which made Paris a prison. We heard about the cold,
famine and desperation. The wealthy had left long ago.
The poor remained to be starved into submission. That
winter was the worst in memory. They said Death had
two helpers in Paris. Hunger and cold. But it would get
worse. Hatred towards those who capitulated and gave

in to Bismarck fired patriotic zeal against the National Assembly and the rich bourgeoisie.

The Commune became an open sesame for the poor. Citizens showed themselves to be worse than soldiers. Madness erupted the May day the Versailles troops marched into Paris. It was like sending a huge fly-swatter into a swarm of mosquitoes. A man was worth no more than his shoes and the buttons on his uniform. Versailles shot its prisoners, and in Paris they declared that for each head that fell they would chop off three in the holy name of revenge. Paris was in flames.

Destroy, for life is short! Happiness will come later in a new society!

Finally the National Assembly declared Thiers a hero. He had let 30,000 people be liquidated.

Meanwhile, I went from Frederiks Hospital to Bredgade like a hermit in a windowless tower. The only thing that really made an impression on me was a recurring nightmare that Dina was in Paris. I saw her in Père Lachaise cemetery in a heap of corpses after the executions.

Night after night I saw her try to dig her way out of the pile of bodies. Then slowly but surely get pulled back into it. In the end I saw only the tip of her foot sticking out.

I do not remember ever noticing it, but I must have. The nail was missing on the little toe of her right foot.

After a while I had a closer relationship to my dreams than to what happened at the hospital.

Life was simply a question of getting through different subjects. The new remedy for sleeplessness, chloral hydrate, with its blessings for mankind and medical knowledge. Ether anesthesia. Or the subject of syphilis. Its primary, secondary, and tertiary symptoms. The cold fact that manifestations of syphilis in the circulatory and nervous systems were insufficiently known, making treatment inadequate. Although you could use quicksilver salve externally. Or calomel

346

internally. In both instances, the aim was to cause a flood of spit, so that for at least 15 days, 25 at most, the patient would discharge 3–6 pounds of viscous spit per day.

The night Dina's foot disappeared in the pile of corpses, I dreamed I turned myself in for the Russian's murder. The sheriff took it the way you would expect. He was furious that he had someone like me in the family.

The next day I did morning rounds in the wards with the whole group of interns and planned how to get through the legal proceedings. A young man with a wounded leg lay in bed number two. He had probably been in my dream, because he looked terrible.

The blanket was lifted aside and a new student from the autumn class was assigned to hold up the man's foot. Warm moisture and an indescribable stench hit us. Aksel would apply a new steaming oatmeal compress. But first the large abscess on the wound had to be inspected and commented on. The professor squeezed out great amounts of green pus.

The student holding the foot began to sway a little. I was standing on the opposite side of the bed, so could not react. But I managed to think:

'It's only a matter of falling. Then you're out of the dance.'

We heard a harsh thud as the student hit the floor.

'Carry him outside!' said the resident surgeon.

This was the last we heard of him. It was that easy. Just fall.

When I imagined my trial, it was like listening to long dull lectures about tuberculosis, which could be treated with asphalt oil. If you were treated early!

I already felt cold disdain for the judges. Who of course would believe my explanation.

It made no difference. Prison or tuberculosis. I dismissed the thought as a farce about suffering. To be human was to suffer. And to be ridiculous. I could not expect to avoid it.

For a while the students and interns stood along the walls in the corridors during their breaks talking about the Neanderthal man. I did not much appreciate having such discussions for the sake of discussion. The superficiality of standing in a corridor disputing one's evident lack of knowledge was nothing to live or die for. My goals were simple, but genuine, I believed.

I do not know when I first realized the Russian had returned. Through her. Through the court proceedings. The nightmares were often confused. One night I was an insect trying to creep under piles of old leaves to save myself. No matter where I crawled, it was to no avail.

She did not write! Why the devil didn't she write? Had I ever done anything to her? Except for something I could do nothing about: I once saw what she did.

At first I mingled my grotesque anxiety dreams with the professors' stream of words. Or allowed them to propagate between the lines in F. L. Bang's textbook, *Praxis Medica Systematice Exposita*. It was from 1789 and hopelessly old-fashioned. I read it as a curiosity, to have citations to pound the table with when I wanted to document the world's complete folly. That matched my mood.

Everything was a matter of theoretical illness and absolute death. Nature, the trees, flowers and animals were a Utopia. You did not see them much there among the cobblestones and tall brick buildings. Even the large trees in the parks and along the streets were already dead. All that was needed was a war. A spark from a match. Leaving nothing but charred remains. That fascinated me. I looked for fires, street fights and tragic newspaper headlines, like an old pimp who haunts houses of pleasure long after all pleasure and profit are gone.

*   *   *

It was October 1871.

Karna and I did not have many conversations. She did not carry on conversations. Not with words. Her eyes did. And her hands.

But on this day we had a conversation of sorts. Later it became an answer book for me.

It was very early Sunday morning. We were walking in the rain from Frederiks Hospital. She had been at the hospital all night and I had been carousing with Aksel and a few other interns. I wanted to make her happy by being at the gate when she came out in the morning.

The smell of autumn pervaded the empty, gray morning streets. I walked with my hands buried deep in my pockets and my jacket open. The front of my shirt was already wet. Water dripped from my shoulders. From my nose and my hair.

She carried a large, torn umbrella. But I refused to share it. You had to be a contortionist to walk under an umbrella with Karna. She walked in fits and starts, like a restless animal. And might suddenly stop short, so you risked getting an umbrella spoke in your eye.

I tried to continue the discussion about war and peace that I'd had in the cafes. That is, I talked and she listened while thinking her own thoughts.

'I never understand how people can have enemies,' I said, and then continued:

'The more I learn about humans, the less I understand the word enemy.'

She stopped and looked at me as if I had asked to what extent rain was a just phenomenon. Then she took out a handkerchief and blew her nose slowly as she extended one foot and saw her sole was loose. Examined it carefully. Then she said:

'Do you have anything to eat?'

'Yes. Are you hungry?' I said bewildered.

'Do you have a bed and food?'

'Yes . . .'

'Nobody beats you?'

'No . . .'

'Then how could you understand the word enemy?'

She had irritated me before. Her practical, absolute manner. She could be silent for hours, only to suddenly throw out one of her earthbound hypotheses. Which proved impossible to refute.

'I've seen the horrors of war,' I said sullenly.

She made no reply, and began walking.

'If you don't want to discuss ethical approaches to problems because you're a woman and uneducated, that's fine with me. We can just keep quiet. Or we can talk about wounds and diarrhea and maimed bodies,' I said sulkily.

'Have you never needed anything, Benjamin?'

'What do you mean?'

'When you talk about your home, about your studies, about . . . about everything, it's as though it's all something you do out of . . . curiosity. Not out of necessity.'

I stared at her. She had attacked me as if I were a spoiled dandy. Hadn't we seen people die together?

'Every time I want to discuss something with you, you answer by attacking me. Personally!'

'Excuse me!' she said.

Her voice was weary. She began walking. Her footsteps struck the wet cobblestones forcefully, and were sent back to me like little slaps on my ears.

'Do you have enemies, Karna?'

'Yes.'

'I don't mean people you've quarreled with, or people you're annoyed with. But real enemies? People you could imagine killing!'

'Yes.'

'Who?'

She kept walking. I stopped and grasped her arm. Rain poured down on us. The bottom of her skirt was completely soaked. Her hair hung wetly in her face despite the umbrella. Her eyelashes were stuck together in tiny bunches that dripped down her cheeks.

350

For a moment I was outside it. Somehow I knew I would always remember this: Karna's eyelashes heavy with rain.

Now and then you get a feeling that what you see or experience is just a repetition of something you experienced before. Without being able to explain or understand it. I knew I would experience again Karna's eyelashes stuck together. Or remember them so clearly it would be an experience.

'Who?' I repeated.

'It's a long story,' she simply said.

'Tell me,' I said.

'No, not now.'

'Why not?'

'It's raining. I'm cold!'

'And if it weren't raining?'

'I'm tired, Benjamin.'

I said no more. All right. She was tired.

The church bells began tolling the hour. Six chimes each. They answered one another with different rhythms and in various tones. We walked across St Annae Plads as we usually did when coming from the hospital. The city was already awakening.

When we reached Store Strandstraede the day came tumbling out of entrances, through windows and doors. An arm here, a foot there. A listless face beneath a hat, an umbrella, hair.

Day and night mingled their smells. Stench. A full chamber pot got emptied in the gutter as we went past. At the same moment a newborn shaft of light thrust between the rows of houses.

It must have been the shaft of light that made me think about Anders and Dina's wedding. The dull sound of church bells from within the stone walls. The ceiling was so very far away. The organ. It did not swell, the way books said. It boomed. I had a father! I sat in the front pew and saw Dina come down the aisle with Anders. They were both pale. Deathly pale. Dina's eyes had no pupils. They disappeared in the shafts of

351

light streaming through the windows. The leaves of the big trees outside cast shadows on the two who walked down from the altar. They held onto each other while the shadows danced on their faces.

I stood in the church wishing Anders and Dina and I would laugh together.

I have not given up that wish yet.

So I took Karna's arm and leaned under the torn umbrella. There was a hole right above my forehead.

She looked at me. Gravely, somewhat blankly. Maybe I should have asked how she was? Asked if, despite everything, she was glad there was no longer war in Denmark? Asked if I could do anything for her? But, after all, she had said she was tired.

The church bells stopped ringing. We were silent too. I wanted her to talk to me. Church bells always made me think absurd thoughts. Now it occurred to me I could ask her about communion. I remembered that it seemed frightening to me that people received a bit of bread and a sip from the chalice. That the parson commanded them to eat and drink Jesus's body and blood.

Everyone looked unhappy when they filed down from the altar. They were supposed to be rid of their sins. But they looked as if they were condemned to death. Did they know it was not so easy?

'Have you taken communion?' I asked Karna.

She looked at me bewildered.

'Why do you ask?'

'I'm thinking about the church at home.'

'How so?'

'I'm thinking about sin.'

'Whose sin?'

'Mine,' I lied. 'Do you think forgiveness of sin is possible?'

'Yes, but it's such a bother to do it that way . . . To go to church for it.'

She sighed.

'Yes,' I agreed.

352

'If women had started that business of going to the altar to get forgiveness for sin, they'd have put long tables and benches in churches, so you could sit and rest while you felt your sin melt away. The way it is now, it's short and cold. About like releasing sperm!'

It was not the first time she said such things. Not even Cecilie would say that sort of thing.

'Oh Karna!' I said, artificially indignant. Then I laughed. Relieved because she gave me a reason to laugh. She did not laugh.

We had come to her entrance. She closed her umbrella and shook it weakly. The veins on her hands were blue and visible against her light skin. We walked through the large, wretched entrance.

The rear courtyard was full of smells. Fried pork, morning coffee, old garbage. The inhabitants' clothes lines were stretched from window to window above our heads. Up towards the sky I saw a batch of oblong cloths hanging in the rain. It occurred to me that perhaps Karna was out of humor because it was her time of the month.

At that moment the sky opened and the sun created red rips in the cloths. It was the second time they were colored that month.

As if she guessed my thoughts, she said dully:

'You can't come in with me. I need to sleep.'

I tried to put my arms around her. But she twisted away, and at the same time lifted her face towards me. Defiantly. For a moment I thought it was the rain. Then I saw. She was crying.

I could have asked her. If she was unhappy about something. If it had anything to do with me. But I did not do that.

I heard her footsteps. Saw her back. Bent forward in her well-worn coat. Her loose sole shuffled a little. It sounded like a cripple walking.

A slight breeze made the cloths on the line tremble gently. It had stopped raining.

*   *   *

353

It is strange to think that if I had asked her, perhaps I could have accepted it. But probably I could not have accepted it.

For a long time she had not gone along with anything I planned. My serious, theoretical conversations drowned in her everyday problems and tasks. Whenever I tried to elevate everything, the same thing happened. We did not speak the same language. But I thought I tried.

I was wet and tired, but went straight to Peters Inn and let my clothes dry on my body while I ate a solid breakfast.

Afterwards it was easy to figure out that she knew about the baby that morning. I do not know if she was fond of me. She did not talk about such things. Nor did I. Maybe it was the same for us both. You can never know what is love and what is loneliness.

I never learned who her enemy was.

I did not force her to do anything. Never promised her anything. Why should I be the enemy?

I liked her. Desired her, yes. But in reality I knew nothing about her. Or about her family. Knew only about the two small rooms where she lived with her grandmother and brother. And now I also knew she had an enemy.

In many ways, she was a pleasant acquaintance. She filled an emptiness in me. She did not ask about being protected, getting engaged, or having attention.

She never complained that I sought her company only sporadically and usually spent my time with fellow students. I had no idea what she thought.

As I sat chewing cheese and ham that morning, I decided to stay away from her for a while. Our strange exchange of words depressed me.

'I'll stay away from her,' I told myself. 'If that's what she wants.'

CHAPTER 12

It was just by chance of course, but that morning when I returned to my room a package lay inside the door. As if my life were a well-directed play. I forgot Karna.

The package was addressed in Anders's large erratic handwriting. The sturdy paper was criss-crossed with twine. The postage generously paid so I would have no problems.

I hung my jacket on the hook by the door and kicked off my wet boots. Then I took the package to the table by the window, broke the wax seal and impatiently cut off the twine.

Inside was a large tin box from the store. There had been tobacco in it. Anders knew much about how products could be damaged if they were not properly wrapped.

A special atmosphere spread from the tin box to me. Images of Reinsnes. Smells that endlessly begot other smells. It made me dizzy. I had to sit down while I unpacked the contents.

I was a boy again. Suddenly I could see Stine's face clearly. And her hands as she folded clothes she had brought in from the line. Dried by sun and wind, sprinkled with dew.

The smell of the stable, hay, earth. Fragrances in Oline's kitchen. The scent of sour dough and salts of hartshorn. Of flour and open bottles of fruit juice. Of burning firewood. The special smell when the men carried barrels of water into the back entry in early spring. Odors of icy slush and wet mittens coming through the back door.

Suddenly I remembered the time I carefully put my tongue on frozen iron. To show I was a real man. And the parlors at Reinsnes: *krumkake* pastries on stemmed glass plates. Cigars. The sweet smell of tablecloths stiffened with sugar. Dust. So light. Just a hint in the winter drapes at Easter time. The upstairs hall: lavender and stiffly rolled linens in the cupboards. The braided bark baskets under the roof containing Stine's rose petals and herb mixtures. The dry, safe smell of the ash bucket that should always have the lid on it. The toilet buckets before they were emptied early in the morning. The smell of people who lived under the same roof. Traces of what everyone knew about everyone, but did not talk about.

And Hanna! Sweet perspiration and wet hair. Wool stockings. The fresh scent of her skin! Which I had not known anywhere else. Which she was spreading around in Lofoten now.

I was suddenly overwhelmed with longing. For Hanna. For a chance to undo the times I acted as if I owned her.

In the midst of the images and smells rising from the tin box lay the Bible. The one that was always on Dina's writing desk before she left.

I do not know what I had expected. But the first thing I felt was disappointment. I did not realize it was she who sent the Bible until I read the letter from her inside it.

I stood with the Bible in my hand, opened it and felt the warmth from it as if from a living being, and then I saw the letters. Two letters.

One was from Anders. I skimmed it quickly before unfolding the other.

It was written in a strong resolute script.

At first I was not sure it was Dina's handwriting. I wanted it to be! Wanted it so much my hands trembled.

Then I doubted it. Admitted to myself that I was unable to recognize my own mother's handwriting. Tried in vain to remember the account books and order sheets. But could not.

However, from the contents I realized it must be from her.

Dear Benjamin,

I am sending you Hjertrud's book so you can have it or keep it for your descendants. I would be grateful if you came here to get the cello. It is not being used. It would be better off at Reinsnes. But the trip is probably too long.

Dina

The letter contained no information, except for where I could find the cello. The signature was almost illegible, as if purposely distorted.

Lack of sleep and my emotional state made me scarcely able to see. I paced back and forth across the room for a while. Then I sat down and wrote a letter to Dina.

After a polite, cold beginning in which I thanked her for my grandmother's Bible, which I would take care of even though I did not know what I would use it for, I wrote:

'As for the cello, I will not come to get it. I passed my final examinations with top grades, and am now doing an internship. After receiving your letter this morning, I made a decision. I will go home to give myself up to the sheriff and confess that on an autumn day in 1856 I deliberately shot and killed the Russian, Leo Zjukovski, with a Lapp rifle. Then I will take whatever punishment they give me. Perhaps I will get a milder sentence because I was just a child when it happened. I will say I was out of my mind with jealousy because the man came and took my mother from me and threatened to bring her to Russia. They will surely believe me. I will ask Anders to inform you. When everything is over, you can take the cello and come home.'

At the bottom of the page I wrote my Copenhagen address. Then I put on my wet jacket and went out to mail the letter.

At first I felt a sort of triumph. An intoxication. Which turned into anxiety when it dawned on me that I had condemned myself.

Søren Kierkegaard! What was it he wrote? I did not remember his exact words, but the meaning was clear: as he turns inward, he discovers freedom. He does not fear his fate, because he perceives no further task, and freedom is his salvation. Freedom to not do this or that in the world, to be king or emperor of the present, but freedom to know within himself that he is free . . . He does not fear whether others consider him guilty. His only fear is the fear of being guilty.

I was not guilty. But now I began to fear people's judgment. Deprivation of bodily freedom. Degradation. I shuddered at the realization that I had reason to doubt Dina would, or could, save me from guilt. And if she did it? Came home? Then we would both be destroyed by people's judgment.

But now at least it was done. The letter was written and mailed. I had told her what I intended to do.

Back home in my room, I sat down and began paging through the Bible. The delicate pages were dog-eared. The gold leaf was nearly gone. There were underlined passages and various bits of paper stuck between the pages. The first passage I opened to was the third chapter of Ecclesiastes:

'To every thing there is a season, and a time to every
    purpose under heaven:
a time to be born, and a time to die;
a time to plant, and a time to pluck up what is planted;
a time to kill, and a time to heal;

a time to break down, and a time to build up;
a time to weep, and a time to laugh;
a time to mourn, and a time to dance;
a time to cast away stones, and a time to gather stones
together;
a time to embrace, and a time to refrain from
embracing;
a time to get, and a time to lose;
a time to keep, and a time to cast away;
a time to rend, and a time to sew;
a time to keep silence, and a time to speak;
a time to love, and a time to hate . . .'

At the beginning of the passage some words were
pencilled in the margin: 'To Benjamin, son of joy'.

I staggered to the bed.

After a while I could hear a man crying in the
room.

I stared into a snake's narrow eyes. The snake was
Mother Karen's picture of Man's fall from divine grace.
The coiled body turned into a sling, ready to attack.
The tongue flickered right in my face. Then I felt the
bite. My fear had icy teeth. It tore my flesh and
breathed on me so I dared not move. Meanwhile, the
poison began working. I was trapped and unable to
defend myself. The room whirled around. I realized I
was holding something in my lap. Hjertrud's head
lay there. We were trapped in each other's image.
Everything happened both slowly and quickly. We
fell through years of events. My years and her years.
Hjertrud's saliva rose like fountains from her mouth.
Balancing at the tip of each fountain were air bubbles
that contained pictures. Dina was in the pictures. I was
in the pictures. I did not want Hjertrud's head in my
lap. And I did not want to be in Hjertrud's bubbles.
Everything was just dread and disgust.

But I did not escape. The bubbles with pictures in
them stuck to me. My face. My hands. I was both the

person who had to receive the bubbles, and the person inside them.

I awoke just before midnight. It was quite dark. The scant furniture was silhouetted like gloomy shadows on the walls. A crack of light sifted through the curtains. I had trouble breathing.

A dream still remained in my head and body, but I remembered it only as cold damp dread.

My glance swept across the table to the tobacco tin from Anders. Beside it lay Hjertrud's black Bible.

She got boiling lye poured on her and died much too early. It was a gruesome death. Not really real. Almost like a fairy tale filled with terror and horror.

Once while listening to a lecture on treating burns I remembered the story and felt a vague horror. The kind you feel when you look at a war scene in a painting. Or in a tapestry. Worn, sun-bleached threads create a pattern from another time.

I knew little about her aside from the story of her death. Dina never talked to me about the accident. She had been so young after all. Maybe she could not remember it even if she wanted to.

Once in a while Oline talked about it a little. But then it sounded as if the worst thing about the accident was that it happened just before Christmas. You could not ask the sheriff about such things. I learned that early in my childhood. He had to be protected against his anger, his sorrow, his galloping heart and his nervous stomach.

So Hjertrud had remained as someone scalded to death just before Christmas long before I was born.

I stumbled between the bed and the table where the Bible lay. The air was glass dust I had to inhale. I was still beside myself. I was a person I had never known. A thought not yet thought. A gene not yet used. And at the same time, a festering pustule of guilt.

I was in Hjertrud's pain. In the longing for something

to cling to. After all these years, Hjertrud's pain and Dina's fear of being caged had found me.

I had written to Dina and taken it on me. It was mine.

I slammed down the inkwell cover, shook the curtains and paced around the room to frighten away the dream. I wanted so much to be in Jacob's pictures. He must have some good pictures. I wanted to be little again, and longed for Jacob. Wanted him to come out of the black picture frame.

But he did not come. He had no skin, no voice. Was just a constant smile and a flat, handsome paper face.

I heard someone call for his father somewhere in the room. Or in my head. The shouts spread into the dim night light. As if they were a secret.

I performed surgery on the Russian's head. Worked so hard the perspiration flowed. Sawed, bored and sewed. Bandaged. Then I put him in Dina's cello case and set out towards unknown cities to find her and deliver the whole Russian. I tidied him up and rubbed his cheeks to give him more color. He was better than new. Because in the operation I got rid of the scar on his cheek. It was not a nightmare. Just a sweaty dream.

I realized the dream tried to get me to do precisely this. To look for her with the healed remains of the Russian's corpse.

I struck a match and lit the lamp. I was thirsty. The water in the carafe was old. But I drank it. Tasted iron. Blood?

I read the letter from Berlin once more. Then for a while I sat and observed myself. From outside. As if I were making a doctor's call at a madman's home and had to make a diagnosis.

Disappointment over the letter was just a reaction, a superficial infection in the outer layer. But the terror of accepting the guilt for the Russian was incurable.

In the midst of everything I realized I had not reported for duty at the hospital at the correct time.

I lied to the hospital directors, saying my mother was ill and alone in Germany, and bought a ticket to Berlin.

It is possible I regretted my heroic letter declaring I was going to report myself for murder. But I cannot recall admitting anything.

I believed I would meet her. She owed me a meeting before I turned myself in!

I thought when I knew where the cello was, then I knew where she was.

That was how I crossed the border into Bismarck's despised country. That was how I learned that when you do not find the one you seek, you can take revenge on someone else. And that was how I came back carrying Dina's cello, without having met her.

As I sat on the train to Copenhagen, she was flattened between the rails and the wheels. Hour after hour she sang continuously:

'Hate me, Benjamin! Hate me intensely! Hate me out of your life!'

I tried to get it to make common sense. Had to. Told myself I had read too many of the old philosophers and had become caught in the Greek tragedies. But in reality the tragedies did not exist. Only army generals and corpses.

The Russian should have been the great tragedy in my life. With the result that Dina was taken away to prison. And I went around at Reinsnes as a murderer's son.

Actually it became the event from which I dated everything. This was the only reality to which I related, no matter how many thick books I read. No matter what medical secrets I might discover.

Bismarck reportedly said: 'I couldn't sleep. I've hated all night!'

I told myself that hate was as fickle as love. It faded and disappeared in the boring sea of small insignificant events that make up a human life. When all was said and done, life was a question of getting out of bed

362

in the morning. Of making compromises with body
and soul in order to keep afloat. Sometimes you experienced joys worth remembering. But distinctly
important events were as unusual as a pearl in an
oyster. They often began with a grain of sand that
chafed and chafed. Sometimes the sand crystallized
and became a pearl even though you could not see it.

I could comfort myself by saying: 'You were the only
witness when Dina shot her lover. What of it? Do you
know who you'd be without that event?'

CHAPTER 13

When I returned from Berlin I concentrated on my duties at Frederiks Hospital. The demands of an intern's life did not leave much time for private life anyway. Morning rounds at exactly 7:35 in P ward.

When Saxtorph arrived everything must be ready to go. The resident surgeon, interns and medical students filed into Q ward. Then into the three M wards. We interns wrote the professors' endless dictations into the records. Then we had clinical lectures and examinations. After ten o'clock we often had to go to the 'church', which was what we called the operating room. After that came visits to the patients in private rooms.

I was glad I did not live at the hospital. Most interns lived in the pavilion above the pharmacy. It was nice enough there. But I got tired of people so quickly. I ate at the hospital when on duty, but otherwise hurried home to Bredgade.

Even the friendly shouts to Madam Frederiksen made me irritated or nervous. And I discovered other sides of myself too. Once I gripped quite hard a self-important dying man who kept shouting orders in a squeaky voice. As if we interns and nurses were his lackeys. It felt indescribably good to have him shrink in my hands and hiss like a lemming. But he did not get a chance to report me. When I arrived at the hospital the next day he had already been taken to the corpse building, which was next to the bath building and the quartermaster's small garden. I thought about

364

him when I rounded the corner and went home for the day.

'Now his body is lying in there,' I thought.

Contact with death and odors of disintegrating life fitted my mood. I isolated myself with my books and my work. It was important to feel how little life was worth.

Aksel shook his head when I began taking my morning shower in the bath building. A few times during the winter he picked icicles off the hair on my neck during lectures.

'You've always had a tendency to exaggerate. But I didn't know it included self-torture,' he whispered with a shudder. But I was clean.

Aksel teased me about my hermit existence, as he called it when I did not attend parties. I said it was because I did not feel like getting drunk.

Sometimes I went to Kongens Have and sat on Anna's and my bench. An utterly futile action. She was never there. The closest I came to her was one afternoon when I sat looking at the rime on the trees. The wind rattled the remaining stiffly frozen leaves. Then I saw her floating towards me. I knew it was just a childish fantasy. But it was nice anyway.

Aksel rarely talked about her. But occasionally he did.

'I was at Anna's parents' home on Thursday,' he would say. Quite naturally.

'Oh,' I replied.

Or I asked:

'Was the food good?'

Once in a while I read Kierkegaard's *The Hidden Life of Love*. But I could not make his tenets jibe with the desperate longing he revealed. Was it because I knew he had renounced love?

Women. Large open wounds of sex wherever I saw them. I took them with me and did grotesque things with them. In dream images. But I tried to stay away from their reality. You never knew how to make them disappear when you could no longer stand them.

I tried to discuss this with Aksel. He was clear:

'You're a worn-out whoring billygoat!'

I struck back of course. That was like me.

'You'll be in another category in a few years, Aksel,' I said smiling. 'Men who take women's bodies with them, but never bother about the women or the dreams. Your career and comfortable living will give you a paunch. Because you found a rational use for your belly as well as a woman's. A temple for appetite and sperm. If someone speaks to you about love in fifteen years, you'll talk about the latest medical discoveries. Or bread prices. I pity the poor woman's body that's with you!'

'I hear your spite, brother. But where's your sting?' Aksel said laconically.

'Haven't you noticed that married women always seem to be looking for something that got lost in the pantry? Or in the sauce? It's painful to see . . .'

'What about Benjamin Grønelv's own interest in women's bodies?' Aksel interrupted with a sneer.

'My interest in women isn't unique. But my unwillingness to haul them with me like miscellaneous cargo is probably more unusual,' I said.

'Yes, and this unwillingness became quite evident years ago. When Karna came to Copenhagen to look for work. But that didn't stop you from going to see her when you found it convenient, even if you winked at others in between,' he replied dryly.

'The hardest blows come from those closest to us,' I said to put an end to it. He had won the round.

'You can say that again,' said the fellow who usually presented himself as Denmark's worst preacher's son.

I could have asked about Anna. Just to tease him. Instead he asked:

'Do you still see Karna?'

'She's working when I'm free, and she sleeps when I'm working. How could I?'

'I'm just asking.'

'Thanks for your efforts!' I replied.

I could have said he did not have a monopoly on Anna. But that would not have helped. He had a monopoly on Anna.

On Christmas Eve I saw Karna.

It was a long time since the autumn day I walked home with her from the hospital. I had seen her a few times from a distance. But had not gone to visit her.

The operating room had been turned into a church and decorated with pine boughs. Behind the lectern stood a lighted Christmas tree. Pine twigs were stuck into the students' inkwells. So they were useful during the holiays too. Practicality was the first commandment even at Christmas time.

Down by the railing around the operating table was an old organ. It sounded like a street sweeper with a bad cold. To my annoyance, the clumsy tones moved me and made me think about Christmas at Reinsnes.

Then I saw Karna. There was snow in her hair and on her shawl. As usual, she somehow radiated unhappy healthiness. She glanced at me before taking her place to join the singing. I returned her look. It took no more than that. I began growing bigger as I sang Christmas carols with folded hands.

When the worship service was ended, I walked over to her. She had gained weight attractively. Was more buxom. It made it easier to smile at her. I took her hand somewhat cockily. It was damp and trembled slightly.

Her face was pale, almost white. With lovely peach-colored cheeks. Her blond hair was still damp with melted snow. Solemnity and calm surrounded her. She was the only person I knew who could be dead tired and still have sparkling eyes. Today they sparkled more unhappily than I could ever remember.

'It's a long time . . .' I said quietly.

She did not reply. Just looked at me. That made me uneasy.

A couple of interns who also were spending Christmas in the city waved to me from the door. They had talked about having a beer at a neighborhood pub.

I felt uncomfortable. Knew I should not just toss off a polite comment. Karna deserved more. My cursed conscience made me stand there a moment longer.

'Is everything all right?' I asked.

She still said nothing. There was something about her eyes. It was too much. I cleared my throat and was about to say goodbye.

Then she did something strange. She opened her threadbare coat. Like a little girl wanting to show off her fancy dress and watching to see what I thought.

But the dress was not new. I remembered it from the previous winter. It was becoming. Yet it was no reason to open up her coat.

Then I saw. Her abdomen bulged. It was not simply good health! She stood here on Christmas Eve itself and showed me what was wrong with her belly.

What did Benjamin Grønelv think then? Did he think: is Karna going to have a baby? What should I do about that?

Possibly. The seconds went by terribly fast. I took a couple of breaths. My friends waved again from the door. And I? I bowed politely, kept my eyes on her eyebrows, wished her a merry Christmas, and left.

But her belly had already begun to knaw at my brain.

As we sat drinking dark beer, I thought a few times: she probably wanted to warn me. She got into trouble with another man. And could not bear to tell me about it. That was why she had not contacted me all this time. Of course that was why!

After Christmas I heard she had been fired due to shameful circumstances. A few times I thought about going to visit her. After all, we were old friends, or whatever you would call it. But the cursed fact is: I let her belly devour my brain without doing a single thing.

But I was going to prison for murder! That was the whole meaning of my life.

Sometimes I asked myself simple, but dangerous, questions:

'What if Dina is really dead? What if that's why she didn't write and say I shouldn't confess to the murder?'

The answer I gave myself was always the same:

'Dina isn't dead. Why should she be dead? She just doesn't want to make herself known. Thinks she can control my life, the way she tried to control us all. But she's wrong!'

'And what will you accomplish by taking all the blame?' I asked myself.

'I'll force her.'

'Force her to do what?'

'To see me . . .'

'And what good will it do if she sees you?'

I got no further. Because I had to give myself a little boy's answer.

I developed a sentimental habit. Read passages in the old Bible like a preacher. And I also wrote a letter to Johan about theological questions. Reproached him between the lines for having been in Copenhagen at the same time as Kierkegaard and not mentioning a word about it when he came home. I did not do this to put Johan on the spot, but because I thought Dina would not like that I contacted him. If I could not correspond with Dina, then I could correspond with Johan.

His reply was friendly, but short. He had celebrated Christmas as Reinsnes with Anders. It had been a 'blessing', despite the uncomfortable winter travel. With regard to Kierkegaard, Johan looked forward to discussing the madman's writings with me when I came home. It was sad of course that Kierkegaard had to die so young.

He ended the letter with many thanks for letting him hear from me and with: loving thoughts to you in the Royal City from your brother Johan.

Karna's belly was not scientific hypotheses. Still it gnawed at my brain constantly. I set out for Store Strandstraede a few times, but changed my course on the way.

I saw it on him before we did morning rounds at the hospital. He threw his jacket two meters through the air and made it land nicely on a hook on the wall. Something had happened.

Anna had come home.

'She's become a damn good English interpreter,' he boasted.

'Oh? Then maybe you should try to get into the diplomatic corps for her sake?' I said.

The joy in his eyes froze. He said no more and slunk away.

When we were assigned to work together in the laboratory it brought us unbearably close to each other. The light in there was crazy. And the room always made me think about alchemists who wanted to make gold. And sold themselves to the devil to do it.

'I didn't mean to hurt you,' I said tentatively.

'I'm tired of you,' he declared.

'Excuse me!'

'I thought you were over all that,' he said.

'I thought so too,' I lied.

'If you're not, everything will go wrong.'

'I'm just envious,' I said. 'You're so damned . . . so secure!'

He accepted it!

'Let's have a beer together tonight!' he said amiably.

'But she's home, isn't she?'

'Yes, but she's got enough to keep her busy,' he said.

We continued making gold at Frederiks Hospital.

That evening we went to a pub that had a female

singer. Aksel liked to be right next to the stage. Smiling. As if she were singing just for him.

'She wears short skirts,' he said cheerfully as we stumbled in.

'Should I ask her to put on something else?' I grinned.

'Don't be so awful on a Saturday night. She's a good singer,' he said.

A thick cloud of tobacco smoke surrounded us. She stood on a small platform high enough above the worst smoke so that we could see her mouth move. Adding to the fun was a wretched male person at an old out-of-tune piano. A gentleman in a bowler hat and lorgnette thought Aksel was taking the singer away from him and began chattering furiously in the midst of the song.

'Shut up, man!' said Aksel, pleased to be attracting attention.

When the man did not give up and tried to push Aksel away from the platform, I gave him my cigar and tugged Aksel's arm.

'Sit down!' I said.

'Why?'

'You're making that gentleman angry.'

I got him to sit down. But he was in a fighting mood. Especially because the singer gave him long, loving looks.

'Sing the song by Bøgh! Do the song about Copenhagen!' he shouted, and threw kisses to her.

The gentleman in the bowler hat was clearly displeased.

She leaned forward and looked at Aksel, then she signalled to the piano player, who switched to another melody. Aksel got what he wanted. She sang for him:

There's no other city so cunning and sly
In music and nonsense and clowning and jokes!
Eight nights of the week, how the hours fly by
With Tivoli swarming with young and old folks.

The city will have twenty theaters soon.
I'll just let it happen! And only will say:
A girl in each cellar pub singing a tune –
Even Babylon didn't have that in its day!

Afterwards Aksel shouted for her to sing about love. He should not have done that. The man in the bowler hat got his friend to take charge. He snapped his fingers at a dog of indeterminate breed lying under the table. The dog was large and threatening. Especially when it leaped out and bared its teeth.

Aksel gave in. He had an impressive flair for giving up at the last moment. But his spirits sank, so we had to drink a lot of beer.

CHAPTER 14

The pounding was inside my head. I was a barrel being pounded. Inside and outside at the same time. A barrel with a definite zinc taste. I opened my mouth. Dry! Opened my eyes. Could not see clearly. I held out for a little while as I tried to orient myself in the pounding barrel.

Then I realized that someone had come in. Quick uncertain steps, heavy breathing, and an adolescent boy's voice saying my name while the landlady whined in the hall.

The first thing which registered when I opened my eyes was that I lay with my cheek against a pair of somewhat dirty feet. They were not mine of course. Aksel lay on his back staring stupidly at the boy in the doorway. We lay with our feet in opposite directions, Aksel and I. He had simply dropped off to sleep without my noticing it.

'I was here before. You weren't here,' the boy stammered, waving his arms.

I tried to climb over Aksel onto the floor. It took a while. Like most of life's serious situations, this one was completely idiotic.

'It's Karna! Hurry up! She's ripping apart!'

Aksel was a sandbank.

'It's Karna!' the boy repeated.

I got myself out of bed. Dunked my head in the water bucket to wake up, and drank at the same time. Swallowing underwater was fine, because that way I did not choke.

'Grandmother said I should fetch you, so we don't have to pay a doctor.'

I got my bearings while I dried my head. Pants, shirt, jacket. Medical bag. I must have known what it was about. Cannot recall asking the boy anything.

He and I had spoken to each other a few times during the period I used to walk home with Karna. But I did not remember his name.

Aksel swung into action. Movements like an angry bull. Copied my dive into the water bucket. Shook himself dry. A walrus in a rush.

'I'll go with you,' he announced.

There was nothing to say.

We must have slept until late in the day. Because shadows patted my face mercifully as we ran. Spring was an accursed time. We took only a few minutes. But it felt as if I raced through an entire life. Everything flickered. Someone had pounded nails into my head.

When we got to Store Strandstraede I expected to hear Karna's screams out in the street. Women usually screamed. But silence wailed over the whole block.

I had been present at births twice. In one case the child was stillborn, it's true. But that was a relief because the mother was unmarried. Three births were regarded as a good introduction. I clung to these statements, while my heart hammered its way out of my body.

'There's so much blood in there,' the boy warned as we rushed into the courtyard.

She lay with her hands chiseled into the bedposts. Her knuckles were white. She seemed to have just one goal: to hold fast to her own bed.

Her nightgown must have been white. Now it was a gray covering pulled up almost under her arms. There was not a dry spot on it.

Her body was arched over the mattress. In the midst of a contraction. The desperate birth opening looked at

374

me accusingly as Grandmother, who was kneeling by the bed, stood up and screamed:

'Help her! Help her!'

I met Karna's bloodshot eyes. But she did not see me. I was nobody. Her mouth was open. I could see she wanted to scream. But no sound came.

Mechanically I did what I had learned. Aksel assisted in a way. We were two pitiful schoolboys trying to put their lessons into practice.

The child lay with its back to the opening. I had no idea if it was alive! I don't think I even thought about that. I just had to get it out, before it tore Karna apart.

'Hot water!' Aksel said to the old woman.

'We've had hot water here for hours,' she wept.

'Run to Frederiks Hospital and ask them to send an experienced maternity doctor. It's a matter of life and death! Two lives!' Aksel whispered to the boy, who was already on his way. He was dripping with sweat. He had been running before.

The contractions came without pauses. There was far too much blood. I tried desperately to get hold of the slippery bundle. The head? Damn it, there must be a head somewhere?

My sparsely equipped medical bag was useless here.

'It's the umbilical cord . . . holding back the baby,' Aksel said in a low voice.

I stared at him. What did he mean?

'The umbilical cord. A knot. That must be it. Probably around the neck.'

Aksel spoke as calmly as possible. But it was nothing to depend on. He would probably faint.

I did not dare take the chance of using force. Aksel had made me realize some sort of life existed in there. For several minutes I was simply an observer. Almost hoped Aksel would faint, so something would happen.

It was now I should have done the little I could. Said I loved her. But all I did was increase her pain.

I was her executioner. Right from the first embrace, I was Karna's executioner. I washed my hands and cut her open. Stuck my hand and lower arm into her. The sweet blood fumes knocked the breath out of me. But I stayed upright. On my knees.

I had seen Tomas do it a few times with cows and sheep that had a difficult time.

Now she was only breathing and muscles. She tore herself apart. And I helped. In order to get it over.

'It's daylight now,' said Grandmother, gripping Karna's hand.

'When did it start?' I heard Aksel ask.

'Yesterday morning sometime. She was alone . . . I got here about dinner time.'

I had to get the baby turned. How can a hung-over craftsman turn a baby in its mother's womb?

'Should I try?' Aksel asked.

But I heard his voice, and shook my head.

'No,' I said, as my hand followed the bundle into Karna's body again.

That was when she gave up. Lay there, still and lifeless.

'Make her wake up,' I shouted roughly.

I heard the gentle slaps, but did not see them.

'Use water!' I gasped.

I heard the water. It splashed on her almost tenderly.

Grandmother wept.

'Dear, good, precious little Karna,' she sobbed.

But Karna was tired of war. It had lasted for years. She wanted no more of it.

'Push!' I hissed between my teeth.

Aksel pressed down on her poor body. With all his strength. Paused and pressed again.

'It's completely stuck! Push, Karna! PUSH!'

The Executioner commanded.

And at last she seemed to wake up.

She did what I said. Pushed out everything.

Her breath. Her wide open eyes.

You can avoid thinking about it. Think about other

things. But you do not forget it. The smell of the struggling body. The fumes. The strength of her belly against Aksel's sturdy arms.

First came the cry. It did not come from her mouth. It came from her belly. Hung like thousands of sharp, quivering knives in the walls and ceiling.

I held out my arms. Cupped my hands like saucers. Like a little boy ready to catch a ball. My eyes were riveted on the place it would fall. A defiant ball with its back to the world!

I no longer saw Karna. Just heard the silence like a distant storm. When I unwound the small body from the umbilical cord, my eyes met an ancient human gaze. A direct, coal-black stare. A red aura with blue and white lightning surrounded the little head.

A soft nearby sound built a nest in my ears: the gentle plop as the tiny being landed in my hands like a great sigh.

Then everything stopped for a few seconds. The movements in the room froze, as if they had entered a predetermined picture for ever.

Silence.

Until, almost as a reflex, I grasped the poor bluish, slippery thing by the ankles and kept slapping until it gave in and let out a sound. I stood up with the little creature dangling above Karna's body.

But Karna's face was shattered. It went to pieces before our eyes. She lay absolutely still. Her hands let go of the bedposts. Her knees arched feebly towards the ceiling. Round and childish. With a small hollow in the middle of the kneecap.

A groan escaped from what were once her lips. Her eyes were closed.

Was this Karna?

A thick red river flowed from her. Dripped onto the scoured wooden floor. Followed its own course. Created its own intervals of time along the bluish umbilical cord that still connected her to the baby. Then the river came in spurts. Found paths here

377

and there, and wandered away in the bed. The river from a hidden world. A world for executioners to hide in.

Aksel was busy tying the umbilical cord. Thought we had completed the first masterpiece. He had learned to tie umbilical cords.

Later you can always let yourself say: poor Benjamin Grønelv! A trained doctor. And a man. He saw people die when he was still a boy. Met death on the battle-field, and together with Karna in the field hospital. Still, he was unprepared. And no one had taught him that while there is still time you must say:

'I'm a coward, but I'm fond of you!'

Nor did I know that the reason you must say simple but necessary words is not to ease the other person's death. It is to make it easier for you to die yourself.

Grandmother took the naked bundle of humanity and wrapped something around it. It was a girl. A tiny serious creature who already had stamped me with dark distrust.

Aksel leaned over Karna. His words came evenly. A comforting purling sound. Refreshing. As when some-one pours water into a glass before the eyes of a thirsty person.

I stared at Karna's river. Red. Spasmodic. Spurting. Powerful. I threw my arms desperately around her pelvis. Lifted it to try to stop the flood. Sat like that a long time. To force life to remain in Karna's body. Get her to fight again. But everything became a fog in which I lost my bearings.

In despair, I tried to find salvation in Aksel's eyes. But he shook his head. Although of no relevance, I noticed the stubble on his face was unusually coarse. His pores came towards me disgustingly. Nausea rose in my throat. The walls flattened out and rose again. It made me furious.

A crazy voice suddenly screamed into the room:

'Don't touch her! Don't touch her! Karna! KARNA!'

Then I felt an arm around my shoulder. I shut my

eyes tightly to keep everything at a distance. Meanwhile, time began passing without Karna.

When I opened my eyes, Aksel was leaning over to straighten her childish knees. Then he hid the dried river under a sheet.

The back of his shirt was soaked with perspiration and shook slightly.

I was just an observer who happened to pass by. Karna! You must not condemn me! I didn't want it to be like this. It was just life that rushed towards you so grimly. If I could have loved you in return, I would have. Do you hear me calling you? You didn't say anything, did you? You didn't blame me? Didn't tell me to take care of you? If you had said something, then at least I would have known something – could have given you an answer!

Maybe you were the one I should have had? Maybe you were even the one I wanted? Why didn't you force me? Then at least I'd have had to make a choice. Why didn't you push me away? So I could say I tried.

Do you think I didn't see you? That I could have done more for you? Come sooner? But I didn't know you needed me, did I? I couldn't take you to Reinsnes. You understood that, didn't you, Karna? Do you think I knew you were going to have a baby, but didn't care? How could I know that? You said nothing to me! And if you had said something, Karna, how could I be sure the child was mine?

How can a man know?

Karna?

CHAPTER 15

The most interesting thing about the time that followed was that the hours apparently piled up outside my body with no meaning whatsoever. Finally the pile got so high I realized it would crush me if I did not do something.

I do not know how I got to Bredgade, nor what was said betwen Aksel and me. But I remember he made me get up after some days. I also remember he brought me bread and a bottle of wine in a paper sack.

'What day was it?' I asked, as he poured wine into a water glass.

'What do you mean?'

'When we went to Store Strandstraede . . . ?'

He leaned far over to make sure he did not spill.

'April 23rd,' he said finally.

'I see,' I said, without looking at him.

He said no more.

'St George's day,' I murmured.

But that did not seem to matter.

A little later, Aksel said:

'I told them at the hospital that you have a terrible cold. But you'll be there Monday morning. At 7:30 on the dot. To make rounds. Operating room from 10 to 11 as usual.'

I nodded. He finished off the wine bottle before he left. He probably had his own concerns. Anna, for example.

*　　　*　　　*

The day the landlady came and demanded her rent, I realized it was not over yet. The world still found much fault with me. She was unmerciful. She thought I was sick, she bellowed. But now she realized I could not pay my rent because I had drunk up all my money. She also shouted that my room stank. That I did not empty my toilet bucket. That I had to move.

I counted out some bills for her. She sniffed in the corners and moved towards the door with unmistakable warnings.

'Do you have children, madam?' I asked as politely as if I had never seen her before.

She gaped. It was quite remarkable to see. I understood from her open-mouthed expression that she wished me no ill. That made me bolder.

'Have you given birth?'

'I don't understand . . . ?'

'Neither do I,' I said amiably.

'You miserable wretch! Trying to talk your way out of the unemptied toilet bucket. You're a pig, Benjamin Grønelv!' she raged.

'Yes. And an executioner!' I said, and thought: 'It's good to say that.'

She stared at me with a horrified look, and mumbled something about insanity before she left and slammed the door behind her.

I had to smile. It should be as natural for people to cry as to smile, I thought. My whole face was stone. Dropped into the deeps.

Since I was up and there was still enough light, I decided to shave. I went into the courtyard with the full toilet bucket and the empty water bucket. Emptied the one the landlady had scolded me for. She was right of course. It stank. Women are often right. But they do not have to say so. That's unnecessary. One knows it, after all.

As I stood by the pump letting water stream into the zinc bucket, I noticed the same zinc taste as the morning Karna's brother awakened Aksel and me. What was it he said?

'It's Karna!' he said.

The zinc taste grew stronger as the bucket filled. The water flowed profusely. I turned off the spout. But that did not help. The sound was still there. The water flowed and flowed.

Only after I got to my room again, shut the door, and said aloud, 'Now let's get us shaved,' did the sound subside a bit. It helped to say 'us'.

I opened my mouth. Let air stream through it. Breathed in and out as if for the first time. Went to the window, opened it. Repeated the breathing exercise. While shaving I realized, after cutting myself three times, something was wrong with my eyes. I could not see where my skin stopped and my beard began. The doctor looked at me coldly in the mirror. Made a diagnosis: overexertion and an unbalanced emotional state. Ergo: mentally disturbed.

Interesting!

'But I've been lying in bed for days! Why should I be worn out?' I derided myself.

'Mental disturbance can occur somewhat later. It's merely temporary in nature,' said the offended doctor.

'And what should I do in the meantime? Walk around with a half-shaved jaw covered with cuts?'

'You'll see, everything will be better once you do something about what you don't understand,' said the doctor.

I immediately felt better.

I know I did not expect to be received like a hero. But neither did I expect to be received like an enemy.

Karna's brother opened the door when I knocked. He stared at me silently and sullenly. From inside came a strange brittle sound. Like someone breaking twigs. A baby crying.

'I thought maybe I could . . .' I said, not knowing what to say.

Grandmother came. Looked me over. Then she said curtly:

'The funeral was yesterday.'

I nodded. An ant had gone astray up the wall. Now it was struggling to crawl between the wall and the door frame. That was remarkable. An ant? Here in the middle of the city? How did it survive?

'Your friend came! With flowers!' she said accusingly.

'There's an ant,' I said amiably.

The boy stretched his neck through the doorway. Stood gaping, looking alternately at me and at the bustling ant. The woman dried her eyes and took two small steps towards me. Squinted at me from beneath bushy white eyebrows.

'Don't burn all your bridges, you might need them later,' she said suddenly, and drew me inside.

I think we had a conversation. I do not remember much of it. I think she asked if it was my friend or me who was named Benjamin.

'It's me. My friend's name is Aksel.'

'Then you're the father of the poor little thing,' she said listlessly.

I do not know if I replied. I only know the child was crying behind the curtain. Strangely stifled cries.

Maybe it was suffocating? That was for the best. Karna was not here after all.

'I'd hoped it was the other one,' Grandmother said bluntly.

I nodded.

'He's more suitable. From a better family. He's got quality. He came with flowers. He cried at the grave.'

I nodded again.

As the old woman lowered her eyes and sighed, I suddenly saw she had the same nose as Karna. Small and straight with well-formed nostrils. You could want to touch one nostril.

I raised my hand. But let it fall again.

'It's dying from starvation,' she said.

I was still looking at her nostrils.

'I have to put the baby somewhere. I can't keep her here. I'm old. The boy needs food and clothes too. He can't earn much. Now that Karna isn't here . . .'

She put her hand to her eyes for a moment.

The baby's crying stopped. I thought:

It's probably suffocated. Air passage blocked by a blanket or cloth. Blue face. Mouth and eyes wide open. Tiny hands clenched.

The doctor knew. Had seen stillborn babies.

'Do you know where I can take the poor thing?' she asked.

I shook my head.

She put her face in her hands again. Made sounds.

'They shouldn't have walled up the window at Frederiks Hospital. The window for the most pitiful ones . . . the ones nobody could keep.'

You had heard about the 'drawer'. A window by the stone bridge had been walled up. In the old days people could leave their unwanted children there, ring the bell, and run away. On the bell were the words: 'Salvation for Unfortunate Children'.

'May I sit down?' I asked, and took a spindle-backed chair by the table. There were two other spindle-backed chairs.

She followed, and sat down across from me. Blew her nose in a rag she pulled from her sleeve. The skin on her bare underarms was pale and loose. Became folds when she laid her arms on the table and twisted the rag around two fingers. I found it touching somehow.

'I didn't get anybody to come from the hospital,' the boy said stiffly, and left. You could wish he had stayed. The air was so heavy. The old woman's despair smelled sickeningly sweet.

'I guess you're not going to start being a father?' she said into the air after a while.

I do not think I managed to answer.

'That's to be expected,' she said bitterly. 'They don't

384

do that. Certainly not when the mother dies . . . the fathers don't exactly stand in line. Certainly not.'

'What can I do?' asked the doctor as politely as possible.

She raised her head and looked at me. Her contempt was so obvious I recoiled.

'Do you have any money?' she asked.

'Not much.'

'I owe for the funeral. It wasn't much of a one . . . Poor Karna . . .'

'What do we owe?' I asked brusquely.

Grandmother answered obediently.

'Ask them to send the bill,' I said.

'They do that without asking.'

'All right. But ask them to send the bill to Benjamin Grønelv at the widow's home on Bredgade.'

Just then the bundle on the bed started crying. So it had not suffocated.

'What do you do with it? When it cries?' I asked.

Grandmother sighed, blew her nose again, and padded over to the curtain in front of Karna's bed.

'I give her a mixture of sugar water and milk. But she doesn't tolerate it.'

She brought a bundle to the table and put it in my arms. It moved. The warmth from it spread up my arms and into my throat.

'We need to find someone who wants her,' Grandmother said from the stove. She was warming something in a pot.

'I haven't done the scrubbing at the dry goods store since Karna . . . I can't go any longer without skillings for bread and milk. We owe for two weeks,' she added.

'I'll get some money,' I said, staring down at the small angry face in the bundle.

Sickle-shaped locks of black hair stuck to the sweaty head. The bundle arched itself like an eel and made grimaces and sounds. With each cry its mouth opened like a baby thrush. At first it seemed to just take in air and be satisfied with that. Then the puckered-up face trembled with injustice and the sound came with frightening rage.

'That's quite a sound,' I said tentatively.

'The child is healthy and well-formed,' said Grandmother. 'That's not the problem. But she can't tolerate food. It's too strong. I wish I knew someone to nurse her for a few weeks . . .'

The old woman began to weep again.

'Maybe there's someone at one of the hospitals,' the doctor said comfortingly. 'I'll investigate.'

The doctor took complete command of my life. Sent me humbly begging to get mother's milk for Grandmother's bundle. I dropped in on the midwives at Frederiks Hospital and Kommune Hospital. I begged and pleaded. Collected charity in small drops. Told a heart-rending story about Grandmother and the baby and the mother who died in childbirth. In the end, the nurses and midwives knew the story so well that all I had to do was hand them the bottle.

Every day Grandmother asked if I had met anyone who needed a little girl in good condition. And I shamefully replied that I had not found anyone.

During this time I saw Aksel only when we were on duty at the hospital. But one evening when I got home I found him lying asleep on my bed.

I decided to start locking the door when I went out.

'What are you doing here?' I asked.

'Sleeping,' he said with a hostile look.

I took off my jacket and walked over to the table by the window. His eyes followed me. Then he stretched, sat up, and started looking for his shoes under the bed.

When he only found one, he just sat there holding it in his hand. Leaning forward. I could not see his face.

'What do you want?' I asked.

'Why are you avoiding me?'

'I'm not avoiding you.'

'You're not? Then why don't I ever see you at the

usual places? Why aren't you ever here? Why don't you come looking for me any more? Is your accursed conscience bothering you? We were together when . . . when poor Karna. That wasn't my damn fault . . .'

'Shut up!'

'No, I won't. We need to talk about this.'

'There's nothing to talk about. She's not . . .'

'I don't want to talk about Karna. For that matter, I didn't know she meant so much to you. You kept that well hidden!'

I do not know whether it was what he said or the way he said it, but I rushed at him. A ridiculous attack. He held me in the air by my waistcoat until I calmed down. The waistcoat, however, got ruined. A moment earlier it had a silk back with a painstakingly sewn half belt. When I felt the floor under my feet again, I took off the waistcoat and stared at it.

Aksel stood in the middle of the room, his arms dangling.

'Don't make me angry,' he said.

'You've got a damn cynical way . . .'

'I think I learned it from you.'

'I see!' I said.

'Do you have any beer here?' he asked.

'No, it just gets hot these days.'

'Can we go somewhere and have a couple?'

'No, I just got home. I need to sleep.'

'You've slept for at least fourteen days!'

'No, I haven't,' I said indifferently, and lay down on the bed. It still had an indentation from Aksel.

He sighed and sat down on the chair by the desk. Half turned away from me.

It got very quiet over there. I closed my eyes and hoped he would leave. Then suddenly he said, as if talking to himself:

'Anna doesn't want me.'

Even from behind closed eyelids you could tell the shadows in the corner behind the bed were blue! A carriage rumbled past the window. The horses' hooves thundered against the cobblestones. Dina! Dina rode on the rocky beach. I heard the thundering. A series of small booms in my ear. My body lay on the bed. But I myself was a lump inside Aksel's head. There I heard his words again. They hung in the air. Trembling, waiting for me to take them.

I swallowed them whole.

'What does she want then?' I heard myself ask.

'I didn't ask, but it's not exactly a mystery.'

'It's not?'

'No. Because she told me that you two . . . That you . . . That she'd slept with you!'

I raised my head from the pillow and tried to breathe calmly.

'She said . . . Anna said . . .' I stammered. But I could not deny or confirm anything. It was too unbelievable. Women did not say such things! Not even Cecilie could have said such a thing when it was not true. Anna? No!

'Damn it all!' I mumbled after a while.

He turned and looked at me. I was dog shit at the fish market.

'How many are you going to go through before you give up?' he said as he blew his nose. 'I didn't know you were so deceitful, so contemptible, such a damned swine!'

'I see,' I said. And kept thinking about what Anna had said. Thought and thought. Until the words fell from my mouth:

'Why did she say that?'

He stared at me furiously.

'I guess she's more honest then you!'

The room grew deathly silent. Then he broke down:

'Just make sure she doesn't die in childbirth before you've gone to the altar together. That would be an ugly mess. Damn you, you wretched Norwegian dog!'

I took it lying down. Could understand very well. Aksel. Dear Aksel! Dear, dear Aksel!

'It's not true!' I burst out.

'No, that's maybe an exaggeration. But not much,' he said between his teeth.

'I mean, Anna. It's not true. I haven't slept with her. Never. I . . .'

He gave me an icy look.

'Are you trying to get out of it? You want to make Anna a liar in order to keep me as your friend? You want everything. To have your cake and eat it too. You're worse than I thought. I ought to plaster you to the wall in this miserable . . .'

'You've got to believe me! It's not true.'

He came towards the bed. So threateningly that I rose on my elbows. He looked me over. Up and down! But mostly in the eyes. I thought: 'He's going to grab me now. All right. Then it's all over.'

'And what do you think she'd gain by telling me such an obscene lie?' he snarled hoarsely, as he tried to maneuver his body tight against mine.

I was not enjoying myself. His rigging hung loosely above me. Giant booms. The sails were not lashed securely. They could land in my face at any moment.

'I don't know,' I said.

He did not hit me. Nothing happened. He kept staring at me.

'Well I'll be damned,' he said at last. Calmly.

I sat up completely, feeling relieved. Fumbled on my nightstand for a pipe and tobacco.

'You believe me then?' I said eagerly. Much too eagerly.

'Believe? I believe you've got more holes in you than any old boot I ever knew, Benjamin Grønelv! And you've been my friend for years! If it's really true she's lying? Then you must realize she's got a reason? How dare you betray her to me? Why don't you take it on yourself like a man? You chicken-heart!'

He snatched the pipe and tobacco from me, went back to the chair, and took a long time filling and lighting it.

'You're right,' I said finally.

Aksel rolled his eyes behind the pipe smoke.

'I've wanted to, it's true,' I said without looking at him. 'Wanted more than anything in the world: to sleep with Anna.'

'Then we still have something in common,' he countered dryly, without even a tiny spark of lewd emotion.

At that moment I could understand why I was fond of Aksel. I thought about that even when he continued his cynical speech. I do not know if what he said even registered with me. It purified me. Made everything simple and complete. At the end he gave me a coup de grâce:

'What do you plan to do with Anna?'

'You know perfectly well she doesn't want me either,' I said.

'But if she did?'

I sighed and shrugged my shoulders.

'Then I'd take her to Reinsnes.'

A mean sneer lit up Aksel's face.

'I must say! You're improving! I'll personally be your second when you ask her. It will be a pleasure to see you finally act like a man.'

I saw no reason to reply to such things.

'And if she actually wants to go up to that icy wilderness?' he asked.

I got the feeling he had set a trap for me.

'That won't happen,' I said firmly.

'Why not? When she willingly loses her honor and virtue by lying for your sake?'

'I can't be responsible for what she says to you!'

He nodded. Sat there nodding awhile.

'Just think! Benjamin has discovered how simple love is. He wants love right at hand, but won't exert himself for it! He can't be responsible for what Anna says. And he can't imagine why she says it! But! He thought he'd like to sleep with his friend's fiancée. That's his gospel of love and friendship. Congratulations!'

He got up to leave. Reached the door before I pulled myself together.

'Are you leaving?'

'I haven't been here,' he mumbled.

'We're not friends any more?'

'Not today!' he said wearily.

'You won't tell her . . . that I denied it?' I begged.

He gave me a pitying look.

'No,' he said curtly.

Now it was his turn to avoid me. Even at the hospital. I followed the routines as best I could in the surgical division with Saxtorph. A life of rules and carbolic vapors.

Each day I tested my manhood by defying all propriety and going to the Maternity Hospital to beg for milk for the baby in Store Strandstraede. I delivered the milk to Grandmother's door. Sometimes I heard the child crying inside.

In May, Aksel and I began a six-week course to get 'jus practicani' as obstetricians without really becoming friends.

There was no word from her. Dina.

You could plague yourself with thoughts about how Aksel and Anna might be strolling along the lakes now, or going to Tivoli. It definitely made you weary. I wanted to sleep all the time.

On Bredgade I emptied the toilet bucket attentively, as if it were the most important thing in life. I also tried to find out how I stood financially. Realized I must ask to extend my internship until I went home. Home? Did that mean I thought I could avoid going to court?

To my credit, I will not deny that I seriously considered writing or telegraphing Anders to ask for money for Karna's grandmother. The strange thing was, the more I thought about it the less I wanted to actually do it.

I reviewed the last conversation between Aksel and me, word for word. His accusations. Also tried to reconstruct my last meeting with Anna. But somehow it was as if these things no longer concerned me.

I took out Kierkegaard's books. Not because I wanted to read his work, but because I wanted to escape myself.

Fear and Trembling: Problemata: '. . . Only he who draws the knife obtains Isaac. He who will not work, has no bread: he will be deceived, as the gods deceived Orpheus with a specter in place of the beloved, deceived him because he was lovesick and lacked courage, deceived him because he played on the cithara and was not a man . . . He who will work gives birth to his own father.'

These were all welcome hypotheses for controlled feelings.

CHAPTER 16

One evening I went to the Apothek because I could stand no more of Benjamin Grønelv. And absolutely no more of the widow on Bredgade.

The moment I saw him, I knew how much I had missed him. Aksel sat under a kerosene lamp. In a corner, alone.

I walked over to his table. Hesitantly. He nodded dully when I sat down.

'Well, well, so you're visiting old Kannikestraede?'

'I need to see if the new whippersnappers at Regensen have beards yet,' I said.

He nodded darkly.

'No, there aren't many beards!' he said after a while.

'I'll get this round,' I offered.

After our drinks came and he still showed no sign of life, I said:

'Having a bad day?'

'I'm laughing myself to death,' he replied.

'It's that bad?'

'Yes!'

I sipped my drink and watched the people. It occurred to me I should take off my overcoat. Did so, and sat down again. He still just sat there saying nothing.

'Well!' I said invitingly.

'Don't shout!' he shouted, so loudly it startled a waitress with a tray.

'You want to kill me? Or somebody else?'

'I don't kill people,' he said firmly.

'What's the problem then?'

'That's the problem!'

I suddenly understood what he was saying.

'Yes,' I agreed. 'That's the problem.'

For a while we sat looking in different directions, as if we did not know each other.

'I went to the funeral. Good God!' he said suddenly.

I was on guard.

'Yes?' I asked.

'She thought I was you . . . Damn it, I had to make her understand it was you who . . .'

'Thanks for your kindness! But why bring this up now? To torment me?'

'All right, all right! Cool down!' he bellowed angrily.

I took it calmly. Was careful to avoid his eyes.

Then he started again:

'Have you seen her?'

'Who?'

'The baby,' he said.

'Yes,' I said tersely.

'Does she look like you?'

'Stop it!' I begged.

And a little later, I said:

'I'll get us a schnapps!'

'Feeling generous today?' he asked disdainfully.

'Yes,' I said.

'Do you see Anna, too?' he asked, looking off into space after we got our schnapps.

'No, do you?' I countered.

'Yes,' he replied, sending me a furious look.

There was nothing to say to that.

'I'm going home soon,' I said.

'Yes, you must be in a hurry now,' he said dryly.

I rose to leave despite my full schnapps glass. This was enough. Put on my coat. His eyes followed me.

'Well, all right,' I said, and nodded goodbye.

He sat as if he did not realize a farewell was occurring.

'Your mother? Still living abroad? Is she feeling all

394

right now?' he asked, as if we still sat across from each other.

'She hasn't been sick,' I answered.

'But that was why you went to visit her . . . in Berlin.'

'I didn't see her,' I said evasively.

'You didn't see her?'

I kept standing.

'No!'

'But you brought back the cello . . . I thought she was so sick she'd stopped playing. She played the cello, didn't she?'

'Yes, for a while. Studied with a maestro.'

'That's what I thought. And then she quit?'

'Yes.'

'Is she finally going home too?'

'No.'

'Sit down, man! You've got no reason to be angry! I have!' he shouted.

I shrugged, and sat on the edge of the chair.

'Strange women up there near the North Pole, aren't they?' he said, and laughed somewhat uncertainly.

I did not reply.

'Is she great? A virtuoso?' he asked.

'I don't think so,' I said evasively.

'What does she say?'

'Nothing.'

'Don't you ask?'

'I told you I didn't see her! You don't ask someone you haven't seen since you were a boy.'

'Do you mean your mother simply left you?'

'Something like that.'

'Good Lord! When? How old were you?'

'I don't remember exactly . . . Fourteen . . .'

'I'll be damned . . .' he murmured, stroking his beard. 'And I once thought I knew you! There's a lot one doesn't know . . .'

I did not answer. But I understood the hint.

'I didn't know she'd been gone so long. Was it just the cello-playing? Or was there a scandal?' he asked.

'The cello-playing. As far as I know,' I lied.

We sat in silence for a while. Aksel covered the schnapps glass with his hand for a moment. I looked at my own hands. Neither of us had done much manual labor. But my hands were not built for it. Not very strong compared to Aksel's. I had inherited Dina's long fingers. But what did I know? Jacob might have had fingers as long as from here to Øresund! Aksel's hands looked as if they had been switched from a smith's baby to a preacher's child at birth.

'You mean you didn't find her? That you don't know where she is?'

'Something like that.'

'Did you try? Or did you just pretend?'

'Stop it! Do you think I went to Berlin for nothing?'

'You weren't gone long.'

'She wasn't there!'

He stroked his beard madly.

'What if you went looking for her? Now!' he said

His voice was a whisper through an open window at night.

'Why should I?'

'To find out if she'll see you. Find out how she is.'

'I already tried. I don't care how she is any more!'

He stared at me, then shut his eyes tightly and grimaced.

'Hell, you don't fool me! There's not a day since she left that you haven't thought about her!'

'Oh . . .'

'Isn't that right?'

'Well . . . yes. From time to time . . .'

'We'll go!'

'We?'

'Yes, you need a second in this duel. And I need to get out in the world! Young women shouldn't be the only ones who get out in the world, while we ruin ourselves with work!' he sneered.

'I don't have any money for a trip.'

He sighed a little, and formed his mouth into a fleshy funnel while he thought further.

'I'll try to arrange it,' he said finally.

'No, I can't borrow money.'

I talked about how terrible it was to borrow money from people. He looked at me awhile. Then he pounded his fist on the table.

'You're a coward! You don't dare to look for your mother! You're afraid she'll send you away!'

The room suddenly turned upside down. Aksel was a detestable, stinking cadaver I had to escape from before it was too late.

I rose unsteadily to leave, but he reached out his arm and held me down.

'I'm going to Berlin with you!' he said decisively.

'What made you decide that?' I asked, and noticed he was lighting one of the professor's Havana cigars.

'Does it matter?'

'Yes.'

'Why?'

'I have to know your reason If it's to take revenge on Anna, or if it's because you think you'll help me.'

'It's neither. Just a totally selfish desire to travel abroad,' he replied.

I reached out my hand. From old habit, he let me borrow his cigar. I took a couple of puffs and gave it back.

'Let's get out of here,' I said, and drained my glass.

He was remarkably co-operative. We started walking in his direction. Towards Valkendorf.

'Even if I wanted to go to Berlin, I don't have the money,' I said.

'Can't you get some?'

'No. I mean, I could ask Anders. But I don't know how things are at home. And it takes time.'

'I can arrange a loan for you,' he said confidently.

'Where will you get the money?' I asked.

'From my mother,' he smiled.

'Without saying what you're going to use it for?'

He shrugged.

'She'll assume I've run up some debts.'

'Why are you so set on doing this?'

'I already told you.'

'It's to keep me away from Anna! But I'm leaving soon!' I said.

He stopped and gripped my arm.

'It's not just that! You're a fool if you don't understand. I don't think I can do anything more about Anna. Not yet. If women can travel, so can I!'

'All right,' I said.

After a few steps he stopped again and took hold of my arm.

'I was there tonight. At Anna's,' he laughed. It was not a nice laugh.

'Did you have fun?'

' Not especially,' he admitted. 'Shall I tell you why?'

'Well . . .'

'She didn't eat dinner with us. Anna got a severe pain that made it impossible for her to sit at the table. Benjamin, I swear I didn't even offer to make a diagnosis. It was too obvious. But I comforted her parents, like the well-mannered fellow I am. And Benjamin Grønelv hovered over the waters like a restraining spirit!'

'I'm sorry,' I mumbled.

'That's all right,' he retorted quickly. 'You're forgiven for everything.'

'You're much too young to be so bitter,' I said.

But he did not even try to respond in a similar tone. We had walked past Valkendorf long ago.

'I'm not going to see her any more,' I said, and kicked something lying in the street. It proved to be bigger and harder than I thought.

'Oh yes you will! You're going to see her!' he said furiously. 'And each time, you'll get more and more cured. When you're alone with her you'll talk about me. And when you're with both of us, you'll laugh. You'll be my friend and my best man. In return, you can be damn sure I'll get money and find your mother.'

We were between two street lights. All I saw was his hand holding the glowing cigar.

'Is this what you call friendship?' I asked.

'You're damn right!'

'You decided in a hurry how you'd buy me, didn't you?' I said.

'Yes, I think fast. But I'm not buying you. I need you myself.'

'Is it so obvious that you're the right one . . . for Anna?'

'Yes. I've told you that before. It's been the two of us since we first met. Anna and I were six and eight years old. We've known it the whole time. That it would be us. It's beautiful. Serious. It's not something anyone is going to come and ruin.'

'You've never talked about . . . about love. I thought it was a practical arrangement.'

'And if I'd used great words about love, then you wouldn't have tried with her? Is that what you mean?'

What could one say?

'Then you wouldn't have tried with her?' he repeated, and blew thick smoke rings over our heads. He had the upper hand.

'I don't know,' I admitted.

He charged ahead like a bull with its horns towards the ground. Quite a distance. Without saying anything. But then he said:

'Imagine that! You admitted it!'

The sky had clouded over completely, and the first large raindrops fell on us as we passed the man on horseback immobilized for ever at Kongens Nytorv. The wind rustled loudly in the trees around the statue, and Aksel's hair stuck straight out. A shoeshine man who was out late pulled his cart past us at a mournful pace. A couple of solitary flashes lit up the sky.

'Look!' said Aksel. 'The fireworks in Tivoli!'

'Yes,' I said dully, and stuck my hands into my pockets.

We looked at each other as the rain hit the cobble-stones so hard that water spattered around us.

'We need to find shelter. Where's the nearest pub?' he said.

'Remember, we have to be in the operating room tomorrow, Aksel!'

'That's just like you! First you wait until late at night to meet me. And when I'm finally here, you're tired. And that's before we've even started. When are we leaving on the trip?'

He enjoyed having the upper hand.

We were surely a strange sight as we walked the streets in the rain. Siamese bodies with separate brains who were still dependent in every way.

The first pub we came to was a lugubrious place on Ny Adelgade. There we managed to sweep our disagreements under the rug and lay great plans. About Dina.

The first schnapps tore at my intestines and reminded me I should eat something. But since Aksel had been well fed at the professor's elegant table, I did not bother with food. Besides, Aksel insisted they only served sausages seasoned with arsenic in such places.

But at least I got warm. Our wet overcoats hung on a hook to get smoked and dried. The room was thick with pipe smoke and coarse faces under the lamps. Our sorrows fell under the table. Little by little we became uncontrollably happy. Both of us. After numerous glasses of schnapps we were drunk too. Aksel made a little speech with each schnapps. All to the effect that he was the apple of his mother's eye. And that he would certainly arrange a loan. When our internship was over, we would go to Berlin.

I asked him to stop repeating this lest I think it was nothing but drunken nonsense. He replied by giving me a thorough analysis of his mother's great weakness for him. Due not only to his charming appearance, but also to his tender soul. Which she insisted was just like her own.

I was beyond weariness and hunger. I was an early Judas sitting at Jesus's knee hearing how he would save us both with the help of his contact with a higher power. In Aksel's case: his mother.

After convincing me how easy it was to charm a person with the inborn defect of being a mother, he began asking questions about Dina.

'After all, I need to recognize her if I meet her when you're not there!'

At first I felt dubious, because I could not tell him anything that came close to the wonderful mother love he had within his reach. So I chose other ways. And I got carried away by my own story. I heard that myself. It was not my mother I described. It was a woman. Dina. Whom I had thought about for years. Who made people change when she entered a room. Especially men.

I told about the parson, who nearly always came to Reinsnes without his wife. About Niels, who hanged himself out of unrequited love. About Anders, whom she abandoned. About the Russian, who shot himself before our eyes because he could not have her.

Somewhere I crossed some boundaries. I believed what I was saying. Aksel's shining eyes under the lamp. The loud rustle of voices around all the tables. The warmth in my body. The feeling of being friends with Aksel again. Everything helped to add color and spice to my story.

Now and then Dina walked across the farmyard with her brow furrowed and her face impassive. But I pushed the image away. Set her on Blackie and let her race across the fields. I let her play Mozart until the cobwebs danced on the ceiling above us. And Aksel sighed. I let her light the candles at Christmas. Lean over the five-branched candelabra. So close that her hair caught fire. And I let her sail into the Sound like a devil.

It did not matter that I had no stories about her falling for Benjamin's charm. I described her astride her horse without a saddle, on a sheepskin. Described her at the prow when the cargo boats set out to sea. Or when she welcomed the Lofoten men. Told about the time she and I sailed alone across the open sea to buy a horse.

Aksel listened without making his ironic comments. He let himself be drawn into a kind of intoxication. I think we sat there and were both in love. Not with Anna. With Dina!

Once Aksel said:

'Are you talking about your mother? Or someone you dream about meeting?'

'It's a person we'll both meet!'

'Maybe I should have someone like her?' he said suddenly.

I drained my glass and smiled arrogantly.

'She certainly wouldn't loan us money.'

He looked at me and pounded his fist on the table. We toasted each other thoroughly.

'Come to Reinsnes after she comes home!' I said hospitably.

'With Anna?'

I did not hesitate.

'With Anna!'

We staggered cheerfully out into the night. It had stopped raining. But everything was dripping. We wandered about in an appendix inside the huge whale's belly. It was fragrant and stank.

The gaslights looked down on us softly. The streets were almost deserted. But dull sounds from the whale's distant digestive system reached us like dark secrets. Siamese bodies. Shared arms and legs. Reeling and chuckling, with mud far up our trouser legs.

'What the hell happened to that shoeshine man? I desperately need to beautify my dogs!' shouted Aksel towards the stiff rows of houses.

402

'Shhh, otherwise the fellow will come and put us in a cell,' I warned.

'Put us in?' sniveled Aksel, stopping short in the middle of a gutter. A blissful smile spread on his face. Then he whispered so loudly you could hear it across the street:

'Now we're going to go and knock on the madam's window in Peder Madsen's Passage!'

I was suddenly sober. The stench from the gutter struck my brain like a club. The golden story hours were over. Revulsion began its march towards me. Dizzy and nauseated, I shook my head.

'I'm too exhausted . . .' I said as despairingly as possible.

I heard Aksel's whistling long after we parted company. As I steadied myself against walls and brickwork, words sang in the back of my head:

'Come to Reinsnes with Anna! With Anna . . . With Anna . . .'

Anna sang to me.

CHAPTER 17

A few days later, an envelope awaited me when I came from the hospital. I guessed it was from Aksel. But it was from her. Anna! A 'specter' from Kierkegaard's writings. She did not want to come to my lodgings, but she wanted to meet me in A Porta at Kongens Nytorv at six o'clock that evening. If I did not think it important to come, that was all right, she wrote.

I was not enthusiastic about the meeting place. A snobbish women's tea room and pastry shop where people went to be seen. But that in itself was something. It meant she was not afraid to be seen with me. Not only did she lie to Aksel about the most intimate things, she encouraged the lie.

As I reread the letter, I realized I had not seen her for ages.

It was only four o'clock, and already my hands felt clammy. Should I get dressed? That was the answer! So I dressed as nicely as possible. Polished my shoes with blacking. When I had finished, it was barely five o'clock.

I knocked on the landlady's door and asked if I could do anything for her. An errand, or . . . ?

She looked at me wide-eyed, then smiled almost amiably.

'You're not dressed for that. Have a good time!'

I wondered if she read the letter before giving it to me. It had no seal. I felt annoyed. But I did not know if it was because she perhaps read the letter, or because she was so patronizing. In any case, I said quite offended:

'The toilet bucket *is* emptied!'

'My goodness!' she replied.

'The woman who brought the letter said she came from a professor . . . what was his name again . . . ?'

She smiled blissfully. As if she and I had a secret.

'That's the worst part!' I said as ironically as possible.

'Don't be impudent, young man. I'm like a mother to you after all these years. And now you're soon going to leave . . .'

That gave me a reason to say good evening and leave the house.

I arrived first and found a table by the window just to see her coming. She seemed like a stranger. It was probably the London clothes. I could not see her face. The window was too dusty.

She looked around the room hesitantly. I stood up to greet her. Could not see clearly. Simply sensed the light, loosely draped outfit with Anna's body inside. But it was very elegant indeed. Without being overloaded with lace, buttons and pins as was fashionable. Perhaps that was why she looked older than she was?

When she got closer, I thought she seemed about to cry. I kept my eyes on the angels painted on the wall above her head. That did not help much. The potted palms on pedestals, the chairs and tables, it all whirled around. I shook her hand. But that was nothing to hold onto. Merely confusing. Like when someone tickles you under the chin with a blade of grass when you are stretched out on the ground with your eyes closed.

You could tell yourself Karna was dead. She did not see it.

I did not ask about Aksel. Not just because I felt she expected it, but more because I could not get the words out of my mouth. I felt nauseated, which was not how I should feel. Aksel was right. It was not her fault. You could not point to a single thing that cast blame on Anna!

But she had asked to see me in order to tell me something. It must be something important. There was no point in me trying to guess what it was. But it did not make me blameless in Aksel's eyes. Nor in hers either.

She seated herself on the chair I pulled out. Her face lay in shadow under her bonnet's brim. Even so, I felt her gaze. Straight at me. A bit childish. Anxious?

She seemed tired and a little pale, thought the doctor, while I followed the movements of her breasts when she breathed. Down at her neckline. Lost myself in the remarkable bow of her upper lip. When she opened and closed her lips a few times, making a dimple appear at each side of her mouth, I felt the dimples transplant themselves into my groin. I had unconsciously stretched my hand across the table. But she did not reach towards it.

Neither of us had said a word when the waiter arrived and asked what we wanted.

'Just a glass of fruit juice for me, thank you,' she said, slowly pulling off her gloves.

I ordered two glasses of fruit juice, and the waiter disappeared.

'You saw me coming?' she asked with a nod towards the window.

'Yes, I saw you coming.'

We were both silent awhile.

'I had to meet you alone. Of course it's not . . .'

'Yes?'

Her mouth opened to say something. Then it closed and narrowed. Were it not for the two dimples at the corners of her mouth, I would have thought she regretted coming.

'To talk about Aksel and you, without Aksel hearing?' The words slipped out of me.

'No. And yes!' she said defiantly. As if she had just realized that this was indeed the case.

I made an exaggerated gesture with my hand.

406

'The fact is . . . I have something to confess. And something to reproach you for.'

'Take the reproach first.'

My heart was silent in my body. That was abnormal. Only a moment ago it had pounded so loudly I could hardly hear the carriage wheels outside.

'You told Aksel my plans. I confided in you and wanted you as an alibi. And you betrayed me.'

'That must have been long ago?'

'You told him I wanted to go to London.'

'Wasn't he supposed to know?'

'Yes, but it must have hurt him to hear it from you.'

'Then maybe you shouldn't have told me?'

'Maybe not,' she admitted stubbornly.

'I thought you were a free person.'

'How naive can a man be? When did women become free? Papa is the only man I know who . . . He's even fighting for women to be able to study . . . medicine!'

'I'm sorry,' I said smoothly.

'You're sorry!' she exclaimed.

'Not about the professor! No, no! I'm sorry I told Aksel!'

I sipped my fruit juice.

'I took revenge,' she said.

'Oh?'

'I told Aksel I went to London because I willingly let myself be seduced by his best friend.'

She spoke very rapidly. Still I understood every word. I already knew about it of course. But my amazement was genuine. I was stunned that *she* told me this.

She bent over the table quickly, and took a long sip of fruit juice. Her bonnet was a bit crooked. It had a knob of gathered material at the back. That looked idiotic now, sticking straight into the air. When she looked up again there was a red stripe along her upper lip. Right above the dimples. I wanted to let my index finger follow the stripe.

'Why did you say that?'

'For two reasons: I got revenge. And I made myself so impossible that Aksel won't have me.'

'Why are you telling me this?'

'Because it's good that you know.'

'Couldn't you rather have told Aksel you didn't love him?'

'No.'

'Why not?'

'Because it's not true.'

'I see. You don't want to marry him. But you love him?'

'Yes. Everyone who knows Aksel loves him. Don't you?'

'That's not the same.'

She fumbled with something in her lap. Her gloves?

'What do you think of me?' she asked. Barely audibly.

What did I think of Anna? How in the world could I explain what I thought of Anna?

'I think you're not . . .'

'What?'

'For me. That it's better if . . .'

'If you just . . . leave again? And then I'll be good enough for Aksel?'

Her eyelashes cast long shadows. The arch of her forehead. Her nose. The indentation under her nose. Her chin. It made me heavy. With desire. To own her. To hear her say completely different things from what she actually was saying. I wanted her to say wild, intense things. With naked hips and round arms around me, and her bonnet pointing towards the ceiling.

I was about to ask if we could find a place without so many people. But of course I did not dare. And suddenly it was much too late.

She laid her two bare hands on the table with the palms up, as if wanting to receive something. Then, looking straight at me, she said quietly:

408

'This Karna? Who died in childbirth? What did she mean to you?'

Her eyes. Had I seen them before? Naked. With a quivering muscle in the right corner? The pupils. Dark and intense.

A potted palm stood behind her head. Its shadow created a branched pattern on her cheek and shoulder. As if someone had clawed her long ago and a dark scar remained.

I looked down at the table.

'I don't know,' I whispered. My organ hung shamefully in the corner.

'You went to her while you met me?'

'No.'

'Why do you say something you know isn't true?'

We appraised each other. But could not be enemies. I picked up my napkin and leaned across the table. Then I moistened it against my lips and carefully wiped away the red line of fruit juice.

She shut her eyes tightly and sat motionless until I had finished. Then she leaned against the back of her chair and looked straight at me again.

'As someone who meets one woman while keeping company with another, do you think it strange that I love Aksel but don't want to be part of his family and his life for ever?'

'No, it's not strange,' I said.

Outside, a lively group walked noisily by. It gave me a welcome opportunity to escape her gaze and look out the window. But it did not last long. You had to stay in the room you were in. Even if you did not know what to say.

She drank the rest of her fruit juice. A red stripe appeared again. I tried to smile, but could not.

'Do you remember when you stood in front of me in the park and said you loved me?' she said, speaking very fast.

I nodded.

'Did you go straight to her afterwards?'

'No.'

'Why not?'

'Anna!' I begged.

'Is that always how it is, men say they love you but go to someone else?'

'I can't answer for all men . . .'

'Just answer for yourself.'

My blood. It struck me in the face. I wanted like the devil to slap her for that. To press her beneath me until her words stopped! Until she grew utterly still in my arms.

'Our . . . our relationship isn't so certain,' I said.

'Explain how you see it.'

'It's not so simple . . .'

'Start somewhere.'

You could imagine you trusted her. Told her everything. Even things I did not really know myself. And if I dared to expose myself like that? Now? Did I have anything to lose?

'Aksel, to begin with,' I heard myself say.

'He's my concern.'

'He's my friend.'

She gazed at me from beneath lowered eyelids. Confound it, didn't she look lustful? Even if she was the professor's daughter? Yes! Anna was flirting with me. Sending me glances! She said nothing for a while. We simply looked at each other. I felt she had not even heard the words: 'He's my friend.'

Then she broke in with a whisper:

'Do you remember Peer Gynt? The Bøyg? Do you remember the Bøyg?'

I swallowed.

'I remember Peer best,' I said. 'What do you mean?'

'You say one thing and think about something completely different. You want everything to go perfectly. So you can avoid . . .'

'That's not true!'

You could actually toy with the thought of escape. Escape from Anna. Her words. You could look longingly towards the door when someone opened it and walked out to the street.

'Was it just nonsense . . . what you said you felt for me . . .'

'No!' I interrupted.

'Then tell me what you want!'

'I want things to go well for you. For Aksel and you.'

She silently mimicked the words with her mouth. Her eyes slowly filled with tears. Then she began pulling her gloves through the palms of her hands. Time after time. The same, almost desperate, movement. I started counting. Six. Seven. Remembered I had performed such rituals as a boy when everything seemed threatening. I used to count all sorts of things. In order to stop at a particular number and be saved. But I had to be in a certain position in relation to the danger.

When she reached her number and stopped, I said:

'Life isn't like reading books.'

'Isn't it?' she said.

What could you say?

'This Karna . . . Her baby? It's alive, isn't it?'

She knew about it! I should have seen that when she came in the door! Aksel told her. Or she guessed it herself when he told her about Karna and the baby. Of course! And now what? Could anything be worse?

'It's alive,' I said.

'And you didn't intend to tell me? Despite what you said?'

This had become too ugly. This was not the way love was supposed to be. An unpleasant interrogation in a cafe.

'What good would it do to bother you with it?' I said.

'Bother me!'

She rocked slowly back and forth on her chair. Suddenly I felt an intense dislike. Towards myself. And therefore towards her. The one who could sleep!

'What hurts most . . . is to despise someone,' I heard

411

her say somewhere above me. Then I realized she was walking towards the door.

At last I could do something concrete. Run after her. The waiter stopped me firmly. And at first I did not realize he wanted payment for two glasses of juice. I dug the coins out of my pocket in confusion.

When I came outside, she was standing holding onto a lamp post. I threw my arms around her without stopping to realize we could cause a public outrage at Kongens Nytorv.

'Anna, can you forgive me?' I whispered.

'I can't forgive you for how you are,' she said simply, and pulled herself free.

You were surprised she did not cry. She should have cried.

We walked aimlessly towards Østergade.

Suddenly I knew this was one of those moments I would carry with me. Walking beside Anna. Perhaps one day I would think: I walked with Aksel's Anna that evening.

Of course I could also not think about it. But I would never forget it.

'How will I make you understand?' I said.

She did not look at me. Just walked. Straight ahead.

'I understand. It's you who doesn't understand! I have . . . have . . . And you still don't understand!'

'Why you wanted to meet me?'

'That too.'

'You're courageous, Anna. I can understand why Aksel wants you.'

She stopped short and looked at me. Then she raised her hand and slapped my face. People stopped and stared.

I could not take my eyes from her bonnet. In her haste she had cuffed its ears too. It was crooked for a moment, and then hung over her shoulder by its ribbons.

'And you?' she screamed. 'What do you want?'

But she still did not cry.

I covered my face with my hands. It was all I could do. The mistake could not be corrected. I must just let time pass.

Again you longed to say something that would make her excuse everything. After all, Karna was no longer there. But to actually say it . . .

She calmed down while I helped with her bonnet. My cheek stung from her slap. That way she was very close.

Things could not get worse, so I ventured to take her arm when we began walking again. Felt the material of her sleeve against my hand.

I should have known she was not finished yet.

'What are you going to do with the baby?' she asked into the air. Her voice was whisks in a metal container.

'I?'

'Yes, you!'

'I've chased around to all the midwives in the city to get milk,' I said.

'And that's enough?'

'Things are better now . . .'

At that moment she began to cry. As if it were wrong that I got milk.

We had come to Amager Torv. An omnibus and three horse-drawn cabs were lined up lazily in the shadow of some broad marquees. A vegetable seller still sat taking an afternoon nap under her umbrella. She had put an old *Adressavisen* over her face. The newspaper flapped disrespectfully each time she exhaled, and stuck to her face with a snoring sound when she inhaled. All to the great enjoyment of a couple of boys scurrying about.

I needed so much to have something to laugh about. Why couldn't Anna and I laugh? I leaned over her and attempted a smile. But she did not look at me. I was a hole in the air.

'I have to go home,' she said.

'Why?'

'Aksel and I are supposedly taking a walk . . . He'll meet me at A Porta and go home with me for dinner.'

413

You could think about her having used Aksel! As a chaperone, in order to meet me! Instead, I somehow felt smothered. Something became dead tissue somewhere. It had to be cut away. You could call it jealousy. Or loneliness. If there was any difference?

'So you need to leave . . .' I mumbled, and turned to accompany her back to the cafe.

'You're so . . .' she said unsteadily, without finishing her sentence.

I did not ask what she meant.

'Will I see you again?' I asked instead.

She stopped and blew her nose in a tiny handkerchief. Suddenly she appeared indifferent. Completely calm. You could not even see she had been crying.

'That's up to you to decide,' she replied.

I did not ask what she meant. It was not the right time.

Østergade was an endless street today. I said nothing. Just held her elbow respectfully. When I saw Aksel turn into the cafe with long strides I let go of her and stopped walking.

'Thank you for meeting me,' I said politely.

She hesitated a moment, reached out and touched the front of my shirt. Quick as a flash. Then she turned and left.

'Bless you, Anna!' I called after her in a low voice.

I do not know if she heard me. She gave no indication.

A dog loped up to me and rubbed against my legs. I leaned down and patted it a few times. The sky had begun to turn violet. The Holy Ghost church bells rang. Seven chimes.

Anna had been with me a whole hour!

CHAPTER 18

Aksel lived at the new Valkendorf collegium. Not just anyone got a place there. In 1588 King Frederik II decreed that Hvide cloister on Regent Valkendorf's land should provide housing for sixteen poor, industrious students. But history changed many things. The old cloister was torn down and a new building constructed.

Aksel was neither poor nor industrious. But he lived there nonetheless. Behind a solid front portal, well-trimmed hedges and a flagpole. With his own entrance from a corridor. It was heaven for a student or intern.

Two days after seeing Anna, I went to remind Aksel that we had a trip to make. I had not seen him at the hospital.

Like me, he did not lock his room. I went in and settled down on the bed. With my shoes on and one of his cigars for comfort. I took a nap, and when I awoke Aksel had not appeared.

Hearing another resident walk past, I stuck my head out the door and asked if he knew where Aksel was. He had gone home for a few days, I was told.

Dusk had already crept into the building. I resolutely lay down on the bed and lit another cigar. After a while I realized Aksel had gone home to get money for the trip. So he took everything seriously after all!

She must have moved almost without a sound. I did not notice her footsteps until the door opened and she stood there, breathing hard. Anna!

When she saw me, she just stood there. With both hands behind her back. As if holding the door against unknown enemies.

'Benjamin!' she exclaimed.

'Yes.'

You could imagine you were lying in Aksel's bed dreaming about Anna. But you were not dreaming. She was real.

'What are you doing here?' she asked. The words came slowly as she took a breath and let it out.

'I was waiting for Aksel. They say he's gone home for a few days. And you?'

'I came to visit Aksel,' she said.

'You do that often?' I asked, trying to sound contemptuous.

'It happens.'

'Do your parents know . . . ?'

'Why do you ask?'

Her gaze was veiled. The darkness of the walls seemed such a crazy blue. I got up from the bed. That was an impossible place. I put out the cigar. The small room was a shell. Around Anna and me! I had her. Near me. Alone. And no one could see us.

A giant wave came from the deep and lifted me with it. I stumbled across the room. Put a hand on either side of her neck and fastened her to the door with my body. Found her mouth while I pressed her between the door and me. Pressed without putting my hands on her!

I locked the door. Yes, it was I who locked the door.

'No!' she said when I closed my arms around her and kissed her again.

'No!' she said when I repeated her name over and over.

She definitely said no. But she was with me! I felt her with me. I had learned 'no' did not always mean no. But I did not know I was so strong. Or did I know? Did I enjoy it? In Aksel's room. After a while, in Aksel's

416

bed. On his rough striped bedspread with clear marks of shoe blacking and cigars.

My strength forced a place on a flowering field. The fragrance! Dear good God, how fragrant it was in Aksel's room! Anna! Skin. Material. Hair. The walls were packed in dull brown soil. The ceiling was so easy to carry. For someone strong. She was so easy to reach.

Even if I remembered she came to see Aksel against the rules, it was not how things actually were. Because she was with me!

And you could imagine she too had been longing. You wanted to show her she had been longing. For me!

This was no wet, secret dream. One of those I would awaken from weakly satisfied, but without having used my body. My arms. What in the world did I use these two damn arms for before?

And my hands. My hands had to do such good deeds. Everywhere at once. Breathlessly I tried to run through all her gardens. Leaped over every fence and gate. Picked blooms in every flower bed.

'No!' she said.

But wasn't that just music? Of course it was music! Her voice. It did not matter what she said, because she had music within her.

'No,' she said again.

But her 'no' was outside my boundaries.

At the moment I felt her finger press my right eye until everything grew black and nauseous, I heard she was crying.

You could tell yourself you should have done things in a nicer way. More calmly. More lovingly. It was not like that. You did not know you were so strong.

I had to stop because of my aching eye. Blink again and again. The pain heightened my desire, but it held my strength in check awhile.

Then I realized I had toppled Anna onto the bed. It was all disorderly. Her elegant clothes. Everything. But it smelled so confounded sweet!

I lay with one hand under her jacket and blouse and noticed she had stopped crying. There was something amazingly soft in there. Her skin. Warm as holding Stine's baby eider ducks.

I kept thinking she would try to get up. But she lay utterly still. Terribly still. I raised an eyelid and looked straight at her closed eyes.

Then I began moving my hand. Slowly. Expecting she would defend herself against my hands. But her arm wound itself around my neck while her hand crept into my hair. It helped so much! That she had her hand in my hair.

I had not expected that. There was forgiveness in it. Karna's hands came between us. Powerless. For brief moments. But that did not matter.

I had to kiss her again, even if she got angry. When I opened my eyes once, I met an animal stare. Timid, furious, frightened, delighted. Everything. I burrowed my head into her to escape Karna's blood. I swallowed and struggled. My organ was so goal-oriented it hurt. I restrained myself. Found her skin with both hands, but restrained myself.

Her hat tumbled to the floor. I made an idiotic movement with my arm to pick it up. But she kicked it away with her foot. Her comb fell out and her hair tumbled down.

Then she did it! I could not think while she did it.

Ripped open the buttons of her blouse, tore at laces and hooks in her underclothing. Then they lay there. Anna's breasts lay there! Like two suitably large round pieces of halibut lying on a beach in the dark.

You did not have to believe it. Because now things were as they once had been. I could look at them in peace and quiet without their running away. They were not very large. But golden, with small dark nipples. Different from those I had seen before?

Why do you try to ruin things for yourself in sacred moments? Why did I lie here with Anna and make comparisons? With whom? The madam in Peder

418

Madsen's Passage? Or the girl with the velvet ribbon around her neck and ugly blue spots on her breast in Magstraede? Or the lonely wife in Berlin? Or the tanner's Andrea! Good God, how you can complicate sacred moments! Karna's soft generous bosom with large spreading nipples? While Anna's breasts lay in my hands?

And Anna? Did she see me? My thoughts? Did she realize I was comparing her with all the others? Did she see how little I had learned from them? Because it was mostly done out of compelling necessity. Does one even do such things out of love?

Desire? Anna! Can desire be love?

I did not ask. Desire was a stallion. It could not be stopped. It jumped over fences and leaped across ramparts. This was the finish. This was what my hands and body did to fulfill a longing.

What happens to fulfilled longings? No matter what, I will long to do it again. Specifically with her!

Anna had to be the braver one. Anna! The professor's talented daughter. I fumbled with her face and hair. Caressed naked skin. The exciting transition from thin material to skin. The edges. The lacings. The buttons. Her buttocks had a fine viscous surface. Like touching the plush of the old chaise longue in the smoking room at Reinsnes. I so wished I could see her naked. Feel the skin around her waist.

At first I did not dare to touch her opening. You could go so far as to sigh and feel you were almost there. But I did not dare. What if it now proved that the whole time she had fooled me into believing she wanted to? Only to push me into the dark again?

At the brink of disaster you always make a choice.

I chose Anna's opening. And just when I held my breath and was about to thrust into her, she pulled back. Her animal eyes tried to tell me something, but I could not meet her gaze. Was already swimming through a deep dark sea.

Her eyes pleaded. I regained my senses. The thought! You had to think the thought. Had to understand, even if you felt pain down there. That I was the first. Not Aksel? Not anyone!

My desire, which had pounded in my ears and forced its rhythm throughout my body, grew still. You could call it confusion. Or tenderness? You could think about what to do now. And that you never had anyone for whom it was the first time.

You could ask, but you would have to ask fast. How do you ask?

Our eyes floated into each other while her silky legs wound around my naked hips. Then she pressed her stomach against me and held my buttocks.

I heard my groan, and the room disappeared. There was only one place in the world: hard and wet and soft.

Anna's willingness to bear pain came between us. She did not utter a sound. It was just a matter of making the movements. You had certainly made them before!

But I could not do it. Shrank inside her. When you had everything, and it was just a matter of doing it, you shrank. I felt her hand along my back under my shirt. While I thought desperately about the thrusts. The wild, blind thrusts I should make in Anna.

I could think about it until I blacked out. But I could not do it. Finally we lay absolutely still. She lay under me and stroked my face with her fingertips.

We lay together without looking at each other. Gradually I could make out the furniture in the room. The walls. It occurred to me I should pull her skirt over her.

'Benjamin,' she simply said.

You could not know what that meant. So I fumbled for her hand. To somehow make everything good again, I started in with everything: the buttons, the hooks, the lacings.

'Benjamin,' she said again.

I waited. But could say nothing. We sat on Aksel's bed with our arms around each other. She looked down at herself with shame, and drew her blouse over her breasts.

My pungent body odors filled my nostrils. The ugly beside the beautiful. The man in Aksel's bed. Beside Anna's body. What had I done? My throat grew slimy.

Someone went by whistling under the window.

Once we held our breath as somebody came up the steps and shuffled down the long corridor. We were probably both thinking the same: he's coming! Aksel. Now we've crushed Aksel.

When all was quiet again, she crushed me:

'Now you can go to the barmaids. Now I'm like them!'

You should be prepared that women can be so awful.

'Anna, Anna . . .' I begged, and drew her close.

But I saw it clearly. My offense was written in red letters on every wall! I had ripped Anna's self-image to shreds. What was Anna now? Why did you have to tear women to pieces? I could not wish it undone, and I had probably never done anything worse. Anna! On Aksel's bed while he was getting money to go and find Dina.

I do not know how, but words came which I did not even realize I knew. I spoke haltingly, but got the words out:

' "Behold, you are beautiful, my friend; behold you are beautiful! Your eyes are doves behind your veil; your hair is like a flock of goats, moving down the slopes of Gilead . . . You are all fair, my friend, there is no flaw in you. Come with me from Lebanon, my bride, come with me from Lebanon!" '

Her hands fell into her lap and she lit a small candle for me in each of her two blue eyes.

When I had whispered the last words, she sniffled a little, raised her hand and brushed it across her face. Then she buttoned her blouse up to the neck. As she gathered her hair under her hat, I saw the nape of her

421

neck was golden too, and her mouth was trembling. I do not know how unhappy she was. I could have asked. But then I would have had to bear it if she started to cry. I would prefer to think that she too felt a lonely longing to possess the forbidden for a little while. Just a little while! That her body was longing! And this longing was stronger than unhappiness and betrayal? Stronger than what we felt for each other?

I should have talked to her about it. But how? I sat on Aksel's bed, with time and space a taste of blood in my mouth. That was probably why I recited those great words. About love. Or whatever it was?

She could have said, 'You won't escape this time, Benjamin.' But she did not say that. We helped each other with the essentials. Clothes. Hair and shoes. Clung to a common concern for each other. We felt so guilty we had to drown it in mutual tenderness in order to bear it.

'Now at least we know who we are,' she said when she was ready to leave.

As she opened the door, a draft from somewhere caught a strand of her hair and blew it towards her hat brim. For a wild moment I repeated: ' "Come with me from Lebanon, my bride, come with me from Lebanon!" '

But when she was gone, I realized I had not spoken a word.

CHAPTER 19

Three days after Valkendorf, Aksel still had not shown up. He must have given an excuse at the hospital, because nobody asked about him there, even though this was the end of 'jus practicandi'. And I did not dare to ask.

I said to myself that Anna had told Aksel everything. That it was just a matter of time until he came to Bredgade and pasted me to the widow's wallpaper.

I realized I was making a penitential journey when I went to see Karna's grandmother. I promised again to get her some money. Karna's brother and I made a few milk runs together. That is to say: I went to Maternity Hospital, and he took the milk home with him.

The last day at the hospital Aksel turned up with complete equanimity. The moment I saw him, I knew Anna had not said anything. After the final ceremony in the 'church' with speeches and an untuned piano, he came over and clapped my shoulder.

'I've got the money!'

I do not know how people like me should behave. It was new to me in fact. To be someone like that. You can make excuses and say it took five minutes before we sat together under the trees in Grønnegården. And once we were sitting there alone, Aksel was so terribly happy. Went on and on about his good mother. He felt he owned the whole world.

You can't always tell things the way they are, for

heaven's sake! We see that time after time here in this world.

I could not bring myself to go out drinking to celebrate. Not with Aksel. Complained of feeling ill. He and the others threatened to come to Bredgade to check on me if I did not show up later that evening. Then they went off to Valkendorf or Regensen. Their singing shattered the air long after they were behind brick walls.

You could stand there on the cobblestones and curse being born an idiot and a scoundrel. Or wander through the streets. You could go up to Anna's door three times without knocking. You could watch the shadows lengthen and tell yourself:

'Now you can go to Nordland and say you killed your mother's lover! You spent a little time in Copenhagen. But that's over.'

I could still sit in pubs for a few days drinking Danish beer and thinking everything was futile. But then I would have to stop eating hot meals. Because Karna's grandmother needed all the money I could spare.

For one crazy moment I sat on a bench and believed I was saving money to get my clothes cleaned and buy new boots so I could go to Berlin with Aksel. But that was impossible now. To travel with Aksel.

The city was dusty and hot. At the corner of Østergade, Amager marketplace opened before me. People and animals steamed in their own warmth and the sun's heat. The shadows were still short. Those who could, sought refuge along the tall buildings. Harnessed to a buggy by a lamp post stood a gleaming black horse, lazily eating from a feed bag while the driver dozed under the carriage hood.

At the exact moment I remembered walking here with Anna, I was sure she came out of the tailor's. But it was someone else. I had seen Anna several times. Was ready to rush over to her. But it was always someone else. Sometimes I left without investigating whether it really was she. That way I had her. A little.

A water wagon thundered past, sending cascades of water over a flock of street urchins who used the chance to cool off.

The Amager market women sat behind wooden tables heaped with vegetables and potted plants. Some had umbrellas. Others drew their kerchiefs into a point above their faces as sweat ran off them. The gutters stank. Passers-by held their noses while they walked on planks across the worst ditches.

As I crossed the street, an omnibus drove away. A group of men in top hats sat on the roof. As if molded into the air. With no will to live. While clouds floated behind the rows of buildings. Inside the ombibus sat the women. Motionless. Like wax figures. Afraid of melting in the heat.

I wandered along Gammel Strand and looked at the fishwives. A habit I had developed. Perhaps the fish smell drew me there. Or the fact I sometimes could not bear to meet people I knew.

The distance from Bredgade across Kongens Nytorv was usually just far enough to clear my brain. But not today. At the corner of Store Strandstraede I had to face a guilty conscience: should I see to Karna's grandmother? Or?

I won.

At Højbro a young servant girl walked past with a gleaming fish in her basket. A tantalizing scent of cheap toilet water blended with fresh perspiration and fish. She had opened her jacket in the heat. Her breasts swayed under her thin blouse. Two overripe fruits. I must have stared at her. Because she lowered her eyes and hurried past. I could not help turning around. Heaviness spread in my groin. And loneliness.

I walked among the fish stalls hearing the shouts of broad-hipped women in kerchiefs under the umbrellas. Went close to them and met their direct gaze, until the tanned faces broke into a smile. Their mouths opened and their hands fumbled for the smooth smelly wares. They wiped slime and fish scales on their aprons after each sale.

I strolled a few 'side streets'. Past open windows with plump arms and stiff, cheap smiles. It was late afternoon now, with plenty of shadows in the corners. Then the women appeared.

'Now you can go to the barmaids! Now I'm like them!' resounded to my footsteps until I lowered my eyes and walked past.

On my way home I noticed the date on a newspaper, and it became important to recall what Mother Karen's calendar stick said about 17 June.

I did not remember until I got back to my room and saw the landlady had put a letter on the table. From Anders. As I opened it, I remembered: 17 June. Bottolfs mass. 'The earth that has rested this year must be plowed now, because all the roots are loose and can easily be pulled up – and later rot.'

The room was stiflingly hot. A heavy smell of fried onions seeped in from the kitchen. It made me more nauseated than hungry, although I had eaten nothing all day. I tossed my jacket on the hook by the door and took the letter out to the courtyard.

Anders had not sent just a letter. He sent a large sum of money without my asking for it. Karna's grandmother would be happy about that, and I could still travel home in first class.

He began with a careful overview of the people at Reinsnes. Stine and Tomas. The children. Hanna, who became widowed in late spring and therefore moved home with her son.

It was hard to imagine Hanna as a widow with a child. For a moment I saw her in my mind. A small dark figure with a steady gaze and stubborn expression. But the image slipped away. I could not hold onto it.

Had not thought about her for a long time.

Anders wrote most about the good herring fishing.

Reinsnes boats had been unbelievably fortunate. And they had sold so much more than in previous years. Speculation and changing business conditions had ruined many boat owners, but not him, he wrote in his square stiff handwriting.

He never mentioned the word 'loan' in his letters. He called it necessary resources. Now he had the upper hand on this 'bad practice'.

I could imagine him as he sat there in the office at the store sipping rum from the old hand-blown glass with a chipped rim.

He wrote enthusiastically about the new telegraph office at Sandsøy. And there was a telegraph office in Tromsø too. It was marvelous. Like magic, you could say. It made the world very small. He urged me to telegraph when I would arrive. He thought it was such fun to get telegrams. I could send it collect if I was short of money. Times were good. Large herring were God's gift to both rich and poor in the north. There was good weather at sea beyond Bjarkøy, and the herring were thick beyond Malangen. But one had to go out and take them, because they did not come near land.

He wrote matter-of-factly that he had bought a roof over their heads in Strandsted, and had hired people to salt herring. He believed in that business. As long as you did not lose your head in the herring entrails. People were happy for the income and easier to do business with. Taking out fire insurance to show you were a big shot had become an epidemic. They had done it at Reinsnes too. Anyway, the people and cattle were fine and healthy.

Letters from Anders were from another world. When you read them you always felt you had forgotten something.

Some days are like no other days.

This day did not begin with the ceremony at the hospital and the realization that our training was finished. Did not begin when Aksel and the others disappeared around the corner, nor with the compulsive thought about Mother Karen's calendar stick and the letter from Anders.

The day began late in the afternoon. Behind the wooden fence that separated the water pump from the cats and garbage kegs. A large willow tree created a comforting oasis together with the water pump. Water always dripped from the spout. Trickled constantly. Like a secret spring from within the earth.

The three tall buildings surrounding the courtyard were the skeleton for all sorts of dormers and out-buildings. They leaned over the courtyard to create living space for more and more people. Stairways, external walkways and bay windows created good shade on a day like this. High above, stockings and shirts fluttered cheerfully on clothes lines, casting shadows on the red brick wall. Flower boxes tried to give the impression of an idyllic spot. Windows were open, and the sounds of people and objects merged into a disjointed cacophony. Life, it was called.

The bench I sat on was solid enough. But still, I seemed to be swaying. The shadows, the rustling tree-tops above me. Four clouds floating in the sky. It all flickered and pressed against my eyelids. Now and then the hinges on the front gate squeaked. I could not see the entrance from where I sat. But after a moment the upper part of a head might appear above the wooden fence. If the person was a certain height. Or wearing a hat.

I dozed a few times and thought I saw Anna. Fleetingly. A pale straw hat with a soft brim. The sun intensified her golden skin. It lasted just a fraction of a second. Like when leaves cast restless shadows on your eyelids. Then I was alone with a faint breeze.

I was reading the letter from Anders for the third time when someone came through the front gate. Light steps. Immediately afterwards I heard Madam Frederiksen's loud voice through the window on the first floor.

'Yes, he's home. He's sitting on the bench by the water pump.'

Anna! It must be Anna! I had conjured her to me!

I closed my eyes tightly and pretended to be asleep. The rustle of a skirt was unmistakable. Her shadow fell on me, but I did not respond. It was a game. A game that sent me floating. I grew out of my body. Was a tree with branches in the sky and roots in my groin.

I could tell by the silence that she stood looking at me. But I did not open my eyes. She would have to touch me before I responded. Had to come over to me. And I would be innocent. She had to come to me, as she had come to Valkendorf. This time she had to come to me!

CHAPTER 20

'Benjamin,' a voice called from somewhere above me.

The voice? Where had I heard it? A wave. Slow. The voice was fragrant. Had such a crazy light. It hurt. Wrecking bars pried at my eyes. Something hard seemed to hit me again and again on each temple.

Then suddenly I was a child sitting on a black horse being led across the fields. She stood beside me wearing a yellow suit and a wide-brimmed beige hat and said:

'Benjamin!'

Without my doing anything to make it happen, I stood up beside the bench. I probably thought I should go to my room and sleep a little. The heat was stifling. Anders's letter was completely wet in my hand. When I spread my fingers it stuck to my palm.

There was something wrong with the face. You could tell yourself it was just a matter of starting to walk, and then everything would dissolve and be exactly as before.

Because if it had been reality, you would have known what to do. Because you had planned it since you were a boy! Everything. What you would say. What she would answer.

Then the voice came again. A sea breeze? Here in a Copenhagen courtyard? A banal longing? That said:

'Benjamin . . . don't you know me?'

Then the pendulum began to swing. Slowly at first. Then steadily faster. You could grasp it to hold it still.

But then you just got caught on it and had to swing with it.

So you swung from side to side. Far into outer space. Finally, so fast that you had to sit down. But the wooden bench was unsafe, so it was best to stand up again immediately.

A cool wet hand on my forehead. Running water nearby. Why didn't someone fix the water spout? Why was everything so undependable? Why didn't you go to bed before it was too late?

The fragrance was stronger now. You had to raise your hand to protect yourself. To end this. The hand laid itself on her breast. Her jacket was open. Warm skin through thin material. Her face! So close. Could you touch it?

I could not help saying:

'Mama!'

I repeated it again and again. The years were erased. Everything was where it had been and always should be. Before the Russian. I dissolved within my own body. I clung to her. Whimpered.

She held me tight. I do not know what happened. Do not know what I said. Just that she held me tight. And that her pale eyes looked at me. Calmly. Somewhat introspectively, as if she could not quite bear to look. Somewhat in wonder, as if she thought:

'Yes, it's him!'

She saw me!

She had not yet said anything. Except: 'Benjamin . . .' And: 'Don't you know me?'

Still, we went into the building together as if we had agreed for years that we needed to hide ourselves. Up the stairs. Through the smell of fried onions.

Once in my room I hung over the end of the bed for a while. Stared at her. Then I stumbled to the open window and back again. Still staring.

She took off her suit jacket and hat. Then she sat down on the bed with a sigh.

431

Somebody threw a ball against the wall. I counted the thuds. Twenty-one. Then everything was silent. Infinitely silent.

You could imagine this was the blessedness of death. In the midst of this death, widow Frederiksen came and offered iced tea or soda water to young Grønelv's mother.

Dina said thank you and asked if we could have it brought here. We had so much to talk about – if the landlady did not mind.

Madam Frederiksen certainly did not mind.

'This young man has studied so hard, he's worked himself sick. He hasn't been himself,' said Madam Frederiksen, making it clear that she kept an eye on things.

You could get the impression that you were a person of consequence in the house.

The soda water arrived in the nicest glasses from the large front cupboard.

Dina's voice was in the room again. Brushed past my ears like wind. Small, insignificant words. Tiny questions. About whether I really had been sick. About whether there were any places nearby to eat.

Eat?

Somewhere inside me was a broad, quiet river. Everything floated on it. Everything she said.

And the pale eyes? Were they like that? So clear? How could I have hated them? How could I ever believe she was guilty? Guilty of what?

I could hold her hands tightly to atone for everything. But when I met her eyes the river carried the words:

'You must see Karna's daughter!'

She smiled.

How simple everything became then. Simple! Until she asked:

'Karna's daughter?'

I think it was then I understood Dina was real.

She sat looking at me. Questioningly. God and Dina looked at me. I began to tremble.

Finally I managed to shake my head and say it was nothing. Absolutely nothing! And the river flowed on with her words. They were small bubbles that came from the bottom. From old logs lying in the deeps and slowly turning into earth. From small fish hiding along the shores. You could see them glisten beneath the water's surface.

But then suddenly she rose and went towards the door. I ran after her. Gripped her arm hard. Pulled her back.

'Don't go! Don't go! This time you mustn't leave, Dina!'

My voice had a menacing tone. I stared at her threateningly as she tried to twist from my grasp. But her eyes were calm. Terribly calm.

'I'm not leaving, Benjamin! I just have an errand in the courtyard.'

'Oh no! No! You've got to stay here!'

She closed her eyes a moment, then opened them and looked at me. Almost affectionately.

'Then we'll go together,' she said.

I released my grip.

'Afterwards we'll go somewhere and get something to eat,' she added as she put on her hat.

I positioned myself between her and the door. She walked over to the cello case and laid her hand on it. Said nothing. Just showed she had seen it.

'Well?' she said. 'Aren't you going to put on a jacket too? So you look like a decent fellow.'

I did as she said.

She stood in the middle of the room, ready to leave, and glanced around it a few times.

'So both you and Johan have lived in this room?' she said.

'Yes,' I mumbled.

'Do you like it here?'

'I live here,' I said.

As we were about to leave the room she said:

'You're speaking Danish?'

'Yes.'

'To me too?'

'To you too.'

She was walking ahead of me, so I could not see her face. But I had a feeling she smiled. I should not have answered her like that. I should have added a bit of humor. Said it had become a habit. Anything at all.

The Canal Cafe. She read aloud the menu posted on the door, as if I were blind. I studied her skin. Her ear lobe with a pearl in it. The lines around her mouth. Her hairline. Her breasts. Her waist in the long, tight-fitting jacket.

She was older. Thinner than I remembered. The furrow between her eyes? Wasn't it deeper before? Strange. Did she think more good thoughts now? I felt childishly jealous. So I shifted my glance to her temples. They had a trace of white.

At a table far back in the restaurant I found some balance again. Found a technique of focusing my eyes on the base of her nose. That way I escaped. When she turned her head just slightly, the well-defined bridge of her nose appeared. The high cheek-bones. Her mouth had almost no Cupid's bow. I did not remember noticing that before. But there was a deep hollow above her upper lip. As if some finger had pressed an indentation there to make up for the carelessness with the Cupid's bow. The corners of her mouth turned up the way I remembered. Or did they do that just for me? Because I knew?

Was I really afraid of her? Now that she was here, I did not know what to say to her. All the reproaches and accusations I had formulated these years, where were they now? Where the devil were all the words? Why didn't I look her straight in the face and tell her what I thought?

She ate the same food I did. Ham and cheese, dark

bread, and strong beer. We chewed in silence for a long time. I devoured her with my eyes between each mouthful. She was more discreet. Several times she laid her hand on my arm.

'Don't eat so fast!' she commanded.

I stopped. She was giving me orders. I had to smile at that. But from then on I chewed as nicely as I could. Even so, I finished long before she did.

'You should have seen my friend Aksel!' I burst out eagerly. As if I were a schoolboy who finally realized how to entertain the grown-up.

'What about him?' she asked.

'He has a way of consuming raw eggs and schnapps . . . I'm sure he didn't learn that at home. He's from a parson's family . . .'

I stopped short, and blushed. Heard how ridiculous it was. I had not seen my mother since I was a boy, and one of the first things I told her about was Aksel's eating.

I saw laughter in her eyes. That made me braver. With a full stomach and a tankard of strong beer in my blood, I looked at her openly. Wanted to irritate her. Make her uncertain. Angry. I could hold her again if she got so angry she wanted to leave.

'I got a letter from Anders this morning,' I burst out. 'Everything is happening today! Do you want to read it?'

She shook her head and took a swallow of beer.

I drew the letter from my jacket pocket and pretended not to understand.

'I'll read it!' I said eagerly, smoothing out the paper.

'No!' she said loudly.

'Why not?'

She held up her hand with a deprecating gesture.

'You're a coward!' I snarled.

The moment the insolent words were out I realized they were not said in Danish. That made me even more furious.

'So be it,' she said slowly, without mentioning that I was not speaking Danish.

'Haven't you read any of the letters we sent you?' I asked between clenched teeth.

'I read them all. But I was by myself then. Everything in its time, Benjamin.'

'Really?'

She leaned forward on the table and rested her chin in both hands. The corners of her mouth turned up, but her eyes were serious.

'Put the letter away. It's to you, not to me,' she said.

I began to read aloud.

I thought she would get up and leave, so I could create a scene. But she just sat looking at me.

I tried to find the right tone as I read and at the same time watched her. It was not easy. For a little while the words flew between us like insects. Neither of us wanted them. In the middle of the letter I realized she was right. Because Anders disappeared. He was just a tool in the battle against Dina.

I folded up the letter. Folded and folded. Over and over again. Until it was just a small mound of paper in my hand. As it lay in my palm, the paper seemed to want something. It tried to unfold itself again. Small scratching wings against my skin.

'Tell me about yourself instead. Whatever you'd like me to hear,' she said.

'Why?'

'Because now I'm here and can listen.'

It was so strange. Her language. So long since I'd heard it. I was annoyed that it affected me. She spoke as though she came directly from Reinsnes. Today. And had never been away.

'I've finished my medical studies. I've bought my doctor's bag.'

'What an accomplishment, Benjamin! I didn't think you'd study to become a doctor . . .'

'Is there anything wrong with being a doctor?'

'No, it's wonderful! But I thought you'd rather read novels and things like that.'

She said it! She praised me! Still, it was all wrong. She should not say it like that! Why did she say that about novels? Why the devil did she say that?

I stood on the beach and watched Dina run up the tree-lined avenue. Up to the Russian's body. I stood with my feet in the ocean and leaned forward to drag the boat ashore. Alone. Now she reached the Russian. I stood down here with my feet in the ocean. The boat was much too heavy.

Waves of nausea rolled over me. Ham, cheese and dark beer threatened to come up and out.

'Is that all you have to say? Didn't you get the letter saying I was going to report myself to the authorities?' I asked.

'I got the letter.'

'So you know! Everything!'

'Nobody knows everything. But I know enough to be here. I hope you haven't reported it yet?' she said.

Was she talking about the weather?

'Damn it, are you talking about the weather?' I said.

'No,' she said.

She slowly wiped her mouth with her fingertips and leaned back in the chair. Her eyes crept into the shadows.

'It isn't your burden, Benjamin. Do you know that?'

'The burden is there . . . No matter whose it is.'

'And so you want to punish yourself, Benjamin? Because I didn't let myself be locked up?'

By this time most of the other customers had gone. Still, she was talking too loudly. I had to make her speak more softly. People could hear . . .

'You left,' I whispered.

The corners of her mouth turned up again. A smile? Or what was it? Karna's baby hanging from my hand, upside down, just before it cried the first time. The corners of its mouth!

Dina leaned across the table and held both my wrists. Tightly.

'Yes, I left you, Benjamin. I'm sure it feels like that.'

So she had said that too! She sat here. She held me!

I still stood with her hatbox in my hands. I still sat in a tree furiously shouting after her as she was rowed out to the cargo boat.

'Why did you send me only an old black Bible? So I would think you were dead?'

She did not reply immediately. Smoked-stained walls and ceiling locked us in with each other. A cone of light shone across the room, allowing a glimpse of Christiansborg castle through a somewhat dirty window.

'I suppose I thought . . . It was the only thing I could give you. I wanted you to have . . . peace,' she said uncertainly.

I could not give the contemptuous replies at the tip of my tongue: 'How nice you sent the Bible!' And: 'You could have sent a Bible to Anders too! He might deserve it.'

I said neither. Instead, I looked down at my palms. Examined the lines carefully.

'Did you know I was in Berlin?'

'Yes. And I knew you took the cello.'

'Why didn't I get to meet you?'

'I didn't know you were coming. I was in Paris . . .'

'I don't believe you!'

We were silent. For a while we just looked at each other. Then she simply said:

'I see.'

Life was empty now. Completely empty.

'Have I lied to you, Benjamin?'

'I don't know. You have at least not said things!'

'That I was going to leave? I said that!'

'I don't remember.'

'That's understandable. It would be too hard.'

She twisted a small thread from her blouse sleeve between her fingers, looking at me the whole time.

'Why did you come now?' I asked.

'I had to . . . make you understand.'

'Understand?'

'Yes. You can't take upon yourself something you haven't done.'

'What do you mean?'

She took her time. Then said clearly and softly:

'It wasn't you. One autumn day Dina Grønelv shot and killed Leo Zjukovski with a Lapp rifle, while Benjamin Grønelv stood on a hill and saw everything. Since then, Benjamin has been motherless.'

Her face froze. Her eyes were open channels in the ice.

She said it! She sat here and said it! Still, it didn't make things good.

'Is that enough now, Benjamin?'

Can anyone answer such a question?

Everything got so quiet. I saw the sounds, but heard nothing when the waiter piled fourteen plates on the shelf.

'Thank you for not giving up. I had to come,' she said.

She said it! I heard her say it!

The river flowed again. Everything floated. Dina too. A woman no longer completely young, who floated on a river among her words. Who tried to maintain some dignity, even if she knew it was hopeless.

We were the only customers in the cafe. The waiter scurried around in a coarse white apron and made it clear he wanted us to leave. I was afraid this person would ruin everything by talking to us, so I started fumbling in my pockets for money to pay the bill.

She was quicker. Found money in her purse.

I looked at the picture on the wall. A sailing vessel in a dark frame. I could imagine that when everything was over, when the river had taken both us and our words out to sea, I would still see in my mind the ship in the Canal Cafe. While I was doing something completely different. Like opening a book.

439

Out on the street, she took my arm and said cheerfully:

'You've grown. A lot!'

'And you've shrunk a little,' I countered as lightheartedly as possible.

It helped. We kept walking and smiling hesitantly at each other. The sun was setting. It bathed Slottsholmen, the church towers, and the highest roofs towards the west. Turned red brick to gold. Curtains of light, dust and shadow, thin as crêpe, hung between the buildings. Layer after layer.

'At this time of year the sun never sets at Reinsnes,' she said.

'That's right.'

'It would be nice to have salty sea breezes and night sun,' she added lightly. All too lightly.

I knew what she was really saying.

She hailed a carriage going by.

'I need to get my luggage at the station, and then find lodgings.'

Now she was like she was in the old days. Practical, brief and energetic.

'Let's go to the sea. Do you know some places?' she said.

'It depends on what you want, and what you can pay.'

'It should smell of soap and sea, have clean towels, and two beds.'

'Two?'

'Two!' she said firmly. 'You're so big now.'

'Do we have enough money to go outside Copenhagen?' I asked. But I could hear how eager I was.

She was already bargaining with the coachman. We would fetch her baggage and stop at Bredgade to get some necessary things for me. Within a few minutes she had agreed on the place and price. The coachman knew just the place. His brother rented out a small house by the sea north of Klampenborg.

'We can take the train,' I said.

She turned to me. Was exactly as I remembered her. Dina from Reinsnes.

'That's a bad way to do business! To entice the seller into revealing where to find the wares, and then cheat him of his profit. Besides, I don't want to rub knees with strangers, or listen to fat matrons who want space for all their baggage and dogs. I've had enough of riding in train compartments for a while.'

When we got to Bredgade, I went in alone. Madam Frederiksen rushed into the hall with many regrets and a sweaty nose. She would have liked so much to invite my mother and me for dinner.

'. . . but unfortunately my sister is sick, and I must hurry out to Roskilde to see to her. That trip is a nightmare, and . . .'

She kept talking while I tried to explain that we had already eaten, and that we were going to the country for a few days.

Then she began her admonitions about toilet buckets, fires and locking doors.

I hastily threw some clothes and a few books into my sailor's bag while she stood talking in the open doorway. Suddenly my eye fell on the cello behind the bed. I grabbed it too, and noisily moved towards Madam Frederiksen with both hands full.

'The keys!' she reminded me. And the next moment she let out a cry, an entreaty to God. It was so unusual that I stopped.

'Something wrong?'

'No, no, it's just that the young man, the one you see so often . . . he was here looking for you.'

'Aksel? The tall fellow with lots of blond hair?'

'Yes, yes, Aksel. He asked me to tell you he'd be back. This evening.'

My first thought was that he knew nothing about Anna and me. But then it struck me that this was

441

precisely what he did know. I stood there with the cello in one hand and my sailor's bag in the other.

'How did he look?' I asked.

'Oh, like always. Nicely dressed and . . .'

'I mean, was he upset or anything?'

'Not that I could tell,' she answered in surprise.

It would be just like Aksel to hide his fury, I thought. Now I might as well crawl into the ground. Or into the sea.

I ran past Madam Frederiksen and down the stairs.

'The keys?' I heard her shout after me.

'Yes! Have a good trip!' I shouted back.

'What should I tell your friend when he comes?' she shrieked.

I stopped. And tried to think fast.

'Say I've gone north to Klampenborg with my mother! Just say my mother is here!'

The truth was best. He would hardly come looking for me and paste me to the wall like wallpaper when he knew Dina was there.

She made no comment about my dragging along the cello.

When we were outside the city and driving by the sea, she said:

'It might have been nice to just settle down here. By the sea, you know.'

'In Copenhagen?'

'In Denmark. There's something about it. The language. Everything. Closer . . .'

'Yes,' I said.

The coachman's back was dark with sweat. He hummed softly. I noticed that he raised the whip so its shadow danced above the horse's head. But he did not strike the animal.

We drove between rows of large trees. The shadows turned them into cool green fairy-tale animals. They owned the sky.

There were so many things I wanted to ask about. But I did not know where to begin.

'When did you start speaking German? I mean, speaking German so people understood you?'

She thought for a moment.

'Once I woke up after I had dreamed in German . . . and there was someone there I could talk with. Something changed then. I realized I'd never had anyone to talk with . . . about my thoughts. Not in Norwegian.'

With those words she took all my pawns off the chessboard. I did not dare to move.

'It's not just the language . . . You see, people almost never meet each other. And so of course they can't talk to each other. Today I think you and I really met, Benjamin.'

She sat looking at her hands.

'I was so afraid to meet you. And then it was so wonderful . . . You've got just a slight Danish accent. Not much, considering how many years you've been here. It feels like coming home with all my thoughts, son.'

She said it! She actually sat there and said it! It was not just something I imagined. I wanted to stand up in the carriage and laugh out loud. Instead, I said:

'Have you ever seen so many big trees in your life, Dina?'

'Oh yes! But it's always nice to see . . .'

Blue shadows chased across her face as we drove under the trees.

And suddenly I was walking in the rain with Karna. Walking with Karna and remembering Dina as Anders's bride in the stone church. With leaves casting shadows on her face. Time did not exist. Everything wove together: Dina as a bride. Karna with rain dripping from her hair and eyelashes. Dina in the carriage with me with sunlight flickering on her face.

I knew that even if I did not think about it, I would never forget it. I would never know why the images belonged together. Why I remembered those particular images together.

'Were you fond of Anders?' I asked out of the blue.

She hesitated a little.

'I'm still fond of him. But you see . . . So much happened in between.'

'The Russian?'

She nodded.

'And you, Benjamin! Anders was yours. Was the person you had.'

'We could have shared him surely?'

'Could we?'

'Did you marry him for my sake?'

'Why do you ask?'

'Because you're finally here, so I can ask.'

She thought for a moment.

'No,' she said firmly. 'I got married for my own sake! But you could put it like this: I wouldn't have married Anders if I hadn't seen he could be good for you. And for Reinsnes . . .'

'Later, after you left, did you think about . . . how things were for him there?'

The carriage swayed violently. We rode over some branches lying in the road. The coachman reduced the speed and stood up to calm the horse.

She turned to me while holding herself fast in the seat.

'Benjamin, I know you've had to take sides, against me and for Anders. It can't be otherwise.'

What could I say? After a while she added:

'But I thought about how things were for him. Every day. Every single day I thought about how things were for all of you.'

CHAPTER 21

The house we rented was right on the beach. It was actually an old boathouse. One room, with only the most essential comforts. Beds fastened to the walls behind a checkered curtain. A table and chairs. A fireplace. We got water from a barrel that was filled once a day. The owner ran an inn, and his son brought us supplies on a handcart.

The hours flowed into one another. Now and then time stopped completely. The sea gazed kindly at us. While we revealed ourselves to each other, powerfully, like the breakers around the skerries at home. Crashed down and were drawn in. With tremendous force. Only to withdraw again. Far, far out. Each into our own deeps.

We spent the first night drinking together like old friends. Several times she laughed aloud. Her laughter seemed so strange. Until I realized I did not remember her laughter. Dina did not often laugh at Reinsnes. I had to ask her about that.

'No, we didn't laugh much there.'

'Were you always unhappy?'

She looked at me. Straightened the tablecloth and moved her glass slightly.

'Unhappy? No . . . not exactly. But there was a lot to think about. A lot to be done. And you weren't grown-up . . . We probably didn't laugh at the same things, you and I? That's probably the reason . . .'

'Also the Russian?'

'Also the Russian,' she said.

'Do you mind if I ask something?'

'Maybe it's best to get it over with?'

'What do you mean?'

'You've probably got a lot against me, Benjamin. It's natural that you ask questions. If I can give you answers . . .'

'Are you going to Reinsnes with me now?'

'No.'

'Why?'

'My life isn't there any more.'

'If I turn myself in, so you can be safe? Will you go then?'

'No! And you mustn't turn yourself in! That's just something you came up with to force me to come back. It's a . . . a stupid *sacrifice*.'

She poured more wine. The glasses were already more than half full.

'Anders has to be alone the rest of his life?' I asked, and avoided the word sacrifice.

She set the bottle silently on the table.

'Don't try to live other people's lives! I think your own is hard enough!' she said brusquely, and avoided the name Anders.

It was she who made the conversation safe again. Asked me about student life. I told her. And drank wine quickly. Talked about Aksel. She asked little questions in between, but mostly she listened. And smiled.

It made me feel secure. I wanted to talk about Anna. But did not mention her. Not yet.

Once late that night I shouted to her, even though we sat right across from each other:

'Play, Dina! Play!'

She shook her head. But she was still smiling. I think she needed games as much as I.

We spent the next day getting oriented to the landscape and walking the restlessness out of our bodies. I waited for her to share her thoughts. But daylight locked all doors. When she opened the wine bottle after sunset the second evening, I nodded again towards the corner where I had set the cello.

'Why did you want me to get the cello in Berlin?' I asked.

She sat down and filled both glasses to the brim. Then she raised hers to her lips and drank.

'I probably needed an excuse to meet you,' she said unexpectedly.

'Couldn't you just come? Like you did now?'

'I considered that . . .'

'And the cello?'

'I wanted you to take it to Reinsnes. I hadn't played for a long time.'

'Hadn't played! But you left in order to learn to play!'

She gave me a quick look.

'I liked to think that, yes. After a while I realized that wasn't how it would be. Instead, I'd listen and see.'

'Haven't you played since you left?'

'In the beginning. I found the man where you got the cello. He rid me of my worst habits. Things started to go well. Then something happened . . . They disappeared. Everyone.'

I stared.

'Who?'

'Hjertrud, Jacob, Leo. It was over. They didn't want to be with me any more.'

Her eyes were naked.

'You do understand, Benjamin? Don't you?'

'No. The dead should leave us in peace!'

'The dead are us,' she said simply.

'No! Don't say that!' I exclaimed angrily.

'There's no other way to say it. When the dead leave us . . . then we have to do penance. So I stopped playing.'

The room became icy cold. I swallowed. She gave me a penetrating look. But I would not go along with her. Suddenly I remembered various things I had heard as a child. Words not meant for me. About Dina's madness.

447

About her nightly seances in the summer house. Where she held masses for the devil!

'You're joking . . .' I said dully.

She was bent forward slightly. As if asleep.

Then she began to speak. Her voice sounded as if she were reading something from a book. The words settled on my face like snowflakes. Tiny pressure against my skin and eyes melted and evaporated. Fragile. Nothing to consider keeping.

'The screams used to wake me up. They stuck in my head. They ate up my thoughts. She got no peace. Was always dying. She was the slit belly of a poor sheep. Everything came out. I thought she threw a little button down from heaven. It was just a small shell I found on the beach. But beautiful heavenly colors. She was in the lonely eagle that circled above the roof. She watched over me. But at night she screamed. Gave me her screams somehow. What could I do? I couldn't get them out. They got stopped up here inside. And the sheriff tore down the wash house. Maybe that was it, I didn't have anywhere to go. To get them out. The wash house was driven onto the beach at ebb tide, and the place it had stood got overgrown with thickets. As if nothing should exist any more. When Dagny came, they moved Mama out of the main house. Her picture. The way she looked when she was still in one piece. They threw it out. Then we went to Reinsnes, to be with Jacob. What else could we do? Lorch had to go to Copenhagen. I couldn't forgive myself for it. That I let them take Lorch. I could have set the house on fire, I could have stuck a knife into the sheriff, so he'd understand. The music, Benjamin. Lorch was in the music. So I had him in a way. The important thing was the music . . .'

She stopped. Outside, the ocean breathed. An immense rhythmic breathing.

'You've never talked about it . . . before?'

'I think I stopped talking the day they dragged me into the snow outside the wash house. The day I

448

scalded Hjertrud to death. When I found words again, there wasn't much to say. People rushed around. Everything was destroyed.'

'It was an accident! It wasn't you!'

'Whatever it was, it was!'

I shivered. She still went around with all that! She still went around with it!

I could have asked if that was not enough. Why the Russian too?

'How old were you?'

'Five.'

'You can't say it was your fault. You were five years old!'

'Guilt doesn't depend on age.'

'But you were a child.'

'We're all children.'

'You should have talked to . . . to somebody about . . . everything.'

She laughed briefly. I did not like it.

'That wouldn't have undone anything. Talk? To whom?'

'Surely somebody was there?'

'No.'

So it began long before she carried me in her womb. Had I thought it all started when the Russian lay between us in the heather? That she could not stand the days and the nights? When I heard her tell this, I felt as if our life together began when she stood in the snowstorm hearing Hjertrud's screams. Maybe she shouted for someone to see even then. But I did not see anything before the Russian lay there.

And then it just got worse.

The room grew silent.

People came from Reinsnes and lined up on the table between us. Became pieces in a chess game she alternately played against herself and against me. And the Russian? Was he the castle that fell?

She had always been quite a good chess player. And

449

I knew she tried to protect the pieces she did not expose to me.

The whole time she talked as if it concerned someone else.

'You must have missed Hjertrud, didn't you?' I said.

She looked at me thoughtfully. A long time.

'Do you ask that because you've missed me?'

It was my turn to gain time. Yes, she was playing against me now.

'Maybe,' I admitted.

She nodded.

'I had to take Hjertrud with me. She had nobody else.'

'Who do you have?'

'Don't ask!'

She withdrew into herself. I felt rejected. Surely she could give me what I showed I could receive!

'You didn't die! You ran away!' burst out of me.

'You can certainly say it that way. I had to.'

'The judgment? Were you afraid of the sentence?'

'The judgment?' she said into the air. As if it were the first time she heard someone say the word.

'I only know certain things can't be changed. But thank you, Benjamin! Thank you for the letter saying you intended to turn in yourself in my place. When I got that, I had to let myself see you.'

'Is that enough, Dina? To thank me?'

'It's what's most important, I think. To have someone living after you who knows why everything happened. Maybe you'll understand . . . a little better . . . when you have a child yourself.'

Somebody stuck a thumb into my eye. Hard. She had checkmated me. Even so, I said nothing about Karna's child. My child. Not then. But all the pores in my body knotted together. Tried to lock me in. Still, her words made things more orderly between us. I admitted to myself that it probably would not have helped Benjamin Grønelv to have a mother in prison. Not then. And not now. But I could not say that.

450

'Why didn't you write, so we'd have known where you were?'

'I wanted it to be impossible to come and get me. Just as you stay here in Copenhagen without writing home. Because you don't want anyone to come and get you?'

She had noticed that Anders wrote he was waiting for a letter.

'Maybe we should just let people come and get us?' I said.

'And who would that be best for?'

'Anders, for example.'

'You have a good heart, Benjamin,' she said.

Then she rose, walked over to the door and opened it. Dawn was already a light stripe in the east. After a while she closed the door, turned, held up her hand and waved. As if she already stood at the railroad station about to leave.

Then she went to her bed.

I do not know how long I had been asleep when she awakened me.

'You're shouting in your sleep,' she said above me.

'Karna,' I said, still in my dream.

I sat up slowly.

'It's Karna! She died!'

Dina's face and hair. Morning. A silver of light entering through the small window. She folded back the cover and stuck her feet under it. Then she sat with me.

'She died. In childbirth!' I screamed.

And a little later:

'She died! That's what happens to those we touch, isn't it?' I whispered.

The moment I said it, I realized it was true.

'And the baby?' I heard her ask.

'With a grandmother who can't keep her.'

I sat with my head in my hands waiting for her to say: then take her to Reinsnes!

451

But she did not say that. She rose and walked over to the window. Fumbled for matches and lit the stump of a paraffin candle. It took a long time. The contours of her body were clearly outlined through her white nightgown. It made me remember the years that had passed. It made everything empty.

Still without saying anything, she came back carrying the candle and watching it carefully. She set it by the bed and crept close to me again. The flame flickered now and then. It gave out a faint glow. After all, it was already daylight.

Had I expected her to give an order? A moral tongue-lashing? A solution?

'Why don't you say anything?' I finally asked.

'Sometimes it's best to light a candle first.'

I wiped my face. My skin had shriveled. I should never have told her!

'I didn't want it that way. I didn't know . . .'

I felt like one of the stray dogs that stole into the back courtyard looking for carrion, water and bitches.

'Of course not,' she said.

'Do you understand?' I sniffled eagerly.

'Yes.'

Immediately, the room became a bit warmer. Safer.

'Tell me about Karna!' she said.

I shook my head.

She sat for a while, then nudged me. In a friendly way.

This was the second round. She had won the first without my noticing. She had begun to line up the playing pieces.

'Tell me about Karna!' she repeated.

'I met her in a military hospital during the storming of Dybbøl. She was strong and quick and . . . The men were fond of her. But they . . .'

'And you?'

'I don't know. Good God! That's the problem: I don't know!'

'But the baby is yours?'

'I don't know.'

'Who else's could it be?'

She had already taken the first pawn.

'You don't know everything, Dina.'

'No, I realize that.'

I shifted my position. She was too close. As if I had said that to her, she got up and opened the door. The ocean rustled in silver. Sea birds owned the light and air out there.

'Benjamin! I'm standing here listening,' she said with her back to me.

Then I brought out Karna. She carried a bundle in one hand and her torn umbrella in the other. She finally came. Dina received her. The bundle was opened and examined. Dina called it: your child. It was frightening and quite unreal. But strangely enough, the shame lessened.

Meanwhile, the sun rolled in to us. A great white shield with the sea washing behind it. The light swallowed us. Made us ethereal. Without faces. Without skin. We were tangent to each other. Surrendered ourselves. Our bodies and words flowed into each other while I poured Karna's life over the whole room. Finally everything grew still.

Then it happened: Dina walked across the room with firm steps. Opened the cello case. Looked at the instrument. Touched it.

The wind rumpled the broom growing by the door-step.

Then, in one flowing movement, she put the instrument between her thighs, leaned forward and drew the bow. She tuned long and thoroughly. It was strange to see. The cello and Dina wept together. She had the tears, the cello gave them sound.

I remembered something I once read: the wonders are always there. But only for the person ready to receive them.

*   *   *

Old Petter Dass hymns. Mozart. Christmas songs. Wild dance melodies. Once she stopped and swore softly in German.

'Bach!' she shouted in explanation.

It sounded imperfect and choppy. But she began again and again. Snorting like a caged animal.

I took a salty dip in the ocean and got dressed outside behind the wall. The whole time I heard the cello. Calm and warm, I went inside to fry pork. Cut thin slices and laid them close together in the pan. The smell wafted towards the open door.

Her eyes followed me as she played. She sat behind the cello with bare feet, wearing only a shift.

We ate in silence and then she began to play again. Still without getting dressed.

Late that afternoon I had to help her wind cloths around the fingertips of her left hand. They were raw.

'I should have taken my medical bag. Salve,' I said.

She smiled.

'It will heal soon,' she said.

As if that were a cue, or maybe because I was afraid to lose her to the cello again, I said abruptly:

'There's someone else.'

'Someone else?'

'Her name is Anna.'

'Oh,' she said, looking at the bandages.

I was an idiot. But that did not help. It had to come out somehow.

'The fact is . . . Damn, what a mess!'

I attempted a laugh. A laugh could not hurt.

'So Anna won't see you because you've become a father,' she said as cheerfully as if talking to a boy who had stolen a sweetmeat.

'Anna is engaged to Aksel.'

'Who is Aksel?' she asked.

'The one who eats raw eggs . . . I told you . . . The only friend I've got.'

I expected her to laugh. That would have been appropriate. But she did not do that. She said:

'You've made good use of your time, Benjamin!'

I could crawl under the floor where it would be nice and dark.

'Anna? What sort of family does she come from?'

I fell into the trap and willingly told about dinner with the professor's family and that Anna had been in London.

Dina nodded and checkmated me again:

'She sounds like a good catch!'

I had myself to thank.

'It's not that!' I shouted. 'Good Lord, Dina!'

'It's easy to love those who bring a great deal. I certainly should know that!' she said dryly.

'Dina!'

'What does he say? Aksel?'

'You can imagine. He'll probably . . .'

I could not bear to go into the details. And she did not seem interested either. I should not have mentioned anything. Should not have become sentimental just because my mother arrived from the past. I locked up what happened in Aksel's room. And that Aksel wanted to get money to help me go to Berlin.

Finally I felt so lonely that I asked bluntly:

'What do you think?'

She moved her rag-covered fingers. One after the other. Braided them over one another. As if it were a matter of life itself.

'Things like this don't exactly make men greater than they are,' she said honestly.

It was an open move at least.

'What does Anna say?' she asked after a while.

'I don't know.'

'Maybe you should ask? Maybe you're the one she wants.'

'What should I do? I can't shoot Aksel, after all!'

When I met her eyes, I realized what I had said.

'No. Maybe Anna can shoot Aksel for you,' she said.

'Or me . . .'

'Or you,' she said.

455

She shifted her position a little. Her knee touched mine. I straightened my back to avoid it.

'Is it a life and death matter with Anna?' she asked.

'Sometimes it seems that way. With Aksel too . . .'

She nodded.

'Maybe the hardest thing is what you can't do anything about. Karna. You have to take her with you.'

I was checkmated again. And she still had not given me any advice.

The days and nights flowed into each other. Afterwards I remembered just fragments of conversations, images, sounds. They all crept into each other, over each other, covered each other, clarified each other.

As we walked along the beach she sniffed and sighed. Occasionally she bent down and picked up something. A shell, a bit of sea glass, a piece of driftwood, a blade of dried grass. We did not say much. I thought about Karna.

When we got hungry, we ate at the landlord's inn and exchanged ordinary words about things around us. In the midst of this I asked:

'How do you make your living?'

She chewed and swallowed. When she began to speak it was as though she were talking to herself.

'Things turned out well. I'm better at numbers than most people. So I've managed. If there's one thing people want, it's those of us who can keep accounts. They think that makes them secure.'

She told little things about her life. About the house she lived in. The leaded panes of colored glass she had installed in the bay window. Like in the glass verandah at Reinsnes, I thought.

She talked about the man who owned the house where she lived. She saw him occasionally. He bought plots of land, drew architectural plans and calculated costs. Built. Not just in Germany. He was very capable. Had grown up in France. For several years she helped him with his accounts and was paid partly in shares of

456

stock. They understood each other. Knew where they had each other. Traveled together.

'You went to Paris with him?' I asked.

She smiled then.

'Yes. So you believe I really was out of the country?'

'I think so.'

'Good! Then we've made progress.'

We ate for a while without saying anything. Then I asked:

'So you have a good life?'

'Good?'

'You aren't in any need?'

'No, I'm not in any need!'

As we walked back to the boathouse, I asked:

'Would you have married the man who builds houses if Anders didn't exist?'

'No,' she said firmly. 'That's the good thing about a stinking mass of humanity like Berlin. You don't have to think about whether the parson and God are teamed against you. You're alone . . . With God.'

She had explained herself clearly. But I felt happy too soon. Suddenly she said:

'Would you have married Karna, if she hadn't died?'

These confounded surprise moves!

I shook my head. That put various things in place.

The rain came. Large, heavy drops on the window and thatched roof.

Then she told me about the cotter's farm at Helle. I had heard before that she had stayed there. But thought it was just for a few days. Just as Oline wanted no talk about my shameful birth in the summer barn, people at Reinsnes never talked about Dina's stay at Helle. Even Tomas did not talk about Helle, although he came from there.

'How did Tomas come to Reinsnes?' I asked.

'Tomas came to Reinsnes because I sent for him,' she replied.

457

For a moment it appeared she would talk about it. But she held back.

She mentioned Lorch constantly. She wished she knew where his grave was. He had died in Copenhagen.

'He taught me all sorts of things,' she said.

'Maybe we can find his grave, if you stay in Copenhagen awhile?'

She smiled then, and nudged me.

'Oh Benjamin . . .' she said.

Thick sea fog hid the world.

Dina inspected her fingertips before breakfast and began to play. Occasionally she laughed aloud and made grimaces. Sometimes she hummed, or sang old Petter Dass hymns. I mostly lay on my bed looking inward at myself.

Suddenly, in the midst of a hymn, she stopped and put down her bow.

'That's enough!' she declared.

I said nothing.

'Hungry?'

'Well, yes.'

'Let's do something about that.'

'Here?'

'No. At the inn.'

After our meal we walked along the beach letting foam and salt water wash over our bare feet. The sun was back again. Dina had tucked up her skirt with a shawl tied around her waist. Even so, it slapped wetly on her legs.

'Did I dream it? Or did you say it? That you were there when the baby was born?' she asked with her back to me.

'Yes, I was there when Karna . . .'

'When the baby was born?'

'I caught her in my hands.'

'That's quite a job for a man,' she murmured.

Was there scorn in her voice? No. Amazement.

'Men probably don't often . . .' I mumbled.

'Oh, I don't know,' she said with a smile. 'Anders probably has the knack, and Tomas could certainly have done it,' she chuckled.

'In fact, Tomas sat outside the door when you were born. And if Oline hadn't come to the summer barn . . . maybe . . .'

I bridled. And peered at her with curiosity.

'And my father? Jacob?' I asked.

She turned towards me. Instantly serious.

'No!' she said brusquely.

'He went hunting, I've been told. Was used to blood . . .'

'Such a task has little to do with hunting. Blood?'

'I meant my father probably could stand blood, since he was a hunter.'

'Jacob could stand blood. And he went hunting. But he could never have done such a task. But you don't need to be like him. Jacob isn't your father.'

Silence lay thick around us. Drowned out the sea birds. The waves abandoned their element. Rose towards me. Became hands that gripped my throat and squeezed. A steamboat struggled out there too. The light was knives. I shut my eyes tight. JACOB ISN'T YOUR FATHER!

When she began speaking again I did not hear her words. Not for a long time. But I saw her face. Her mouth. Her lips moved. Her eyes? Was she Dina? Who talked to me about something I could not comprehend? Why did she say such things?

Then she put Tomas on the chessboard. For years he was the piece she protected. Now he moved towards us. Carrying his poles. From the fields at Reinsnes, across the sea, and through the strip of thin mist. I was forced to understand his looks. To forgive him for not revealing himself.

Karna and the baby were a stopper in the whole thing. Made it impossible to judge harshly. Rage evaporated and turned into weariness that paralyzed everything. I had become an old man. It was too late. Too late to get a father.

I know nothing about the time. It went by on its own. But once, much later, I asked:

'Why do you tell me this now? Why?'

'Because I realize the time is right.'

Only once in my life had I been on the small cotter's farm Tomas came from. A swarm of people and animals. The smell inside the cramped cottage. A mixture of sweat and milk fresh from the cows. Smoke from the open hearth. I dimly remembered a thin, sinewy man with a crooked back and white hair and mustache. And a red-haired, energetic little woman with kind eyes and quick movements. Suddenly they were there. Inside my body. In my bloodstream! This was the source of half my heritage. Benjamin Grønelv was a bastard with a false name and inheritance.

She had borne this secret all these years. She had made fools of us all. You could hate and condemn. But it would not change a thing.

I could not look at her. She was no better than the whores who . . .

'Now you can go to the barmaids! Now I'm like them,' Anna said. She had come onto the chessboard. Now she threatened the king.

Did it never end? It was too horrible. And amidst everything, Karna came with the bundle and her torn umbrella. She silently leaned over Aksel's bed and watched the game. As Anna threatened the king.

I did not say a word until I got control of myself. Then a thought struck me:

'But . . . then Mother Karen isn't . . .'

'No.'

'But Mother Karen is the one I take after. That's what I've always heard. It's impossible that Mother Karen . . .' I heard a pitiful little boy's voice say.

460

'You do take after Mother Karen! No one can change that,' she said.

Then it came! My rage rolled me in tar and feathers and stinking old cod livers. It twisted and tore me and sprinkled salt in all the cracks and sores. It did not start behind the confusing thoughts. Where I was going to pieces. No. It started in my stomach. A stone of nausea. I could not vomit and get it out. It was too compact. Too enormous to pass through my throat and esophagus. It would crush my teeth and tear the uvula out of my throat. I wished I could cry. Howl. But I could not. Instead, I quickly reflected on who my family was. And I, who had never seen any real point in having dead Jacob as a father, was now furious as a little child that Dina had erased Mother Karen from me and, with a few words, turned me into a cotter's boy on Sheriff Holm's estate.

'Who knows this?' I whispered in Danish in a voice I had never heard before.

'Nobody,' she said.

But I heard the tiny hesitation. It was just the way she took a breath. Still, I heard it.

'Nobody?' I repeated angrily.

'Tomas had his suspicions. But the church records clearly say Jacob Grønelv.'

'Tomas knows?'

'He can never be sure.'

A tall female stranger with her dress tied up around wet legs and dark hair graying slightly at the temples held both hands around the handle of her parasol. Tightly. A little silk tassel hung from one spoke. The wind slapped it against her cheek. The look that met mine was direct. Straightforward.

'Men can never be sure about such things. You've probably had that thought youself?'

The sea birds had quieted. The beach was deserted. We were the only two people in the world. The air hung heavily above our heads. It seemed the whole universe obeyed the law of gravity, just to press me down.

We had wandered far. A few words lay between us. But no forgiveness. No solution. No comfort.

I did not want comfort! The little boy from Reinsnes dragged poles across the fields without knowing it was his father walking beside him. The devil must be in women!

Finally I asked wearily:

'How could it happen? With Tomas? Why him?'

'How could it happen with Karna? Why her?'

Bewildered, I replied in utter seriousness:

'It was the war, Dina.'

She drew her head from under the parasol and looked at me. Almost innocently.

'That's it exactly, Benjamin! It was the war.'

'Was Jacob dead when I was conceived?' I asked, knowing it was an impermissible question.

'As far as others were concerned, yes. But not for me,' she said.

'So you were unfaithful to him?'

'Yes, I was unfaithful.'

'Were you unfaithful before he died? With Tomas?'

'No! Everything in its time. Then it was he who was unfaithful.'

She sat down on a large log. The wind had loosened her hair and was playing havoc with it.

A new thought popped into my head:

'So Johan isn't my brother?'

'No.'

'So actually he should inherit Reinsnes along with Anders?'

'No!' she said, almost angrily. 'Nobody can change what's written in the church records.'

'Are you sure, Dina?' I asked.

'Reinsnes is for the person who deserves it. For a while, that was me. Now it's Anders. If Johan had been the right person for Reinsnes he'd have been there long ago.'

462

'He's a clergyman. And you were there, after all.'

'I had to earn my right to Reinsnes,' she said.

'And so do I? Is that what you're trying to say?'

'I thought I said it clearly enough.'

I wanted to ask who would have Reinsnes in that case. But I realized it was not up to her. It was up to me.

'Johan can still lay claim to Reinsnes.'

'He's too afraid to do that.'

'Afraid?'

'Yes. Afraid of God. Afraid of Jacob. In the end, he was afraid of me.'

'Why?'

'Because he realized he wanted to have me. But he imagined God didn't agree.'

'Dina! Johan?'

Suddenly I remembered certain things. Johan getting so furious that he hit me. What was it I said to him that time?

Dina's eyes became two merry slits when she saw my expression.

'Yes. That was in our youth,' she laughed. 'He was older than I, for that matter. I came into the house as his stepmother. That wasn't easy for any of us. I remember he promised to write to me from Copenhagen . . . The worst thing isn't being afraid, it's not understanding you must do precisely what you're afraid of doing. Then you're rid of it!'

That night all the fathers came. Jacob, Tomas, Anders. I did not know what to do. They all wanted me to plead their case. With Dina. About something I did not understand.

When I awoke I felt as if I had not slept for several weeks. I brought firewood, bread and milk. Made coffee. Dina sliced the dark loaf. We sat down near the stove, Dina under a large shawl. Her eyes were still heavy with sleep. She seemed to blend with the sea out there. At first, not much was said. I sat thinking about whether I should tell her about the dream. Then she said:

'In the end, there's only one thing you need to decide, Benjamin. To go on. You can't always take people with you. There are people everywhere. It's just a matter of seeing them. I met one inside the wall in Paris. I remember thinking: if she weren't such a ruined woman, I'd like her for Benjamin. As if you should be guaranteed to have unspoiled . . .'

'When were you there, Dina?' I broke in.

'When Bismarck arrived. But I got out. I couldn't think in several languages. And Paris was the wrong place to think in German.'

She laughed harshly.

'It taught me a lot. It's not hell that's bad. It's human beings.'

'Tell me about Paris!'

She shook her head.

'Anyone who is confined, is in hell. Some people are confined by sickness. In their bodies. You've seen some of them, I'm sure. But maybe it's worst for people confined inside their heads.'

I felt very uneasy. She sat looking at me.

'You're afraid, Benjamin? You've been afraid a long time? Afraid of going to court?'

'I? *You* must have been afraid?'

'Sometimes. But not seriously. Not until the letter came saying you were going to turn yourself in.'

'You can't stop me, if I want to!' I said.

'Yes, I can, Benjamin. And you won't make me do that.'

She looked straight at me. Not threatening. Just wearily.

'Don't you regret it, Dina? Don't you ever regret it?'

'Should I sit here after all these years and trouble you with my regrets, Benjamin?'

'But you do have regrets?'

From somewhere outside came a trickling sound. Water splashing against stone.

Her eyes did not resist. Held nothing back. Like the gaze of the child who was Karna's and mine.

'Regret is for people who think it's that easy.'

'Haven't you ever needed . . . needed forgiveness?'

'Who'd have enough power to grant that forgiveness?'

What could you answer. Except to say: God.

'Was it because of love? That you shot him?'

I forced myself to ask the question.

'Love . . .'

She pronounced the word as if tasting it. As if it were the first time she heard it.

'Yes?' I said.

'Tell me about love, Benjamin!'

I swallowed.

'I don't know anything about love,' I finally replied.

CHAPTER 22

The seventh day Dina whistled as she got dressed.

She announced that the sun was out and we were going to Dyrehaven. To stand under the trees with the deer. Life was not just fog, she declared cheerfully.

We strolled to the inn and ate at the rough wooden table in the yard. Two hearts were carved into my side of the table. With the initials B and D. I pointed and smiled. Dina cocked her head and laughed.

'It's strange about names,' she said absent-mindedly. And a little later:

'What's her name? The baby's?'

I was unprepared. The truth was, I did not know. Had not thought about it.

'Maybe you should think about it. Names do something to people.'

I did not reply. She read from the newspaper about preparations for midsummer celebrations of St John's Eve. We finished eating.

'Maybe you should find out, Benjamin?' she said.

'What do you mean?' I asked, pretending not to know.

'The baby's name.'

'Will you go there with me, Dina?'

I realized I had thought about it the whole time. Wondering if I should ask her. And what she would answer.

'That depends.'

'On what?'

'Whether you're interested in giving the baby a name.'

'And if I'm not?'

'Then I've no reason to go there.'

'Are you saying . . .'

'It's not me that has to say!' she interrupted, and prepared to leave.

Copenhageners took trains and steamboats to St John's Eve celebrations. Klampenborg swarmed with summer dresses, parasols and wide-brimmed hats – and panting gentlemen in overly warm clothes and hats stuck to their heads. But the sounds were cheerful. Voices and horn music. A man carrying sugar sticks in a basket on his stomach walked through Bellevue shouting his wares. Both he and the sugar sticks were about to dissolve. The sun was everywhere. Moisture rose from the horses harnessed to rumbling carriages containing respectable families. The dust got into everything. Burned your eyes.

An elegant rider wearing spurs and carrying a whip strutted past. I noticed him look at Dina. She had on a pale green dress with a fluttering cape over it. Filled with childish jealousy, I told myself the fellow certainly couldn't afford to buy a horse. He just wanted to show off in a riding habit.

In the middle of the square strolled a young couple. The woman was pushing a baby buggy. An idiotic contraption with three wheels. Were it not for the buggy's folding top, you might mistake it for a coffin on wheels. Narrow at the foot. Black. With a cloth over it. And no sign of life.

Dina pointed to the Bellevue Kro pub.

'No, not there! Let's get out of here!' I said crossly.

She did not reply. But I noticed her look.

Later we took a ride along Strandveien in an open carriage. The coachman let us each have a beer from the basket under the seat. Dina drank hers with great equanimity and a skill every brewery worker would

467

envy. Then she lit a cigar and leaned back. Took a few drags and passed it to me. She enjoyed the ride so openly I did not need to say a word.

After we got out of the carriage, and were walking under the trees, she talked about the avenue of rowan trees at home and the birches in the garden. And the mountain ashes. We laughed about us both loving trees so much.

Everything was poignant, ridiculous and unreal. You could imagine saying to someone in the future: it was the evening Dina and I strolled in Dyrehaven in Klampenborg. On St John's Eve!

The evening named after John the Baptist. Somehow I thought about both Tomas and John the Baptist. Simultaneously. Finally I saw them in my mind. A waking dream. A figure kept emerging from the shadows. At one point I would have sworn he was as real as we were.

The huge oak trees had unfolded their leaves long ago. Thick as leather. Over by a fence, John the Baptist bent down. In Tomas's form. Gathering earth's gifts after the winter. Stern and silent, wearing a camel-hair cloak and a leather belt. Did he find his grasshoppers today? Or was it a day for wild honey? What did he think about our pagan St John's Eve customs? He who raised symbols to cleanse and purify lonely humans, did he see Dina and me? Did he see us celebrating with beer bottles and cigars, even if everything was confused and the baby had no name? Did he see that good and evil are there? In humans. In nature. Did he already see us when he admonished us the first time he baptized with water and redemption? Did he see Dina, who did not believe in regret? In forgiveness? Did he see the clover was juicy and green? Did he smell the fragrance of roses and flowering elderberry? Did he see it was not time to gather fruits? Did he know he was my father? Did he understand I needed time? Did he realize it had been such a cursed winter?

*   *   *

'Dina, do you understand I need time?' I asked.

She was leaning against a tree trunk with her eyes closed. And she did not open them when she replied.

'Time isn't something you need. It's something you perhaps may get.'

I comforted myself with John the Baptist. That was no comfort.

'I need a horse,' she said after a while.

'Should we go to the road and hire a carriage?'

'No, just a horse,' she breathed.

'Do you know there's a Danish tradition that a witch and "Old Erik" the devil will appear tonight, on St John's Eve? They'll ride a broomstick to faraway places. To Bloksberg! And Hålogaland. So one should put a rowan branch outside the door for protection when they fly by,' I said.

'Then they're out late, because it's starting to get dark,' she chuckled.

'They say if you want to know about these journeys to churchyards in Hekkenfel, Bloksberg or Norway, you should sit by a crossroads at midnight. Under a harrow that has no spikes. Then you may see people you know fly off on a broomstick thinking they're invisible. That's how you see witches . . . and are amazed at who they are.'

She pushed her hat to the back of her neck and looked up at me. Her body floated in all that green as the swaying treetops showered down gold coins. They struck her face first, then her shoulders.

I went closer and gently grasped her shoulders. To see if she was real.

'Do you believe witches are evil?' she asked.

'Why do you ask?'

'Because I think you were wondering.'

I could try to make everything good again by bending down to her and saying something nice. But she smelled expensive and strange. That man who designed and built houses? Did he buy expensive perfume? Why didn't I ask?

Suddenly she laid her cheek against my chest and said:

'Please don't think I'm evil, Benjamin!'

I dropped to my knees and put my arms around her.

'I don't,' I whispered.

The sky had darkened. The sun's last rays were gleaming glass pillars among the tree trunks. Green colors turned to brown and delicate blue. I let myself be drawn in. To where nothing was real or unreal. It simply was. Peace.

We found a tent where they served food and drink. The celebration had begun. People arrived in groups. Whole families. Bands of young people. Students and sweethearts close together. And clinking picnic baskets.

You cannot always know why you say or do certain things. I began talking about Kierkegaard's writings. About Abraham's sacrifice. About some of my thoughts. She let me talk. I do not know if she got anything out of it. But sometimes she nodded. Once she smiled to herself. It was when I reproached Abraham for having shirked his responsibility by not telling Isaac he was to be sacrificed.

'Sacrifice serves no purpose. People can't make sacrifices without getting something in return. Abraham wanted favor in God's eyes. He was no worse than others. He just had to make a great sacrifice so God would see him,' she said.

'It's not that simple, Dina. It's a question of faith!'

She looked at me and broke into a smile again.

'You've studied so much,' she said.

'Haven't you heard of Kierkegaard?'

'Maybe. But if so, I've forgotten. But stories from the Bible . . . you can't forget those.'

Perhaps I could try to share thoughts with her after all. So that after everything was over I could say: 'We, my mother and I, sat at Dyrehaven and ate onion soup and talked about Kierkegaard and Abraham's sacrifice of his son!'

I tried to remember Kierkegaard's exact sentences. But I only remembered his words about the paradox of faith. I recited them as I stared at a point between her eyes:

' "What a tremendous paradox faith is. A paradox which can transform a murder into a holy act pleasing to God. A paradox by which Isaac is returned to Abraham! A paradox which no thought can encompass because faith begins where thought leaves off." '

She sat with her hands folded in her lap and her eyes closed while I haltingly got through it.

When I had finished, she said without opening her eyes:

'I didn't get him back. Maybe I didn't have enough faith? Or maybe the thought of you, Benjamin, became so strong my faith disappeared . . . The thought that actually you were the sacrifice.'

I had said the word: murder. And she understood everything.

'Murder? What is it? War isn't murder? Sacrifice isn't murder? Then what is murder?' I asked.

'It always depends on who judges. Everything I did became a judgment placed on you. That's not how it should be.'

Nature lined up all around us.

After sunset we strolled to Kirsten Pils Kilde. The old wellspring of the gods. According to legend, a glass of spring water was good for body and soul. That evening there would be a market, speeches, singing and dancing near the spring.

On one hill some young people were lighting a bonfire.

'They're lighting a bonfire to keep the witch away,' said Dina.

I was sorry I had mentioned the word witch. But it was too late now.

When we got closer, I recognized some students from Regensen with their sweethearts and friends. They had lashed a tar barrel to a pole. With great noise and commotion, they lit the barrel and watched the flames lick towards a towering heap of logs and straw. Little by little, the flames from bonfires in the distance responded.

I had thought about it. That I might meet people I knew. Together with Dina. Perhaps I was so childish I even wanted it to happen. With the questions that would result.

A group of girls joined hands and danced in a circle and sang. I gradually recognized Adam Oehlenschläger's words:

We wander in the shadow
Mid grasses pale and green,
Where wild flowers grow
Saint John's wort we glean.
Little herb so fair
Grows so verdant there,
Grows so clean and pure,
Unhonored and obscure.

In kitchen garden rows
We plant the herb again.
From crevices it grows
And twists away, and then
If it takes root and thrives
We will have happy lives.
And if it dies, 'tis true,
We all will die then too.

If none of us are here
Alive with joy and cheer
When summer comes next year
And wild flowers appear,
Then, marked by a plain cross,
Beneath the churchyard moss,

Pale in the grave we lie.
Life has passed us by!

Saint John's wort we glean
Where wild flowers wait
Mid grasses pale and green
And tree trunks tall and straight.
Little herb so fair
Grows so verdant there,
Grows so clean and pure,
Unhonored and obscure.

Gaudy market tents had been set up on both sides
of the road. Like a counterpoint to Nature and the
melancholy song. A couple of drunken men staggered
over for a friendly discussion with a coppersmith. The
smith soon gave up and went his way with a deafening
clatter of copper baubles and scrap in his handcart.

In one tent a young bare-legged girl was selling pots,
plates and jugs. She shouted in a bright happy voice
that her jugs were the best for fetching water from the
spring.

It seemed the bare ankles and fresh face attracted
customers more than the prospect of life-giving spring
water. Men crowded in front of her stall. I did too.

Afterwards I fetched spring water and poured it over
Dina's and my hands. Then I threw the jug with full
force against the stones, as legend decreed.

The girl's business was flourishing. The same was
true in the 'eight-skilling shop' where one bought small
gifts for those at home, or for a sweetheart one had for
the evening.

Musicians got the dancing started on a flagstone
paving. All around, people had settled down with
picnic baskets. Some had elegant white tablecloths and
blankets to sit on. Others sat down just anywhere.
Students and young girls with chaperones sat close
together around baskets, bottles and glasses.

I had just told Dina I wanted to buy a bottle of wine,

when someone rose and came towards us. Laughter and voices disappeared.

Anna! Glided hazily before me. When she realized I was not alone, she stopped short.

I was grateful for the twilight. And knew I could not let Anna just stand there on the path. I drew Dina over to her and said:

'Dina, this is Anna. Anna, this is my mother, Dina.'

If Dina was surprised she hid it well.

I had automatically switched to speaking Danish. She did not seem surprised by that either.

They shook hands. Anna stared. That was real enough!

'So you're Anna! You're Benjamin's Anna!'

I had never thought this scene could take place. Everything became totally absurd when Aksel's voice was heard from the podium just in front of us. He was concluding a St John's Eve speech:

'On this light summer night when Nature's forces are at their height, we bless the sparkling elements which ever cleanse and never age, but eternally rejuvenate and bring new life: fire and water. Fire and water!'

I was not the only one who listened. Dina was a listening animal. Aksel's large blond head in the torchlight. Like a wild faun. Just come from the dark forest. Ignoring that Aksel was mine, she took him all for herself. I saw it on her. And I did not want to see it.

The applause and shouts of 'Bravo!' for Aksel's speech almost drowned out Anna and Dina's meeting.

And I? I was an insect. An insect in Aksel's room at Valkendorf. An insect on Anna's body. Or in Dina's hat feathers.

The past few days drifted out of reality. I could stretch out my hand and take hold of thin air. Dina was gone. As she always had been.

Someone rushed past with a sparkling torch. It illuminated us. A large golden gleam on Anna's face.

'Benjamin hasn't said a word about his mother visiting him,' she said.

'No, I didn't tell him,' said Dina.

You could stand there mute. And watch them both as Aksel's tall figure climbed down from the podium and came towards us. His shadow was about as cheerful as a courtroom trial.

I realized the moment was carved into my life for ever. In my old age, if I lived that long, Anna's, Dina's and Aksel's isolated words would be essential elements: 'Now we know who we are' . . . 'You're Benjamin's Anna' . . . 'Fire and water' . . .

Afterwards everything went so fast.

Aksel took both of Dina's hands and leaned towards her with ridiculous deference. As if he had stepped out of a pitiful chivalric drama.

At first all I could do was try to determine if Anna had told him. About us. But if she had, he was playing for high stakes, while awaiting the chance to chop me into mincemeat.

As we walked a little distance behind Anna and Dina he whispered:

'To think she just came! God, what a mother you have! We'll go to Berlin with her!'

But I still could not be sure he did not know about Anna and me. I had a feeling those two, Anna and he, had an agreement: to revenge themselves by exposing me! With Dina as a witness.

Now everything was ruined. Dina suddenly became a woman who had wandered in to be Aksel's witness. She became the center.

CHAPTER 23

The evening became a macabre masked ball. Songs alternated with discussions.

Dina discussed Bismarck's villainy with my Danish student friends! With mature decadence. Related brief episodes about the madness and depression in Paris before Napoleon III was taken prisoner.

I remembered she would not talk about those things to me. She recited clever verses ridiculing the Prussian army leaders. In German! We sat in a circle around the baskets and bottles. One fellow named Jens had graduated with Aksel and me. He was Aksel's friend more than mine and lived at Valkendorf. Had a tendency towards brooding. Dozed off now and then. But when he said something in professional discussions, he was a champion.

Claus Clausen was from a merchant family, seemingly carefree, and had the university's best baritone. He appeared to be Sophie's escort this evening.

Anna did not say much. I do not know how I managed it, but she sat between Sophie and me. Wearing the mask of Aksel's slightly neglected sweetheart? Sometimes she leaned towards her sister and said something I did not hear.

A torch illumined her right ankle. I thought she would pull down her skirt. But she did not. Quite the contrary. Once she stretched her body towards Sophie and the bottom of her skirt crept up her leg.

I had never seen Aksel's mask before. It was a dish filled with honey to attract Dina.

Between Claus and a blond creature they called Janna sat a tall, dark-haired law student with eager eyes. Otto. He had an impressive mustache, considering his age. And was one of the many who showed off more than he studied. You might just shrug it off. He had this awkward, apparently naive manner that often makes people think status seekers are harmless.

Now he was practically in ecstasy over Dina's satiric verses. And wanted her to repeat the words about Bismarck who spent his nights hating and, implicitly, was a bad lover.

'Enough is enough,' Dina said with a smile.

Then Otto began telling about Georg Brandes's scandalous love for a much older woman, Caroline David. It made him the center of attention. The story was well-known, how the woman left her husband and children and came to Brandes's public defense of his doctoral dissertation 'The French Aesthetic in Our Time'. It sounded as if she did it all in one afternoon while everyone else took a nap.

Anna interrupted him angrily:

'Stop it! Brandes gave us Mill's book, *The Subjugation of Women*. Without his translation, I'd never have known that book existed! And now they're even going to start a women's organization here in Copenhagen. Had you heard that?'

'It doesn't mean we need to accept that he lives a spineless life with an old woman! And that he talks to groups and encourages suicide and broken marriages! Ugh!' said sweet Janna, laying her hand on Otto's arm.

She was the daughter of a well-known Copenhagen confectioner, and looked like a pastry. Marzipan covered with frosting and decorations.

For a while the discussion focused on what ethical demands could be placed on famous men. Men who should be an example for us all. Janna adamantly believed one should make greater demands of such people than of other mortals. Claus maintained this was typical women's talk. The pastry got insulted, and declared it was not she who brought up the subject.

Sophie defended her, and said Claus should distinguish between women's talk and an academic discussion, but in fact students spent more time singing and drinking than discussing.

Objectivity reached a climax when the law student burst out:

'But you don't have to do everything so damned openly as this fellow Brandes!'

Throughout the exchange, Dina watched each speaker in turn. With the same expression she had had when she studied things in the market stalls earlier that evening. Finally she said:

'Well, well. So a married woman came and listened to the young genius, Georg Brandes, discuss French aesthetics. Was the woman wearing only underwear?'

'Of course not,' said Janna dismayed.

'I must say you discuss important things in Copenhagen! Take care Mr Brandes doesn't get weary of it and move . . . to Berlin!'

There was a painful silence. Then Sophie began talking feverishly about dancing.

I noticed Aksel's eyes on Dina. I let myself be drawn towards it, even if it was unbearable. It was like walking towards the summer barn on dark autumn evenings. Or spying on the servants in the hayloft after the hay was brought in. He noticed me looking at him. Then he asked Anna to dance.

I saw them in the lantern light. They looked good together. But she had been for me! At Valkendorf. Just for me.

Her skirts. Her ankles with a blue flower embroidered on her stocking. Her stocking's edge. Her breath. Her scent. I sat in the grass thinking about it. The intensity. The craving. To find my way into her. Inside.

When they returned, I could see everything was not as it should be between them. Unable to control the vile joy that exploded in me, I leaped up and asked her to dance.

She was breathing hard from dancing. But her mask was on. The carefree, innocent one.

'I should have brought my dance card,' she said in a high, unnatural voice.

But she went with me. We passed the blazing bonfire on the hill. A couple of fellows stood guard with buckets of water. Laughter and shouts from the bodies moving in the dark mingled with the music and the fire's crackling.

I floated away with her. Anything could happen! You could imagine tomorrow did not exist. Just tonight. Midsummer Eve.

I kept us out of sight from Aksel and the others as much as possible. Her body was fragrant. Or was it elderberry?

I could dance with Anna while the intensity lived its own life. Spread. Filled my head. My groin. My arms hardened around her. She was soft. I could not hide that my organ stiffened against her. She did not pull away.

I said her name. Again and again. Could find nothing else to say.

The people around us wore their happiness masks. They added sounds. They laughed. Snickered. Flirted. Lanterns swung in the breeze. The bonfire sent sparks and smoke towards the lusterless sky. The music bound people together. They were worms that twisted around each other. Clung together and pushed away.

I was already in Anna. She realized that. She paused and got out of step. I could not feel ashamed. Wanted to have her. Anna! She would be mine! With her naked golden face.

'Say it! What you said at Valkendorf,' she whispered.

At first I did not understand. Had forgotten. Felt only the intensity that pushed everything else aside. It had but one goal. I wanted to lead her away from the others.

479

Into the forest. Wanted to hide myself in her. Inside her. Right now.

'Say those beautiful words you said to me!' she gasped.

I heard the expectation in her voice. Among all the undulating worm bodies.

Then I saw Aksel and Dina dancing. This was a night for witches and demons. Infernally powerful. And green. Much too green.

Dina's hair had tumbled from under her hat. Her skirt swirled straight out. Aksel's arm around her waist. She tilted her head back and laughed. Towards Aksel!

I had seen it before in an undulating memory. When? Several lives ago? The Russian's life? My life?

I could not bear it. It was too awful. I made it ugly myself. But that did not help. I let myself hate. Everything and everyone. Dina. Aksel. They were in the way. Indispensable. But in the way.

'Say those beautiful words you said to me at Valkendorf!' Anna pleaded again.

Her arm bound me to earth. My brain was a hollow tree trunk. I could not remember the words from the Song of Solomon. She wanted some words from me. Couldn't I give her some words? She waited. She looked at me. But I could not. Just stood there and squeezed her. Tightly, tightly.

Then she turned her face away. As if she had to bear the shame of my stony organ.

I tried to lead her through the crowd. Not to the others. Not to the idiotic student group. To their singing. The glasses. The emptiness.

'Let's go for a walk by ourselves,' I said breathlessly.

'No,' she said curtly.

I could have recited those words. Instead, I took her arm and led her through the crowd.

I do not know where it came from. Suddenly it was just there. Cold fury.

480

'Are there others on your dance card besides Aksel and me?' I snarled.

She stopped short in surprise.

'Why are you so rude?' she said.

'I shouldn't be here,' I said.

'I shouldn't either!'

'Let's walk under the trees . . . there . . . a path!'

'Don't be an idiot!' she said, and pulled me forward while looking over her shoulder.

Probably looking for Aksel and Dina?

I saw myself floating with sparks and soot above the bonfire. Disappointment. Shame.

'Pardon me!' I heard myself say.

We stopped to let a group of country folk in clacking wooden shoes pass by. When we started walking again, she looked behind her and said:

'She's beautiful. Your mother.'

I pulled myself together.

'Yes.'

'I think Aksel likes her,' she said, turning around again.

'Yes.'

When we had almost reached the others, she said:

'Aren't you going to ask if I like her?'

'Do you like her?'

'Yes, but you're spoiling it.'

'How?'

'You're so angry. It's as if you don't want your mother to have anyone admire her. It's as if you don't want anyone to have anything.'

What could one say to that?

When we sat down under the lanterns with the others, I tried to make things good again. Put her shawl around her shoulders. But she pulled it off with an impatient gesture. I could not see her face.

An eternity went by before Dina and Aksel came back. And when they came, they were dissolved in laughter and familiarity.

Suddenly I heard my own triumphant voice:

'We've talked about it, Anna and I!'

I heard it was crazy of course. But we played so many male games, Aksel and I. We were friends. Old friends. Especially on Midsummer's Eve! I'd show them that!

'We've talked abut it, Anna and I!' I repeated, more subdued. 'The two of you are coming to Nordland in August. To Reinsnes!'

Dina was leaning on Aksel's arm. Her skirts flowed out around her.

I did not look at Anna.

'What a fantastic honeymoon!' said sweet Janna.

'Who's going to marry whom here? It's not quite clear,' Claus broke in ironically.

Aksel completely ignored the insult, and said to me:

'Wonderful, but then you must convince Dina Grønelv to be there too!'

There was a tremor behind the calm voice. Did we finally understand each other?

'I'll go on ahead to Reinsnes and get my house in order,' I said as lightly as possible.

'No, leave that to others. We want you on the trip! Don't we, Anna?'

Anna did not reply. She stood up. A moment later she had disappeared among the trees. The silence in her wake blocked all my pores. My organ was a puppy against my thigh.

Dina's skirt rustled. She stood up too, and said quietly, but clearly:

'It's late. Thank you for the nice evening!'

She leaned towards Aksel and said something I could not hear. He rose hastily. I forced a faint smile.

Then she laid her hand on my arm.

'Go and find Anna. See that she gets home safely. All right?'

I got to my feet in confusion. But she had already left with Aksel. I had forgotten how she managed everything her way.

The party began to break up. Everyone was thinking

their own thoughts. Anna had fled. From what? Janna and Sophie began putting the glasses and leftover food into the picnic baskets, Janna chattering nervously and Sophie grimly silent. The others tried to talk about ordinary things. Otto attempted a joke about the witches' night.

I felt feverish. Stumbled off to find Anna. After half an hour I gave up and went back to the picnic spot. She had still not returned.

Sophie was there alone with one of the baskets. The others had gone to find a carriage. She scolded men in general, and Aksel and me in particular. Aksel had promised on his honor to get them safely home before midnight. Now it was already long past twelve! Aksel and Anna had flown off in separate directions. And she was left with all these picnic things.

I took the basket in one hand and her arm in the other. She repaid me by making angry gestures with her parasol and began to cry.

I let her scold me.

We found Anna by the spring. A stony figure in light drapery. A modern ghost. She did not cry, but scowled at us as if we were her enemies.

Sophie begged her to come with us. I begged her to come with us.

'I'll find a carriage,' I said, wondering if I had enough money to pay the coachman.

Anna shook her head and pursed her mouth as if she wanted to spit at me. My body was diffused with shame. But my brain was working.

'Please leave us alone a few minutes,' I whispered to Sophie.

She walked away a short distance. But where she could easily hear every word that was said.

'You can't blame me for what Aksel says and does,' I said as calmly as possible.

Anna did not answer. Just stood there and stamped her foot.

'I'm sorry I said that . . . that I had talked with you about going to Reinsnes.'

'You're a monster!' she snarled.

'Yes, well . . .'

'You have no shame! I never want to see you again! Neither of you! I'll tell you what you are, you and Aksel. You're parasites! You live by compromising women. Devour us – skin, hair and everything – and toss any remaining shreds into the gutter! You regard nothing as holy, and take nothing seriously. I hope things go really, really badly for both of you!'

'Anna. Please forgive me. I'll take you home now. And you won't have to see me ever again.'

'Yes, yes, let's go,' chanted Sophie desperately, walking towards us.

Had I not been so beside myself, I could have laughed at the utterly idiotic scene. Aksel's scene? His revenge because he thought he had lost? Or was it mine? My scene, because I had lost?

The carriage bumped along through the night. Beneath dark trees. Now and then I heard the sea. Foam licked the shore out there in the darkness. The sky was full of stars.

I could imagine she was on her way to Bloksberg with him. She was going with Aksel to Bloksberg!

I had been banished to the front seat with the coachman. Why did I tell that idiotic lie?

I turned towards Anna. Shouted through the noise of wheels and hooves, not caring that the coachman and Sophie heard:

'Are you angry with me, Anna? Or with Aksel? Please! What's wrong, Anna?'

It was awful. I told myself she would never speak to me again. She would get out of the carriage and go into the house on Store Kongensgade. And then away, away! I was still turned towards the back seat.

'I'll tell you what's wrong, Benjamin Grønelv!' I heard her say through the darkness. 'I'll tell you, even if it's too late! You're such a coward you don't dare to admit you love me. You two men flip coins over me, and take turns winning! It's a fine story, Benjamin Grønelv! God help us, what a fine story! Go back home where you belong. Let me never see you again! Because I'm ashamed of what I feel for you!'

'People don't say things like that, Anna!' sobbed Sophie.

I wanted to leap over the coachman's seat and hug Anna close. I wanted to convince her she was mistaken. That everything would be fine. That I would love her until I died. If she just believed me. But I said nothing. Because she was right.

We had come to Store Kongensgade. Lights shone threateningly from the sitting-room windows.

'They're still up,' said Sophie anxiously.

'I'll go in with you and explain why you're so late,' I said.

'No, don't!' snarled Anna.

I did not reply. But paid the coachman what money I had. He looked angry, so I turned quickly and carried the basket into the yard. We approached the lions on the second floor.

The professor strutted around in a quilted dressing gown. He began by bellowing, but eventually took things nicely. I explained as best I could that Aksel was detained. And that we got delayed because there were no carriages to be had. When he let himself be convinced without questioning what detained Aksel, I asked to speak with him. Alone.

'It's very late for conversations,' he said. But he lit the lamp and gestured that the women should leave.

Sophie stole past me with a wan smile. Anna turned to her father and protested:

'He has nothing to say that I can't hear!'

'Anna!' her father said tersely, and pointed to the door.

She did not look at me. I merely sensed her warm breath as she brushed past.

The professor went to a cupboard, took out two schnapps glasses and filled them from a bottle. I struggled with a cough that had settled in my throat. It both wanted to, and did not want to, come out.

'Well?' he said. 'Out with it! What's going on?'

I coughed again. Swallowed a little schnapps and came right to the point.

'Aksel and I are rivals. For Anna. It's hard for Anna. Aksel and I have been friends all during our student years. It makes everything impossible. My mother has suddenly come to town. I haven't seen her for many years. It's confusing. But it's no excuse for my acting stupidly several times this evening. Anna is angry.'

'What stupid things did you do?'

'I was rude to Anna.'

He looked at me as if he were about to make a diagnosis, but could not fully make up his mind.

'You brought the women home . . .'

'Well, yes. That was only reasonable.'

'And Aksel?'

What should I say? That he had gone to an empty boathouse with my mother? No.

'Anna was angry with him.'

'Why?'

'Actually, she was probably angry with me.'

He filled a pipe and lit it. His cheeks became deep holes when he inhaled.

'Are your intentions serious, young man? Is that why you've come here?'

That was it. I should have expected this turn in the conversation.

'It's obviously no use,' I said.

'Confound it, what kind of an attitude is that?'

If I said I had seduced Anna in Aksel's bed, maybe he would have thrown me out. Or said we'd damn well better see to it that we got married. If I had told him about the baby, he might have shown a bit more understanding, but thrown me out anyway.

Had I said either of those things, I would have been brave.

I said neither of them.

Still it took several glasses of schnapps. The professor listened attentively. I was a sinner. But the professor was not a clergyman, he was a surgeon. Not a word of reproach.

Daylight had come, and the red plush furniture became too visible. I could see the seats were shiny where people most often sat. The wing chair in the corner had a greasy stripe along the armrests. A slightly shabby, cozy, intellectual room. Not as bourgeois as I thought the last time I was there.

'So what are you going to do, young man?' he said finally. As if he still needed a small detail before he could say what was wrong with me.

'I'd just like the professor, who is close to Anna . . .'

'You want me to plead your cause?'

'No, no! It's impossible.'

'So we agree. What then?'

'What advice can you give me, Professor?' I said.

'Go back to Norway. Give Anna a chance to forget. If she marries Aksel, that will be best for everyone. Young women have their own way of seeing things. But Anna is strong-willed. She's already wept her way to getting six months in London. But if you're serious, talk it through with Aksel! I've never seen such idiotic complications. You're both grown men! Ready to go into the world and practice medicine,' he said, and smothered a yawn.

'Do you believe in love, Professor?' I asked.

I met his eyes. Saw the glimmer of a smile. Not unfriendly. Turning his glass between his fingers, he said:

'Hmmm, love . . . I assume you mean my own involvement . . . I don't know very much about you. It's to your credit that you come here to talk with me, even

487

if the hour is a bit unusual . . . But I can't tell if you're doing it out of love. I don't know if you're in debt. If you can support a wife. I don't know if Anna could be happy up there in Nordland with its dark winters. But . . . I won't oppose it, if that's what Anna wants. On the other hand, her mother certainly will oppose it. But Anna . . . is stubborn. Terribly stubborn. It could be the death of you. That's what I know about love at the moment.'

He smiled as he drained his glass.

'Now we must get some sleep. The world can't be saved in one night,' he added, holding out his hand to me.

The next moment, Anna stood in the doorway. Her usually golden face was pale and drawn. Her eyes wide.

'Anna! Aren't you in bed?' the professor exclaimed.

'I heard every word,' she said.

'I see. You listened at the door? And so?' he said.

'You two are bargaining about my future as if I were a piece of furniture.'

'Now, now,' said the professor.

'I'm not going to Nordland. Not for a trip, and not to get married! Men's intrigues are too trifling for me! Too tedious. Do you hear? I don't want to become part of Aksel's clergy family either! I want to go to London again and see something besides this.'

It was the Midsummer Eve witch! Everything about her was in disarray. Her elegant, impeccable dress was wrinkled. Her hair disheveled. Her bare feet stuck out from beneath her skirt. The lace on her sleeves and at her throat drooped, as if she had been out in the rain or dew. Her slender fingers were clenched tightly around strong thumbs. She held them in front of her like a shield. Her breasts were bellows pumping hard. Pulling themselves out and then in again.

I had never seen her so beautiful.

'I'll give the two of you ten minutes to sort things out.

Then I'm coming to lock you out, young man,' said the professor, and left the room.

'Will you come with me to Reinsnes anyway? Anna?' I begged before he had shut the door.

She looked me up and down. Swallowed.

'Will you stay in contact? After I leave?' I continued.

'I don't know! I'm tired of you. Both of you. Immature puppies!'

I tried to take her hands. But she stepped back. Put her palm in front of her like a shield.

'What I can't forgive you for, is what you did to Karna without telling me about it,' she said.

I could hear that she absolutely would not cry.

The red velvet tore loose from the furniture and pressed into my throat. In the midst of suffocating I felt dead tired. That was something at least. Maybe I even felt relief. Relief that she did not cry, but scolded me instead. That she did not cling to me and say: take me with you!

In any case, I shook her hand with great dignity when the professor entered.

As he accompanied me to the door, I realized he had misunderstood everything. He said:

'I guess I've seen it the whole time. Where things were going. Ever since the first evening you were here. I'd hoped for Aksel and Anna. That would have been so right. So simple. But Anna is so . . . You won't have only easy days with her, young man. She's proud enough for you both. So there's no point in you being proud.'

There was no reason to disagree with him.

CHAPTER 24

I do not know what happened in the boathouse. Because I went straight to Bredgade. I even slept after a while. Aksel and Anna? Anna and I? Aksel and Dina? Anna and I?

What could I have done? I was so weary. How weary can you be? From things you yourself set in motion.

Three days and three nights passed. I had obtained two large crates in which to pack my books and few belongings. They were stacked in the corner by the door. Brown, solid. I was sitting on the bed smoking my pipe and the church bells had variously just chimed three, when I heard her talking with Madam Frederiksen somewhere in the house.

The next moment she stood in the doorway to my room. Radiating vitality. Her colors were clear. Her movements gentle. Her scents filled the room. Heavy and light at the same time. Salt and spices. The stable smell had disappeared in Berlin.

I knew I could not count on her to smooth my life.

The days in the boathouse were gone too. Or had they ever existed? Were they just something I imagined? Because I so desperately needed them?

'I brought your satchel and the cello. Asked the coachman to put them in the courtyard,' she said.

I nodded.

'How did it go?' she asked bluntly.

'With what?' I purposely spoke in Danish.

'Anna.'

'Not very well,' I said.

'But you found her, and got her home?'

'Yes. And you? Did you get Aksel home?'

She had come over to the bed. Now she turned on her heel. As if inspecting the fences around her. I had crossed one of her boundaries.

She was exactly as before. But I was not. I was not a little boy she could hold firmly by the back of the neck when rage and disappointment overcame me. I was a medical-school graduate. Benjamin Grønelv. I was not subject to her will!

'No! Quite the contrary!' she said, and turned to me again. Her eyes, clear as glass, emitted circular waves. They hit me.

I said nothing. But met her gaze.

In the silence I thought: the image of her now is burned into me for ever. This precise moment. No matter what happens, I must take it with me.

She sat down, completely calm. Straightened her neck as though she had set a heavy water jug on her head. The movement was more gentle than unyielding, but it said: don't try to bend me!

Her nose was in profile. Pulled her face up fearlessly. It contrasted with the soft cleft between her chin and lower lip. While she was still being created and had not yet found her form, someone had placed a finger there very lovingly and left an indentation. The furrows by her mouth and between her eyebrows made her features softer than I remembered. But what did I actually remember? Had I had a clear image of her?

'Were you able to talk? With Anna?'

I shook my head.

'I drove back with Sophie and Anna. Sat in the same carriage. Anna scolded me.'

'Did she have any reason?'

'Yes, I think so.'

'Do you want to talk about it?'

'It was a lie . . . what I said before she ran off. About

agreeing that she and Aksel would come to Reinsnes. I don't know why I . . .'

'But surely that wasn't the only reason she scolded you?'

'No.'

She looked at me and waited.

'I was there. Aksel wasn't there . . . He didn't exactly act as if he was engaged.'

You could get back at her a little. She shrugged.

'No, not exactly. But it gave you a chance, didn't it?'

'This isn't buying and selling!'

She examined me carefuly. From my shoes on up.

'Not for Anna, no. But for you? For Aksel?'

'Don't make things so ugly.'

'They're not beautiful! You're about equally good, Aksel and you. And Anna is trying to work things out. Certain things tell me she may be a better merchant than either of you two . . .'

'Dina! Don't drag Anna into the mud!'

'You're mistaken, dear Benjamin. I'm trying to make her visible. If she gets dragged into the mud, I think you'll be in the mud too. It's the eyes seeing her that need to purify her.'

Suddenly she looked around the room and changed the subject as if the conversation was over.

'Crates? You're packing?'

'Yes.'

'You're leaving?'

'Yes, soon. Aren't you?'

She did not answer. Walked around the room once before sitting down at the table by the window. The light behind her made her face dark.

'I imagine you're not planning to invite Anna to come to Reinsnes with you?'

'I asked her,' I said.

'What did she say?'

'She didn't give me an answer.'

'But she didn't say no.'

'No . . .'

492

'Do you care about her?'

I nodded.

'Is it your honor that makes things difficult? Because of Aksel?'

'No. I thought so . . . for a while.'

'Are you afraid she won't be happy? That she'll leave? That she'll find life too confining up there? For a long time now you've thought it would be too confining for *you* too, haven't you? You're hesitating . . .'

I forced myself to meet her gaze. But had no desire to answer. Still I hissed through my teeth:

'You're hardly the right person to . . .'

'That's true,' she interrupted quickly, paging through a book lying on a crate.

'You're afraid she'll leave you again?'

I did not answer.

'You're afraid she'll leave you?'

'Yes!' I said angrily.

'I don't know why I said that . . . I haven't reasoned it out yet . . . But there are two things we know. One is death. The other is that we'll be abandoned. One way or another. Abandoned.'

I thought: the worst defect in human intelligence is that it blindly depends on the eye . . . and compensates for the emptiness and white spots with the other senses. So we always see only one side of the world. The external. In small as well as large things. And because we're so used to measuring everything with our eyes alone, we forget the other sides. I knew very little about Dina's inside.

But what I said was:

'Fatally abandoned!'

'What do you mean?'

'To escape it, you chose to be the one who left,' I replied.

'It may seem that way to you.'

'Was it the right choice?'

'The only people who make choices are those who risk choosing the wrong thing.'

'And the others?'

'They do nothing. And whatever they get, isn't theirs.'

Suddenly starting on a new track, I said:

'That's why you did it? Leo?'

I could tell she was trying to say something. I waited. For her to pull through. It took time.

'It was being . . . abandoned,' she said slowly.

'And you see it was a wrong choice,' I said after a few moments.

She did not answer. She rose and began pacing the room as she cracked the outer joint of her index finger. It was an unpleasant sound.

She ended up by the wall. Leaned her forehead against it a moment. Then she threw back her head and screamed:

'I see that! I see that!'

She turned and slid down the wall until she was sitting on the floor with her arms around her knees.

I could have gone over to her. Could have sat beside her. But she was so distant. Unreachable.

'Come here, Benjamin,' she whispered from the wall. 'Come here.'

Finally she said it.

She held her arms around me. A long time.

'Aksel?' I asked.

She smiled a little.

'He'll manage!'

'You chose him away from Anna,' I said.

She looked at me as if judging how much I could stand. Then she simply said:

'Yes.'

'Was it for my sake?' I asked.

'No! For my own sake!' she replied quickly.

We were still sitting on the floor. My back began to ache.

'I leave for Berlin this evening,' she said.

I nodded. A small bird tried to perch on the window ledge. Its tail created a restless, impatient shadow

494

above her head. The bird scratched lightly on the window frame. She turned her head towards the sound. I held my breath. I had experienced exactly this before.

The bird flew away and she turned to me.

'But first, there's one thing . . . I want us to go there together . . . To your child.'

We walked to Store Strandstraede. Through the tumbledown gate that screeched in distress if you barely touched it. The courtyard was no more inviting than usual. It rose around us like stage flats. A dilapidated crow's nest. Where people driven by their housing need had used intelligence and creativity to add to the building, expand it, find places to fasten floorboards. To add height and width. It seemed ready to topple on us if we merely breathed on it. An ingenious system of steps – with and without railings, landings, projections and covered balconies. They all leaned against each other in a vital symbiosis. It felt like a house of cards. As if everything would fall down if you removed even one plank.

Clothes lines stretched between the covered balconies, displaying gray, worn out sheets and un-mentionable rags slightly camouflaged under petticoats and pillowcases. Sunlight shimmered on uneven windowpanes and colored the sounds. People's private lives assaulted us from innumerable open windows. The light did its best to play colors and shadows against each other to improve the stamp of poverty. But it was like looking at the world through a piece of colored glass.

A large, aggressive cat wove around Dina's legs. It embarrassed me. As if everything in there was mine. As if I were responsible for all the dirt and decay. In a corner stood baskets, boxes and crates filled with garbage and trash that had not been hauled away for days.

Once I thought this courtyard was heavy with desire.

Karna!

Outside the cellar apartment with ants in the door frame, Grandmother had tried to brighten the place with a flower box brimming with red geraniums. It hung defiantly on a couple of crooked hooks under the only window she had.

The moment I knocked, I began wishing I could leave. I was sorry I had given in and taken Dina here.

We stood by Karna's bed and I looked down at the half-naked little body. Dina stretched out her hand to the fist in the swaddling clothes. Grandmother quickly told the sad story. I already stood on the scaffold. The ax was on its way down. I heard the whistling sound of gleaming iron.

'How old is she now?' Dina asked, looking at Karna's grandmother.

'Two months exactly,' I answered.

They both looked at me. That was all right. Certain dates one remembers.

I could imagine Dina suddenly losing her composure, as she did earlier that day when we sat on the floor. I could even imagine her sweeping the baby off the bed and declaring she wanted to take it with her. To give the child a home. Thereby making the sacrifice that would free us both. Life for life. Leo for the child. I knew women do such things.

But she did not.

The baby woke up and groped in the air until she found the finger I held out to her. Like an animal with night vision that uses instinct and antennae when the day comes too quickly. She squeezed tightly and held fast, staring at me with wide eyes.

I had not seen her for a long time. But now I saw her: one eye was brown and the other was blue!

And Tomas came towards me. Across the fields at Reinsnes. He climbed laboriously over Grandmother's geraniums and came in through the window. Dragged himself across the wooden floor with years of dirt imbedded in its grooves. He carried hay-drying poles behind his neck. Carried, carried. His neck bowed to the floor. He tried desperately to look at me from beneath his curly red hair. It had traces of white at the temples. He wanted to tell me something. But gave up. Time after time. The stack of poles teetered, and almost fell, each time he straightened up to show me his face. He was alive. Terribly alive. Sweat and soil. He did not look at Dina. He looked at me. Wanted to tell me something, but could not.

I was six or seven years old. Walking behind Tomas on a path in an outlying field. The path to the summer barn. The sweet scent of ripe blueberries filled the air. There were always such big berries around the summer barn. Because the animals emptied themselves here, I had learned. Blue clumps hung on the bushes along the path. Up the hills. Shining with dew or rain. Or large and dull in the shadows. God had chosen precisely these berries and given them a velvet covering. I threaded them on a straw as I walked. You could feel safe in their fragrance. You did not even need to feel happy. Just safe. Tomas's back cast a large shadow in which I could hide. Light flickered between his legs. In rhythmic fits and starts. From side to side. Always on the way into new days.

The fragrances were the day itself. The day was the blueberries along the cattle paths. The day came from the sea when I waded on the beach with a salty wind tickling my nostrils. The day stood still when I stole into the barn where the fragrant smell of hay was packed into the shaft from the loft.

I stood by Karna's bed and thought: 'What am I, Benjamin Grønelv, doing here in Store Strandstraede?'

My brain registered this simple question while the odor of a baby became terribly evident.

I was right in the middle of it. And my life became very small and inevitable.

* * *

Grandmother had welcomed Dina like a queen. Offered her port wine in a small glass with a chipped rim.

She had probably also felt a hope. That Dina would take the poor baby. Feverish red spots appeared on her cheeks when she told how she had cared for her grandchildren since they were small motherless creatures. She talked about herself as if she had already died of old age. And she wove in little facts about how hard life was for people without the means or health to care for their families.

'She tolerates a mixture of milk and water now. She's healthy as a fish!' she assured Dina. And a little later:

'She's growing fast . . . needs some clothes . . . I don't know where to turn . . . good people don't grow on trees . . . she's lost all her hair, poor thing . . . it was so black, and curly as an angel's, when she was born . . . like embroidery on her head . . . Madam should have seen . . . I can't believe it . . . poor Karna . . . I can't believe it . . .'

'Does she look like Karna?' Dina asked.

Grandmother hurried over to the chest of drawers and got a framed photograph of Karna. Karna sat under the glass smiling. It was misleading. Karna so seldom smiled.

'What will you name her?' Dina asked, looking intently at the photograph.

The air was heavy, and I thought I would not hold out. But I did.

Dina did not prove to be a savior. She stood there with that attentive, but coolly distant, manner wrapped around her like a membrane. Was present with unyielding sensitivity. Still, she stood outside. My dreams of a mother as a regretful, penitent being lay trampled in the dust. She was a woman who happened to be leaning over Karna's bed and who picked up the little one and laid her in my arms. Slowly.

'She's dirtied herself,' said Karna's grandmother, making it sound as if it was my fault because I happened to be holding her.

*   *   *

Then I laughed. I stood there with the smelly baby in my arms and had no idea what to do with her. But I laughed. I had already made a decision. It was madness! And probably the first choice I ever made.

We were back at Bredgade, standing by the door ready to go to the railroad station. Dina with her traveling bag and I with her suitcase. Then I took the cello case in my empty hand and said:

'You must take the cello with you, Dina!'

She stared at it.

'No!' she said.

'Yes! I'll take little Karna and Hjertrud's book with me. You take the cello! Then we're even.'

The carriage that had come to fetch us rumbled into the courtyard. Hesitantly, she took the cello case.

'All right. Bless you, Benjamin! So now we're even!' she said, hastily turning her back to me.

Everything was so crazy. She sat with the cello between her knees and stared at the rooftops as we drove. I happened to think about a reindeer doe with a fawn that wandered down to Reinsnes one spring. There was so much snow. It roamed at the edge of the forest to find lichen. Shy. Quick movements. Always on the move. Away from some danger? From people?

I helped her out of the carriage and into the arcade of the railroad station. The arched roof was a shell over us. In a semicircle far ahead the trains could come and go. From there they traveled straight into the dangerous sky.

The sounds: voices, train whistles, crates being dragged. Everything was meaningless noise from another planet. When the whistle blew and the train began to move, she shouted through the din as she tried to reach my hands through the window:

'Bless you, Benjamin!'

Then she was gone.

499

*　　*　　*

I saw her. She sat somewhere under a high gray bridge playing the cello while the world went to pieces around her. She lifted her head and spoke to me.

'Benjamin, it's all right if you judge me. Harshly, if you want to. It's all decided. Love and sorrow. It's taught me everything I know. The music . . .'

'But what about people, Dina? What about me?'

'I take you with me.'

She leaned forward and hid her face. Her movements were light and free. Her shoulders gentle. Her fingers and wrist an extension of the strings. Music sprang from the instrument.

'Sorrow will be your instrument. Use it! It's given to you so you'll see who you are!'

The sky cleared. Reddish light colored the bridge. I closed my eyes. Felt weary.

'Haydn's cello concerto, Benjamin. Whether the orchestra behind me is large or small, I must play the whole piece! It's a matter of life itself!'

She was so close to me now. The wide sleeves of her dress rustled faintly. The material slid loosely up her arms when she drew the bow. Made her alternately naked and clothed.

The cello owned Dina's lap. I clung to her knee instead. Laid my cheek against the dress material and felt music flow through her body and her bones. To me. Now it was mine.

I thought: now she will say that Benjamin is too big to cling to his mother's knee. But she let me stay there. Taken up with her own concerns. She attuned her ear and listened inwardly to her own tones.

Then the orchestra began to play. I did not know it was there. In my own head. I felt the drumheads split. Blood trickled from my ear canals. It dripped on us both in time to the music. The pain subsided.

Then it was over.

I let go of the beat.

EPILOGUE

In marching home from Mount Moriah thou hadst no need of a panegyric which might console thee for thy loss; for thou didst gain all and didst retain Isaac. Was it not so?

Fear and Trembling – Johannes de Silentio

I stood under the huge shield of the roof and stared after the train. The sky ahead was a leaden half-moon which swallowed both her and the powerful, smoke-spitting snake that slithered out of my small life.

When I finally turned around, Aksel stood a few steps behind me, a wild look in his eyes.

'Well?' I said.

'She didn't want me to come here.'

'No?'

'She wanted to say goodbye to you alone.'

I did not reply. Started moving towards the exit. He went with me. I probably pitied him. Or myself. Knew what lay behind it when people said things like: 'She didn't want me to come here.'

Later, as we sat with beer steins in a pub on Vester-gade, he said into the air:

'It's over . . . the game is over.'

'Yes,' I agreed.

'I'm going to leave too,' he said.

'Going home?'

'Berlin.'

Something tumbled from a shelf inside my head.

'No!' I said firmly.

'Yes!'

'You can't do that!' I declared.

'I'll show you!'

'You may have to pay for it . . .'

'I can stay there alone twice as long as you and I together . . . for the loan I got. But I'll find something to do.'

I reached out and grabbed him.

'No, it's not that! That's not it! I mean . . . it's not the money!'

He laughed scornfully in my face.

I had to prevent him from going.

'She's dangerous!' I said.

'You're damn right, she's dangerous!' he said helplessly.

'She can't stand it . . . being abandoned.'

He looked at me curiously. Then countered:

'I thought you were the one who couldn't stand being abandoned.'

'That's true. But *she's* the dangerous one.'

Did I have to say it? To save him from going to Berlin and becoming a broken fingernail? I should probably say: 'She shoots people like you, who come only to learn and to play!'

'She doesn't have the attitudes towards right and wrong that they have at your parsonage, Aksel . . . Do you understand . . . ?'

'If she did, I'd never have known her!' he shouted happily.

I drew a breath. A deep breath of air. I needed an entire hurricane.

'He was bigger than you, much older and wiser,' I panted.

'Who?'

'The Russian.'

'The Russian?'

'The man she shot! He didn't realize she couldn't stand to be abandoned!'

So it was done! I had dug an animal's grave for her.

In Aksel. It would probably be well hidden beneath thick green leaves for a while. Until it was too late for her to save herself. Some day when the moon danced over distant rooftops in Berlin, she would tumble in. And even as she fell she would know: Benjamin did this.

Across from me sat a strong, blond man with wide eyes who ran the tip of his tongue over his lips. A long time. Then he said angrily:

'You're making this up, Benjamin, so I'll stay away from her!'

I noticed he could not bring himself to say 'your mother'. He said 'her'. I would have done the same, I thought, and replied:

'No, quite the opposite. Since I was eleven years old, I've found many strange ways to avoid saying it to anyone.'

I could see he was trying to imagine the consequences of what I said. But he failed.

'Be that as it may. I'm going to her!' he said firmly.

'There was a lot of blood. As much as with Karna. But it was his head. He lay in the heather. I stood looking at him. It was such a nice autumn day. Sunshine,' I said informatively.

'Stop it!'

'All right,' I agreed.

We were silent.

'I've actually known her all my life. Not just those few days . . . do you realize that?' he said calmly. There was something almost meek about the blond man.

'Has she . . . ? Does anybody know?' he added.

'You and I.'

He just sat there.

'You shouldn't have told me!' he said finally.

'Probably not.'

'I can't let her just disappear. I won't let you frighten me away! Do you hear!' he said a little less meekly.

'I tried at least!'

503

He threw back his lion head and licked foam from the bottom of the beer stein.

'Don't go to Berlin!' I begged.

'Don't be childish,' he said.

'You've only know her a few days!'

'I've been waiting for her for ever!'

'You're the childish one! Can't you hear that?' I attempted.

'If so, it's my own concern!' he said angrily.

'Don't go!' I pleaded.

'I can't help it!'

'It's madness!'

'Then let me experience madness!' he raged at me. 'Let me escape your morals and rules! Do you hear! *You* have no right to talk, damn it!'

'And Anna?'

'I've written her a letter and wished her all the best, whatever happens to her.'

'How nice of you,' I said caustically.

'You think so?' he asked, equally caustically.

We sat like two weary stevedores at the end of their shift. Our arms hung limply.

'There's something I need to tell you. You can paste me to the wall. But I need to tell you anyway,' I said.

'Yes, I can imagine.'

He tried to give me one of his old derisive grins. It did not work.

'It's Anna.'

'I know,' he said.

'What do you know?'

'In my room. At Valkendorf.'

'Did she tell you?'

'No, that wasn't necessary. I found my half-smoked cigars and her comb in my room.'

Some minutes passed.

'You acted like you didn't know a thing at Dyrehaven,' I said.

'Did I?'

'Damn it all!' I exclaimed.

'How was it?' he asked.

I felt my face burning.

'How was she? Anna?' he asked, refusing to give up.

'I can't talk with you about that,' I said huskily.

'That figures. Waiter! Let's have another round!'

I thought it best not to take part in his conversation before it was necessary.

'Are you taking Anna with you?' he asked with new beer foam in his mustache.

'No! The baby!'

He wrinkled his forehead and gaped.

'You can't be serious, man!'

A little later he mumbled, as if to himself:

'How will you manage that? The baby? What will you do with it?'

'Please . . . please,' I begged.

'All right.'

A pack of stevedores clattered in. They had received their wages and owned the world.

I decided to leave Aksel to his fate. Nodded.

'All right. I'm going to miss you,' I said sentimentally. In a voice full of rust and old blood. It had lain under the rich soil of the battlefields at Dybbøl for years. Now it had been dug up. Not particularly heroic.

He nodded. His face had grown in the last twenty-four hours. It was very large.

'I remember the first time I met you . . . You had such a good appetite for raw eggs . . .'

I put my face in my hands. It was flowing. The whole sewer system, thin as hairs. The finely tuned garbage my blood circulation set in motion. The artery from our student days. Singing under the trees in the Regensen courtyard. All the sinful nights. The one with the madam in Peder Madsen's Passage. And the afternoon when I betrayed him in his bed. Now he had his day of reckoning. We were even.

We could not give everything. I had to stop it. Now! So I said:

'It's been fun. Great fun!'

505

'Yes, the game is over . . .' he mumbled.

After a while he said:

'You're like her. But she's more beautiful.'

I heard his cartilage crack when I punched him in the face. He squinted a little, then hit back. Hard.

A few seconds later I sat with my hands full of blood from my nose. It felt good. We sneered at each other.

I knew I would feel the stony impact of his fist the rest of my life.

This was the text for 15 August on Mother Karen's calendar stick: 'Today the sap returns to the tree's roots.'

Anders stood in the office down at the store thinking that summer was lasting a long time. It had been blessed with sun and easterly winds. Having just come home from Bergen, a part of him still floated out there between sea and sky.

His vest was unbuttoned and his shirt was open at the neck.

Hanna bustled through the open door. She had long been indispensable in the store. Now she rushed into the office and thrust a telegram into his hand.

'A messenger just brought it,' she said, and was gone again.

Anders rose from his chair and held the folded paper in front of him. Squinted. Then he opened it and tried to read. Squinted again. The letters floated before his eyes. He shifted the paper from close to further away to distant. Several times. Finally he gave up and took out his spectacles, as he called them. Then he spread out the telegram and read solemnly:

'Send a woman to meet me. My little motherless daughter and I need help. Arrive Bergen on 7 September if God and weather permit. Will stay at our usual lodgings. All is well. Benjamin.'

Anders carefully sat down again. Pushed his chair out a little from the old office desk to gain time. Put everything in place. Glasses in the glasses case. One foot over the other. His free hand brushed through his white mane before coming to rest in his lap. But suddenly he stuck out his strong chin and laughed loudly and boyishly. Then he got up and went into the store. Standing in the middle of the floor, his feet wide apart, he read the telegram.

The clerk stood in a white cloud above the flour bin, ready to use the tin ladle. Hanna held the large tailor's scissors. Ready to cut five meters of leather for a woman from the islands. The scissors fell. Through a shaft of late sunlight.

Then Anders shouted in the same tone as when he announced it was all clear for the herring seine. Joyous, calm and concentrated:

'Bless my sinful soul, what a great thing that tele-graph is! Where will I find a woman who'll take the first steamboat to Bergen?'

Karna! Shall I tell you about Mother Karen? About how her scent has gone with me. And her magnifying glass. I still have it. She doesn't need to be my grandmother. As long as I can take her with me. I've already packed our crates of books. They're going to Reinsnes.

It's strange that I know so little. I don't know any-thing about love. Do you hear? That's probably what's wrong with me. Maybe you saw it already when you were born? Karna!

I'll take you with me. Carry you. Do you think it's possible, Karna? That it's not a cursed sacrifice? That it's to save myself?

Do you think it's true there is a time for everything?

How can one forget so quickly, Karna? What are we made of, we who forget everything? The field hospital? The bodies. The battlefields. We bound up the stumps. Or saw the men bleed to death. Did it do nothing to me? Karna! Did it bring us a hair's breadth closer to love? If not: what good was it? Have you seen a cranium stuffed with newspaper?

I won't forget when you were born. But maybe

I've already forgotten. Because it was so terrible. So beautiful. The red river you caused made me forget you. I got so frightened I forgot you, Karna. Can you understand that? Even the sorrow made me forget you. Because I had to go through it alone. Do you think I'll be able to remember you through everything? So I can tell you about your mother's hair. Tell you there was a hole in her shoe. And that her umbrella was torn.

Do you think I can ever tell you about my faithlessness? I don't think so. I gave up before I began. Can you understand that one can be such a coward? And yet, I know I'm not evil. I'm not evil. Do you hear! But people forget so quickly.

That's why I know nothing about love. I've sensed it. With iron and blood in every footprint. I know that. And still I forget.

I would have liked to be spared all the bother with you. I've already forgotten you several times. Forgotten you because of sorrow. Forgotten you because of joy. Forgotten you because I couldn't bear to think I killed your mother. I carry you both with me.

You hold tight when I reach out my finger to you.

You don't ask me yet who I am.

Do you think I'll have forgotten everything the day you ask?

THE END

DINA'S BOOK

Herbjørg Wassmo

'THE GREATNESS OF THIS BOOK IS ITS GUT-WRENCHING PORTRAIT OF A WOMAN FOREVER IN THE GRIP OF HER PAST'
Los Angeles Times

Set in Norway in the mid-nineteenth century – a land of short, blazing, idyllic summers and dark, frost-rimmed winters, of mountains, bear-hunts, and hazardous sea voyages – *Dina's Book* centres around a beautiful, eccentric and unpredictable woman who bewitches everyone she meets.

At the age of five Dina unwittingly causes her mother's death. Blamed by her father and banished to a farm, she grows up untamed and untaught. Her guilt becomes her obsession: her unforgiving mother haunts her every day.

When she finally returns home she is like a wolf cub, tamed only by her tutor, Lorch, who is able to reach her through music. Married off at sixteen to a wealthy fifty-year-old landowner, Jacob, she becomes sexually obsessive and wild. Jacob dies under odd circumstances and Dina becomes mute. When finally she emerges from her trauma, she runs his estate with an iron hand. But still Dina wrestles with her two unappeased ghosts: Jacob and her mother. Until one day a mysterious stranger, the Russian wanderer Leo, enters her life and changes it forever . . .

'A MASTERPIECE THAT LIGHTS UP THE SKY LIKE A MEGASTAR'
Verdens Gang, Norway

'AN EXPLOSION OF A BOOK – A UNIQUE TALENT AND A WONDERFUL EVOCATIVE POWER'
Politken, Denmark

'A NOVEL THAT WILL STAY WITH YOU FOREVER'
Kristianstads-bladet, Sweden

'RICH HUMOUR AND ASTONISHING EVOCATION OF PLACE AND SENSATION, THIS IS A TEXT ONE CAN SMELL AND TASTE'
Patrick Gale, *Daily Telegraph*

0 552 99673 4

BLACK SWAN

A HEART OF STONE

Renate Dorrestein

'A LITERARY NOVEL WITH A DARK SECRET IN ITS HEART THAT
MAKES READING COMPULSIVE'
Kate Atkinson

Precocious Ellen is the only one of the four close Van Bemmel
children who dreads the arrival of the new baby. She has told her
parents to call the baby Ida, the ugliest name she could think of, and
is secretly afraid that the curse she has put upon the unborn child
will come true. Her parents, eccentric and devoted to each other,
seem to the outside world to be loving and caring, but after one of
the children has a shocking accident a horror descends upon this
happy household which leads to a disaster even Ellen is powerless
to prevent.

Twenty-five years later a pregnant Ellen returns to the family
home, where she is haunted by the voices of her dead family. She
imagines the questions her own child will one day ask: 'Mummy,
why don't I have a granny? Why no grandad? No uncles or aunts?
Why not?'

A Heart of Stone is an elegant, passionate but chilling novel from
Holland's bestselling writer.

'A WONDERFUL FRESH VOICE WITH A STARTLING AND
ULTIMATELY REDEMPTIVE TALE TO TELL. HER WRITING IS
SUPREMELY CONFIDENT AND INTIMATE. *A HEART OF STONE* IS
A LITERARY NOVEL WITH A DARK SECRET IN ITS HEART THAT
MAKES READING COMPULSIVE'
Kate Atkinson

'NOT ONLY HIGHLY EMOTIVE AND COMPELLING, BUT
HUMOROUS TOO. I COULD NOT PUT THIS NOVEL DOWN'
Marika Cobbold

0 552 99836 2

BLACK SWAN

EMOTIONALLY WEIRD

Kate Atkinson

'THE LUSTRE, ENERGY AND PANACHE OF HER WRITING ARE AS
STRIKING AS EVER . . . FUNNY, BOLD AND MEMORABLE'
Helen Dunmore, *The Times*

On a peat and heather island off the west coast of Scotland, Effie
and her mother Nora take refuge in the large mouldering house of
their ancestors and tell each other stories. Nora, at first, recounts
nothing that Effie really wants to hear, like who her father was –
variously Jimmy, Jack, or Ernie. Effie tells of her life at college in
Dundee, the land of cakes and William Wallace, where she lives in a
lethargic relationship with Bob, a student who never goes to lectures,
seldom gets out of bed, and to whom the Klingons are as real as the
French and the Germans (*more* real than the Luxemburgers).
But strange things are happening. Why is Effie being followed?
Is someone killing the old people? And where is the mysterious
yellow dog?

'BEAUTIFULLY WRITTEN . . . BRIMMING WITH QUIRKY
CHARACTERS AND ORIGINAL STORYTELLING. KATE ATKINSON
HAS STRUCK GOLD WITH THIS UNIQUE OFFERING'
Time Out

'A TRULY COMIC NOVEL – ACHINGLY FUNNY IN PARTS –
CHALLENGING AND EXECUTED WITH WIT AND MISCHIEF . . .
AN HILARIOUS AND MAGICAL TRIP'
Meera Syal, *The Express*

'SENDS JOLTS OF PLEASURE OFF THE PAGE . . . ATKINSON'S
FUNNIEST FORAY YET . . . IT IS A WORK OF DICKENSIAN OR
EVEN SHAKESPEAREAN PLENTY'
Catherine Lockerbie, *The Scotsman*

0 552 99734 X

BLACK SWAN

A SELECTED LIST OF FINE WRITING
AVAILABLE FROM BLACK SWAN

99313	1	**OF LOVE AND SHADOWS**	*Isabel Allende*	£6.99
99820	6	**FLANDERS**	*Patricia Anthony*	£6.99
99734	X	**EMOTIONALLY WEIRD**	*Kate Atkinson*	£6.99
99860	5	**IDIOGLOSSIA**	*Eleanor Bailey*	£6.99
99832	X	**SNAKES IN THE GRASS**	*Georgia Blain*	£6.99
99824	9	**THE DANDELION CLOCK**	*Guy Burt*	£6.99
99854	0	**LESSONS FOR A SUNDAY FATHER**	*Claire Calman*	£5.99
99888	5	**A TRIP TO THE STARS**	*Nicholas Christopher*	£6.99
99686	6	**BEACH MUSIC**	*Pat Conroy*	£7.99
99715	3	**BEACHCOMBING FOR A SHIPWRECKED GOD**	*Joe Coomer*	£6.99
99767	6	**SISTER OF MY HEART**	*Chitra Banerjee Divakaruni*	£6.99
99836	2	**A HEART OF STONE**	*Renate Dorrestein*	£6.99
99587	8	**LIKE WATER FOR CHOCOLATE**	*Laura Esquivel*	£6.99
99910	5	**TELLING LIDDY**	*Anne Fine*	£6.99
99851	6	**REMEMBERING BLUE**	*Connie May Fowler*	£6.99
99681	5	**A MAP OF THE WORLD**	*Jane Hamilton*	£6.99
99893	1	**CHOCOLAT**	*Joanne Harris*	£6.99
99796	X	**A WIDOW FOR ONE YEAR**	*John Irving*	£7.99
99867	2	**LIKE WATER IN WILD PLACES**	*Pamela Jooste*	£6.99
99859	1	**EDDIE'S BASTARD**	*William Kowalski*	£6.99
99737	4	**GOLDEN LADS AND GIRLS**	*Angela Lambert*	£6.99
99861	3	**IN A LAND OF PLENTY**	*Tim Pears*	£6.99
99918	0	**MUSIC FOR THE THIRD EAR**	*Susan Schwartz Senstad*	£6.99
99819	2	**WHISTLING FOR THE ELEPHANTS**	*Sandi Toksvig*	£6.99
99780	3	**KNOWLEDGE OF ANGELS**	*Jill Paton Walsh*	£6.99
99673	4	**DINA'S BOOK**	*Herbjørg Wassmo*	£6.99